# THE FLAME TREES

by

Baden James Scholefield

THE FLAME TREES

ISBN: ISBN: 978-1-7638032-2-0 Hardcover

ISBN: 978-1-7638032-3-7 Paperback

Copyright © Baden James Scholefield.



This novel is a work of fiction. Names, places, events, and incidents are either the product of the author's imagination or used fictitiously. Any resemblance to persons, living or dead, or actual events is purely coincidental.

There are scenes in this manuscript that could be considered disturbing, and certain characters' attitudes and language could be considered racist. The author has used language that is to be considered historical in its use, and while it may offend some people, he has tried to tell his story as it was in those days, and he apologizes for any perceived offence Any language or attitudes depicting racism are purely meant to be seen as a part of the plot of this fictional work and in no way reflect the thoughts or personal views of the author.

# Legend of the Pearl

*There is an ancient Japanese legend that says when the earth is troubled, the moon weeps and her tears fall from the heavens into anxious seas. Ryujin, the tempestuous god of the sea, summons oysters from the ocean floor to gather and hold them safe, for one day, as if by magic, a perfect pearl will form.*

From a plaque that once hung on the wall of the offices of 'Taylor House Pearls' in Broome in 1912.

# Dedication


*This novel is dedicated to my wife Judy
and my children Shannon and John.*

# Contents

# Prologue
## Dawson House

Darwin, Northern Territory
November 11th, 1997

The old man drew on his pipe. He exhaled and watched the smoke drift out over the well-tended gardens below. He glanced up at the sky; it had been raining on and off for most of the night, but finally, it seemed to have cleared. Honeyeaters and tiny friarbirds flitted about among the trees. The sweet smell of the frangipani flowers coming up from the garden reminded him of days long gone. The old man liked to sit and watch the late-afternoon traffic pass by along East Point Road. People seemed to be in such a hurry to get to where they were going these days. He preferred it the way it was when not everyone owned a motor car.

A pair of rainbow lorikeets flew up in a blaze of colour and landed in the bent old flame tree that shaded most of the driveway. They sat together like lovers, preening themselves and pecking at each other. The misshapen old tree had always taken pride of place in his garden at this time of the year. Its flowers were like fire against the bruised late-November sky. Alexander palms and yellow hibiscus bushes lined the paved driveway that passed under the old tree and up the side of the house to the garages beneath the stately old weatherboard home. Coconut palms lined the roadside opposite, the sea beyond the unbelievable blue of the tropics. An old pearling lugger lay at anchor out in the bay, its mast swaying from the low waves that rolled past and lapped quietly along the narrow beach.

The old man was suddenly woken from his reverie by the sound of a familiar voice from somewhere just behind him.

'I'd better be off then.'

He put down his pipe, took his cane from the side of the chair and stood up.

'What was that, Alice?' He asked the Aboriginal woman looking at him from the front door. He'd become a little hard of hearing of late.

'I've finished the cleaning and the ironing. There's some nice cold ham and a bowl of salad in the refrigerator for your dinner. I'm all done for the day, so I'd better be off. I have a few things to do at the shops before I go home,' his housekeeper announced.

'Thank you, Alice,' the old man replied.

'I'll see you in the morning then,' the Aboriginal woman said, patting his arm as she went past and down the steps.

Alice loved the old man. He'd always been so kind to her, not like some she knew. She had been his housekeeper for so many years now that she had lost count. She went down the driveway with her old carry-bag in her hand, smiling.

'I'll see you tomorrow then, Alice,' the old man called after her.

'It's your birthday tomorrow; I'm going to get you something nice from the shops. It's something I saw there last weekend,' Alice replied, in a voice loud enough for the old man to hear.

'Don't you go wasting your money on me, Alice? You have a family to look after, and don't you forget it,' the old man called back.

'It's my money, and I'll do what I like with it,' Alice yelled, looking back and laughing.

'There's nothing I need, Alice—nothing at all. You just keep your money for yourself.'

'Goodbye, you grumpy old bugger,' Alice called back in frustration as she went to where her bicycle leaned against the old flame tree. A carpet of red flowers had fallen on the ground around it; some lay in the cane basket attached to the handlebars. She put her carry-bag on top of them, wheeled the bicycle down to the roadside, waved just like she always did, and rode off.

The old man sat back down, leaned his cane against the chair, and re-lit his pipe. It would be quiet now that Alice had gone. He preferred it when she was there. She brought the old home to life, rushing about, chatting with him, singing, and doing her work.

Just for a moment, he felt lonely, but it soon passed. He drew on his pipe and continued to watch the traffic go by along the busy road. A while later, he got up, reached for his cane, and went inside. He left the front door open and closed the fly door. There was a nice breeze coming across from the bay. He wandered into the sitting room.

The old house was filled with the old man's memories. Two comfortable cane chairs and a wonderfully carved teak sofa he'd imported from Singapore long ago sat in comfortable order on the magnificent Persian rug. An ancient cedar-bladed ceiling fan with a discoloured brass boss was turning slowly on the cracked plaster ceiling. Bookshelves lined one of the walls. An antique French clock sat in pride of place on one of the shelves, surrounded by leather-bound volumes of poetry and the classics. Across the room, two huge ebony elephants with yellowed tusks sat on either side of a hand-painted porcelain pot that held a magnificent bamboo palm swaying slightly from the breeze coming through the open windows. An elaborately carved Balinese screen stood partly folded next to the old piano. Lotus flowers carved into the beautifully figured teak adorned its delicate panels. The old man's cane tapped on the floorboards as he went across the room and pressed one of the piano keys. He smiled as he remembered the woman who had played it so beautifully so long ago.

A few moments later, he went across the hallway to the dining room. He loved this room. *She* had chosen its furnishings and the artwork long ago. *She* had ordered the dining table and chairs and the elaborate sideboard from an English mail-order catalogue not long after the house had been built. They were made from Jamaican mahogany and had been sent at great expense from London long ago. He went over and stood in front of the painting that hung above the sideboard, an abstract work done by William Roberts and painted in 1924. It had been one of her favourite things. He straightened the solid silver candleholder that didn't need straightening and moved away. Several small photographs in gold-painted frames sat nearby. They were of his dear wife. He didn't look at them. He knew they would make him feel sad.

He left the dining room, went along the hallway to the master bedroom, and opened the door. He looked in at the neatly made brass bed. He hadn't slept in that bed for more than thirty years—*not since she had passed*. He went in, his cane tapping on the floor. Tiny scratches marked the floorboards from the many times he had been in this room. It was *their* room once—long ago. He walked to her side of the bed. Some of her things still sat on top of the bedside cabinet: a small mirror, a hairbrush, and a Bible. He ran his fingers over the Bible, smiling again as he thought of her. A painting hung above the bed. A waterfall crashed down through an ancient landscape of red cliffs and bush-covered valleys. It was titled '*Waterfall on the Prince Regent River.*' It was dated 1933 and done by a lesser-known Australian artist, Isabella Montinari. *She* had found it quite by accident in an art gallery during one of their shopping visits to Melbourne in 1958.

The old man sat on the edge of the bed and opened the bedside cupboard. He took out a small jeweller's box and held it in his trembling fingers for a few silent moments; then he opened it. Inside was a golden pendant on a thin gold chain. The pendant was round and about the size of a gold sovereign. In its centre was a magnificent red stone, and around the outside were strange but beautiful Cyrillic symbols. The old man rubbed his fingers over the ruby and smiled as he remembered the two women who had worn it so long ago. Strangely, the ruby felt warm to the touch of his fingers. He put it back in its little box, clicked it shut, and returned it to the bedside cupboard.

A while later, he got up, went into the hallway, and continued to the kitchen. This room had hardly changed since the home had been built more than seventy years ago. The cement-plastered walls had been painted a soft green, a colour *she* had chosen long ago, but now faded and dull in places. The cabinets were a deeper green, well worn from years of use, as were the hardwood bench-tops, now badly chipped in places. An ancient wood-burning stove sat in a massive brick chimney against one of the external walls. A *Dreschler* wall clock hung on its smoke-stained chimney breast. It hadn't worked for more than thirty years. Three tiny, hand-painted green porcelain monkeys sat together on the narrow mantlepiece. Their beady black eyes had watched all who had entered this room for the last 73 years.

The old stove hadn't been lit for more than 30 years. A modern gas stove had been installed on the wall opposite, next to the new two-door refrigerator he'd ordered from a brochure Alice had shown him just before Christmas two years before. A small wooden dining table and four chairs sat in the centre of the room. Alice had set a place for him, as she always did. A glass bowl of water sat in the centre of the table. A yellow hibiscus flower floated in the water. The old man smiled; she was always surprising him with little things she thought he might like.

On the far side of the room, a little breakfast nook jutted out into the side veranda where delicate potted ferns grew and hanging baskets hung from shady rafters. Leadlight windows in pale green and rose pink lined the upper sections of its five walls. A Tiffany lampshade in the same colours as the windows hung above its little round table. The old man went to a side cabinet, moved his cane to his left hand, and poured himself a glass of sherry. He took the glass and went back out to the front veranda.

The traffic along East Point Road was quieter now and the sky darker. It would soon be raining. He sat down, took out his old pipe, and lit it. As he exhaled, he felt a familiar pain in his chest. He tried not to think of it and sipped his sherry. Out on the bay, the old lugger was rocking about at her mooring a little more now, and bruised clouds lined the distant horizon. It was quieter now, almost dark. The leaves of the old flame tree were flicking about, whispering in the cool breeze coming across from the bay.

A crow suddenly glided in on the salty breeze and landed silently in the old tree. To the old man, it seemed to be watching him. It sat there for a while and then flew off. Its mournful call echoed through the garden. The old man felt a familiar sadness pass through him as he sipped his sherry. He was alone again as another day ended.

A while later, he took his cane and went down the veranda steps. The perfume from the frangipani trees was stronger now, filling his senses with precious memories as he hobbled across the lawn. There was a place in the garden that *she* had loved—a place where no one walking by could see them as they sat together. Long ago, he'd instructed a young carpenter they knew to build a small arbour there. It was set among cane palms and white-flowering hibiscus bushes. He remembered her tying a spindly bougainvillea cutting to one of the posts and explaining how that one day it would grow to cover the rafters with its red flowers. His gardener had cut it back only recently; it had become overgrown and unruly. He smiled as he remembered her kneeling there, dirt on her knees, talking to him as she planted it. It was covered now with carmine-red flowers that seemed to glow in the evening light.

He hobbled over to the little cast-iron seat and sat down. A sudden flash of lightning made him look up at the sky. Peals of thunder rattled off in the distance. The pain was still there in the centre of his chest. He would rest for a while; perhaps then it would ease. He put his cane on his lap and leaned back. Raindrops began to drip through the bougainvillea, spotting his freshly ironed white shirt. He loved the little, white-painted arbour, even though some of the paint was beginning to peel from the rafters in places. He closed his eyes and tried to remember his wife's beautiful face. As the years had passed, it had become more and more difficult for him. And then he remembered her eyes, her beautiful, smiling eyes. They were the darkest brown, almost black. A moment later, he gasped and fell back against the seat. The pain had suddenly become much worse. For a moment, he thought he might choke. He tried to get up, but he fell back again, dropping his cane to the flagstones.

A sudden bolt of lightning lit up the garden with a strange, flickering blue light, and just for a moment, he thought he could see someone standing near the hibiscus bushes, but his vision was blurred from the rain, and he couldn't be certain.

Another bolt of lightning lit up the darkness . . . *This time, he was certain!*

A tall, beautiful black woman was standing just beyond the hibiscus bushes. She was wearing a pale green silk kaftan that shimmered each time the lightning flashed!

She had her arms out. She was reaching for him!

'*Oh, Kasiah . . . Is that really you?*' The old man called out.

The rain was pouring down now, soaking him. Thunder rattled through the rain-soaked garden like distant gunshots.

The old man struggled to his feet and staggered towards the indistinct image of the woman he had known and loved from long ago, standing near the dripping hibiscus bushes.

'*Oh, Kasiah . . . It is you . . . Where is my Tessa? I can't see her! Is she with you?*'

* * *

The following morning, just before eight o'clock, Alice Rowe, the old man's housekeeper, leaned her bicycle against the old flame tree. Last night's rain had battered even more of its flowers to the ground. The lawn was carpeted with its red blossom. The Aboriginal woman's pretty cotton dress was damp at the back from the water that had flicked up at her as she'd ridden her bicycle to the old man's home. She took her carry-bag from the basket and started up the driveway. She had his present carefully wrapped inside . . . She noticed the front door was open!

*Something didn't seem right! The old man always locked the front door at night!*

She went up the steps quickly, noticing the half-empty sherry glass and pipe on the table next to the old man's chair. She hurried through the open door and along the hallway to his bedroom.

*The bed was still made! Where could he be?*

She turned and opened the door to the bedroom opposite. It was empty as well. Somehow, she knew it would be.

She hurried on to the kitchen . . . *He wasn't there either!*

*Had he fallen somewhere?*

A terrible chill gripped the Aboriginal woman's heart as she rushed about the old house, searching. But he was nowhere to be found . . . She ran back to the front veranda and looked out over the gardens.

It was then that she saw him!

The old man was lying on the wet grass near the little, white-painted arbour. A lorikeet was drinking rainwater from a puddle nearby. She ran down the steps and across the lawn to where he lay.

His clothes were soaked, and his body was still. She kneeled and slowly turned him. Her breath caught in her throat. His skin was deathly pale, and his white hair lay flat across his wonderful old face . . . *He was dead* . . . His eyes were closed, but strangely, there was a faint smile on his lips.

The Aboriginal woman sat back on the wet grass next to the old man's body. She reached out, took his hand in hers, brushed away some blades of grass from his fingers, and burst into tears.

# Part 1

# Chapter 1

# An Unexpected Call

Eight days later
Adelaide, South Australia.

Charlotte Dawson put down her mobile phone. She had just received a call from a solicitor's office in Darwin. The caller had informed her that she was to receive an inheritance from a person unknown to her and suggested that a meeting in their offices in Darwin would be advisable as there were details that needed to be explained in private by one of their partners, Mr. Paul Rosenberg.

Charlotte's first thought was that the call was a scam of some sort, and she very nearly hung up on the caller. But she thought for a moment—the woman's voice had an Australian accent—that much she was sure of. Perhaps she was being too cautious. She asked the woman if she could tell her something about the inheritance and who it was from. The woman explained that their senior partner, Mr. Rosenberg, would explain it all when she arrived.

'Is it necessary for me to travel all that way?' Charlotte asked, sounding mildly annoyed. 'I'm a schoolteacher here in Adelaide, and it may be difficult for me to get away on such short notice. Apart from that, I have no family or relatives living in Darwin from whom I could inherit anything.'

'Mr. Rosenberg has instructed me to tell you that it is most important that you meet with him here in Darwin. He will explain everything when you arrive,' the woman insisted.

'Is Mister Rosenberg able to come to the phone?'

'He's in a meeting at the moment,' the woman explained.

'This is terribly inconvenient. We have exams at my school in a few weeks. I'm awfully busy at the moment,' Charlotte replied.

'I have been instructed to tell you that it is of the utmost importance that you travel to Darwin. If you would like help with the travel costs and accommodation, I'm authorised to pay for bookings on your behalf,' the caller added.

'No, that won't be necessary but thank you for the offer. It's just that it's so inconvenient right now.'

'I'm terribly sorry about that,' the woman replied.

Charlotte thanked the caller and told her she would ring her in the morning to tell her what she intended to do. She sat looking at her phone, wondering why it was so important for her to travel all that way. She was annoyed that the woman wouldn't give her any more information. She hit the shortcut to her mother and waited.

*   *   *

Charlotte Dawson was a schoolteacher in the southern city of Adelaide. She was 33 years of age, tall, and an exceptionally beautiful woman. Her hair was long and naturally blonde. Charlotte kept herself in great physical shape with regular exercise at a local gym, and regardless of the weather, she spent every morning swimming in the sea near her flat in Glenelg. She was a long-time member of the Moseley Beach Club's swimmers' group.

Charlotte had never married, although she had been in several serious relationships, none of which had ever worked out for her. She was a strong-willed and thoroughly independent woman, which was probably one of the reasons her relationships struggled.

Apart from swimming, Charlotte's other great passion was horse riding. She spent most of her Sundays with friends at a riding establishment in the Adelaide Hills, near Mount Pleasant. On Sunday evenings, she could usually be found enjoying a meal and a glass of chardonnay at a nearby restaurant. Charlotte Dawson was a capable and well-liked teacher at her school, loved by her female students and lusted over by most of her adolescent male students.

* * *

A moment later, Charlotte heard her mother's voice.

'Charlotte, my dear girl. Is everything all right?'

'Mum, I've just received the strangest call from a solicitor's office up in Darwin.'

'Is there some sort of problem, love?'

'No, I don't think so. But I've been told that I am to receive an inheritance of some sort.'

'An inheritance . . . From whom?'

'I have no idea. It couldn't be Dad's father; he died here in Adelaide years ago. What little he had, he left for Dad. I still miss Dad terribly, Mum.'

'I feel the same way, dear girl . . . And just what have the solicitors asked you to do?'

'They want me to fly up to Darwin for a meeting as soon as possible.'

'And will you be going—?'

'It's what they've advised, Mum. But that's all they would tell me.'

'It all sounds rather mysterious,' Charlotte's mother added.

'It certainly does.'

'What have you decided?'

'I think I should go, Mum. I have a feeling it could be important. I'll ring them tomorrow morning and tell them I'll be on the first available flight. I'll have to let them know at the school; someone will need to take my classes for a few days.'

'Surely, it's not necessary for you to travel all that way.'

'That's what I said to the woman who rang me. I think there may be more to it than just money, though—that's if there's any money left after the solicitors have gotten through with it.'

'I hope there is nothing illegal about it, Charlotte. A lot of funny stuff goes on up there in Darwin. It's so close to Asia, you know.'

'I'm sure there's nothing for you to worry about, Mum.'

'Ring them again and ask them to tell you what it's all about.'

'The woman insisted that I travel up there. She said it was important. I think I should go.'

'How long do you think you will be gone then?'

'I have no idea . . . A couple of days—three at the most, I would think,' Charlotte replied.

'Let me know if you want me to go over to your flat and check on things for you.'

'Thanks, Mum. I will. I'll ring you from Darwin after I've met with them.'

'Bye then, love.'

'Bye, Mum.'

*   *   *

Late the following afternoon, Charlotte Dawson arrived at the offices of Rosenberg and Gately, solicitors, in the central business district of Darwin. It was the beginning of the wet season. It was hot and humid, and it had rained heavily during her taxi ride in from the airport. She was shown into an air-conditioned office to wait for Mr. Rosenberg and informed that he shouldn't be long. While she waited, she checked her mobile phone. There were no messages, and she wasn't expecting any. It was just a force of habit. She put her phone back in her bag and looked around the fashionably decorated office. Chrome-framed law certificates adorned the walls. A huge plastic monstera plant sat alone in a hand-painted China pot in a corner of the spotless room. Cool air hummed down from a vent in the centre of the white-panelled ceiling. Charlotte thought of Adelaide and her job. She had contacted her school from the Adelaide airport and told them she would be away for a few days on urgent family business. She apologised and assured them she would contact them as soon as it was taken care of. But she couldn't help it; she felt guilty leaving on such short notice.

'Ms. Dawson, I'm so glad you decided to come. We have much to discuss.' Charlotte heard an educated male voice coming from behind her to disrupt her thoughts. She turned toward the door.

'Mr. Rosenberg,' Charlotte replied, getting to her feet and taking the outstretched hand.

'That is correct. But please—just call me Paul.'

Charlotte studied the man shaking her hand. He was about sixty years of age, perhaps a little more. He wore an off-white tropical suit, bone-coloured shoes, and a dark green, open-necked shirt. His face was well-tanned from the tropical sun, his greying hair was neatly barbered, and he was smiling.

'Please sit down again and make yourself comfortable, Charlotte. Did you have a pleasant flight?'

'Yes, I did. Thank you, Paul.'

'It's quite a distance,' the solicitor replied. 'I have done it many times.'

'I'm hoping you can tell me why I needed to come all this way, Paul. Surely, we could have discussed whatever needed to be discussed over the phone.'

'I felt it would be much better if we met in private, Charlotte. There are things of the utmost importance that I need to discuss with you,' Paul Rosenberg advised politely, going behind his desk.

'Should I be concerned?'

'Certainly not, my dear,' the solicitor replied, pulling a thick file from his top drawer.

Charlotte could read the neatly typed words at the top of the file from her side of the desk.

*To be discussed in person with Ms. Charlotte Dawson of 37 Pier Street, Glenelg, Adelaide, South Australia.*

'Would you like some tea or coffee before we begin? This could take quite a while, I'm afraid.'

'A cup of coffee would be most welcome,' Charlotte said, staring at the file.

'There is nothing for you to worry about, Charlotte; I can assure you of that. I'll get us both some coffee, and then I'll explain.'

The solicitor clicked a switch hidden from Charlotte's view and ordered coffee. Then he took out his glasses, opened the file to its first page, and began reading.

A few moments later, there was a tap on the door.

'Come in, Penny,' Paul Rosenberg called out.

An attractive woman of about thirty years of age came in carrying a tray containing a pot of coffee, two small white cups, and a bowl of sugar cubes. She placed them at the end of Paul Rosenberg's desk and turned to leave.

'Just a moment, Penny,' Paul said, looking up.

'Yes, Mr. Rosenberg?'

'Charlotte, this is Penny Kendal, my secretary. She spoke to you on the phone yesterday.'

Penny Kendal gave Charlotte a smile. 'I'm pleased to finally meet you in person, Miss Dawson.'

'Thank you, Penny. I must apologise if I sounded a little abrupt on the phone.'

'I understand completely,' Penny replied.

'Penny will help you over the next few days with some of the details of our discussions,' Paul Rosenberg added, looking down at his file again.

Penny gave Charlotte a nod of confirmation, smiled, and left the office.

Paul Rosenberg poured two cups of coffee, slid one toward Charlotte, and nodded toward the sugar bowl.

Charlotte shook her head.

The solicitor picked up the page he'd been looking at, adjusted his gold-rimmed glasses, and was silent for more than a minute while he studied the file. 'Do you have some means of identification with you, Charlotte?' He asked finally.

'I have my driver's licence. Would that do?'

'Yes, of course. I'm sorry about this.'

The solicitor took the licence, wrote down the license number, nodded his thanks, and passed it back to Charlotte and continued with another question. 'Charlotte, do you know of, or have you ever heard of, a man by the name of Henry Archibald Dawson?'

'No, I don't believe so.' Charlotte replied, taking a sip of her coffee. 'We have the same surname. Are we related in some way or another?'

'All in good time, Charlotte . . . All in good time.'

Charlotte put down her cup. She noticed her fingers were trembling a little. She watched the solicitor's face as he continued.

'Charlotte Dawson, I have to inform you that we at Rosenberg and Gately have been appointed by the late Henry Archibald Dawson to be the executors of his last will and testament, and as such, I have to discuss the details of the will with you.'

'I must say, Mr. Rosenberg, I have no knowledge of this man at all,' Charlotte remarked.

'The very first thing you must do for me, Charlotte, is read this letter,' the solicitor announced, sliding an envelope from his file and pushing it across his desk.

Charlotte picked it up and looked at the words handwritten on its pale cream manila front.

*In the event of my death, this letter is to be handed unopened and in person to Ms. Charlotte Dawson of 37 Pier Street, Glenelg, Adelaide, South Australia.*

Charlotte turned the envelope to open it and noticed it was sealed with a spot of old-fashioned red wax. The imprint on the wax was in the shape of a boat of some sort, perhaps a pearling lugger. She looked at the almost perfect cursive writing. She could tell it had been done with an expensive fountain pen. She took the letter opener Paul Rosenberg offered her and slit it open.

'This is all very mysterious, Paul,' Charlotte remarked, passing back the letter opener.

'It is part of the instructions that I have been asked to follow,' the solicitor replied.

Charlotte slid out the pages of personally monogrammed paper, sat back, and began to read. . .

Henry Archibald Dawson, Esq.

Dawson House, 8 East Point Road.

Darwin, Northern Territory.


*To: Ms. Charlotte Dawson*

*37 Pier Street, Glenelg*

*Adelaide, South Australia.*


*My dear Charlotte.*

*This letter will most likely come as a great surprise to you, as you will probably not have heard of my existence. Let me explain. Your grandfather, Paul, on your father's side, was my younger brother. Your grandfather and I were born here in Darwin long ago. Paul and I grew up in a very violent and abusive home. Our father was an ill-tempered man who drank far too much. As boys, we were subjected to regular beatings for little or no clear reason. It was a terrible time for both of us. When our dear mother died during the influenza outbreak of 1912, our father lost what little control our mother had had over him, and he became even more abusive. After a particularly violent evening, Paul and I secretly decided to run away. I was sixteen years of age at the time, and Paul was fourteen. It seemed to us that our father was blaming us for our dear mother's death for some strange reason or other. Early the following morning, Paul and I were quietly packing to leave, terrified should our father find us doing so. As it happened, we need not have been concerned. Our father, in a drunken stupor, had hung himself in our woodshed during the previous night.*

*After the council organised our father's funeral, we were taken from our home and placed temporarily in a boy's home in Nightcliff until we could be fostered out. We had only been at the home for a few days when we decided, once again, to run away. Paul managed to get a job helping a camel driver cart freight down to Alice Springs. From Alice Springs, he hoped to get to Adelaide and start a new life there. I decided to head across to Perth and try to find a future for myself in that city.*

*Paul and I were never close, even as boys. Our personalities were vastly different. Paul was the quiet, steady type, while I was not. I suppose that as we continued with our lives, the memory of our brutal childhood was something that both of us wanted to wipe from our thoughts completely. We never wrote, and over time, we drifted apart. I imagine that this is quite difficult for you to understand, Charlotte. But they were difficult times.*

*I knew little of what became of Paul and only found out many years later that he had reached Adelaide, married, and had a son there. Of course, I was very pleased for him. The later news of his death came as a great shock to me, and then to learn of your father's sudden, unexpected death as well, came as an even greater shock as I was considering contacting him.*

*Unfortunately, Charlotte, I have never been blessed with children, although I was married for many years to a wonderful woman whom I still miss terribly. There have only ever been two women in my long life, and I loved them both with all of my heart and more, but there were no children from either of those relationships.*

*After your father's untimely death, I decided to contact an investigation agency in Adelaide to make discreet enquiries to find out if there were any surviving members of my brother's family. The agency contacted me soon after with the news that my brother had a granddaughter. I apologise if you feel I have taken liberties doing this, but I needed to find out. You see, Charlotte, you are the only surviving member of my family.*

*I have led a long and hard-working life, and I have dealt with the tragedies that have befallen me to the best of my abilities. Other than losing my dear wife and one other, I have few regrets. Over this time, I have gained a modest amount of wealth, and in the event of my death, I have decided to bequeath all that I have to you. I have been told that you are an intelligent and capable young woman. A popular teacher in your* chosen field and of admirable character. I believe you to be a fair-minded person, and I have been informed that you support your widowed mother to the best of your ability.

My solicitor, Paul Rosenberg, is a good man whom I trust implicitly. He will give you all the details of your inheritance and guide you through what needs to be done. I sincerely hope you make good use of what I have left you and that it brings you much happiness. I do, however, have a couple of simple requests for you to follow, Charlotte, and I hope you will not mind doing them for me. I would like you to introduce yourself to Alice Rowe, my housekeeper, and David Thomson, my gardener, and thank them on my behalf for their many years of excellent service. I have left two envelopes with Paul, each containing a modest sum of money, for you to give to them as well.

Paul will carry out all the paperwork and the transfer of my assets into your name. I would suggest that you speak to him about setting up a trust for taxation purposes. He is a good man, and I have instructed him to offer whatever help you may need.

Now, to another matter. My housekeeper will give you a set of keys to my home when you meet with her. The home and all that is in it I have bequeathed to you as well. On the ring of keys, there will be two keys that you will puzzle over. You will find they are not for any of the rooms in the home. What I am about to tell you, you must keep to yourself. You must tell no one. In the sitting room, you will find, after some exploration, a bookcase that will open to reveal a narrow staircase that leads down to a secure room beneath the home. There you will find the locks where the keys fit. Among my many treasured things, you will find an old journal and some paperwork that will tell you the story of my long and colourful life. It is all there—the letters, the old photographs, and much, much more. I hope they will be of interest to you. You will find something else there as well, something that my wife and I have treasured and kept for many years, something quite valuable that now belongs to you.

As I write this letter, my only regret, dear Charlotte, is that we have never met in person. But perhaps it was meant to be that way.

Yours sincerely

Henry A. Dawson.

Charlotte folded the pages and looked at Paul Rosenberg. She was silent for some time before she spoke.

'Paul, this has come as a great surprise to me, and it may take me a while to come to grips with what it all means,' she said in a soft voice.

'I expected that. Henry told me that you would probably have had no knowledge of him. Nevertheless, Charlotte, you are now his sole beneficiary. I will have Penny give you a copy of his will, which was signed by Henry in my presence and witnessed by my partner, Terence Gately.'

'Tell me, Paul, will the details on this inheritance take very long to be completed? As I explained to Penny on the phone yesterday, I'm a schoolteacher, and I will need to get back to Adelaide as soon as possible. Of course, I shall be glad to receive this inheritance and the old home and accept it with grace and humility.'

'Charlotte, there is quite a lot for us to get through, and it will certainly take a while. At the very least, four or five days,' Paul Rosenberg explained.

'In that case, I think I should contact my school and explain. Please don't think I'm not appreciative. It's just that it has all come as quite a surprise to me, as I didn't know of Mr. Dawson's existence before today. Tell me, Paul, has there already been a funeral for Mr. Dawson?' Charlotte asked.

'Henry is to be buried tomorrow morning at ten o'clock,' the solicitor replied.

'In that case, I think it is only proper that I should attend the funeral. After that, I shall need to make arrangements for my return to Adelaide as promptly as possible.'

'Charlotte I'm not sure that you fully understand what I am telling you. Our office has handled Henry Dawson's financial investments and legal requirements for many years. At the time of his death, he was quite a wealthy man. His assets, while not including his home, artwork, and furnishings here in Darwin, are estimated to be worth more than fifteen million dollars.'

'Oh, my goodness—! Did you say . . . fifteen million dollars?

Are you quite sure?'

'Yes, Charlotte, I am quite sure. You are, as of this moment, a very wealthy woman.'

'I don't know what to say,' Charlotte replied, bursting into tears. 'Oh, my goodness, what a wonderful man.'

*　*　*

Charlotte was to spend that night in a city hotel that Penny Kendal had booked for her. The first thing she did when she was shown to her room was to ring her mother. She spent more than an hour explaining what had happened at her meeting with the solicitor.

'My goodness, Charlotte, how wonderful for you,'

'I'm still in shock, Mum. So much money, and a home as well.'

'Have you seen the old place?'

'I haven't yet. Mr. Dawson's funeral is to be held tomorrow morning. Perhaps after that.'

'Do you think you will attend, my dear?'

'Yes, Mum. Mr. Rosenberg is picking me up at the hotel in the morning,' Charlotte replied.

'Isn't it strange that your grandfather never told us about his having a brother up in Darwin? I'm sure your father knew nothing of him either.'

'It seems the two brothers grew apart years ago. In the letter Mr. Dawson left me, he says they had a difficult childhood and were never close, even as boys.'

'What will all this mean for you, my dear?'

'I've decided to ring the school tomorrow and hand in my notice. Mr. Rosenberg says the paperwork and transfers will probably take quite a while to get done—quite possibly two or three weeks. It won't be fair to the school if I stay away for that long. There is so much to do. There's a share portfolio, government bonds to transfer, and several bank accounts. One in Singapore, he tells me. He's been extremely helpful. It's all been quite overwhelming.'

'Will you need a financial advisor to help get you through all of it?'

'I'll be using Mr. Rosenberg's office. He's offered his services. He's familiar with inheritance laws and trusts. He's looked after the old man's finances for years. He seems very competent.'

'How wonderful for you, Charlotte. I'm glad he's looking after you, my dear.'

'I'll ring you tomorrow night, Mum, after I have been to the old man's home. I have no idea what it's like yet. Being quite old, it could be awfully run down,' Charlotte implied.

'What do you think you will do with it?'

'I suppose I will have to sell it. I'm looking forward to seeing it, though. There's some old paperwork and bits and pieces in a room the old man has asked me to look at.'

'Take some photos and send them through, dear.'

'I will. I had better go, Mum.'

'All right then, love. Goodbye for now.'

'Bye, Mum.'

# Chapter 2

# The Old House

The following morning, Charlotte was picked up from her hotel by Paul Rosenberg.

'Good morning, Charlotte. I hope you managed to get some sleep last night,' he said, shaking her hand in the hotel lobby.

'I hardly slept at all, Paul. I still can't believe my good fortune. I must apologise for being impatient and flippant with you yesterday morning. Thank you for putting up with me,' Charlotte said as they went outside.

'Don't concern yourself. It was to be expected.'

'All the same, I do apologise,' Charlotte replied.

Paul opened the car door, and Charlotte climbed into the front seat of his dark blue BMW.

'It was such short notice to have to come all this way. Perhaps I should have spoken to you personally on the phone. I've been so busy over these last few days,' the solicitor added, pulling away from the kerb into Darwin's morning traffic.

'Is there to be a church service for Mister Dawson?'

'No, there won't be, Charlotte. We're heading directly to the cemetery,' Paul replied.

A short while later, they left the air-conditioned car and walked through the gates of the Darwin cemetery. It was hot and humid, and it looked like it might soon rain.

'That must be it over there. I think we may be a little late,' Paul said, taking Charlotte's hand.

They hurried over to where a coffin was being taken out of a dark grey hearse. Apart from the funeral director and his helpers, there were only two others at the gravesite. One of them was an Aboriginal woman of about sixty years of age. The other was a slightly younger white man.

'I'm not sure, but I think the Aboriginal woman is Alice Rowe, Henry's long-time housekeeper, and I'm guessing the man next to her is David Thomson, his gardener,' Paul whispered to Charlotte as they hurried to the gravesite.

'I have a couple of envelopes for them in my case back at my hotel. Should I speak to them after this is over?' Charlotte whispered back.

'You're meeting with them this afternoon at the old house. It may be better to leave it till then,' Paul replied in a low voice when they arrived at the gravesite.

They stood together and were silent while a grey-haired priest stepped forward to read the eulogy. When he finished, there was an awkward silence for a few moments, and then the Aboriginal woman went to the graveside. She was stone-faced and silent as she reached into her carry-bag and took out a cardboard box filled with yellow hibiscus flowers and red poinciana blossom and let them fall into the grave. When she finished, she went back and stood next to the man they thought was the gardener.

The priest then asked the little gathering if anyone would like to say a few words.

As Paul Rosenberg went forward, Charlotte noticed the Aboriginal woman staring at her from across the graveside. She smiled in return but received no response.

Paul Rosenberg began: *'My name is Paul Rosenberg. I have handled all of Henry Dawson's legal and financial affairs for more than twenty-five years, and over that time, Henry and I became good friends. Henry was a man I have always had the greatest respect for. He was a very private person, and he had very few friends here in Darwin. He and his wife, Tessa, came to live here many years ago after spending their earlier working lives in Broome, Western Australia, where I am told they ran a successful pearling business. Tessa's parents, the Taylors, were well-known in the pearling industry during those years. After the death of his wife, Henry was never quite the same. I suppose you could say he became a recluse. But he was a good friend, and he will be sadly missed by those of us who knew him well. He is with his dear wife now, the woman he loved for so long. God bless you, my friend, and may you rest in peace.'*

When Paul stepped away from the graveside, the Aboriginal woman went forward again and stood there silently, looking down at the flower-covered coffin. A moment later, the man she had been standing next to went to her, stood with her for a few moments, and then took her hand and led her away.

Paul reached for Charlotte's hand and took her to the grave, so they could both say a silent prayer for the old man. While they prayed, Charlotte noticed the adjoining headstone next to the freshly dug grave. She read the sad words chiselled into the white marble.

*Tessa Dawson. Born 1897 . . . Died 1962.*
*'If my love could have saved you, you would have*
*lived forever.'*
*Henry.*

'I think we should go now, Charlotte,' Paul said finally, startling Charlotte.

'How sad it all seems, Paul. I wish I had known this old man as well as you did,' Charlotte remarked.

'I'm quite certain you would have liked him just as much as I have. But I had better take you back to your hotel now. I have to get back to work. Would you like me to book you a taxi for your trip out to Henry's old place when we get there?'

'I can take care of it. Thank you for bringing me here today, Paul. It's been very sad, but I'm so glad I came.'

'We have a lot to do over the next few weeks, Charlotte. I will personally introduce you to Heny's bank managers and his stockbroker. I know them all personally.' Paul explained when they arrived back at his car.

'You've been a huge help, Paul. My sincere thanks for that,' Charlotte replied.

Charlotte said goodbye to Paul Rosenberg outside her hotel, assuring him she would see him at ten o'clock the following morning. She went back to her room, showered, changed her clothes, and went for a stroll along Smith Street, the long main street of Darwin. It was hot and humid, but the city seemed pleasant. She strolled past coffee shops with plastic tables on the footpaths filled with chatting tourists, past women's clothing stores filled with summer's latest fashion, and silent glass-fronted office blocks. Her mind was spinning. She went into a café, ordered an orange juice with ice, sat at a table and tried to gather her thoughts.

Twenty minutes later, she found a taxi near a city hotel. She asked the driver if he would take her to East Point Road.

'What number, love?' the driver asked as they pulled away.

'Oh . . . My goodness, I'm not sure. Do you know the home of Mister Henry Dawson?' Charlotte replied. She couldn't remember if Paul had given her the number. If he had, it had slipped her mind. She felt silly for not remembering.

'I sure do, love. A nice old place, down the end of the road and right across from the bay. I wouldn't mind it meself. It'd be worth a fair bit these days with the way house prices are going up here in Darwin.'

'Did you know the old man?' Charlotte asked.

'I can't say I did, love, but everyone knows the house. They call it Dawson House. It's an old colonial weatherboard. It's a beautiful old place and a great spot. They get real nice breezes coming across from the bay out that way.'

A short while after they drove away, Charlotte noticed the sea on her left. It was calm and unbelievably blue. A few minutes later, the taxi driver pulled against the curb.

'That's the place over there, love. Nice, isn't it?' He announced, winding down his window.

'Yes, it certainly is. It looks lovely. Now, how much do I owe you for the fare?' Charlotte asked.

'That will be twenty dollars neat, love.'

Charlotte paid the driver and climbed out. The taxi driver swung his car around and drove off.

Charlotte stood by the side of the road and looked over at the old home. A huge flame tree covered with fiery red flowers was partially obstructing her view. She noticed a bicycle leaning against the twisted old tree and a Toyota utility parked further up the driveway. Tall, elegant palms lined the driveway. The lawn was a perfect green and wonderfully cared for. She crossed the road and stood in the shade of the bent old flame tree. It was shaped like an umbrella, with some of its limbs almost touching the ground. A carpet of red flowers covered the lawn beneath it and part of the driveway. On her left, nestled among some low flowering bushes, Charlotte noticed an ancient brick letterbox with a discoloured brass plaque that read: 'Dawson House.' She looked up at the old home again. She could see it more clearly now. It was a magnificent two-story Australian colonial, white-painted, and of perfect proportions. The walls were weatherboard, although there was some red brick visible on the lower floor. The roof was steeply pitched in the style of the time and painted a dark colonial green. A weathervane in the shape of a pelican sat atop one of the gables. Some of the roofing iron was a little rusty here and there, and the paintwork was showing signs of age, but it was a beautiful old home, helped in no small way by the wonderful gardens and shady trees. A double-sided set of steps in the tropical fashion of the day led up to the wide veranda, which carried around three sides of the upper story. Charlotte noticed two people sitting at a table, watching her as she continued up the driveway. She saw them get up and start down the steps.

'Hello there. I'm guessing you're Alice and David,' Charlotte called to them as they approached her. She'd recognized them from earlier that day at the funeral of the old man.

'G'day there,' the man replied. The Aboriginal woman said nothing.

'My name is Charlotte Dawson. I'm the granddaughter of Henry Dawson's brother. I'm so glad you are here today. I need to speak with you both.'

Neither the Aboriginal woman nor the white man replied.

'I wonder if you'd mind introducing yourselves?' Charlotte asked. She was beginning to feel embarrassed and uncomfortable.

'Oh, I'm sorry about that, Miss. I'm David Thomson. I used to do all the gardening here. This is Alice Rowe. Alice did the housework and cooking for Henry. I apologise for seeming a little standoffish. You see, we're both still coming to grips with the old man's passing. He meant a lot to the both of us.'

'I have something for you,' Charlotte replied awkwardly. She was feeling embarrassed and nervous for some reason or another. She felt as if she was intruding. She took the two envelopes from her handbag, went forward, and reached out with them.

'We're both all paid up, Miss. The old man always paid us a full week ahead. We've just been here gathering up our stuff,' the man said, taking the envelopes, looking at them, and then passing one to the Aboriginal woman. 'As I said, the old man meant a lot to us, Miss.'

'It seems that you both meant a lot to him as well, David. Mister Dawson has instructed me, through an inheritance letter, to thank you for your many years of service and give you those envelopes. I would keep them in a safe place if I were you. He has given each of you a cheque for one hundred thousand dollars.'

Alice sat down on the lawn and burst into tears.

The gardener looked at her for a few seconds, then he knelt to comfort her. He had a lost look on his face.

'Do you think we could go inside out of this heat?' Charlotte asked.

'Yes, certainly, Miss,' David Thomson replied, getting to his feet.

Alice got up also. Her dark face was wet with tears. She put her envelope in her apron pocket, went to Charlotte, and took her hand. 'Come with me, Miss,' she said with a weary smile.'

'Thank you, Alice.'

The Aboriginal woman led Charlotte up the steps to the

veranda, opened the front door, and turned to her. 'I'm sorry we both treated you so poorly, Miss. It's all been a terrible shock, you see. We miss the old man so much,' she said, leading Charlotte inside the home.

Charlotte looked along the hallway. She noticed its high ceiling. A wonderful fan-shaped art deco mirror hung on the wall above a stunning mahogany wall stand not far from the front door. An antique bronze lamp in the art deco style of a woman holding a globe above her head sat on the hallstand. A painting of a pearling lugger laid up among some mangroves hung on the wall opposite. More paintings hung on walls further along the hallway.

'Oh, that's alright, Alice. Do you think we could go into the sitting room?' Charlotte asked, turning to Alice.

Alice looked at David and then back to Charlotte. 'We don't go in there much. We could go up to the kitchen if you like,' she said quietly.

'All right then,' Charlotte replied.

The Aboriginal woman took Charlotte's hand again, and they continued along the hallway to the kitchen.

David pulled out a chair from the kitchen table when they got there. 'There you go, Miss,' he said with a polite smile.

Charlotte sat down. She noticed a bowl of water in the centre of the table. A yellow hibiscus flower was floating in it.

'Would you like a cup of tea or a cold drink, Miss?' Alice asked.

'A glass of cold water would be very welcome. Thank you, Alice.'

David Thomson sat down and put his envelope on the table in front of him. He was still staring at it when Charlotte spoke.

'The gardens are lovely, David,' she remarked, to ease the tension while she waited for her drink.

'Thank you, Miss. There's a lot of work needed to keep them nice in this weather,' David replied.

Alice came back and handed the glass of water to Charlotte. 'There you are, Miss.'

'Thank you, Alice,' Charlotte replied, taking a sip of the water. 'I think I should tell you both what has happened over these last couple of days.'

Alice sat down, and they both watched Charlotte's face.

'It has all been a big surprise for me, but it seems I am Henry Dawson's only living blood relative, and as such, he has left his entire estate to me, which includes this lovely old home and all that's in it,' Charlotte began.

Alice and David looked at each other but said nothing.

Charlotte continued. 'I live in Adelaide, down south, and until a few days ago, I had never heard of Mr. Henry Dawson. It seems he and his brother—my grandfather, lost contact many years ago. Henry made inquiries and found out his brother had died, as had his brother's son—my father. He was then told through an agency in Adelaide of my existence.'

'And you say the old home is yours now that the old man's gone,' David said with a confused expression.

'Yes, David. I am now the owner of this wonderful old home.'

'What do you think you will do with it now that it is yours, Miss?' Alice asked, her eyes still fixed on Charlotte's face.

'Call me Charlotte, Alice.'

'That wouldn't be proper, Miss.'

'I won't mind at all.'

'Oh . . . All right then, Miss,' Alice replied.

'I'm not too sure what I should do about the house at the moment. I'll be here in Darwin for the next few weeks. I would love it if you would both continue with your duties while I am here, though. I will pay you both, of course.'

'There's no need to go paying us, not after what the old man just gave us,' David blurted out, smiling at Alice, and looking at his envelope.

'I insist that I pay you both, David. I won't have it any other way.'

'If that's what you want, Miss,' David replied awkwardly.

'Will you be staying here in the old house, Miss Charlotte?' Alice asked, feeling embarrassed by the familiarity of calling the beautiful white woman by her first name.

'Oh . . . I hadn't thought of that. Would it be much trouble for you if I did, Alice?'

'No trouble at all, Miss . . . Err, Charlotte. No trouble at all.'

'Do you have any objections, David?' Charlotte asked.

'I just do the gardens. If the old place belongs to you now, I think you should do whatever you like,' David replied, smiling pleasantly. Charlotte noticed he was holding his envelope in his hand.

'All right then, I'll come tomorrow afternoon after I've finished with the solicitors,' Charlotte replied.

'You could stay in the guest room, Miss. It's roomy, and the second bathroom is just across the hall. It hasn't been used for a few years, though. I could get it ready for you tomorrow morning,' Alice suggested.

'Thank you. Tell me, Alice—how did Mr. Dawson pass away? What happened to him?'

'I found him out in the garden near the little arbour he'd built for his dear wife many years ago. It had been raining quite badly that night. He had a heart attack—poor man.'

'It must have been a terrible shock for you, Alice.' Charlotte noticed tears misting in the Aboriginal woman's eyes.

'It was awful, Miss. David got here soon after I did, and we called the hospital. They sent an ambulance to collect the body. We both cried for ages. He was such a lovely man. It was his birthday. I had his present with me that morning. It was a book about Broome and pearling, where he and Tessa used to live years ago. He would have loved it. I've put it in the sitting room on one of the library shelves.'

How terribly sad it must have been for you,' Charlotte replied.

David stood up and put his envelope in his shirt pocket. 'I'd better be off then. It's been nice to meet you, Charlotte,' he said, nodding goodbye to Alice.

'I had better be getting back to my hotel as well. I'll need to tell them what my plans are,' Charlotte replied, getting to her feet as well.

'I could drop you off if you like. I'm heading home in a minute,' David offered.

'Thank you, David. That would save me waiting for a taxi.'

Charlotte looked at Alice and smiled. 'I just love the old home, Alice. You keep it so nice. Will you show me around tomorrow when I come?'

'Yes, Miss, I'd be glad to. What would you like for dinner tomorrow night? I might have to get some things from the shops.'

'Oh, I hadn't given that any thought. Would you like to surprise me?'

'All right then,' Alice replied with a pleasant smile.

'Thank you, Alice. I hope the three of us become good friends over the next few days,' Charlotte said, pushing her chair in place.

'I would like that, Miss. After all, you're the old man's kin. I think he would have wanted that,' Alice said, getting to her feet as well.

'I'd have to agree with that,' David added, with an awkward smile.

'Thank you both for making me feel so welcome,' Charlotte replied.

'Goodbye then, Miss Charlotte. I'll see you tomorrow,' Alice said, pushing her chair in place against the little round table as well.

Charlotte went over and hugged the Aboriginal woman. 'Goodbye, Alice.'

'Oh, my goodness . . . Goodbye, Miss Charlotte.'

# Chapter 3

# Dawson House Holdings

Charlotte spent all of the following morning at the offices of Rosenberg and Gately with Paul Rosenberg, familiarising herself with the many assets and holdings left to her by Henry Dawson, of which there were many. The share portfolio alone was quite complicated, as a lot of the dividends were still to be paid or reinvested.

'Charlotte, I have been giving a lot of thought to what will be the best course of action for you as we move forward. Many years ago, I set up a company and named it *Dawson House Holdings* for Henry, and it seems to me that the best course of action would be if we simply transferred the ownership of that company into your name,' Paul Rosenberg advised.

'I'm relying on your knowledge of these things, Paul,' Charlotte replied.

'That way, the taxation structures would remain mostly unchanged, as most of Henry's assets were governed by *Dawson House Holdings*. Some, however, were not, and among those are his personal bank accounts, of which there are three. Each was used for different purposes. One was used for the maintenance of his lovely old home and the wages for Alice and David; another was used solely for donations to local clubs and societies just before the end of each financial year. Of course, those donations were tax-deductible and always made anonymously through our office. The last of his accounts is an investment account in Singapore. As you can see by the figures, it holds quite a lot of money, easily transferable, of course.

That particular account has always been assessed separately.'

'This is all quite complicated. Are there any taxation payments still pending?' Charlotte asked.

'No, there are not. Everything is in order as of the end of this last fiscal year. If we can get this transfer of *Dawson House Holdings* done over the next couple of weeks, we should be fine for the following fiscal year,' Paul Rosenberg replied. 'Of course, a lot of this will depend on your personal thoughts and decisions and whether you decide to sell any or all of Henry's holdings and his old home and cut and run, so to speak.'

'I'm not sure about any of it just now. I don't think I want to sell the old home, though. Certainly not for a while anyway. It's such a lovely place. I met Alice and David yesterday and gave them their inheritance. It certainly came as a surprise for both of them. They were so devoted to the old man.'

'Do you think you might move up here then? It could work out financially for you. You could live in the old home and open a small office here in the city to manage your affairs. You could get yourself a nice car. It would all be deductible,' Paul suggested.

'I don't know about that, Paul. I have my mother to think of. My father passed away a couple of years ago. I like to keep my eye on her,' Charlotte replied.

'I'm not sure if you know, but Henry told me some time ago that there is a comfortable flat on the bottom floor of the old place. It may need a bit of work to get it right, but it might be worth considering for your mother,' Paul suggested.

'I certainly love the old place. What a wonderful position! And the gardens are so beautiful.'

'Well then, give it some thought.'

'I certainly will. Fancy that, moving all the way up here to Darwin. I'll have a serious talk with Mum and get her thoughts on it,' Charlotte replied.

'Well, that's it for today. I shall see you tomorrow morning,' the solicitor said, getting up.

'Thank you for looking after my booking at the hotel, Paul. I'll be checking out this afternoon and moving into the old place for a while.'

'That sounds like a sensible idea, Charlotte,' Paul Rosenberg replied, reaching for Charlotte's hand.

*　*　*

Later that afternoon, Charlotte booked a taxi to take her to the old house on East Point Road again. When she arrived, David Thomson's Toyota utility was parked in the same place on the driveway beneath the shade of the old flame tree. He was carrying fallen palm fronds and putting them in the back when Charlotte walked up the driveway carrying her suitcase.

'Hello, Charlotte. I see you've decided to move in for a while,' he said when she got to him.

'I have, David. But I'm not sure for how long just yet,' Charlotte replied.

'Would you like me to take that case inside for you? Alice has the guest room all done for you.'

'I'll be fine, thank you. I don't want to take you away from your work,' Charlotte replied, continuing to the veranda steps just as Alice came out the front door.

'Hello, Miss Charlotte. I'm so glad you decided to come. It'll be nice to have someone to look after again. Can I take your case?'

'I'm fine, thank you, Alice,' Charlotte replied, heading up the steps.

'Well then, you just follow me,' Alice said, holding open the front door.

'I'll see you both tomorrow.' They heard David call out from the driveway. 'I need to get to the dump before I head home,' he yelled, climbing into his utility.

'See you then,' Alice called back.

Charlotte waved, and they watched him back onto the road and drive away.

'There's no air conditioning, I'm afraid, but there are ceiling fans in the bedrooms. The bathroom is just across the hall there,' Alice said when they got to the guest room. She went over and brushed some invisible creases from the bedcover.

'This will suit me just fine, Alice. There's a nice breeze coming across from the bay just now,' Charlotte replied, putting her suitcase on the bed.

'It's getting late; I'll be heading home shortly as well,' Alice added. 'I've left some nice cold chicken in the refrigerator and a bowl of cucumber and mango salad. I hope you like it.'

'That sounds perfect, Alice,' Charlotte replied and began unpacking her case.

'I'll have to show you around the old place tomorrow, Miss, if you don't mind. There is a lot to see. There's a nice flat downstairs. The laundry is down there too, as well as a couple of old storerooms. The garage is at the back. Both of Henry's old cars are in there, all covered in dust. They haven't been used for years. You'll probably want to get rid of them if you decide to sell the place,' Alice explained.

'I'm thinking of not selling, Alice. I haven't made my mind up yet. I may decide to move up here and live in the old place. Would you consider working for me if I did?'

Alice left the window she was opening and went to Charlotte. 'I would love to, Miss. David and I were hoping you weren't going to sell the old place.'

'Well, Alice, it's not certain just yet. I'll need to give it some more thought.'

'That's all right. You just take your time and make the decision that's right for you,' Alice replied, smiling.

'I think I'll take a nice cool shower and go and sit out on the veranda for a while. Thank you for leaving the meal for me.'

'Well then, I'd better be heading off home. I'll see you at eight in the morning.'

'Thank you, Alice.'

'Don't go feeling all alone out there on the veranda. I'm sure the old place will make you feel welcome if you let it.'

'I hope so. Goodbye, Alice.'

'Goodbye then, Miss,' Alice replied.

Charlotte unpacked her case, hung up her clothes, and undressed. She picked up the folded towel on the bed, went across the hall to the bathroom, and showered. Twenty minutes later, she went into the kitchen and poured herself a glass of chardonnay from the bottle she'd packed in her suitcase back at the hotel. She added some ice cubes and went out onto the front veranda. She was wearing the pink silk bathrobe she had bought while on holiday in Hong Kong a couple of years earlier. She loved the feeling of the silk on her naked body. She put her glass on the little table near the railing and sat down in the comfortable old cane chair next to it.

A cooling breeze was coming across from the bay. Charlotte could smell the perfume from the frangipani trees. She had the sudden, strangest feeling that she belonged there on the veranda of the old place. She looked over at the little bougainvillea-covered arbour Alice had spoken of the day before. The place where the old man had died. Blood-red flowers rambled over it and down one of the posts, almost to the ground. Two brightly coloured lorikeets were sitting together on the back of the cast iron seat. She picked up her wine glass, took a sip, and watched them nibble at each other's wings and preen themselves.

An hour later, she got up and went back to the kitchen. She poured herself another glass of wine, sat down, and called her mother.

A few seconds later, her mother answered: 'Hello, Charlotte. How has your day been, love?'

'Busy, Mum—very busy.'

'Where are you now?'

'I'm out at the old house, sitting in the kitchen, sipping a glass of chardonnay at the moment.'

'What's it like?'

'The chardonnay or the house, Mum?'

'The house, silly,' Charlotte's mother replied with a laugh.

'It's quite beautiful. The gardens are so nice. There are shady trees everywhere and pretty little parrots flitting about. The sea is just across the road, and the breezes are wonderful. I can't believe it's mine at the moment, Mum.'

'Is it nice inside?'

'It's lovely. It's quite large. There's even a flat downstairs. I haven't looked at it yet. Some of the old furniture in the house looks quite expensive. You should see the dining room. There are beautiful paintings. The kitchen is a bit worn, but it's nice, and there's a little nook with leadlight windows.'

'Take some photos and send them to me, love.'

'I will, Mum. You would love the place,' Charlotte said excitedly.

'What do you think you will do with it?' Charlotte's mother asked.

Charlotte didn't answer for a few seconds.

'Are you still there, love?' She heard her mother ask.

'Yes, Mum, I'm still here.'

'Oh . . . Good.'

'I'm thinking of moving up here, Mum. I'm thinking of living in the old house.'

'Oh . . . I see.'

'Mister Rosenberg has suggested it. He says it could be an effective way for me to reduce my taxes. I could open a little office in the city somewhere and get myself a nice car. It would all be deductible. He's offered to help me if I decide to.'

'What about your flat and your friends, love? What about your horse riding?'

'I'm thinking it would be a fresh start. I'll miss my friends, though. I suppose I'll just have to make new ones. I imagine there are horse-riding establishments here somewhere. It would mean breaking the lease on the flat and selling my old Corolla. You wouldn't mind helping, would you, Mum?' Charlotte asked.

'Of course not, love. I'll miss you, though. You won't be able to swim in the sea there, you know. There's crocodiles and stingers!'

'I'm sure there's a swimming pool. Mum.'

'I'm certain there would be, I suppose. It's such a hot place,' Charlotte's mother replied.

'You could sell the house and move up here as well. You could move into the flat downstairs. I'd make sure it's nice first.'

'Sell the house—! I'm not sure about that, Charlotte.'

'You'd get a good price for it now. You could even take that overseas cruise you've been talking about for ages.'

'Oh, my goodness, wouldn't that be nice? Are you quite sure about all of this, love?'

'I am, Mum, and the more I talk about it, the more convinced I am that it could be the right thing. There's something about this lovely old home that's helping me make that decision.'

'It's starting to sound like you've already made up your mind to me,' Charlotte's mother replied.

'Would you consider coming up, Mum?'

'Yes, I think I would . . . It would be like a fresh start for me as well. Now that your father is gone, the house doesn't feel the same anymore.'

'I'll have a good look at the flat downstairs tomorrow and see what needs to be done. Some other things need doing as well. Some of the roof sheets are a bit rusty. There are lots of little things. I'll talk to the gardener tomorrow and see if he can recommend a good carpenter.'

'You have a gardener, Charlotte—?'

'Yes, I do, Mum. His name is David . . . And a housekeeper. Her name is Alice. She's nice. They've both worked for the old man for years. 'I'm going to keep them on.'

'If it's such a big house, I suppose it would be sensible. You can certainly afford it now, love.'

I'd better hang up, Mum. I want to take a walk around the old place before I go to bed. Give moving up here some serious thought, though, and I'll speak to you tomorrow evening.'

'I will, love. Don't forget to send some photos.'

'I won't forget. Goodbye.'

'Goodbye, Charlotte. I love you, sweetheart.'

'And I love you, Mum. Goodbye.'

Charlotte put her phone on the table and picked up her wine glass. She drank the last of it and said, in a loud voice, *'I'm going to live in your lovely old home, Henry Dawson. I hope you don't mind.'* She got up, went over, and sat in the little breakfast nook. It felt simply perfect. She loved the leadlight windows and the lampshade. She slid out and walked around the kitchen, opening cupboards and drawers. It needed work, but she loved it—it was hers.

She went along the hallway and opened one of the doors. It was a bedroom—quite a large one. A beautiful brass bed with white porcelain inserts was all made up as if it were still being used. She noticed a woman's things on the bedside cupboard. A hairbrush, a small mirror, and a Bible. She went in and looked at the painting above the bed. The waterfall looked so real that she could almost hear the water crashing down through the cliffs. She read the artist's name at the bottom of the picture frame. *Isabella Montinari.* She hadn't heard of her, but she loved the painting.

She left the bedroom, went across the hall, and opened another door. It was a bedroom as well, but much smaller. A neatly made single bed sat against the far wall. A small lamp sat on the bedside cabinet. She noticed a silver-plated picture frame next to the lamp but facing the bed. She sat on the bed and picked it up. It held a photograph of a stunningly beautiful woman of mixed race. Charlotte guessed her age at a little over sixty. Her skin was clear, dark, almost coffee-coloured. Her smiling eyes were a deep brown, and her dark hair was tied back from her face in a way that seemed to suit her. She was sitting on the cast iron seat in the little arbour out in the garden and smiling lovingly at whoever was taking the photograph. Charlotte turned the frame and read the words on the back. It was in the same flowing handwriting and done with the same fountain pen that had been used to write the letter she had been given in the solicitor's office.

*'My darling Tessa in her brand-new arbour. Summer, 1962.'*

Charlotte could feel tears beginning to mist in her eyes. This was the old man's wife. The woman he had loved and missed so much when he wrote his letter to her. She looked so happy in the old photograph.

'How very sad life can be!' Charlotte thought. She put the picture back on the bedside cupboard, got up, and left the room.

# Chapter 4

# The Secret Room

Charlotte spent the following morning with Paul Rosenberg, attending to more of the paperwork that needed to be done for her inheritance. Paul's suggestion that they transfer *Dawson House Holdings* directly into Charlotte's name was agreed upon and set in motion. Later in the morning, she was introduced to one of Henry Dawson's long-time bank managers. The meeting was business-like and professional, and Charlotte was assured that account transfers would be set up for signing within the next few days. At midday, Paul Rosenberg took Charlotte to a city restaurant for lunch.

'Have you given any more thought to moving up to Darwin and managing your affairs from here, Charlotte?' he asked while they waited to be shown to a table.

'Yes, I have, Paul. I've decided to take your advice. I've given notice to my school and cancelled the lease on my flat in Glenelg. My mother has agreed to take care of things down there for me. I've decided to stay here in Darwin and live in the old house. I've spoken to the housekeeper and the gardener this morning and asked them if they would continue working for me, and they have both agreed,' Charlotte replied.

'I'm pleased for you, Charlotte. If you're thinking you might need an office, there's a small one that's just become vacant on the ground floor of our building that might suit you nicely. I could show it to you tomorrow after we've finished our work if you like.'

'Thank you, Paul. That would suit me perfectly,' Charlotte replied. 'That would mean I could drop in, annoy you, and ask for advice whenever I needed it.'

'You would be more than welcome to, Charlotte, and it wouldn't be an annoyance at all.'

Later that afternoon, Charlotte caught a taxi to her new home. When she arrived, David was trimming the high hedge that separated the property from one of the neighbours. He waved as she went up the driveway. Alice was busy at the stove, preparing dinner for her when she went into the kitchen.

'Hello, Alice. That smells rather nice.'

'I hope you like it. It was one of the old man's favourites. It's curried mangrove crab. I found a couple of freshly caught crabs at a seafood shop I know on the way here this morning. I'll cook some fried rice to go with it and leave it in the oven for you as well,' Alice replied with a good-natured smile.

'It sounds wonderful. Don't forget, you are to show me around the old home before you go.'

'I hadn't forgotten, Miss,' Alice replied.

A short while later, Alice was leading Charlotte around, showing her all the features of the wonderful old home.

One of the last things she showed her upstairs was a door next to the bathroom that Charlotte thought had been a cupboard. Alice opened it to reveal a chute that sent soiled clothing and bedding to the downstairs laundry.

'What a good idea,' Charlotte remarked.

'It works very well. Let's go downstairs now, and I'll show you around down there. The flat has never been part of the main living area, so we need to go out and use the outside stairs,' Alice said, leading Charlotte outside and down the stairs. 'I believe it was originally built for Tessa's mother to live in, but I'm not sure if she ever did.'

'I'm thinking I may have a use for it myself soon,' Charlotte replied, following the Aboriginal woman down the stairs.

'It hasn't been used for years, but I still clean it regularly. There are two bedrooms and a nice little sitting room. There are fans in the bedrooms and the sitting room, but no air conditioning. The kitchen is quite small, but it's nice. The old refrigerator doesn't work anymore. I suppose it's been turned off for too long. I think the wood stove would need to be removed and replaced as well.' Alice advised her as they went from room to room.

'It's quite nice, all considered,' Charlotte remarked, 'but it does need some work. I was going to ask David, but I'm sure you will know, Alice. I would like to hire a carpenter to carry out some renovations. Do you know of anyone that would be suitable?'

'Yes, I think I do. The old man used him last year to replace some of the veranda floorboards. I could ring him for you and ask him to come around if you like. His name is Jeremy Bolton. He's a nice young man and a very capable tradesman,' Alice said.

'I should like to meet him,' Charlotte replied.

'He's a handsome young fella as well, Miss.'

'Now, now, Alice. Just as long as he's a good carpenter, that's the most important thing.' Charlotte said and laughed.

'He's very good at his work, and I'm sure you'd be happy with him,' Alice replied, with a wide smile on her dark face.

'If you could ring and ask him to come around sometime, that would be great.'

'All right then, Miss Charlotte. I'll call him tomorrow.'

'Thank you, Alice.'

'There's not much more to see down here, just a couple of storerooms full of all sorts of old things. Come with me, and I'll show you the old man's cars.' Alice said, leading Charlotte out of the flat and along the side of the old home, where she unlocked two heavy wooden doors.

'I'll show you where these keys hang when we get back upstairs, Miss. I have my own for the front door, but that's the only key the old man ever gave me. It's all I need, though,' she said as they both pulled open the heavy doors.

'Thank you, Alice.'

'The old man didn't want us cleaning his old cars. He said it wasn't worth the time as he didn't drive them anymore. He wouldn't sell them, though. As you can see, they're both covered in dust,' Alice remarked as they went inside.

'How did Henry get to meetings, his doctor's appointments, and business meetings if he didn't use his cars?' Charlotte asked.

'He was almost ninety-eight years old when he passed, Miss Charlotte. He hadn't driven for years. David would take him. The old man paid for David's utility years ago. I suppose it belongs to you now,' Alice replied, switching on the light.

Charlotte looked at the two old cars. One was a four-door Mercedes sedan. It was quite old, and under the dust, she could tell it was a dark blue colour. It looked to be in exceptionally fine condition. The other car was a sports car. It had a small tarpaulin covering the cockpit. Charlotte went to the rear and read, *Porsche 356 A*. It was a bright guard's red colour under all the dust, and for such an old car, it was quite beautiful.

'That was Tessa's little car, Miss,' Alice said, brushing some of the dust from the tarpaulin. 'Henry loved her so much, you know. Her death almost killed him.'

'Did you know her, Alice?'

'Only for a little while. She was very sick when I came here. That was the reason I was hired. She was quite beautiful. It was so sad to watch them together. Henry used to read her poetry and fuss over her so.'

'What was wrong with her, Alice?'

'The poor dear had some sort of cancer. She fought so hard, but it took her in the end.'

'How very sad,' Charlotte replied.

'Henry never spoke to anyone other than me for months after she died. It was a terrible time. She meant everything to him. He has kept her room the same as it was all those years ago. He's never let me go in there to clean. He's been looking after it by himself all this time,' Alice said sadly.

'Thank you for telling me.' Charlotte replied, putting her hand on the Aboriginal woman's shoulder. She'd noticed the tears in her eyes.

'He just loved her so much, Miss Charlotte,' Alice whispered.

* * *

Later, when Alice and David left for their homes, Charlotte went to her bathroom and showered. When she finished, she put on her pink silk bathrobe and went into the kitchen. She turned on the oven and heated the meal Alice had left for her. While she waited, she sat at the table and looked at the ring of keys Alice had left after showing her where they hung in the butler's pantry. She knew the doors that every key opened, except for two. Alice had explained that they probably fit a couple of the old man's trunks down in one of the old storerooms, but she wasn't sure. They were quite different from the others. They were longer and looked a lot sturdier.

After Charlotte had eaten her meal, she washed her dishes. When she finished, she picked up the ring of keys and went into the sitting room. She loved this room more than any other in the old home. It felt like a giant step back in time. She adored the old furniture, especially the two ebony elephants. They were quite large but looked as if they belonged there, standing silently sentinel on either side of the bamboo palm in its lovely old Chinese pot. If only they could talk, what tales could they tell?

She went over to the windows and closed the shutters and curtains. She wanted to find the bookcase that opened to reveal the little passage Henry had told her about in his letter. She was almost certain that Alice didn't know of it when they discussed the keys earlier. After several minutes of pulling at shelves and searching for hidden levers, Charlotte was becoming frustrated. For a while, she thought that the elaborate French mantle clock might have something to do with it, but it didn't.

The bookcases were quite long, running almost the entire length of one of the sitting room walls. A row of low cupboards ran beneath them. Crystal glassware, decanters, bowls, and delicate ivory figurines were set about on small, crocheted mats on the benchtop above. Some were Japanese and looked quite old and expensive, and some were Chinese. She picked up one and admired it. It was Aphrodite, the Greek goddess of love. It was quite beautiful. She set it back down. She then set about opening each of the lower cabinet doors. Some held old magazines, others held even more books, and two of them held paper-sleeved records for the old phonograph that stood alongside the piano. Charlotte crouched down and looked inside the one that only had a few records in it. Somehow, it looked different from the others. The shelf was set back a little. She reached in with her hand and ran her fingers along the underside of the benchtop. There was something there, something metallic—a long sliding bolt. She felt about until she found its folded lever, pulled it down, and slid the bolt sideways. The section of bookshelves above where she was crouched creaked and moved away from the others. She stood up, gripped the shelf, and pulled it slowly open. Inside was a narrow vestibule or passageway.

Charlotte stepped inside. The passageway only went a short distance to a set of narrow concrete steps. On the wall to her left, she saw a light switch. It was of a type she had never seen before. It was round and made from polished wood with a small brass knob for a switch. She noticed the electrical wiring running to it was in a metal conduit of some sort. It looked quite old. She flicked down the switch, and a single light globe of very low wattage illuminated a short flight of six steps going down to a landing with a dull yellow glow. She took an excited breath and went down to the landing. Another flight of six steps went down at a different angle to a short passageway. She went down carefully to the passageway, where she found a light switch on the wall to her left again. She flicked it on. Another light globe on the concrete ceiling lit up the passageway with the same dull yellow light. At the end of the passageway, there was a heavy wooden door with a thick steel lock plate. Charlotte inserted one of the keys. It wasn't the correct one. She inserted the other and turned it. The door opened to reveal a small, windowless room. The walls and ceiling were made of solid concrete. She found the light switch and flicked it on.

The room was about the size of a very small bedroom. A little rectangular table and a single chair sat against one of the walls. There was no other furniture. The room was free of dust, and there were no cobwebs. A small mesh-covered vent was set high on one of the walls. It must have opened into an area somewhere near the garage below the old home. Set into the concrete wall directly in front of her, Charlotte could see a large old-fashioned wall safe.

Her fingers trembled as she inserted the other key and turned it. Nothing happened. In the centre of the door was a large horizontal lever with a clenched metal fist wrapped around it. She wrapped her hand around the metal fist and turned it. Metal pins slid back inside the door, and it opened a little. Charlotte pulled on the fist, and the door swung completely open.

Inside were several metal shelves and compartments. She opened one of the compartments and took out one of the wooden boxes that sat there. Inside were paper sleeves filled with English gold sovereigns. There were more than a hundred of them. She put the box back and opened another. It was filled with even more sovereigns. There were too many for her to count quickly. She put it back and slid out one of the metal shelves. It was lined with dark green velvet. Rows of perfect pearls glittered in the weak yellow light of the room. She opened another shelf. There were more pearls. Some were small; others were larger. Some were pear-shaped, and some were perfectly round. Some were silvery-white in colour, while others had a pale rose colour to them. All of them were quite beautiful. Charlotte had no idea of their value, but she knew they were most likely naturally formed pearls and probably worth a fortune. She opened more compartments, where she found bundles of English pound notes and American dollars.

On the bottom of the safe, Charlotte saw the journal the old man had spoken of and a shoebox full of letters and yellowed photographs. She took out the journals and the shoebox and closed and locked the safe. She wasn't sure what she should do about the contents of the safe, but for now, she would leave them locked away. She picked up the journal and the shoebox, turned off the light, and left the little room. She went back up the steps and into the sitting room, where she latched the bookcase into its closed position. Charlotte's heart was racing with wonderment at what she had just seen in the little room. She was confused, but she decided she would say nothing of it until she had given it more thought. She took the journals and the shoebox back to her bedroom and put them on the bed. She went to her bathroom, took off her robe, and showered again. It had been hot in the little room. After she finished, she went back to her bedroom, switched on the ceiling fan, and sat on the bed. She opened the old, leather-bound journal. It was written with the same fountain pen and in the same flowing handwriting that had penned her letter. The cover page was headed: *The True Story of the Life of Henry Archibald Dawson.* She lay back on her pillows and began reading . . .

# Part 2

# Chapter 5

# Port Of Darwin

October 1913.

Captain Darcy Callaghan of the West Australian State Shipping Lines vessel, the S. S. *Gorgon*, was watching the last of his southbound passengers climb the gangway when he noticed a young lad talking to one of his crew down on the wharf. It was obvious to the captain that the boy was distressed. Now and then, he would point up to the ship, and the crewman would shake his head. The captain wondered what was bothering the lad. He went to the side of the ship and called down to the crewman, signalling that he should bring the lad up to him. Perhaps he had misplaced his family when they boarded. He watched them hurry up the gangway.

'This lad here wants to come aboard and work his way down to Fremantle, Captain. I told him we're not hiring at the moment,' the crewman announced with noticeable self-importance when they got to him.

'Leave him with me and get back to your duties, Foster. I'll deal with this,' the captain advised.

'Yes, sir,' Foster replied and hurried back down the gangway.

'What seems to be the trouble, young man?' The captain asked, turning to the lad.

'I'd like to get down to Fremantle, sir. I'm willing to work for me passage.'

'What's your name, young man?'

'Henry, sir . . . Henry Dawson,' the lad replied.

'Are you running away from someone, Henry?'

'No one, sir. I just want to get down to Fremantle, that's all.'

'Is it family trouble you're in? Has your father been too hard on you, and you've run off? I want you to tell me the truth now,' The captain insisted.

'Me father used to give me and me brother a terrible time, sir. We'd get floggings, regular-like, and after our dear mother died of the influenza, he got a lot worse,' the lad replied.

'And where's your father now?'

'He hung himself in our woodshed, sir.'

'What's happened to your brother?'

'He managed to get a job with a camel driver carting freight down to Alice Springs. He wants to get to Adelaide. A boy told him it's nice down there.'

'How old is your brother?'

'He's just turned fourteen, sir,' the lad replied.

'What about you, young man?'

'I'm sixteen, coming on to seventeen, sir. I'm strong for me size, and I know how to work hard.'

'Have you been working for a living then?' the captain asked.

'I have, sir. I've been working for a wood merchant chopping firewood up until me mother died.'

'And what happened to you and your brother after your father hung himself?' the captain asked.

'They sent us off to a boy's home in Nightcliff, sir,' Henry replied.

'And what was wrong with that?'

'We just didn't like it, sir. They treated us poorly. Anyway, they were goin' to foster us out to different homes and to people we didn't know at all.'

'And just why do you want to get down to Fremantle?' the captain asked.

'I've been told that work is easy to get down in Perth. I thought I'd like to start over down there.'

'Do you think anyone from the boy's home will be out looking for you?' the captain asked.

'I don't think they care one way or another. Like I said, they treated us real poorly.'

'I'll tell you what I'll do for you, young man. I will hire you as a deckhand on board my ship if you give me your word that you won't leave the ship in Fremantle. It will be a full-time position with regular pay, accommodation, and all meals. How does that sound to you?'

'You mean you're offering me a proper job, sir.'

'That is correct, young man. Twelve shillings a week, and all found.'

'I'll take it, sir, and thank you,' Henry Dawson replied.

'And as of now, you will address me as Captain Callaghan,' the captain advised.

'Will do, Captain Callaghan, sir.'

Captain Callaghan called a crew member standing near the head of the gangway over.

'Young man, this is chief mate Derrick Perkins. He will take you below and get you a cabin. You'll have to toss in with one of the other crew. When you're settled, I want you to come back and report to me.'

'What will me duties be, Captain?'

'The chief mate will attend to that,' Captain Callaghan replied. He turned to the chief mate. 'Perkins, this is young Henry Dawson, our new deckhand.'

The chief mate reached for Henry's hand. 'I'm glad to know you, Henry Dawson.'

'I'm pleased to meet you, Mister Chief Mate,' Henry replied, his mind spinning.

'Off with you then,' the captain said, smiling.

'Thank you, Captain,' Henry replied. Feeling the chief mate's hand on his shoulder, he turned and followed him down a narrow steel stairway.

*   *   *

Henry Dawson spent the next year on board the S.S. *Gorgon*, and they were among the happiest days of his life. He soon became a popular shipmate with the crew and, in particular, with the captain, who took a shine to the boy and treated him like the son he'd never been lucky enough to have had.

As time went by, Henry soon became familiar with all of the ports along the Western Australian coast, and he found he loved the sea, with all its unpredictable moods and terrible dangers. From the first day he was hired, he never enjoyed being away from his ship or his friends, even when on a break in Fremantle or Perth.

# Chapter 6

# Henry and the Watermelon

It was on such a trip to the north at the beginning of 1914 that Henry Dawson's life changed forever. They had been steaming for five days since leaving Fremantle on their regular voyage to the coastal ports of the north and then on to Singapore. That morning, they were moored in the little coastal town of Port Hedland. Henry was assigned to helping passengers mount the steep wooden gangway when they returned to the ship after walking the streets of the remote northern town. They were soon to sail when a well-dressed couple arrived at the gangway. The man was carrying a wooden case of fresh fruit they had just purchased from a grocer in the town. He was a white man, of medium height, powerfully built, and around 40 years of age, perhaps a little more. He had dark hair, wore a thin moustache, and was dressed in an expensive, white linen tropical suit, a starched white shirt, a white tie, and off-white shoes. His fashionably dressed wife was a tall black woman of stunning beauty, with long dark hair and dark, smiling eyes.

'Can I carry that to your cabin for you, sir?' Henry asked the well-dressed man, pointing to the wooden case in his hand.

'I'm fine, young man, but my daughter is probably in need of some help. She's behind us somewhere, struggling with the biggest watermelon I've ever seen.'

'In that case, I'll keep an eye out for her, sir,' Henry replied, ticking his little book, and turning towards the last group of ap-proaching passengers as the well-dressed couple continued up the gangway.

It was then that Henry Dawson saw the most beautiful young woman he had ever seen in his entire young life. Like her mother, she was tall and slim. Henry guessed her age at around seventeen, perhaps a little more. Her skin was the colour of the special coffee beans the captain kept in the jar in his cabin. Her legs were long, smooth, and copper-coloured, and her breasts were small under the pretty white cotton blouse that she wore. Even though she was struggling under the weight of her huge watermelon, she walked with an elegant, lithe grace that seemed to suit her. Henry gasped for breath. The closer she got to him, the more beautiful she became. Finally, when she arrived at the foot of the gangway, struggling under the weight of her watermelon, Henry blurted out.

'Your father has asked me to carry that for you, Miss.'

'Oh! I can manage . . . But then, I suppose . . . If Father has asked you to help . . .' the girl said with a surprised expression, hesitating, and then handing Henry her watermelon.

'Thank you, Miss,' Henry mumbled, taking the watermelon from her smooth brown arms. 'I'm Henry, Miss . . . Henry Dawson.' Henry noticed she had the same dark, smiling eyes as her mother.

'I'm Tessa Taylor,' the girl replied with a confident smile.

When they reached the head of the gangway, Henry noticed that the girl's parents were not waiting for her. He shuffled the watermelon from one arm to another.

'What's your cabin number, Miss Tessa?' he asked.

'Number 14,' the girl replied.

'Well then, if you'd like to follow me,' Henry advised and started down a short flight of steel stairs.

'Thank you so much for helping me, Henry,' the girl replied, smiling, and following him down the stairs and into a long passageway.

'It's no trouble at all, Miss Tessa . . . Have you and your parents been on a holiday?'

'No, not really, although we have done some holiday shopping. We've been in Perth on business with Father, and now we're going home,' the girl answered.

'And whereabouts is home, Miss Tessa?'

'We live in Broome. Father says we'll be arriving there tomorrow sometime.'

Henry was suddenly extremely disappointed. They were to arrive in Broome the following afternoon. 'What does your father do, Miss?' he asked to mask his disappointment.

'My father has pearling boats. He exports pearl shell to Europe and America. Have you heard of *Taylor House Pearls?*'

'No, I can't say that I have, Miss.'

'Oh, that's all right. We are quite well known in Broome, though,' Tessa replied.

As they turned into another long passage, Henry noticed a man step out of a cabin ahead of him. It was Tessa's father. He was smiling at his daughter.

'Thank you for being so helpful, young man. I'll take that now,' he said, pointing to the watermelon when they got to him.

'Would you like me to get a knife and some plates from the galley for you, sir?'

'That won't be necessary. My daughter wants to keep it intact until we get to Broome. After we've eaten it there, she wants to plant some of the seeds and see if she can grow one just as big.'

'In that case, I could put it in one of the cool rooms for you,' Henry suggested.

'Are you sure that wouldn't be too much trouble?'

'No problem at all, sir. I could put a tag on it saying it's for a passenger in cabin 14,' Henry added.

'In that case, please go ahead,' Tessa's father replied.

'I'll take care of it right away, sir.'

'What's your name, young man?'

'I'm Henry Dawson, sir,' Henry replied.

'I'm pleased to meet you, Henry Dawson. I'm Duncan Taylor. My daughter's name is Tessa.'

'We have already introduced ourselves, Father,' Tessa said with a shy smile.

'Oh . . . I see.' Tessa's father replied with an expression Henry couldn't quite fathom.

'I suppose I'd better get back to my work now,' Henry mumbled, shuffling the watermelon about.

'Goodbye, and thank you for all your help, young man.' Tessa's father replied, reaching for his daughter's hand.

'Goodbye, Miss Tessa,' Henry said, looking at the girl.

'Goodbye, Henry, and thank you for being so kind.' Tessa replied, smiling and then followed her father into their cabin.

Henry wandered off with the watermelon in his arms, wondering how he was going to survive when Tessa Taylor and her parents disembarked in Broome late the following day.

*   *   *

It wasn't until the following early afternoon that Henry saw Tessa Taylor again. She was with her parents. They were standing at the starboard side railing, watching the rugged Kimberley coastline materialise into the hazy blue distance. The S.S. *Gorgon* was due to arrive in Broome within the hour. Tessa's father was dressed in the same white linen suit he'd been wearing the day before. The only difference was that he was wearing a hat—a fashionable white straw boater. His beautiful wife was dressed differently, though. She was wearing a long, flowing kaftan in several different shades of green. It must have been made from silk or satin, Henry thought, for it seemed to shimmer in the morning sunlight as she moved. Her dark arms were bare, and around her neck, she wore a strange golden pendant with a red stone in its centre that looked like an Egyptian eye. Tessa was dressed in a simple, pale blue cotton blouse, white slacks, and white leather sandals. Her dark, shining hair hung down over her back, almost to her waist, and her smooth brown arms were bare. To Henry, she looked fresh and beautiful beyond compare. He noticed she was holding her mother's hand.

Henry had been searching for them all morning as he worked, but he hadn't seen them until now. He hurried over.

'Hello, Miss Tessa. It's nice to see you again,' he said nervously, waiting for the girl to turn to him.

'Oh! . . . Henry. How lovely to see you again,' Tessa replied with a surprised smile when she turned. There was something in her smile that seemed encouraging to Henry.

Tessa's mother and father turned to Henry as well. They both stared at him. It was Tessa's mother who spoke first after studying Henry for a few seconds.

'Is this the boy who carried your watermelon for you, Tessa?' She said, smiling politely.

Henry noticed her wonderful, smiling eyes again.

'Yes, Mother. His name is Henry Dawson. He was very helpful,' Tessa replied.

'Thank you for being so kind, Henry. I hope Tessa was nice to you,' Tessa's mother said, studying Henry carefully.

'She was very polite to me, ma'am,' Henry replied.

Just then, Tessa's father joined the conversation. 'Hello there, young man. I'm glad we have run into you. I will need to retrieve our watermelon from the cool rooms in a short while.'

'That was the reason I came over, sir. I could give it to you when you depart at the gangway if you like. That's where I'll be working then,' Henry replied.

'That would be appreciated, young man. In that case, we shall see you at the head of the gangway then. And thank you for all your help yesterday.'

Henry noticed Tessa was still smiling at him. He watched her turn and whisper something to her mother.

'All right then, I'll keep a lookout for you when we berth,'

Henry replied, turning to leave.

'Just a moment, young man.' The voice belonged to Tessa's mother.

Henry turned back. He looked at Tessa quickly and then into her mother's dark, smiling eyes again.

'Is there something else I can help you with, ma'am?'

'How long will your ship be berthed in Broome, Henry?'

'For about six hours, ma'am. We have quite a lot of cargo to unload, and then we must catch the tide right,' Henry replied, noticing the surprised expression on Tessa's father's face.

'Are you able to get away from the ship for a couple of hours, Henry?'

'No, not really. But I could speak to the captain if it were important, I suppose. Why do you ask, ma'am?' Henry asked, his heart racing.

'I would like to invite you to our home for tea this afternoon if you can manage to get away for a while,' Tessa's mother said, looking at her husband and then at her daughter's smiling face.

'I would like that, ma'am. I could speak to the captain. I think it should be all right. I could let you know just before you leave the ship. Would that be all right?' Henry asked.

'That will be fine, young man. If you can manage it, my husband will pick you up in our motor car at the entrance to the jetty,' Tessa's mother replied, looking at her husband again.

Henry watched him hesitate for a moment and then nod his head in agreement.

'All right then. I'd better be off. Thank you for the invitation, ma'am.' Henry turned and left quickly, in case Tessa's father reconsidered.

* * *

Captain Callaghan was busy talking to the chief mate, Derrick Perkins when Henry came into the wheelhouse with an excited expression on his face. As soon as the chief mate left, he went forward.

'Can I ask you for a favour, sir?' he began, somewhat breathlessly.

'And just what would this favour be, Henry?' the captain asked.

'Would it be possible for me to have a couple of hours away from the ship when we get into Broome, sir?'

'No, it wouldn't, Henry. We have a lot to do while we're in Broome. You will be needed to help disembark passengers, and after that, there will be cabins to clean,' the captain replied.

'I meant after the passengers have all disembarked, sir.'

'Why do you ask? Do you have some sort of emergency to take care of in the town?'

'No, sir. It's just that I met this nice girl yesterday, and her mother has asked me to have afternoon tea with them at their home in the town,' Henry replied with a disappointed expression.

'A young girl, you say, and what's this girl's name?'

'Tessa, sir. Her name is Tessa Taylor.'

'That would be Duncan Taylor's daughter if I'm not mistaken,' the captain said. 'I dined with them last evening.'

'Yes, sir, that's the girl all right,' Henry replied.

'I see . . . In that case, it might be a good idea for you to stay on board the ship.'

'Why would that be, sir—?'

'The girl's father has quite a hard reputation in these parts.'

'What do you mean, Captain?'

'Duncan Taylor is one of the biggest pearling boat operators on the north-west coast. He has a reputation for being a hard man.'

'I was introduced to him yesterday, and he seemed nice to me,' Henry replied.

'You met his wife, did you—?'

'Yes, sir. She was the one who asked me to have afternoon

tea with them.'

'His wife is a tall, very beautiful mixed-race woman?' The captain added, looking to Henry for confirmation.

'That's correct, Captain. A black woman. She was really nice to me. She thanked me for helping her daughter. I carried her watermelon back to her cabin for her,' Henry replied with a confused expression.

The captain stared at Henry for a moment. 'Perhaps I should tell you a bit more about Duncan Taylor, Henry.'

'Thank you, Captain,' Henry replied.

'As you already know, his wife is a black woman. An exceptionally beautiful black woman. Her name is Kasiah. She is a part Aboriginal and part Macassar woman. She is well known in Broome for her beauty. Kasiah's father came from the city of Kupang, in an area once known as the Dutch East Indies, up on the Savu Sea. His name was Juan Toledo. They say he was a dark, very handsome fellow. He worked as a diver for Duncan Taylor's father, old Angus Taylor. They lived in a run-down old home in Chinatown. A place where hoodoo and witchcraft are still being practised to this day. A part of town where Juan Toledo was comfortable living and where they say he'd become well known for practising his hoodoo as well.'

Henry was wondering why the captain was telling him all this. But he said nothing and continued listening.

'Juan Toledo, Kasiah's father, died tragically, many years ago, from the bends, and Kasiah Toledo was raised by her Aboriginal mother alone. It was said that old Angus Taylor felt partly responsible for Juan Toledo's death. They say he pushed his divers far too hard during those early days. Soon after Toledo's death, Angus began sending money to his wife to help with the raising of Kasiah, her only child. It was rumoured at the time that it was probably to ease his conscience and hold at bay any of Toledo's hoodoo from getting at him from the grave. The story follows that, over the years, Angus began using his young son, Duncan, to deliver money to Toledo's wife on a regular basis. As time went by, the young Duncan fell madly in love with Kasiah, much to the disappointment of his father. Angus tried his best to break them up but to no avail. He had always planned for his son to marry a white woman, preferably the daughter of one of Broome's other well-known, and well-to-do pearling families.

'There was much talk in the town of Broome when the young Duncan Taylor started courting Kasiah Toledo, a black girl from the poorest part of the town. During those times, mixed marriages between blacks and whites were frowned upon. I suppose they still are now, mostly. The day Duncan and Kasiah were to be married, one of the guests at the wedding reception made the mistake of making an unkind remark about Kasiah's skin colour to someone. That comment was overheard by the groom, and a terrible fight ensued, during which Duncan Taylor almost beat that guest to death with his bare fists. I'm told the man has a terrible temper.'

'His wife is certainly very beautiful, captain. I don't think anyone should make remarks about a person's skin colour. It's just not right, and it makes no sense at all,' Henry replied.

'That is quite true, Henry. I'm just telling you all this so that you can understand what sort of man the young girl's father is,' the captain added.

'So, you think it would not be wise for me to go then on account of her father,' Henry replied, his disappointment showing on his handsome face.

'Perhaps it would not be wise, but that is not what I meant. Do you like this girl, Henry?' Captain Callaghan asked.

'Yes, sir, I do. I can't seem to get her out of my mind,' Henry replied.

'In that case, I think you should accept the invitation and just see where it all leads for you. But be very careful how you go with the girl's father.'

'Do you mean I can go, Captain?'

'Yes, I do. But make sure you're back on board by five o'clock this afternoon and no later.'

'Thank you, Captain. I'll do extra when I get back.'

'Far be it for me to stand in the way of young love, Henry. You go and enjoy yourself. But just watch what you say and do with Duncan Taylor,' Captain Callaghan repeated with a laugh.

'Thank you, Captain.'

'Come and see me when you get back and tell me how it all went.'

'I will, sir,' Henry called back as he headed for the door.

# Chapter 7

# Tea with the Taylors

Henry hurried along the Broome jetty. He'd thanked the captain again just before he left the ship for allowing him time away from his duties. He had hurriedly showered and put on his best clothes. He was wearing his freshly laundered beige cotton trousers, a white open-necked shirt, and his best white braces. He hadn't had enough time to polish his shoes, and they were a little scuffed about the toes. His long brown hair hung over his collar in an unruly tangle. He needed a haircut badly.

Henry was nervous. He was wondering what the next couple of hours would hold for him. The captain's story about Tessa's father being a hard man concerned him. He didn't want to say or do the wrong thing. More than anything, he wanted Tessa's parents to like him. He hurried past a horse-drawn cart on its way to the ship and continued along the jetty. A short while later, he could see Duncan Taylor waiting for him at the jetty entrance. He had been hoping Tessa would have been with him, but he couldn't see her. He looked down at his scuffed shoes. He was sorry now that he hadn't taken the time to polish them.

'G'day, Mister Taylor, sir. Thank you for coming to pick me up,' he said nervously when he got to him.

'My car is parked out on the roadside. We have a short walk yet,' Duncan Taylor grunted, turning for the road.

'I don't mind a walk, sir,' Henry replied a little too quickly, as he followed the big man away from the jetty and out onto the roadside.

The only car parked at the roadside near the jetty entrance was a brand-new Pierce-Arrow sedan. Henry had seen a photograph of one in a shipping magazine when he was last in Fremantle. He remembered the archer with the bow emblem on the bonnet. A dark-skinned man was sitting at the wheel, waiting for them.

'In you get, lad,' Duncan Taylor grunted, holding the rear door open for Henry.

Henry climbed in. He could smell the new leather. He wanted to say something nice about the car, but he couldn't think of how to say it. He looked at the man behind the wheel as they pulled away. He was broad-shouldered and dark-skinned. His head was shaved, except for a short, plaited pigtail. There was a thin scar running down his left cheek. Henry noticed strange tattoos on the fingers of his left hand as it gripped the steering wheel.

'We have a distance to go; our home is on the other side of the town,' Duncan Taylor advised, looking at Henry.

'It's a nice car, sir,' Henry finally managed to get out.

'I had it shipped up here a couple of months ago from down in Perth. This is Jago, by the way,' Duncan Taylor said, nodding towards the man driving.

The driver said nothing or bothered to turn his head.

Henry looked out as they sped along the dirt road toward the town. He could see the bright blue of the sea in the distance. It made him feel lonely.

There was an awkward silence for some time, and then Duncan Taylor spoke again. 'I need to have a talk with you while we drive, young man,' he said in a stern tone as Jago turned the big car away from a row of corrugations.

Henry turned back from the sea. He glanced at Duncan Taylor's face, stared straight ahead, and waited.

'I can't say I'm in favour of having you visit with us, young man, and I have advised my wife of my thoughts on this. Tessa is only seventeen years of age. She is not to receive male callers until she turns eighteen, which won't be for another four months. Several young men, all from good local families, I might add, have approached me and asked if they might call, and I have refused every one of them. I am strict with Tessa. She is our only child. I know what you young lads get up to. But I suppose no harm can come from this visit, as I will be watching, and you will soon be sailing, so I have allowed it. But I should tell you right now, young man, if you mistreat my daughter in any way, you will suffer dire consequences. Do I make myself clear?' Duncan Taylor said, with a threatening tone to his voice, just as Jago turned the big car into a long gravel driveway.

'I understand, sir. I have the greatest respect for Tessa. I would never do anything disrespectful. You have my word on that,' Henry replied. He noticed Jago watching him in the rearview mirror. The dark man had a grim, threatening expression on his face.

Duncan Taylor said no more. And they continued along the winding driveway.

Henry took a deep breath, exhaled slowly, and looked out the window. Several Aboriginal men were working in the gardens. One of them was dragging a huge sprinkler on bicycle wheels across the lawn. Water was beating out of it in wobbling arcs. Another man was pushing a wheelbarrow full of palm fronds towards a distant shed. Henry couldn't believe how nice the gardens were. They must have covered more than an acre of ground. Green lawns spread out on either side of the long driveway. Coconut palms lined the sides. Huge umbrella-shaped flame trees and stately tulip trees shaded parts of the wide lawns. Frangipani trees of several different colours were everywhere.

Up ahead, Henry could now see the house. It was beautiful. The roof was clad with galvanised iron, steeply pitched, and painted a deep colonial red. A weathervane in the shape of a pelican sat at the top of one of the gables. A massive mango tree crowded the side of the home that faced the prevailing weather. White-painted steps led up to the wide veranda, which carried around three sides of the stately home. Storm shutters were bolted back on either side of the windows and the French doors in readiness for storms. The house was simply magnificent, helped in no small way by the beautiful gardens that surrounded it. As they drew closer, Henry noticed a narrow, paved path leading away from the house to elaborate arbours covered with bougainvillea and tropical honeysuckle vines.

Jago parked the big Pierce-Arrow in the shade of one of the flame trees and climbed out just as Tessa and her mother came out of the front door onto the veranda.

Henry climbed out, brushing the toes of his shoes against his trouser legs.

'I am so glad you came, Henry.' Tessa's mother called down to him as she and Tessa came down the veranda steps.

Kasiah Taylor was dressed in another stunning kaftan. This time, Henry was certain that it was made from silk. It was deep red, with splashes of gold here and there, and seemed to shimmer in the sunlight as she came down the steps. Tessa was wearing a simple, pure-white linen dress. Her dark hair was tied back from her face in much the same fashion as her mother's. Henry felt his heart race. She looked even more fresh and beautiful than she did when she left the ship.

'Thank you for inviting me, ma'am,' Henry mumbled, suddenly realising how out of place he was, surrounded by such obvious wealth.

'It's our pleasure, Henry,' Tessa's mother replied.

'Hello, Henry,' Tessa said, greeting him with a shy smile when they got to him.

'Hello, Miss Tessa,' Henry replied, trying to gather his senses as he took Tessa's outstretched hand.

Tessa's father took off his jacket, hurried up the steps, and went inside. A few moments later, he came out in shirt sleeves, lighting a pipe.

'Come up and take a seat in the shade, young man. Our housekeeper will be bringing out the tea shortly,' he said, sitting down at a long white cane and glass table.

Jago had disappeared.

Henry followed Tessa and her mother up the steps and sat down in one of the cane chairs. The table was already made. White placemats and napkins had been set in place. Bowls of grapes of two different colours sat on the table alongside a huge bowl of sliced watermelon.

'As you can see, Henry, it hasn't taken Tessa long to cut up her watermelon,' Tessa's mother affirmed, pointing her dark fingers across the table.

'It certainly was a big one,' Henry replied, smiling at Tessa.

'Where were you born, Henry? We need to find out a bit more about you,' Duncan Taylor asked.

'I was born up in Darwin, sir.'

'How old are you, young man?'

'I've just turned eighteen, sir,' Henry replied.

'Are your parents still living up in Darwin?'

'No, sir, they're not. My mother died of the influenza two years ago.'

'And what of your father?' Duncan Taylor asked.

'My father hung himself in our woodshed not long after our dear mother died.'

'Oh, how terrible for you,' Tessa's mother interrupted.

Just then, the Aboriginal housekeeper came out carrying a large silver teapot and a huge plate of scones covered with red jam and whipped cream. They were silent while she poured the tea.

'Thank you, Tarni,' Tessa's mother said to her when she finished pouring.

'And do you have any brothers or sisters, Henry?' Duncan Taylor asked, continuing with his questions.

'I have a younger brother, sir. He went down to Alice Springs with a camel driver. That's when I got my job on the *Gorgon*.'

'It sounds like you have had a difficult start to your young life,' Tessa's mother acknowledged.

'What sort of work did your father do, Henry?' Tessa's father asked.

'Labouring work mostly, sir. He was a terrible drunkard. He used to thrash my brother and me whenever he got himself drunk. After our dear mother died, he got a lot worse. I think he blamed us for her death. He hung himself not long after that, though.'

'Oh! How terrible. And you were both just boys. What did you and your brother do then?' Tessa's mother asked with a shocked expression.

'The council put us in a home for a while. But we ran away soon after that. That's when I got my job with the captain. He's been like a real father to me.'

'How sad your young life has been up until now, Henry,' Kasiah Taylor replied.

'I don't think about it too much these days, ma'am. Not now that I have my job on the ship.'

'Would you like a biscuit or a scone to go with your tea, Henry?' Tessa asked.

'No thank you, Miss Tessa,' Henry replied, nervously sipping his tea.

'After you have finished your tea, you and Tessa should go for a walk in the gardens,' Tessa's mother suggested, smiling at her daughter, and then looking at her husband.

Duncan Taylor shuffled about in his seat. He looked uncomfortable. 'Is that wise, Kasiah?' he said, with a stern tone in his voice.

'Of course it is Duncan. The boy goes back to his ship in an hour or so. Let them have some fun and get to know each other a little better,' Tessa's mother replied with a beautiful smile.

'Come on then, Henry. Finish your tea and let me show you the gardens; they're very nice at this time of the year.' Tessa got up and kissed her mother's cheek. She picked up a slice of watermelon and hurried down the veranda steps.

Henry hurriedly drank the last of his tea and got up as well.

'Thank you for the tea, ma'am. It was real nice,' he said and followed Tessa.

'After you're done with your walk, I'll be taking you back to your ship, young man.' Duncan Taylor advised getting up and going to the veranda railing.

'Thank you, sir,' Henry called up to him.

When Henry reached the bottom of the veranda steps, Tessa took his hand and led him away. 'Come with me, Henry,' she said, and they hurried over to an elaborate, white-painted Japanese archway covered with cape honeysuckle. She led him beneath the arch and then along a narrow path that meandered through the gardens. They strolled side by side past hibiscus bushes of at least a dozen different colours, past cascade palms, and bright red Ixora bushes. In places, tall ferns and clumps of whispering bamboo reached out to brush against their clothing. They were silent for some time, until finally, Tessa spoke.

'Are you glad you came today, Henry?' she asked as they walked.

'Yes, I am, Tessa. I just wish I had more time to spend with you,' Henry replied, his mind racing with affection for the beautiful copper-skinned girl beside him.

'I'm so glad you could get time away from your work on the ship,' Tessa remarked as they passed under a white-painted trellis covered with purple bougainvillea.

Up ahead, Henry could see a small, shaded area surrounded by orange-flowered bauhinia bushes and tall cane palms. A garden seat was set to one side near a little pond covered with water lilies and edged in places with papyrus grass.

'Let's sit here for a while. Mother had a carpenter build this for her last year. She sits here and reads when it's shady like it is now.'

'I like your mother, Tessa. She is very beautiful,' Henry said while they sat together.

'She likes you too, Henry. She told me she likes your eyes,' Tessa replied.

'My eyes! I thought my eyes were just like everyone else's.' Henry said.

'Mother says that the eyes are a gateway to the soul. She told me she saw something in yours that made her very happy. She wouldn't tell me what it was, though. She says strange things sometimes. She's my best friend, though, and I love her so much,' Tessa replied in a quiet but serious voice.

'Tessa, I think you are the most beautiful girl I have ever seen.' Henry blurted out, and he was suddenly sorry then that he had said something so foolish.

'Oh . . . Thank you, Henry. Do you want to know a secret?'

'Yes, of course,' Henry replied.

'I told Mother to ask you to come today, and I'm so glad you came.'

'I'm glad you decided to ask her, Tessa. I haven't been able to stop thinking about you. I wish I didn't have to go back to the ship so soon,' Henry admitted.

'You could write to me if you like,' Tessa said with a shy smile.

'Would your father allow that?'

'If you addressed your letter to our home address, he wouldn't have to know. Mother collects the letters from our mailbox early each afternoon. Father has his mail come to his office.'

'What address would I put on the envelope?'

'Just put my name on it and address it as Walcott Street, Broome, and it will find me easily.'

'Walcott Street. I'll remember,' Henry replied.

'Do you think you will write?'

'Yes, of course.'

'Would you like me to write back to you?' Tessa asked.

'Yes, I would. You would need to write to me at the State Shipping Office in Fremantle and address it to Henry Dawson, crew member, S.S. *Gorgon*.'

'I shall remember,' Tessa replied.

'Do you still attend school, Tessa?'

'No, I don't any longer. My father took me out of school just after I turned fourteen. He wasn't happy with my school at all. I'm not sure why, though. I have a governess now. She lives with us. She teaches me at home. I'm learning French and Greek at the moment. She is very strict, but I do like her. Her name is Juliette. She's French. Mother likes her as well. They sometimes play the piano together, and we sing lovely songs in French.'

'I like the piano. We had an old one in our home in Darwin for a while. My mother would play it for us boys sometimes. She could sing really nicely, too. My father smashed it to pieces one night when he came home drunk. I tried to stop him, but I was too small. He hit my mother that night and broke her cheekbone,' Henry said in a faint voice.

'How terrible. Was your mother all right after that?'

'She was, after my brother and I walked her to the hospital. She had a lot of stitches, though,' Henry replied.

'How terrible it must have been for you.'

'I miss my mother. She was always kind to me. When I was little, she would sit on my bed and tell me magic stories about a place where no one ever hurts anyone.'

'I don't think I could survive if anything ever happened to my mother,' Tessa said.

'I'm glad she likes me, Tessa,' Henry replied.

'So am I, Henry . . . I suppose we should be getting back now. Father will come looking for me if we don't,' Tessa said, getting up.

'Do you really like me, Tessa? I'm just a crew member on a ship, you know,' Henry said in a soft voice.

'Yes, I do, Henry. You must promise me that you will write, though.'

Henry got up as well. He was disappointed that their day together was ending.

'I will, and I promise. Our ship calls into Broome once a month or so, but only if we have freight or there are passengers,' he said.

'Yes, I know,' Tessa replied.

A few moments later, they passed through the Japanese arch and walked across to the veranda steps.

'Did you enjoy yourselves? You weren't gone for very long,' Tessa's mother called down to them.

'Yes, we did, Mother. We had a lovely time. I showed Henry your secret place,' Tessa replied, smiling up at her mother.

'It's not really a secret place, Tessa. I hope you liked it, Henry.'

'It was real nice. I liked the little pond. I saw some fish swimming in it,' Henry replied.

'There are a couple of little rainbow fish in there. They like the shade and the lilies,' Tessa's mother said.

Tessa's father came out of the front door putting on his jacket. 'I'll take you back to your ship now, young man,' he announced, coming down the steps.

Henry noticed the dark man, Jago, was leaning against the Pierce-Arrow.

'Duncan, I would like you to take Tessa with you.' Tessa's mother called out.

'There's not enough room in the car for them both, Kasiah,' Tessa's father insisted.

'She can squeeze into the back seat with Henry. I'm sure she would like to say goodbye to him at the ship.'

Duncan Taylor never replied. He went over to the Pierce-Arrow and climbed in. Jago went to the front of the car; using the crank, he started the motor.

The drive back to the ship was awkward. Tessa's father hardly spoke during the trip except to say goodbye to Henry when he climbed out of the car.

Tessa got out to walk with Henry to the ship, much to her

father's displeasure. As they walked along the jetty towards the ship, she slipped a tiny piece of paper into Henry's hand. When they got to the ship, Henry noticed several of the crew members leaning over the ship's railing, watching him. He felt embarrassed. He thanked Tessa politely for the day, said goodbye to her at the bottom of the gangway, and watched her turn to go back to their car. Then he went on board, leaned over the stern railing, and waved when she looked back. When she was out of sight, he opened the folded piece of paper and read what she had written.

*'Thank you for coming to my home today. I will miss you, Henry Dawson. Please don't forget to write. Love, Tessa.'*

Henry folded the note and put it in his shirt pocket. He would treasure it. Just then, Captain Callaghan approached him.

'You have cabins to clean, Henry. You'd better get to it, lad.'

'Yes, Captain, I'm just on my way,' Henry replied.

'Did you enjoy your afternoon tea with the Taylors, young man?'

'I did, Captain. I think it was the best day of my life,' Henry replied, unintentionally patting his shirt pocket.

'I'm glad you enjoyed yourself. Now off with you,' Captain Callaghan said with a smile.

# Chapter 8

# Travelling North

At just before 6 p.m. that evening, the S.S. *Gorgon*'s hawsers were dragged on board, and the state ship started moving away from the Broome jetty. The tide was an hour from full, and their next port of call was to be the Kimberley cattle town of Derby. Two old Aboriginal women dressed in brightly coloured cotton dresses and several young boys were waving from the jetty. One of the old women had a fishing line in her hand. A bucket of fish bait sat next to where she was sitting. A horse-drawn cart was plodding slowly back along the rail tracks toward the town. Henry was helping secure the gangway in place and lash it down. Captain Callaghan was on the bridge, instructing his first mate at the helm. A short while later, they were clear of the jetty and steaming for Derby.

* * *

When he finished his dinner that evening, Henry hurried to the radio operator's desk and asked if he might have some sheets of writing paper and some envelopes.

'G'day there, Henry . . . Paper and envelopes, eh? I saw you with that pretty girl down on the jetty just before we left Broome. I reckon you must be thinking of writing her a letter,' Mick Davis, the radio operator, said with a grin, handing Henry what he'd asked for.

'Thanks, Mick. I'm going back to my cabin right now to write to her,' Henry replied proudly.

'Would you like some ink and a pen as well?'

'No thanks, Mick. I'm not too good with a pen. I've got a couple of good pencils in my cabin, though.' Henry replied.

'Come back and give it to me when you've finished it, and I'll make sure it gets posted while we're in Derby.'

'I'll drop it back first thing in the morning, Mick.'

*   *   *

The following morning, just after dawn, the S.S. *Gorgon* was steaming down King Sound, approaching the cattle town of Derby. They were arriving with an already-turning tide, which meant they wouldn't be able to sail for at least ten hours.

The tides along King Sound were the biggest in the country, sometimes reaching heights of thirty-five feet and capable of running at more than twelve knots. They had a considerable amount of freight for the town, which included precious goods for the regional hospital, drums of oil and petrol for a local garage, kegs of beer, and crates of spirits for the Shy Poo Hotel.

An hour later, they eased against the oddly shaped Derby jetty and secured fore and aft lines to the sturdy hardwood bollards. The ship's boom was promptly uncoupled and swung out over the forward hold, and the unloading began. Just after midday, their work was done, and the crew was allowed to spend a few hours away from the ship exploring the rough-and-ready cattle town. Most of the older crew members, who were familiar with the town, headed around to the Shy Poo Hotel for a few drinks and a bit of fun. Henry stayed on board, and early in the afternoon, he and another crew member helped station workers load several hundred cattle onto the cattle deck and water and feed them. They were to be unloaded in Darwin and transported by drovers to a local abattoir.

Just after five o'clock, the crew who had gone into the town were back, and the *Gorgon* was slipping her moorings and preparing to leave Derby. They had one more port of call before they were to arrive in Darwin, and that was Wyndham, another cattle town.

It was almost dark, and Henry had just gone to the stock pens to check that the cattle had settled when they were struck by a sudden, unexpected storm from out of the northwest. It was a small but quite violent cell, and it caught them by surprise as it hadn't been noticed on the ship's barometer. The normally benign sea changed suddenly and dramatically, as it often does in the tropics. Huge waves driven up by the storm smashed into the port side of the ship, and dark, scudding clouds raced over them.

Captain Callaghan called for the holds to be secured and any open hatches to be closed. Then he ordered the ship to be turned into the storm, and for the next two hours, the *Gorgon* rose and fell with the waves. Cattle bellowed and swayed about, crashing into the stock railings, their eyes white with terror. Then, as quickly as it came, the storm was gone, and the sea became almost as flat as a millpond. But it had caused them a serious loss of time, and they were late arriving in Wyndham the following morning. The tide was already turning when they moored, and great haste was needed to unload the goods they had for the little coastal town so they could steam out with the fast-running outgoing tide.

*   *   *

Two days later, they arrived in Darwin, where they were to spend a full day in port before heading north again, bound for Singapore.

After the cattle were unloaded and the decks were hosed down and cleaned most of the crew headed into town. Henry went with them. He liked Darwin. After all, it was his hometown. A bustling town on the move already with a population of close to 1,500 people. He hurried along Smith Street, the busy main street, past all manner of shops and rowdy hotels. He was heading to the post office to post his second letter to Tessa Taylor. As he walked, he was thinking about what he had written and wishing he had been better educated. He hoped that Tessa would be able to understand it.

*Mr. Henry Dawson*

*Crewman, S.S. Gorgon*

*State Shipping Services*

*Fremantle.*

*W.A.*


*Dear Tessa*

*I hope you received my first letter. I'm sorry if it didn't make a lot of sense. I'm not too good at letter writing just yet, as I haven't had much experience. Of course, I haven't received a letter from you yet, as we won't be back in Fremantle for some time. But I'm so looking forward to hearing from you when we do get back there. We arrived in Darwin last night, and that's where I'm writing from now. I will go into town to post this to you tomorrow. I hope your mother and father are well. Please say hello to them for me. I don't think your father approves of me very much, but I'm glad your mother likes me, though. She is very beautiful, just like you. I haven't been able to get you out of my mind, Tessa. I know I told you in my last letter that I had a very nice time when I visited your house. It was the best time I have ever had. I know this will probably sound silly, Tessa, but I think fate has helped us to meet. I hope you don't mind me saying this, but I really do like you a lot. I know I am only a simple seaman, but I intend to make a success of my life. One day, if we were ever to marry, I would build you a home just as beautiful as the one your father built for your mother, with wonderful gardens that we could walk together in just like theirs. I am so looking forward to seeing you again. I hope I don't have to wait too long. I have to get off to sleep now, as I have to get up early for work.*


*Goodbye for now, Tessa.*

*Love Henry.*

# Chapter 9

# A Bitter Twist of Fate

## August 1st, 1914

Twenty-seven days later, the S.S. *Gorgon* arrived back in Fremantle. Henry was disappointed that they hadn't called into Broome on their return trip, but it had not been necessary. There were no passengers to come on board there and no freight to be delivered from Singapore or Darwin. They had called at Wyndham for several hours and loaded cattle for Fremantle. Two station owners came on board to travel with the cattle. They then sailed on to Port Hedland to unload goods from Singapore for a local furniture shop, along with bags of rice, sealed containers of noodles, turmeric, cinnamon, and nutmeg for a local grocery store run by an enterprising Chinaman named Mr. Sing. They sailed past Carnarvon and then on to Geraldton, where they delivered more exotic goods from Singapore, including Oriental wall hangings, several beautiful camphorwood chests of different sizes, and several pieces of high-quality teak furniture for a local furniture store.

When they arrived in Fremantle the following morning, Henry went ashore and hurried to his company's shipping offices. The middle-aged woman at the desk looked up at him when he opened the door.

'Can I help you, young man?' she asked.

'I'm Henry Dawson off the *Gorgon*, ma'am. I'm hoping you might have a letter for me,' Henry began.

'Just a moment, and I'll go and check for you. Henry Dawson, you say,' the woman replied, taking off her glasses and getting up.

'Yes, ma'am, Henry Dawson. There might even be a couple of them,' Henry said excitedly, watching the woman go to the back wall, flick her fingers through some pigeonholes, and return to the counter.

'There's nothing here for anyone by that name, young man,' she said, smiling pleasantly, going back behind her desk and picking up her glasses again.

'Nothing at all, ma'am? Are you quite sure about that?'

'I'm quite sure, young man. There is nothing here for anyone by that name. Perhaps you could call again in a day or two.'

Henry stared at the woman for a few seconds in disbelief before he replied. 'Thank you, ma'am,' he whispered, finally turning and going back outside.

What could've gone wrong? Tessa had promised him she would write. Something must have happened to make her break her promise. Perhaps she didn't like him as much as he thought she did. Perhaps her father had found his letters and forbidden her from writing to him. He stood outside the shipping office, wondering if he should go back and ask the woman to look again. But he had watched her go through the pigeonholes. There were no letters for him, and he knew it. He went back along the street towards the docks and his ship.

When Henry got back to the ship, he went up the gangway. One of the crew was hurrying past. He stopped and looked at Henry.

'You better come with me, Henry. The captain wants to speak to all of us. I reckon it might be important.'

Henry and the other crew member hurried to the upper deck, where a meeting was already underway.

Captain Callaghan saw them arrive. 'Fall in, you two, and listen to what I have to say,' he called out as he put on his cap and straightened his tie.

Henry and the other man went over and stood behind the throng of fidgeting, nervous men.

The captain stared at them and was silent for a while, and then he spoke. 'On the twenty-eighth of June in Sarajevo, Bosnia, Archduke Franz Ferdinand, heir to the Austro-Hungarian empire, and his wife Sophie were murdered in the street by a Bosnian Serb nationalist.'

The men started milling about, wondering why something that had happened on the other side of the world should have anything to do with them.

'What's that got to do with us, Captain?' Perkins, the chief mate, called out.

'Hold your tongue, Perkins, and listen carefully. Austria and Hungary have since declared war on Serbia. This, in turn, has brought Russia into the conflict. I am told that Germany has now declared war on Russia and France, and as such, England may decide to enter the war to help the French.'

'What will that mean for us and our ship, Captain?' Another crew member called out.

'Just listen, will you? I have been informed by the Premier's Department that if England enters this conflict, Australia may soon be at war with Germany as well. All coastal shipping is to be stopped until further notice. I've been asked to keep our ship here in Fremantle until I receive instructions from the shipping office. It is possible that we may be asked to help with troop movements. As of now, I have no further information for you, but I will keep you all informed when I can. I would like you all to go back to your cabins for now and stay there until you hear from me in an hour or two. Perkins, I want you to meet me on the bridge in five minutes. Is that clear?'

'Yes, Captain. In five minutes, sir,' chief mate Perkins replied hastily.

Captain Callaghan took off his cap, spun around, and hurried back toward his cabin.

* * *

Four days later, on August 5, 1914, Sir Joseph Cook, the Australian Prime Minister, informed the people of Australia that England had declared war on Germany, and because Australia was a dominion of the British Empire, Australia and New Zealand were now at war with Germany as well. Within hours, thousands of men were volunteering to serve in the expeditionary forces that were to be sent to England to help the mother country in her hour of need. Several of the crew members of the S.S. *Gorgon* had already left the ship to volunteer.

Early that same morning, Henry Dawson was summoned to the bridge of the *Gorgon*.

'Good morning, Henry.' Captain Callaghan greeted Henry with a grim expression when he entered the bridge.

'You wanted to see me, Captain?'

'Yes, I did, Henry. As you know, Australia is now at war with Germany, and because of that, our ship has been requisitioned to help in the war effort.'

'You told us that was likely to happen, sir. What will we be asked to help with?'

'We are to assist with Australian and New Zealand troop movements for England. I have been told there could be horses to ship as well,' the captain advised.

'When will we be leaving, sir?' Henry asked, a grim premonition already flooding his mind.

'We are to leave Fremantle within the hour. Our first mission is to steam to Port Adelaide. We are to have the ship inspected for seaworthiness by the Navy there and have our stock pens altered so we can carry as many horses as possible for the mounted infantry troops of the Light Horse Brigade. On our return, we will be bringing back as much coal as we can carry.'

'Within the hour, you say?' Henry replied.

'Within the hour. As you know, several of the crew members have already left to volunteer, which leaves us shorthanded. Perkins is among them, which means I now have to appoint a new chief mate. As of now, Henry Dawson, you are this ship's new chief mate.' The captain reached for Henry's hand. 'Congratulations, young man.'

'Thank you, Captain. I'll do my best. But can we operate being so shorthanded?'

'The shipping office has managed to find a couple of older, able-bodied seamen here in the town. They will be boarding shortly. We still have our stokers. We'll just have to manage. Navy personnel will be boarding in Port Adelaide to travel with us and help.'

'It's all starting to sound pretty serious, Captain,' Henry replied.

'It certainly is. You can go now, Henry. I still have a lot to do,' Captain Callaghan said, getting up and putting on his cap.

'Just one thing, sir.'

'And what would that be?'

'Would it be possible for me to leave the ship for half an hour, sir?'

'I'm sorry, Henry, but I cannot allow it. Why do you ask?'

'It's just that I'm expecting a letter from that girl I met in Broome. I was going to run down to the shipping office.'

'I'm sorry, Henry. That will just have to wait until we're back in Fremantle sometime in the future.'

'I understand, Captain,' Henry replied, turning smartly, and leaving the bridge.

* * *

The following day, two letters arrived at the state shipping office in Fremantle, addressed to Mr. Henry Dawson, crewman, S.S. Gorgon. The woman in the office remembered the handsome young man who had called four days earlier. She remembered his disappointment when she told him there were no letters for him. She remembered watching him outside her office window. He looked so unhappy. She smiled at the memory and slipped the letters into one of the pigeonholes. Perhaps he would call again sometime during the day.

* * *

For the next nineteen months, more letters would arrive to be put into that same pigeonhole. One day, many months after the first of them had arrived, the office woman looked at the return address on one and thought perhaps that she should return them to the sender. But she decided, after a little more thought, that she would leave it for a while longer. Perhaps one day the handsome young man would call again.

As the months went by, the woman often thought of the young man. She knew some of their company's ships had been sent overseas to help with the war effort. So many things were now being treated on a need-to-know basis with her company, and because of that, she had no knowledge of the whereabouts of the boy's ship, but she hoped he wasn't one of those already killed in the terrible war that was now raging on the other side of the world and claiming so many brave young Australian boys' lives.

# Chapter 10

# A Voyage to Hell

## 1st November 1914

Just after dawn on the first of November, the S.S. *Gorgon* was back from South Australia. In Port Adelaide, she'd been fitted with portable toilets for the soldiers who were to sleep on the decks. The cattle stalls had been enlarged to carry the 400 horses they had on board. Feed, saddles, bridles, and veterinary equipment were loaded as well. Crates filled with live chickens and rabbits were loaded, along with bags of potatoes, turnips, and onions. Several hundred wooden crates packed with tins of bully beef and biscuits were also carried on board. Some were for those on board, and some for the troops already in Africa.

They were moored in the Western Australian southern port town of Albany, along with a large flotilla of other ships. There were 28 ships from the Australian Imperial Force plus 10 ships from the New Zealand Expeditionary Force. More than 1400 men were crowded into cabins, passageways, and onto the decks of the *Gorgon*. Hammocks were strung up wherever possible, and thin kapok mattresses lay everywhere. As the sun rose that morning, the S.S. *Gorgon* was one of the first vessels to steam out of the port of Albany.

The first day of sailing was pleasant for the men crowded on the decks and in the cabins, as the sea was relatively calm, and the breeze was slight. And then the wind picked up, and the seasickness struck. Dozens of men crowded at the rails, vomiting into the rolling waves. Others sat about with looks of utter despair on their faces. Seasickness soon became an epidemic on board the *Gorgon*. The crew was constantly washing the remains of stewed rabbit, chicken, and bully beef from the decks. Chaos followed, and men wobbled about the ship, swaying with the rise and fall of the waves as they tried to find their balance in the long lines outside the portable toilets or the mess tents. Buckets of raw sewage were constantly being thrown over the railing by the crew.

After four days, most of those on board began to find their sea legs. The officers then began exercise routines for the men to keep them occupied. Boxing rings were set in place. Here and there, the sounds of a mouth organ, a penny whistle, or even bagpipes could be heard. A hurriedly built stage was set up where men wearing makeshift dresses played burlesque dancing girls to roars of laughter.

Eight days out, Captain Callaghan became concerned for the safety of those on board. He'd been notified by radio that the German light cruiser SMS Emden was on the prowl. On the 9th of November, one of the Australian warships that were escorting them, the HMAS Sydney, left the convoy to try to intercept the Emden. In a hard-fought battle, the Sydney sank the Emden and rejoined the convoy at their first port of call, Colombo.

The second stop for the fleet was Aden, where they took on coal. They steamed out a day later for their final destination, Alexandria, the ancient city named after Alexander the Great and the birthplace of Cleopatra, the last pharaoh of Egypt. Not a ship was lost during the five weeks they were at sea.

After the men, horses, and equipment were unloaded in Alexandria, the *Gorgon* was to steam for England, where they were to take on supplies for the British army in North Africa. They were then to return to Alexandria, drop off the supplies, and ferry any seriously wounded back to England.

*   *   *

For the next 31 months, the S.S. *Gorgon* ferried munitions and supplies along the north coast of Africa and carried great numbers of wounded back to England. A constant watch had to be kept for

German warships at all times.

On her final voyage, before returning to Australia, she was to take on disabled and badly wounded Australian soldiers in England for repatriation back to Australia. She was also to take on urgently needed medical supplies for her final trip to Alexandria. The cabins and the decks were filled with the shell-shocked, the disfigured, the legless, the armless, and the insane, and several nurses to care for them.

When they reached Alexandria, the medical supplies were quickly unloaded, and the *Gorgon* left port for the long trip back through perilous seas to Australia. The only armaments they had on board were several .303 Lee Enfield rifles and an English Lewis machine gun. During one of their trips along the African coast, Henry and a one-legged soldier practised with the Lewis by throwing empty kerosene drums overboard and blasting them in the ship's wake. Both men became quite capable shots with the heavy machine gun, but because of the limited supply of ammunition, they stopped their practice when ordered by the captain to conserve their remaining ammunition.

Two days after leaving Alexandria, the *Gorgon* was steaming close to the North African coast when a German fighter, a Fokker E1, lifted from its desert airfield. It was just after dawn.

The German pilot banked his plane at the end of the desert runway and prepared to set his bearings for a distant target when he noticed a ship steaming close to the shore in an attempt to stay out of the paths of German warships. The weather was clear, and the sky, almost cloudless. The pilot dropped his aircraft low, hugging the sandhills, as he tried to keep his plane hidden from the crew of the ship as he prepared to attack. Easing back the cocking mechanism on his single Spandau 7.92-millimetre machine gun, he adjusted his goggles and worked his ailerons up and down in sinister preparation.

Men lay about on camp beds and mattresses on the decks of the slow-moving *Gorgon*, oblivious to the existence of the approaching aircraft. Nurses walked among them, attending to their needs.

At the very last minute, the German pilot lifted his plane

above the dunes and raced out over the waves to attack the Australian ship, his machine gun raking the crowded decks of the *Gorgon*, killing anyone in its path. Crippled soldiers were cut to pieces. One of the nurses fell instantly, killed in the maelstrom of machine gun bullets.

Henry had just come out onto the main deck. He'd heard the deafening roar of the low-flying aircraft. He looked up just as it roared over the ship, its engine screaming. He saw the pilot bank in a wide arc to come at them again, and a moment later, he heard the Spandau's deadly rattle as it began to tear another swathe through the crippled men on the deck. Those who could move scrambled for whatever cover they could find; those who could not began shaking their fists and screaming their defiance at the German pilot.

Henry ran headlong into the devastation. Bodies lay everywhere. A legless man was trying to roll off his mattress and get out of the line of fire. The Spandau's bullets tore through him, killing him instantly. Bloodied bits of his body and his kapok mattress stuck against Henry's clothing as he ran past. At that very same instant, Henry felt a sudden jolt of pain in his left thigh; he'd been hit. He staggered on through the dead and dying until he reached the stern railing. He picked up the Lewis machine gun that lay between two unopened wooden crates of bully beef and balanced it on top of the steel railing. Pushing the safety forward, he slapped his hand down on the rotary magazine to make sure it was seated properly and crouched just as the Fokker began to bear down on them for the third time. While he waited, he glanced down. Blood was running onto the deck from the wound in his left leg. Strangely, he felt no pain.

The German fighter levelled out just above the waves. Henry could see the pilot's leather helmet moving about as he worked the controls to keep his plane steady in the light morning breeze. And then he saw his right hand go to the machine gun's cocking lever.

Henry took a sight slightly below the fast-moving aircraft to compensate for the recoil of the heavy Lewis gun and waited for his breathing to steady. He was angry. They were flying the international flag of the Red Cross. The German pilot must have seen it! He waited for just a moment longer, then he took a deep breath and squeezed back the trigger. Holding it in automatic fire, he emptied the Lewis gun at the fast-approaching German plane. The machine gun bucked in his hands, but he held it steady. The stream of .303 bullets tore through the flimsy plane's wooden propeller, ripping the blades apart and sending them spinning into the sea. The Perspex windscreen burst apart as the bullets tore through it and into the face and chest of the German pilot.

The pilot fell forward against the controls, and the Fokker hung in the disturbed air for a split second and then dropped into the sea in an angry eruption of seawater, not more than fifty yards from where Henry crouched with the Lewis gun still smoking in his hands.

A mighty cheer went up from the men across the deck. Fists pumped into the air in a salute to Henry's bravery and skill with the machine gun.

A moment later, Henry fell forward against the railing, dropping the Lewis gun to the deck . . . He was badly hurt!

One of the nurses rushed forward. She'd seen the blood running from his trouser leg onto the deck. When she got to him, she prised his right hand from the railing. 'I need you to lie on your back now, young man. Can you do that for me?' She asked.

Henry fell back onto the deck. He looked up at the sky. The sun was shining through thin white clouds. It looked so quiet and peaceful. He could see a seabird circling high among the clouds. He was almost certain he might soon pass out. All he could hear was the cheering of the soldiers.

'You've lost quite a lot of blood, young man. I need to cut away your trousers and take a look at that leg of yours,' he heard the nurse saying . . . Her voice sounded far off.

Another nurse rushed over and kneeled next to Henry. 'Young man, you've just saved the lives of a lot of people with your bravery,' Henry heard her say. He felt her take his hand in hers. 'You just hold onto my hand now and let Annie take a look at that leg of yours.'

'Alright then, Miss,' Henry whispered back.

The nurse Annie quickly cut away Henry's trousers. Blood was pouring from the wound in his thigh onto the deck. She laid a gauze pad over it to staunch the bleeding and wrapped a long bandage tight around his thigh. Then she took a syringe from her bag, filled it with a dose of morphine, and injected it into his upper leg.

'Let's get you inside so I can clean and stitch up that wound,' she said, getting to her feet and closing her bag.

Several men had moved closer and were watching the two nurses' work.

'Can a couple of you men help us get this young man into one of the cabins?' Annie turned and asked them.

There was a sudden rush of volunteers to help carry the young man, who had just saved many of their lives with his bravery.

*   *   *

A little over an hour later, Annie injected another dose of morphine into Henry's leg. 'That should help with the pain, young man. The bullet that hit your thigh passed right through, but on its way, it took a small piece out of your femur. I've cleaned the bone fragments away and sewn up the wound. We have no doctor on board, so my stitching may well leave some scarring,' she said, looking into Henry's eyes.

'Thank you, Miss,' Henry replied, his voice slurring from the effect of the morphine.

'Just try not to move that leg around too much. I'll come back and have a look at you a bit later. I need to go back out to the deck now and help the other nurses. Goodbye for now, young man,' Annie said, patting Henry's hand and then hurrying away.

'My name is Henry. Thank you for taking such good care of me,' Henry mumbled.

'I'm Annie. I'll be back soon, Henry,' the nurse promised, picking up her bag and hurrying outside.

*   *   *

Henry spent the next week on his back while the S.S. *Gorgon* continued steaming for home. Seventeen disabled soldiers and one of the nurses had been killed in the cowardly attack by the German pilot on the ship that day. Their bodies were wrapped in canvas sheets, bound with cord, and sent to the deep after Captain Callaghan held a short service on the deck where the attack had taken place.

A week later, nurse Annie Edwards took out the stitches from Henry's thigh.

'It's healed up quite nicely, Henry. There will be some scarring, but you will just have to think of it as a reminder of your bravery,' she said, wrapping his thigh in fresh bandages.

'Thank you for looking after me so well, Annie.' Henry answered.

'You may find over time that your thigh gives you trouble now and then. I don't think you will need a cane, but you may have a slight limp,' Annie added with a pretty smile.

'I don't mind, Miss.'

'I suppose you're looking forward to getting home. Have you been keeping in touch with your parents?' Annie asked.

'My parents are both dead, Miss.'

'That's very sad. What about a girlfriend?

'I'm not certain about that. I met a girl up in Broome that I like. I've been writing to her, but I've never gotten any replies.'

'When we get back home, you should see if you can get in touch with her again. Perhaps there was a reason.'

'What about you, Annie? Do you have someone waiting for you?'

'Just my parents in Adelaide,' Annie replied, smiling. She liked Henry.

'Before we get into Melbourne, would you give me your address in Adelaide? I'd like to keep in touch. I could write to you if you like.'

'I would like that, Henry,' Annie replied.

* * *

Six weeks later, they arrived in Port Melbourne. Ambulances and buses were lined up along the wharf, ready to ferry the disabled soldiers away to rehabilitation homes. Journalists came on board to interview Captain Callaghan. They'd been told of the attack on the ship. A naval officer on board the ship had contacted his superiors from Cape Town. Captain Callaghan decided to hold his meeting with the journalists in the crew's mess.

'Can you tell us what happened when you were attacked off the coast of Africa, Captain?' One of the journalists asked him.

'I think you already know most of it. We lost seventeen brave young Australian men and an equally brave young nurse that day. It was a cowardly attack, and it caught us by surprise,' Captain Callaghan replied.

'What about the young sailor, Henry Dawson? Has he recovered from his wounds yet, sir?' Another journalist asked.

'Henry has fully recovered. He is back performing his duties as my chief mate.'

'Can we speak to him?'

'Henry has asked that he be left to his duties. He has no wish to be interviewed,' Captain Callaghan replied.

'There's quite a lot of interest in the country about what happened that day. The lad has been hailed a hero.' The journalist added.

'We are immensely proud of what Henry did that day. But he has asked that he be left alone. Perhaps in a week or two, he might change his mind. But for now, I would ask that you leave the lad alone.'

'Is there anyone else we could talk to about the incident, Captain?'

'If you get back down to the wharf quickly, there may be someone who will talk to you. I have work to do, so I will have to bid you good day, gentlemen.' Captain Callaghan said, standing up wearily and waiting for the journalists to leave him in peace.

*   *   *

Henry was on duty at the top of the gangway, helping disabled servicemen make their way down to the wharf to their waiting families, when the journalists started rushing past him. One of them pushed aside a man on crutches in his eagerness to get down to the wharf. A few seconds later, he watched him walk about among the departing wounded who were waiting to be helped to a nearby bus and ask them questions.

# Chapter 11

# News from the War

### 15th September 1918

**D**uncan Taylor was drinking black coffee and reading a several-week-old newspaper in his warehouse office on Dampier Street in Broome when he turned the page and noticed a news article from the war. *Darwin's brave young son is to be recommended for a bravery medal.* He sipped his coffee and started reading the article.

*First Mate Henry Dawson of the Australian ship the S.S. Gorgon, a ship that was being used during the conflict in North Africa, has been recommended for a bravery medal. His ship, the Gorgon, was returning to Australia, carrying several hundred wounded and disabled servicemen home for repatriation, when, somewhere off the coast of North Africa, she was attacked by a German fighter aircraft. With no thought for his own safety, first mate Dawson, although badly wounded himself, ran through the carnage wrought by the cowardly German pilot and took up a Lewis machine gun. Just as they were about to be fired upon for the third time, he opened fire, killing the German pilot and sending his aircraft into the sea. The ship's captain, Captain Darcy Callaghan, has told our office that Henry has recovered from his wounds and is now back attending to his duties as his first mate.*

Duncan Taylor recognised the lad's name. *Henry Dawson!* This was the same young man who had carried Tessa's watermelon back to their cabin while they were on board the very same ship, the S.S. *Gorgon*. The same young man his wife, Kasiah, had invited to their home for afternoon tea almost four years ago. What a brave young fellow! He thought. He continued reading.

*One of the servicemen saved by the lad's bravery that day had this to say when he was interviewed in Port Melbourne when the ship returned.*

*'It was a bloody mess, to be sure—unexpected as well. We were flying a Red Cross flag at the time. The pilot was sure to have seen it. Seventeen good men and a young nurse were killed that morning by that German pilot in his two cowardly runs at us. The bastard caught us by surprise. Wounded men were screaming everywhere. Some were shaking their fists at the bastard. Those that could, scrambled for cover—those that couldn't were in big trouble. I had shrapnel wounds in my back. I was bandaged up, but I was able to move about. I was trying to drag some of the disabled blokes aside when I saw this young bloke go past me. I could have reached out and touched him. He'd been hit on the last run. I could see the blood all down his trouser leg. I watched him hobble through the dead and dying and pick up a Lewis machine gun at the back of the ship. I watched him lay it over the stern railing. He was calm—really calm. That bloody plane was coming straight for him. I thought he was a goner, for sure. But he waited until he was certain of his aim and then let fly with the whole bloody magazine. Bits of the plane's propeller flew off in all directions. The German pilot copped it—killed instantly he was his plane dropped into the sea, not fifty yards from where the lad was crouching with the Lewis. He deserves a medal for what he did that day, and I hope he gets one.'*

*Lance Corporal Jack Ballinger, AIF.*

Duncan put down the newspaper. Perhaps he should show the article to his daughter. He knew Tessa had been fond of the young man. But he decided against it. His daughter was to be married quite soon. He would have to tell his wife, though. He could never keep a secret from Kasiah. She would always know if he tried to hide something. He smiled as he thought of Kasiah. He folded the newspaper carefully to the article he had just read, put it on his desk, picked up his cup, drank the last of his coffee, leaned back, and thought of his wife.

He'd first met Kasiah as a young boy, delivering money to

Jannali, her mother, on the fourth Saturday of every month. They'd been friends at first—the white boy from the well-to-do pearling family and the tall black girl from the poorest part of Broome. He couldn't remember Kasiah's father, Juan José Toledo, the Negro Macassan diver. He'd been very young when he died. It was said around Broome that he was a shaman of some sort—a spirit medium—a hoodoo man. Many believed he could heal people with his strange potions and magic. Juan Toledo had died from the bends while working as a diver on one of his father's luggers. He had been told many years later that his father had been concerned that something evil would happen to him because of the way he pushed his divers so hard during those early years. His father had always expected as much shell as possible to be brought up from the ocean floor each day by every lugger in his fleet.

After Toledo was buried in the Broome cemetery alongside all of the other divers who had suffered from the very same fate, his father decided to give money to Toledo's wife, Jannali, to help her with the raising of Kasiah, her only child. It was rumoured around the town that it was his father's way of keeping Juan Toledo's black hoodoo at bay.

Kasiah's mother, Jannali, was always nice to him when he delivered her the money. She would smile and invite him inside the run-down old house they called home in a back street of Chinatown, and only then would she take her money. She would give him a glass of water if he wanted one, and sometimes fruit if she had any. As the months went by, Jannali would take him for walks with Kasiah and show them things in the bush out along the edge of the town. He was young, and he never understood much of what she tried to teach him, but Kasiah did. By the time she was ten years old, Kasiah Toledo could read the tracks of every animal and bird they came across, even the snakes and lizards.

It wasn't until they were teenagers that he realised he had fallen in love with Kasiah. That was the day he kissed her for the very first time. They had walked out to Gantheaume Point after school one hot afternoon. The tide was fully in, and they were alone, so they decided to go for a swim in their underwear. Their first kiss was underwater. After that, they kissed several times, sitting on the rocks, holding hands, and watching the waves lap at their feet. It was well after dark when they got home that night, and the fourteen-year-old Kasiah got herself into trouble with her mother. Jannali had been waiting for her on the veranda of their old house. He still remembered the expression on her face as she scolded Kasiah soundly and then sent him home with the threat that she was going to speak to his father. A threat, however, that she never carried out.

But Kasiah Toledo had some of her father's strange ways as well. She believed that at night when you dreamed, you lived a different life. She believed that you entered the spirit world when you slept. A time when you could speak to those who had passed. You could listen to their stories and heed their warnings, for they knew the dangers that the living faced every day of their lives.

But certain things frightened Kasiah. He remembered that she would never look into the eyes of an owl. If she saw one, she would always turn away. He asked her why that was. But she just laughed and changed the subject. He remembered telling her one day when they were teenagers lying together in the sandhills out near Cable Beach, watching seabirds, that she would be burned at the stake in some countries for some of the strange things she said and believed in. Even this very morning, she had acted strangely. She wanted him to stay home and not go to work at all. He remembered their conversation just before he left.

'Duncan, my love, I would like you to stay home with me today. I want you to help me with some things I'm doing in the garden.'

'I can't stay home, Kasiah. I've got a lot of work to do at the warehouse. We have to tidy up and make room for the next loads of shell. We're running out of room with this damn war still raging.'

'Please stay, my love. I don't want you to go today.'

'If you're worried that I might come to harm, don't be. I'll be careful, I promise you.'

'It's just that I saw my mother in a dream last night. She was talking to someone in the shadows. I couldn't see who it was. It was a terrible dream, Duncan. She was weeping, and it frightened me.'

'I always liked your mother, Kasiah. She was very kind to me when we were young,' he'd replied, trying to change the subject.

'I know you did, Duncan, and she liked you as well. But I worry about you. I worry about the way you drive that car of yours. You're always in such a hurry. You drive far too fast. You'll have an accident one day, and what would I ever do without you, my love?'

'I promise I'll drive carefully, Kasiah. But I must go now,' he had replied, embracing and kissing her before he left.

His love for Kasiah had never diminished over the years. If anything, it had grown even stronger. She was his life. She meant everything to him.

He looked down at the folded newspaper again. He knew his daughter had been upset that she had never received replies to the letters she'd secretly posted to this young man all those months ago. Kasiah had told him about the letters one night in bed after he told her he was concerned with Tessa's moody behaviour. After he was told about the letters, he decided he would try to find out what he could about the lad's whereabouts. The state ship, the S.S. *Minderoo*, had started the coastal run again, and he knew her master well. He decided he would ask him if he knew of the lad. But Captain Bradford had never heard of Henry Dawson. He decided then that the lad had probably had a change of occupation. Perhaps he'd gone back to Darwin. But now, after reading this, young Henry Dawson might not have received his daughter's letters at all. If he'd gone off to help with the war effort, that could easily have been the case. Anyway, it was all history now. Tessa was soon to be married to the son of one of Broome's better-known pearling families, George Arthur Peterson, a fine young man.

* * *

While Duncan Taylor was reading his newspaper and sipping his coffee, two of his men were busy moving crates of valuable pearl shell to one side of the warehouse and stacking them high. More room was needed for storage before pearl shell could be shipped overseas to the markets in America and Europe again if the war continued. Under the crates of pearl shell, and unbeknownst to the two men, a deadly taipan snake was slithering further and further away as they worked slowly toward her. She was a huge female, more than nine feet long, and one of the deadliest snakes in the country. She had young beneath the floorboards. She would attack these intruders if they came too close. She'd been hunting for rats. The old warehouse was home to dozens of them. They ate the bits of gristle left on some of the pearl shell. She could feel the vibrations on the floorboards in her long, sleek body as the two men moved closer. She flicked out her tongue, tasted the air, and slithered even further back until she lay coiled beneath the last row of crates.

* * *

Duncan Taylor left the folded newspaper on his desk and got up. He would take it home and show it to Kasiah at the end of the day. She would know whether they should show it to Tessa or not. She often spoke of the young boy who visited them that day. She seemed just as disappointed as Tessa that he had never replied to their daughter's letters. He went through the side door into the warehouse and looked at the two men moving the crates.

'I want this warehouse ready for more storage by the end of today, Jago. We'll have the schooners in tomorrow,' he called out, watching them stack the crates.

'We're workin' as fast as we can, Boss,' Jago, the big Ambionese-Arab, called back.

Jago had been his right-hand man for more than twenty years. He had taken a liking to him when he first arrived in Broome from the Island of Ambon in the Dutch East Indies as an indentured pearling worker. When he arrived, he spoke no English, only Arabic, his father's language, and Malay, the Ambionese language. Over the years, Jago had become devoted to him, and he was never far from his side. But Jago was a dangerous man. A man feared throughout the town of Broome.

'One of you, climb up on top, and I'll start passing them up,' Duncan said, taking off his shirt.

'Righto, Boss,' Jago replied, clambering up the stack of crates.

For the next thirty minutes, Duncan and Paddy, the other

man, passed the heavy crates up to Jago. When they reached the back row, Paddy went over to the canvas water bag for a drink. There were only two crates left to lift.

Sweat was pouring down Duncan Taylor's face and powerful torso when he reached for one of the last two crates and lifted it. At that very moment, his vision was blocked by the crate in his hands, and he never saw the snake.

The taipan was cornered now. She had nowhere to go. She feared for her young, waiting for her beneath the floorboards. She lifted herself three feet into the air and struck.

Duncan Taylor dropped the crate. He'd felt the bite. He looked down. The snake had bitten through his trousers into his right thigh. Its fangs were still caught up in the material. He grabbed the snake and threw it to the floor. It turned and struck him again, twice in the right calf. He stepped back and called out to the man drinking from the water bag.

'Watch out, Paddy, there's a damn snake back here.'

Paddy dropped the water bag and ran out onto the street.

Jago jumped to the floor. A couple of crates of shell crashed to the floor with him. He grabbed one of the rakes they used for the shell and ran to help his boss.

'Stand back. I'll get him, Boss,' he yelled, lifting the rake above his shoulder and charging straight at the swaying taipan. But he was seconds too late, and they watched the huge snake turn and drop through a hole in the floorboards onto the ground below.

'Did he get you, Boss?' Jago asked, hitting the floorboards with the back of his rake in frustration and turning to his boss.

'He got me alright, Jago,' Duncan yelled back, undoing his belt and taking down his trousers. He could see the puncture marks on his thigh. He hobbled back and leaned against some empty crates.

'We better get you in your car, Boss. We better get around to the hospital real quick,' Jago said, taking Duncan's outstretched arm.

* * *

Duncan Taylor was pronounced dead not long after Jago carried him through the hospital doors.

'There was just too much poison!' The old doctor on duty told him. 'There was nothing I could do for him. I'm sorry, Jago.'

For a moment, Jago looked like he might kill the doctor, but instead, he said, 'You betta go and ring his missus.'

There were tears in the dark man's eyes.

# Chapter 12

# Kasiah Taylor

Kasiah Taylor felt the telephone speaker slip through her fingers, swing back against the wall, and hang on its cord. She sat down on the floor. She could still hear the doctor speaking. His voice sounded muffled, but she knew he was still apologising. She started to shake uncontrollably. She wrapped her arms around herself and burst into tears.

Tessa heard her from the lounge. She'd been practising her piano lessons with her governess, Juliette. 'What's wrong, Mother?' she asked from the doorway.

'It's your father—!' That was all Kasiah could manage to get out before she burst into tears again.

'Where is he, Mother? Is he alright? What's happened?' Tessa asked, crouching beside her mother.

'He's been killed, my darling. He's been bitten by a snake in the warehouse. He died in the hospital a few minutes ago. I have to go to him, Tessa,' Kasiah replied, struggling to get to her feet.

'I'm coming with you,' Tessa replied, sobbing, and helping her mother to stand.

'I wanted him to stay at home today, Tessa. I pleaded with him, but he wouldn't listen. There was something dark in the house this morning . . . An evil thing . . . I was warned. I should have tried harder, Tessa.' Kasiah whispered, struggling to remain on her feet.

Tessa put her arm around her mother to steady her. They went into the kitchen and sat down.

'Would you like a glass of water, Mother?'

'Thank you, Tessa.'

Tessa went to the ice chest, poured a glass of water, and took it to her mother.

Kasiah took a sip and stared blankly at the glass. Her heart was broken. Duncan was gone from her life forever. 'Thank you, my darling,' she whispered.

'What has happened, madame? Can I help? Juliette asked in a soft, tragic voice when she came in.

'Father has been killed, Juliette! He's been bitten by a snake,' Tessa whispered to her.

'Oh no—! How terrible, madame!'

'I've got to get to the hospital . . . Tessa, will you come with me?' Kasiah asked, getting to her feet.

'Of course, Mother. I'll get the keys for the car.' Tessa got up, hugged her mother, and went for the keys.

'I will stay here then, madame. I will wait for you to return,' Juliette said, bursting into tears.

Tessa helped her mother outside and down the veranda steps.

'I'll drive, Mother,' she said, her voice trembling, as she took her mother to the Pierce-Arrow.

*   *   *

A little over two hours later, Tessa and her mother were back at the house. Jago had driven Duncan's car back as well. Paddy was with him. They had been waiting for Kasiah at the hospital.

While they were away, Juliette found Tarni, the housekeeper, out in the laundry and told her what had happened. The Aboriginal woman dropped the shirt she was about to push through the wringer and burst into tears. She had known Duncan since he was a small boy. She was a cousin to Kasiah's mother,

Jannali. She put down the rest of the wet clothing and went out to find the men working in the garden to tell them that their boss had been killed by a snake.

*   *   *

Eight people were standing under the old flame tree when Kasiah and Tessa arrived back. They were silent as Kasiah parked the Pierce-Arrow. They watched her climb from the driver's side. Her face was expressionless, and there were no tears in her eyes. Kasiah Taylor was a strong woman. She'd regained control of her emotions quickly. She had faced tragedy before. She was a young girl when her father died on a pearling boat, but she remembered it clearly. Her dear mother, Jannali, had passed away only recently as well, and she had been very close to her mother. Several times, they had lost men on the luggers during bad storms and divers to the bends. She had always known that bad news came when you least expected it. Even though her heart was broken, she was determined not to let it show. She put her hand out for Tessa to come to her side.

Tessa had been crying ever since they left the hospital. The sight of her mother weeping over her father's dead body had been too much for her.

'Hold my hand, my darling,' Kasiah whispered, reaching for her daughter while looking at the solemn group standing in the shade of the old flame tree.

'By the looks on all of your faces, you have heard the terrible news,' she said when they got to them.

'We're all very sorry, Missus.' Tarni, the Aboriginal housekeeper, said in her quiet voice. Her dark face was wet with tears. There was a murmuring of agreement among the rest of them.

'Thank you, Tarni,' Kasiah replied.

There was an awkward silence for a moment, and then Kasiah spoke again.

'I want you all to know that I will be managing my husband's affairs from now on. *Taylor House Pearls* will continue as before. You need not be concerned about your jobs. We must continue with our lives as we did before. It is what my husband would have wanted and expected. Paddy and Jago, please take Duncan's car back to the warehouse and continue with your work for the rest of today. There will be a considerable amount of shell to be stored in the coming days when our luggers and the schooners come back for the lay-up season. But please be careful with that snake still in there somewhere. Jago, please bring Duncan's car home with you tonight. I will come and see you both at the warehouse first thing in the morning. The rest of you, please continue with your work. I will speak to each of you in private sometime tomorrow.' She took Tessa's hand, and they went to the house. Juliette and the housekeeper followed them.

Jago and Paddy went to Duncan's motor car. Jago climbed in and switched on the ignition. Paddy used the crank to start the motor and climbed in. Jago backed away from the old flame tree, turned the car onto the driveway and drove off.

But Ahmed Bin Jago had a strange, lost expression on his face as he drove down the winding driveway of Kasiah's home and turned onto Walcott Street.

# Chapter 13

# The Shipping Office

### 11th November 1918

Captain Callaghan looked at Henry's weary face. He was tired himself.

'Good morning, Henry. Thank you for all your hard work over these last few days. It seems we now have the ship almost back to normal. She certainly looks much smarter now that those horrible portable toilets and mess tents have been removed,' he said to his chief mate.

'Have you been informed by the shipping office about our next assignment, Captain? Henry asked.

'We will not be required to carry out any more operations overseas. I was just notified on the ship's radio a few minutes ago that an armistice is soon to be declared. It will be announced to the public on the wireless before the end of the day. The war will soon be over.' Captain Callaghan said with an attempted smile.

'Thank God for that,' Henry replied. 'Will that mean we'll be returning to Fremantle soon, sir?' Henry asked.

'We're to have repairs done to the deck and some of the superstructure that was caused by that German aircraft done here in Port Melbourne first. We should be able to leave in another two weeks,' the captain replied.

'That's good news, Captain.'

'I'm guessing you're keen to get back to find out if that pretty Taylor girl from up there in Broome has been writing to you.'

'Yes, sir, I am. Although she's probably forgotten all about me by now. It's been such a long time,' Henry replied with an uncertain smile.

'What about that nice nurse who was looking after you here on board? I think she was a bit keen on you, Henry.'

'I wrote to her last night. Annie's really nice, alright, and I like her a lot, but I have to find out if Tessa has written to me. I just can't seem to get her out of my mind, Captain.'

'That's fair enough, Henry. But don't you get too far ahead of yourself? A lot of time has gone by since we were last up there in Broome. As they say, life goes on, young man,' Captain Callaghan said, reaching for Henry's hand. 'I'd like to thank you again for what you did that day when we were attacked, Henry. You saved a lot of lives with your bravery.'

'I just did what I had to, Captain, and no more than that,' Henry replied.

'How's that hip of yours treating you?'

'It's not bothering me too much, sir,' Henry replied.

*   *   *

A month later, the S.S. *Gorgon* arrived back in Fremantle. As soon as the hawsers were secured to the wharf bollards and everything was in order, Henry went up to the wheelhouse.

Captain Callaghan was busy with his log when Henry approached him.

'You needn't bother to ask, Henry. Permission granted. Off you go, and good luck to you,' he said, taking off his glasses and smiling at the young man he thought of as the son he was never lucky enough to have had.

'Thank you, Captain,' Henry replied, spinning about and leaving the wheelhouse.'

Thirty minutes later, Henry arrived at the offices of the State

Shipping Service of Western Australia. He pushed open the door and went inside. He recognised the woman behind the desk. She had been the one he had spoken to the last time he was there.

'Excuse me, ma'am,' Henry began.

The woman took off her glasses and looked up. 'Oh, my goodness, it's you! It's Henry Dawson. How lovely to see you, young man.'

'I don't suppose there are any letters for me, ma'am?' Henry asked, surprised that the woman had recognised him and even remembered his name.

'There certainly are, young man; there are several of them. But it's been almost two years since the last one arrived. I thought something must have happened to you. There have been so many young lives lost in this damn war.'

'I suppose I'm one of the lucky ones, ma'am,' Henry replied.

'The odd thing is, two of them came the day after you called last time,' the woman said as she went to the pigeonholes.

'There are several of them, you say, ma'am,' Henry replied excitedly.

'There are, and I very nearly sent them all back to the return address when the last one arrived. But then I had this feeling you'd call again one day,' the woman said, passing Henry his bundle of letters. She'd wrapped them with rubber bands long ago.

'Thank you, ma'am. It means a lot that you've kept them for me,' Henry replied.

'My name is Laurel Davis, young man. If you don't mind me asking, where have you been all this time?'

'I've been overseas mostly, Laurel. We've been helping with the wounded. We've only been back for a few weeks. We've been over in Melbourne for a bit getting a few things done to the ship,' Henry replied, smiling and looking at the bundle in his hand.

Laurel Davis lifted the hinged partition on her counter and came out. She took Henry in her arms and hugged him. There were tears in her eyes when she spoke.

'I'm glad you got back safely, young man. This war has taken far too many young Australian lives. I'm so glad to hear it's finally over. Now, off you go and read your letters. I hope she's still waiting for you.'

'So do I, Laurel. Thank you for keeping them for so long for me. Goodbye, ma'am,' Henry replied, turning and going back out onto the street.

Laurel Davis went back behind her desk. She was crying when she picked up her glasses.

Pedestrians were rushing past Henry as he stood on the busy street looking at his bundle of letters. Cars were speeding by. A city bus stopped near where he was standing, and its door clattered open. Henry stared at the bus. His mind was spinning with excitement. He needed to find somewhere quiet. He waited for the door to close and the bus to leave, then he crossed the street and headed back towards his ship. A few minutes later, he saw a sign above a door a little further along the street. *The Esplanade Hotel.* When he got there, he pushed open the bar door and went inside. It was quiet, and he was the only one in the bar. He ordered a pint of beer, paid the barman, took his glass, and found a table near a door that read *Cocktail Lounge* in gold-painted letters.

The pedestrians were still hurrying by outside the windows, but Henry couldn't hear them. He sat down, put his beer glass on the table in front of him, and started to pull away the rubber bands from around his letters. When he finished, he laid them out in the order of the dates stamped on them. There were six of them altogether. He looked over and noticed the barman watching him.

'You've got a stack of letters there, young fella. Have you been away for a bit?' The barman asked with a smile.

'I have. I've been overseas for a bit helping with the war,' Henry replied.

'Good for you, young man. Bloody Germans! I'm glad it's finally over. I've just heard it on the wireless from the Prime Minister.'

'So am I,' Henry replied.

'When did you get back?'

'We got back a few weeks ago. We'd been carrying wounded and disabled soldiers back, and we had a bit of trouble with a German fighter. He shot up the deck a bit. We had to get some repairs done over there in Port Melbourne before we headed back here.

'I reckon I read something in the paper about that. What would your name be, young man?' The barman asked.

'I'm Henry Dawson,' Henry replied quickly. He wanted to get on with reading his letters.

'Henry Dawson. You'd be the young man who shot down that German plane and saved a hell of a lot of lives on that ship of yours. I've read about you in the paper. They reckon you should get a medal for what you did that day.' The barman remarked, coming out from behind the bar and putting out his hand. 'I'm pleased to shake your hand, Henry Dawson. I'm Dave Sinclair. I've got a fair idea of what you went through over there, young man. I spent a bit of time over in Africa some years ago meself, fighting the damn Boers.'

'I'm pleased to meet you, Dave,' Henry replied, shaking the barman's hand.

'I'll let you get back to your letters, Henry. You've sure got a stack of them to get through. Are they from a sweetheart?'

'I'm not too sure about that at the moment, Dave,' Henry replied as he watched the barman go back behind the bar. He looked down at the neatly laid-out letters in front of him and picked up the first one. He opened it and began to read . . .

Tessa Taylor

*Walcott Street*

*Broome, W.A.*

*Dear Henry,*

*I was so glad to receive your first two letters. They arrived at the same time, which was nice. I'm so glad you enjoyed yourself when you visited us at our home. It was such fun. It was a shame that it was for such a short time, though. I'm glad you liked our gardens and Mother's little secret place. I sit there sometimes and think of you. I hope your work on the ship is keeping you busy. I think it would be exciting to sail up and down the coast and meet new people when they come on board. I'm so glad you asked me if you could help with my watermelon when we were on board that day. I've planted some of the seeds from it, and they are up already. I agree with you, Henry when you say you think we were destined to meet. I know we don't know each other very well, but I do know that I like you very much. I'm looking forward to the next time your ship comes to Broome. I told you before that Mother thinks you're very nice, but I'm not so sure about Father. When I turn eighteen, he wants me to meet some of the local boys from other pearling families. Some of them have already invited us for dinner at their homes. Mother hasn't accepted any of the invitations as yet. She would like me to make up my own mind about my future. She just wants me to be happy. You make me happy, Henry Dawson. I so hope that we meet again soon.*

*Love, Tessa.*

Henry suddenly felt sad and alone. The memory of his day at Tessa's home had rushed back into his mind. He remembered sitting with her in the little secret place in their garden and watching the rainbow fish swimming among the lilies. It seemed so long ago now. Anything could have happened with Tessa by this time. Perhaps she had met a boy from one of the pearling families like her father wanted. Perhaps she was even married. He opened all but the last letter and read each of them. They were very much like the first, and he loved every word. He could even smell Tessa's perfume on some of them. When he finished, he carefully folded them and put them back in their envelopes.

Then he opened the last one. It was dated twenty-two months ago.

*Tessa Taylor*

*Walcott Street*

*Broome, W.A.*

*Dear Henry,*

*I'm not sure what to think anymore. I haven't received any more letters from you, only the first two. It makes me sad to think that you would have forgotten me so easily. But I can think of no other reason for you not to have written. Your first two letters were so nice. Perhaps you have met someone else. If you had, surely you could have told me. I have spoken to Mother about you, and she told me to be patient. She thinks there may be a reason for your not writing. She said it might have something to do with this terrible war that is going on overseas. If that were the case, I think you still could have taken the time to write to me and tell me. I'm not sure about anything anymore. I'm so disappointed that it has worked out this way. I will take my mother's advice and wait for a while longer. I hope she was right and that there's a simple reason for my not hearing from you.*

*Goodbye for now.*

*Tessa.*

Henry stared at the letter. Captain Callaghan was right—life goes on. Perhaps he'd been expecting too much of Tessa. She would be 21 years of age by now and probably married to one of the boys that her father wanted for her. He felt sick in the stomach.

What should he do? He put the letters together and fastened the rubber bands back around them. He looked at his beer glass. He'd hardly drunk any of it. He got up and looked out the window. It was still busy out on the street. He felt lost. He said goodbye to the barman.

'It's been nice to have met you, young man. Good luck to you,' the barman replied.

Henry went out onto the street. He stood there for a moment, thinking. People dodged around him. An old woman suddenly bumped into him. He heard her mumble something and then hurry on down the street clutching her handbag. Captain Callaghan was right; life certainly does go on. He held the letters tight in his left hand and wandered off towards the Fremantle docks and his ship. Perhaps the captain would know what he should do.

# Chapter 14

# Daffodene

Captain Callaghan was writing a long and difficult letter to his mother in Mount Gambier, South Australia. It had been a long time since he'd written. His parents owned a small dairy farm out on the edge of town. After his father died some years ago, his mother leased out their cows to a neighbour. She'd continued with her daffodils, though. She'd been supplying local florists with daffodils for as long as he could remember. Their little dairy farm out on the O.B. Flat Road was even called 'Daffodene.' He grew up on the farm, helping his father with the cows and his mother with her daffodils. Often, when he felt homesick, he would think of his dear mother. He remembered the William Wordsworth poem that was his English mother's favourite. He put down his pen and sat back as he remembered her reciting it to him long ago while they picked the daffodils for the florist shops she supplied in the town one warm spring day long ago.

I wandered lonely as a cloud.

That floats on high o'er vales and hills,

When all at once I saw a crowd,

A host, of golden daffodils;

Beside the lake, beneath the trees,

Fluttering and dancing in the breeze.

Continuous as the stars that shine
And twinkle on the milky way,
They stretched in never-ending line.
Along the margin of a bay:
Ten thousand saw I at a glance,
Tossing their heads in sprightly dance.

The waves beside them danced; but they
Out-did the sparkling waves in glee:
A poet could not but be gay,
In such a jocund company:
I gazed—and gazed—but little thought.
What wealth the show to me had brought:

For oft, when on my couch I lie.
In vacant or in pensive mood,
They flash upon that inward eye.
Which is the bliss of solitude;
And then my heart with pleasure fills,
And dances with the daffodils.

He missed his dear mother. But so much had happened in his life since those long-ago days. He'd advised her in his letter that he was back in Fremantle, and now that the war is finally over, things should get back to normal. He knew she would have been worried about him. He skipped the part about the German plane attacking them off the coast of North Africa. He hoped that she hadn't read about it in any of the local newspapers. Mount Gambier was a long way from Western Australia. But he couldn't be sure. He was almost finished when he heard a knock on his cabin door.

'Who is it?' he called out.

'It's me, Captain. It's Henry Dawson. Can I come in?' He heard Henry call back.

'Of course, you can, lad. It's unlocked.'

Henry opened the door and stepped inside. He had a lost look on his face.

'Has that young girl gone and left you for someone else, Henry? You don't look too happy, young man.'

'That's the thing, Captain; I don't know. Letters were waiting for me at the shipping office—six of them altogether. It was real nice to hear from her. But the last one was close to two years ago. I think she might have given up on me by now. She said she was going to wait for me to write for a while longer. I suppose I should have written to her from England. But I hadn't even had one letter back from her by then,' Henry replied.

'What do you think you're going to do about it?' the captain asked.

'I'm going up to Broome to find out what's happened to her. She might even be married by now. But I really need to find out,' Henry replied.

'We won't be back on that run for a while, Henry. The *Minderoo* has been filling in for us while we've been off fighting the damn war.'

'Do you think I could get on board?'

It's Captain Bradford's ship. I'll get on the radio in the morning. He's due back here later today.'

'Thank you, Captain.'

'You could work your way up to Broome with him, leave the ship there, and sort things out with the young lass. If it doesn't work out, you could catch the *Minderoo* on her way back down the coast. You'll need to find somewhere to stay, though. There's a couple of reasonable guest houses in Broome, and then there are the hotels, but they might be a bit on the rough side,' Captain Callaghan suggested.

'I hope he doesn't mind taking me on with such short notice.'

'Don't worry about that, Henry. Bradford's a decent man.

In the meantime, you've still got work to do. Get yourself out of here and let me finish my letter.'

'Thank you, sir.' Henry spun around and left the captain to his letter writing.

# Chapter 15

# Taylor House Pearls

Two weeks later, Henry was helping passengers disembark from the S.S. *Minderoo* in the coastal town of Port Hedland, a full day sailing south of Broome. It was the end of the cyclone season. The sky was heavy with dark, slow-moving clouds, and it was hot and humid. They would be leaving Port Hedland just as soon as the last of the freight had been unloaded. When he was finished with the departing passengers, Henry was summoned to the bridge.

'You wanted to see me, Captain?'

Henry liked Captain Bradford. He was a tall man with a shock of white hair and a kindly manner. He was a little older than Captain Callaghan, and to Henry, he seemed very wise. One of the crew told him the captain liked to study the languages and culture of the coastal Aborigines. A peculiar thing to study, Henry had thought.

'Crewman Dawson. Yes, I wanted to have a quick chat. As you are well aware, we will be arriving in Broome with the high tide early tomorrow. You and I will be parting company there. I believe you have personal business to attend to.' the captain acknowledged with a smile.

'Yes, sir. I'll be staying in Broome for a while. But I'm not sure for how long at the moment. I may need to travel south with you when you return, sir.'

'You'll be welcome to, Henry. I'm always glad to help a man

in need, especially one who became a hero on one of our ships during that awful damn war.'

'I'm no hero, Captain. I just did what I had to, and that's all. The real heroes were the Australian diggers who were fighting in the trenches and the Light Horse Brigade. They faced the worst of it: machine guns, gas, and barbed wire. It must have been hell for them. So many were killed. They're the real heroes, sir, and not me,' Henry replied.

'I suppose you're right. All the same, what you did on that day was a very brave thing. You saved a lot of lives.'

'Thank you, Captain.'

'It will be at least another four weeks before we are back in Broome, by the way. I hope everything works out for you, young man. It's a sweetheart, I believe?' Captain Bradford commented, smiling.

'Yes, sir. It's a girl I met over three years ago. Her name is Tessa . . . Tessa Taylor. Her father's a pearler in Broome.'

'Do you mean Duncan Taylor's daughter, Henry?'

'I do, sir. I had afternoon tea with them at their house some time ago.'

'I have some rather unpleasant news for you, Henry.' Captain Bradford said, the smile disappearing from his face.

'What bad news would that be, Captain?'

'Duncan Taylor is dead. He died some months ago. He was bitten by a snake while working in his warehouse, so I'm told.'

'Oh, my Lord! How terrible for his wife and Tessa! Do you know what has happened with them since then?'

'Kasiah Taylor is now managing *Taylor House Pearls*. A remarkable woman indeed. Very capable, I've been told. She's doing very well under the circumstances.

'Thanks for telling me, sir.'

'There's something else, Henry. But perhaps it's better that you find out about that yourself when you visit.'

'Has someone else come to harm, sir?' Henry asked.

'Not as far as I know, young man,' Captain Bradford replied. 'Good luck to you, though, Henry Dawson. I hope things work out for you.'

'Thank you, Captain,' Henry replied, turning smartly and leaving the bridge.

* * *

Early the following morning, the *Minderoo* drew alongside the Broome jetty, and her hawsers were promptly secured to bollards fore and aft, and the unloading of the ship's cargo began. Several horse-drawn rail cars were already waiting at the ready. A narrow-gauge tram line ran the complete length of the jetty to Streeter's warehouses in the town. Apart from freight arriving on the monthly steamers, it was used to cart pearl shell from the warehouses in town to waiting ships bound for overseas buyers.

Henry spent the next hour helping passengers disembark. Some were returning locals. Others were northbound passengers heading into the pearling town for a couple of hours to sample the local delights. A horse-drawn carriage was waiting for them at the entrance to the jetty. The Continental Hotel was usually their first stop, and sometimes the noodle stalls in the town. Time enough to stroll about and wonder at the strange collection of different races and cultures in the thriving but unique coastal town. A town where even the street signs were written in several different languages. In Filipino, Chinese, Arabic, Malay, and, last of all, English. Sheba Lane was another popular destination during daylight hours. A place to buy pearl shell jewellery, tie pins, cigarette cases, strange concoctions and cure-alls, and all manner of other curiosities. But it was a place to be avoided at night when the opium dens, gambling houses, and brothels opened. When dark-skinned prostitutes roamed the dimly lit street, offering their services. A place where the knife often is used to settle disputes. And now, with the luggers laid up along the creeks and mangroves, their crews with their pockets full, it was certain to be dangerous.

* * *

When he had finished his work, Henry farewelled Captain Bradford, and with his battered old suitcase in his hand, he went down the gangway and headed along the jetty toward the town. As he walked, he remembered his trip with Tessa's father the day he went for afternoon tea at their home almost four years ago. How sad it was that he had been killed. When he reached the jetty entrance, he set off for the town.

He was hot and bothered, and his hip was hurting when he finally came to the Continental Hotel. He limped up the veranda steps, went inside, and ordered a glass of cold beer. He swallowed most of it in his first gulp, put the glass on the bar, and looked at the barman.

'I'd like another if you don't mind,' he said, wiping his lips with the back of his hand.

'It's a bit warm out there,' the barman replied, filling his glass.

'It certainly is . . . and humid,' Henry added and asked. 'I'm after the address of a reasonable guesthouse. Do you happen to know of one?'

'There's one not too far from here. It's quite reasonable and not too expensive. They call it the Tropicana Lodge.'

'Whereabouts is it, if you don't mind?'

'It's in Guy Street, about halfway along,' The barman replied, pointing in the general direction Henry would need to take. 'You look like you're new in town, mate.'

'I've just arrived off the *Minderoo,*' Henry replied.

'That's what I thought. You wouldn't happen to be looking for work, would you?'

'Not really. Why do you ask?'

'I need a barman. If you got the job, your accommodation would be taken care of here at the Conti.'

'I'm not sure what I'm doing at the moment. I'll go around and get meself a room and come back and talk to you in a day or so. How does that sound?' Henry replied.

'Fair enough. In the meantime, let me buy you another beer.

You look hot and bothered.'

'By the way, I'm Henry Dawson,' Henry said, putting out his hand.

'I'm Paul Anderson. I manage the Conti,' the barman replied, taking Henry's hand.

* * *

An hour later, Henry was walking along Dampier Terrace on his quest to find the warehouse of *Taylor House Pearls*. He'd booked himself a room at the Tropicana Lodge, showered, and changed into his best clothes. A little further along, he noticed a large, freshly painted weatherboard building. A sign protruded out at right angles from the front wall and hung out over the footpath. The words *'Taylor House Pearls'* were painted onto it in bold green and gold lettering.

When Henry got there, a pair of double doors were open to the street, and two men were working inside. One of them stopped. He'd seen Henry standing on the footpath, staring in at them.

Henry remembered the man. He was the dark man who drove Duncan Taylor's car when he first visited their home. He couldn't remember his name.

'What do ya want—!' the dark man asked.

'I'm wondering if Mrs. Kasiah Taylor is here somewhere?' Henry asked.

'She's in office,' the dark man grunted, pointing to a door that led from the warehouse to another part of the building.

'Is it alright for me to go in?' Henry asked.

'Me knock on door first. What your name, Mister?' the dark man asked, walking to the door.

'Just tell her it's Henry Dawson,' Henry replied.

Henry watched him tap on the door and call out. 'Some fella wants to see you, Missus.'

'Who is it, Jago?' Henry heard Kasiah call back through the closed door.

'He says, Henry Dawson, Missus. You want me to tell him to go away—you busy?' Jago called back.

A second later, the door opened, and Kasiah Taylor came out. She had a wide smile on her face. 'Oh, Henry, how wonderful to finally see your handsome face again.'

'Hello, Mrs. Taylor,' Henry replied.

Kasiah went to Henry and put her arms around him. Henry could smell the perfume on her dark skin.

'Oh, Henry, I've been so worried about you,' she said, releasing him and taking his hand. 'Come inside.'

Henry followed her into her office.

Kasiah Taylor was just as beautiful as he remembered when he first saw her on board his ship. Her dark skin shone like coal lifted from a bucket of clear water, and her dark, smiling eyes were the same.

When they were inside, Henry looked around the office. After the warehouse, he hadn't expected it to be so nice. The walls were lined with tongue-and-groove boards and painted a soft blue colour. The flooring was highly polished hardwood boards. A massive steel safe sat against the side wall that faced the warehouse. Two cedar-bladed ceiling fans were turning slowly on the plaster ceiling. The only window in the room faced the street. It was of obscure glass and covered with a grill of heavy steel bars. The walls of the office were decorated with wooden-framed photographs of pearling boats and their crews. A silver-framed oil painting of a magnificent schooner sailing in a heavy sea hung on the wall directly behind Kasiah Taylor's desk. Henry read the caption: *The Schooner, Mina, circa 1907.*

'I'm so sorry about your husband, ma'am,' Henry said before he sat in the chair Kasiah offered him.

'Thank you, Henry. It was a terrible shock . . . Dear Duncan, you were the love of my life,' Kasiah replied, going behind her desk and looking at the framed photograph in front of her.

'I've only just found out, ma'am.'

'Henry, I would like you to call me Kasiah.'

'Alright then, ma'am,' Henry replied.

'I want to tell you something you will not know, Henry. After Duncan died, I came into this office to tidy up. I packed away most of the old brochures and notes and bits and pieces on his desk into a cardboard box. Only recently I went through the box again and found a newspaper folded to an article that I believe he was going to show me when he got home the day that he was killed. I had completely missed it when I was tidying up, probably because I was still so upset.' Kasiah opened a drawer and passed the folded newspaper to Henry.

Henry read the article. When he finished, he looked into Kasiah's dark eyes.

'You knew that I was sent overseas then?' he replied.

'Yes, Henry, I knew, but only very recently. I was going to tell Tessa, but I decided to wait until I knew if you were still alive or if you came back to us. There is something else you should know as well, Henry. Tessa is to be married soon. She would have been married already, but for Duncan's death,' Kasiah said.

'Tessa's getting married—!' Henry replied, his disappointment showing on his tanned, handsome face.

'I'm so sorry, Henry. She thought the world of you. It's been such a long time. She waited and waited for your letters, you know. But after only two of them came, she never got another. Why didn't you bother to write to her again?'

I thought she'd forgotten about me or found someone else. I never received a reply to my first two letters, and then I was sent overseas. I was gone for so long, and when I came back, these were waiting for me.' Henry pulled his rubber-band-wrapped bundle of letters from his pocket and put them on Kasiah's desk.

'Oh, Henry! I thought that might have been the reason, but I never dared to hope. If only you had written to her at least once again from overseas.'

'It's all my fault. I've certainly messed things up, haven't I? Is she happy, Kasiah?'

'Henry, the Tessa you knew has changed. She is now a very beautiful young woman. She is no longer the impressionable young girl you knew all that time ago.'

'But is she happy, Kasiah?'

'Yes, I think she is. Although I sometimes wonder. Her fiancé, George, is a very fine young man. His family, the Petersons, are one of the biggest operators of luggers in Broome. His father, Sean, is a ruthless businessman. It was only a week after Duncan's death that he offered to buy me out.'

'Are you thinking of selling, Kasiah—?' Henry asked.

'No, I am not. Well, not at this very moment anyway. He is being very insistent, though, and his offer is quite generous.'

'How are you managing on your own?'

'It's the end of the cyclone season right now. Our luggers and schooners are all laid up along the creeks and in the mangroves. My big test will be when they put to sea again. Our crews and divers are reliable and experienced. I don't expect too many problems. You met Jago, of course. He'll help to make sure things run smoothly for me. He was Duncan's right-hand man. His shadow, I suppose you could say. He was very devoted to him.'

'I'm not sure I'd like to get on the wrong side of him,' Henry suggested.

'That is exactly what every man who works for us thinks as well. Our crews are quite frightened of him.'

'I can easily understand that, Kasiah.'

'Jago took Duncan's death very badly, Henry. Paddy told me that he found the snake that killed him that same day. He said he crawled under the warehouse, caught it with his bare hands, and tore its head off. Then he ate part of it raw. Paddy thinks it had something to do with chasing away the evil that visited us that day,' Kasiah said with a shake of her head.

'He ate it raw—! My God!' Henry replied.

'He found her just hatched young and killed each of them as well. After that, he nailed a piece of board under the hole the snake used and filled the hole with molten lead. Paddy told me the lead represents a door—a door now sealed forever,' Kasiah explained.

'How very strange,' Henry replied.

'He's a strange man, Henry. Ever since then, he has followed me everywhere. I suppose it's his way of continuing his work for my husband.'

'It's a good thing to have someone to watch out for you, I suppose,' Henry offered.

'I don't think you understand just how dangerous Jago is, Henry. Every once in a while, a pearl might mysteriously disappear from one of our luggers, only to be discovered in one of the crew's pockets or belongings, or perhaps just a rumour that the theft of a pearl had taken place on one of our boats. Stealing is a practice that will not be tolerated on the boats. More often than not, that crewman would mysteriously disappear. Some would suggest that, most likely, he had just run away to sell the pearl, or perhaps because he was terrified of Jago finding out he had stolen from us. The rumours would soon get around that Jago had probably tracked the man down, cut his throat, and dumped his body in some remote creek out of town. Of course, a body would never be found, and it would soon be conveniently forgotten.'

'Do you believe any of it, Kasiah?' Henry asked.

'I asked Duncan one night after I had heard one of these stories. He assured me that he would never condone any such thing, and then he told me never to speak of it again,' Kasiah replied.

'Where does he live, Kasiah?'

'Jago lives with us, Henry. Many years ago, Duncan had servant's quarters built behind our home. There are several comfortable bedrooms with fans, a bathroom, a kitchen, and a large fly-screened area open to catch the night breezes where they can sit, eat their meals, and smoke. Jago lives there with the rest of our staff. Duncan has never allowed him into our home, and that is still the case today.'

'I suppose you understand him better than most,' Henry added.

'I'm told women are attracted to him, Henry, although I can't understand why. Tessa's governess, Juliette, goes to his bed, and so does Tarni, our housekeeper. Tarni should be ashamed. She's an older woman.' Kasiah explained.

'Are you and Tessa safe with him being so close?' Henry asked.

'Far safer than you can imagine, Henry. No one would dare break into our home with Jago so close. He has a fearsome reputation in the town.'

'What does Tessa think of him?'

'She has always been frightened of him. But he's been with us for such a long time, and she knows he's devoted to us. Strangely, it's comforting,' Kasiah admitted.

'You still have Tessa's governess with you? I thought she would have gone by now.'

'Juliette is part of our family now, Henry. She has nowhere she wants to go. It's the Broome way. She plays the piano so wonderfully well. When we have parties, everyone enjoys listening to her. She is to play for our guests in our garden at Tessa's wedding,' Kasiah said, smiling at Henry. She was so glad to see him again.

'I'm glad your life has not been too disrupted after losing your husband, Kasiah,' Henry added.

'Thank you, Henry. You are very kind. Now, what are we to do now that you've returned to us?' Kasiah asked.

'I suppose I'll go back to Fremantle on the *Minderoo* when it returns. There's a nurse down in Adelaide that I like. She looked after me when I was wounded overseas. It's not the same as how I feel about Tessa, but she's nice, and she likes me,' Henry admitted.

'I read about your injury in that newspaper. You were a hero, Henry. You saved the lives of many brave young soldiers on board your ship. I'm so proud of you.'

'Thank you, Kasiah. But I'm no hero.'

'Henry, I'm going to take this newspaper home and show it to

Tessa tonight. I should have shown it to her sooner. I'm going to tell her you came to see me and that you are here in Broome. She will want to see you. I'm certain of that.'

'Do you think so?'

'Of course I do. Will you come out to our home for dinner tomorrow evening?' Kasiah asked.

'Yes, of course.'

'Where are you staying, Henry?'

'At a guesthouse called the Tropicana.'

'I know the place. I'll have Jago call for you at six o'clock,' Kasiah said, coming around the desk and embracing Henry. 'It's so nice to have you back with us again after such a long time. I've missed you, Henry.'

'And I have missed you, Kasiah. You and Tessa mean so much to me,' Henry whispered, inhaling Kasiah's intoxicating perfume again. He felt her kiss his cheek and murmur something in a language he couldn't understand.

'I will look forward to tomorrow night, then. Thank you, Kasiah,' Henry whispered back.

# Chapter 16

# Dinner With Tessa

Henry was waiting outside the Tropicana Lodge when Jago swung the big Pierce-Arrow into a dusty U-turn and parked at the roadside. He stayed in the car, with the engine still running. Henry stepped off the footpath, walked over, and opened the front passenger door.

'You sit in back, Mister Henry,' Jago instructed.

Henry shrugged with indifference and closed the door. He went to the back and climbed in. Jago put the car into gear, and they pulled away. Henry could sense that Jago didn't want to speak, so he remained silent and watched him drive the heavy car effortlessly through the streets of Broome.

A few moments later, Henry noticed a young, coloured woman with a baby in her arms and a child at her side about to cross the street when she saw them approaching. He watched her grab the child's hand and hurry back to the footpath. He noticed the fear in the woman's eyes. She had recognised Jago at the wheel. A short while later, they turned into the long, winding driveway of Kasiah Taylor's home on Walcott Street.

The gardens were just as Henry remembered them—simply perfect. The flame trees were in full bloom. Their flowers were like fire against the bruised evening sky. The lawns were lush and green. He noticed colourful parrots crowding the rim of a beautiful bronze birdbath that held a statue of Pan in its centre, holding a flute to his lips as they hurried past. Henry couldn't remember seeing it there the last time he visited.

A moment later, he saw the home through the trees. Its imposing façade was partially shaded from the fast-disappearing sun. Sprinklers on long spikes were spraying a fine mist onto a bed of yellow canna lilies near the veranda steps.

Jago parked the Pierce-Arrow under one of the flame trees, and they both climbed out. He inclined his head toward the steps.

'You go up now,' he said in a low voice.

Henry watched him turn and hurry over to a narrow path that led down the side of the house and disappear into the shadows.

Henry's heart was racing. He started up the veranda steps just as Kasiah and Tessa came onto the veranda. He saw them stop and look down at him. Kasiah was smiling, but Tessa's face seemed to hold no expression at all.

Henry thought his heart might leap from his chest. Kasiah had said that Tessa had changed, and she was right. She was no longer the young girl he remembered. She was now a stunningly beautiful woman. She seemed taller and even more statuesque than before. Her coffee-coloured skin seemed smoother and more perfect than he remembered. Her breasts were full, and her body was slim. She was her mother's daughter; there was no denying it now. They were so much alike and both so breathtakingly beautiful.

'I'm so glad you could come, Henry,' Kasiah said, greeting him with an embrace and a kiss on his cheek when he reached the veranda.

'Thank you for inviting me, Kasiah,' Henry replied, turning to Tessa. 'Hello, Tessa. It's nice to see you again.'

'It's been a long time,' Tessa said with a forced smile.

'It's been almost four years since I was last here, Tessa. I suppose the war lasted much longer than we all thought.'

'I suppose it did. Thank God it's finally over now, though,' Tessa replied.

'Let's go inside where it's cooler under the fans,' Kasiah suggested. 'I think Tarni has our meal almost ready for us.'

Henry followed the two women through the door and into the hallway. This was the first time he had been inside the magnificent home. It was cool and quiet. A grandfather clock's loud ticking broke the silence as they passed it. Paintings of pearling boats hung on one of the hallway walls. Japanese wall hangings of wading birds in rice fields with brilliant yellow crests hung suspended on silken cords on another.

He followed them into the dining room. A huge Persian rug covered the polished floorboards on which a magnificent mahogany dining table sat. Beautiful rattan chairs of a high-backed and rounded Oriental design were set in place against the table. Two cedar-bladed ceiling fans were turning slowly on the decorative plaster ceiling. A matching mahogany sideboard sat against one of the walls. A multi-coloured glass vase filled with brilliant tropical flowers sat in its centre. Two ebony figures of naked black women with dark, pointed breasts sat on either side. A painting of a pearling lugger with a helmeted diver standing on the deck hung on the wall at the head of the room. A huge, varnished sawfish was mounted on the wall opposite, its serrated saw, more than five feet long.

At the far end of the room, a door suddenly opened, and Tarni, the housekeeper, came in carrying a tray of food.

'I hope you like spicy food, Henry. Tarni has prepared us her famous fish curry made with a freshly caught blue-bone groper,' Kasiah said, smiling at the Aboriginal woman.

'It sounds delicious,' Henry replied, sitting in the chair Kasiah offered him.

'Are you staying in Broome for long, Henry?' Tessa asked, in an attempt to ease the tension.

'I'm not sure at the moment, Tessa. I'll need to wait at least until the *Minderoo* calls again in four weeks. I've been offered a job in one of the hotels in the meantime.'

'Which hotel, Henry?' Kasiah asked.

'The Continental. I met the manager when I first arrived,' Henry replied.

'George and I go there with friends sometimes,' Tessa added.

'I was sorry to hear about your father, Tessa. It came as quite a shock.'

'Thank you, Henry. It was so unexpected, wasn't it, Mother?'

'It certainly was, my darling,' Kasiah replied.

'I've been told you're soon to be married, Tessa,' Henry said, staring into Tessa's dark eyes.

'Yes, I am, Henry. My wedding is in three weeks. I would have been married already, but for Father's untimely death,' Tessa replied.

'And will you live here with your mother in this beautiful home when you're married?'

'I would love to stay here with Mother. There is certainly enough room. But my fiancé, George, is having a wonderful new home built for us out in the sand hills near Cable Beach. It's little more than a stone's throw from the water, and it's almost completed,' Tessa replied.

'You'll be looking forward to it then, I suppose.' Henry said, looking briefly at the painting of the lugger and then back to Tessa. He wanted desperately to get up and leave. He wished now that he hadn't accepted Kasiah's invitation to dinner.

He glanced at Kasiah . . . She must know how he felt.

'Yes, I certainly am, Henry.' He heard Tessa's reply. 'We are travelling to Hong Kong for our honeymoon. I've been there before, but I was very young. Mother has made bookings for us at a nice hotel in the centre of the city.'

Henry was feeling as if all of his hopes for the future had been torn from him. He knew now that he was still deeply in love with Tessa. But she was to be married. Perhaps he'd been foolish to think he could have had a future with her. After all, he was just a simple seaman. It seemed so long ago now that they first met on the deck of his ship. He remembered her struggling with her watermelon. He must now accept that he is going to lose her. He decided at that very moment that he would take the job at the Continental Hotel, and in four weeks, he would travel back to Fremantle. He would see his good friend, Captain Callaghan, and explain what had happened, and then he would go across to Adelaide to see Annie. Perhaps his future was already being set in place for him as he sat in Kasiah Taylor's dining room.

When the dinner finally came to an end and the small talk was exhausted, Tessa wished him well and went off to her bedroom. Kasiah got up, apologised for her daughter leaving the table so abruptly, and offered to drive him back to the guesthouse.

Nothing was said as they passed through the dark streets of the town. Kasiah parked the Pierce-Arrow near the front entrance to the guesthouse. She left the motor running and turned to Henry. 'I'm so sorry things haven't worked out as you had hoped, Henry. If only you had written all those months ago. I wish there was something I could do for you,' she whispered, reaching for him.

Henry could smell the perfume on her dark skin and feel her breasts pressing against him. He felt as lonely as hell. He wanted to kiss her. 'Thank you for a wonderful night, Kasiah. I will remember it always,' he whispered back.

'You must come and see me before you leave, Henry. You must promise me that you will,' Kasiah whispered, releasing him from her embrace.

'I will. Kasiah . . . I promise I will.'

'Goodbye, Henry.' Kasiah took Henry's face in her hands and kissed his forehead and then his lips lovingly.

'Goodbye, Kasiah,' Henry whispered back, a thrill rushing through him from the kiss. He climbed out and watched until the lights of her car disappeared out of sight, and then he wandered up the path to his room.

# Chapter 17

# The Continental Hotel

The following morning, after he'd eaten his breakfast, Henry walked to the Continental Hotel. When he got there, he went into the office and asked for the manager. A short while later, Paul Anderson came in carrying a crate of Bell's whisky.

'It's Henry, isn't it—?' he said, putting down his crate.

'I'm here about that job, Paul, if it's still going?' Henry asked, shaking the manager's hand.

'Nice to see you again so soon, Henry,' Paul replied. 'It's still available, all right. When do you want to start?'

'Straight away if it suits you. There's just one thing I should tell you, though. I might be leaving in a month.'

'That'll give me a month to convince you to stay, Henry. If you've got your stuff around at the Tropicana, you'd better go around there and get it. Your accommodation and meals go with the job here.'

'I'll head around and get it now. And another thing, I haven't done any bar-keeping before, Paul. You may need to give me some help for a bit,' Henry admitted, shaking Paul's hand again.

You'll pick it up. It's not too difficult. I'll keep an eye on you for a day or two. You can start with me in the front bar tomorrow at opening time. It's quiet in the mornings.'

'I'll be there,' Henry replied.

'Ten o'clock sharp, by the way. Time enough to have your breakfast. The food's pretty good here as well. The cook's my wife, Cheryl.'

'Sounds good. I'll go and get my stuff and see you a bit later then. Thanks for the job, Paul,' Henry replied sincerely.

'No problem, Henry. I'll see you when you get back. I'll show you to your room then and give you a good look around the place.'

*   *   *

The next few days passed by quickly for Henry. There was so much for him to learn, and he was kept quite busy. He was surprised by how much he enjoyed working at the *Conti*, as it was locally known. It was a family-run business, and Paul and his wife Cheryl made him feel right at home. Henry heard no mention of Tessa Taylor or her mother for those first days, and he was glad of it, although at night when he lay in bed, he would think of Tessa and how much he had loved her and how sorry he was that things hadn't worked out as he had hoped. For such a long time, he had dreamed of seeing her again, and when it finally happened, he'd learned she was to be married. He was hurt, but he realised that he must get over it and get on with his life.

However, one late afternoon, things changed. He was working in the front bar with Paul when four young men dressed in tropical whites strolled into the bar.

Henry went to serve them.

'Four pints of beer, barman. It's unbearably hot outside, so make it quick,' one of them said, slapping a pound note on the bar.

'Coming right up,' Henry replied with a smile and started filling fresh glasses.

'You're new here, barman. What do we call you?' the same man asked.

Henry heard one of the others comment, 'Barman should be good enough for any barman in this town.' Then he heard the four of them laugh as they picked up their glasses.

'Barman is fine with me. But if you're interested, my name

136

is Henry Dawson,' Henry said, pushing the man's change over the bar.

'Henry Dawson, eh! So that's your name—is it?' the man who'd ordered the drinks asked with a menacing tone.

'Barman is still okay with me if you'd prefer,' Henry added and started to move away.

'Hang on there, barman. Would you be the same Henry Dawson who's been upsetting my fiancé?'

'And just who's your fiancé—?' Henry asked.

'Don't get clever with me, barman. I'm George Peterson. I'm talking about Tessa Taylor.'

'I'm glad to know you, George. Yes, I know Tessa Taylor. But the last thing I would ever do is upset her,' Henry replied sharply and moved away to another customer.

A few minutes later, George and his friends were waiting for their glasses to be filled again.

Henry went back to them.

'We'll have another round, Dawson,' George Peterson grunted, 'and make it quick.'

'Coming right up, George,' Henry replied, smiling, and taking their glasses.

'I've got a piece of advice for you, Dawson,' George Peterson grunted, slapping some coins on the bar. 'Stay away from Tessa or my friends, and I might just call on you one of these dark nights.'

'It's starting to sound to me like you're not the sort of man that deserves a woman like Tessa Taylor, and if you think your threat has me worried, George, think again,' Henry replied, putting George's change on the bar and moving away again.

'We shall see about that, barman,' George Peterson hissed.

A short while later, George and his friends finished their drinks and left without another word.

'What was all that about?' Paul asked Henry. He'd heard some of George's comments from further up the bar.

'It seems I've upset one of your local gentlemen,' Henry replied.

'That George Peterson is a bloody snob. He's marrying that nice Taylor girl. I feel sorry for her. You knew her a couple of years back when her father was still alive, didn't you?'

'I did, Paul. But that's all in the past now,' Henry replied.

'That's a pity. She's too bloody good for that arsehole, George Peterson.'

'I think I'd have to agree with you, Paul,' Henry replied.

'We'll be closing shortly, Henry. How about you and I have a couple of drinks out in the beer garden after we've locked the place up?'

'I'll be in that,' Henry replied.

*    *    *

Three days later, it was Saturday. It was late in the afternoon, and Henry had just finished work for the day. He grabbed the book he'd borrowed from Cheryl from his bedside cupboard, took a towel from a drawer, and walked down to the town beach for a swim and some well-earned rest. It was hot and humid, and the sky looked threatening. There had been some concern for the last few days that a cyclone was brewing somewhere off the coast, but nothing had come of it as yet.

Henry found a shady spot beneath an old tulip tree, a short distance back from the beach. He left his book and towel, took off his shirt, and went down to the beach for a relaxing swim in the crystal-clear waters of the Indian Ocean. An old Chinese man was fishing a little further along the beach. He gave the old man a wave as he waded out into the low waves. The old man took off his hat, smiled, and waved back.

A while later, Henry left the water and went back to his shady tree. The old Chinese man had gone. He lay down and picked up his book. It had been a busy week. He opened the first page and started reading. He was tired, and it wasn't long before he fell asleep, only to be woken a while later by sand flicking up at him from the beach. He sat up and looked at his wristwatch. He'd been asleep for more than two hours. It was almost dark. He looked at the sea. In the early moonlight, it looked like a slowly moving mirror. Low waves were rolling up against the beach, glistening like millions of tiny, precious stones as they broke against the wet sand. Quite suddenly, it started to spit with rain, a grim portent of what was to come.

Henry got up and put on his shirt. He shook the sand from his towel, picked up his book, and started back toward the hotel. He was almost there and just about to cross the road when the lights of a motor car appeared from behind him. It braked suddenly and stopped at the last moment. Henry turned and watched four men climb out and step into the dull yellow beam of the car's headlights.

'Well. if it isn't Henry Dawson, the smart-mouthed barman.' He heard George Peterson hiss. 'I think it's time for my good friends and me to show you what happens when you interfere in a gentleman's private affairs in this town.'

Henry dropped his book and towel onto the road and waited. It was completely dark now, and the street was quiet. The only light was coming from the headlights of George Peterson's motor car.

George Peterson stayed where he was, leaning on the front of his motor car, while his three friends left him and came at Henry.

The odds weren't good, but Henry knew how to look after himself. Growing up during tough times and in a rough area of Darwin, he had learned how to look after himself.

The biggest of the three men came straight at Henry first, confident he could finish him quickly. That was his first mistake. Henry's straight right fist caught him on the jaw, and he collapsed to his knees on the roadside. His second mistake was not getting out of the way of the next punch.

The other two men stopped for a moment and then came on. One moved to Henry's right, the other to his left, still hoping for a quick victory. They came at him together, their fists held high.

Henry bunched his fists and waited. These men weren't fighters. They were the sons of rich men. He crouched, and a vicious right hook took care of the man on his left. As he came up, the man on his right threw a punch. Henry blocked it and hit him hard in the face with his left fist. He fell to the ground as well, blood pouring from a broken nose. Henry stepped back and watched them struggle to their feet and stagger back toward George, nursing their broken faces.

Henry was out of breath now. Sweat was trickling down his face and back, saturating his shirt. He stared at George Peterson and waited for him to come at him.

'So, it seems you can use your fists a little, barman. But let's see how you go against a good sharp knife.' George Peterson hissed, pulling a pearl-handled switchblade knife from his trouser pocket, opening it, and moving slowly forward.

Suddenly, from out of nowhere, a dark, powerfully built figure appeared in the dull beam of the car's headlights.

'You drop knife real quick, Mister George, or you be real sorry.' Henry heard him say . . . It was Jago.

George Peterson dropped his knife and hurried back to his car. His friends were already climbing inside. Henry saw his face in the headlights as he looked back. It was ashen with fear.

A few seconds later, they were gone.

Henry heard Jago's footsteps approaching him. He couldn't see the expression on his face because of the darkness, but he heard his voice for the second time that night.

'You go home now, Mister Henry. Them fellas give you no more trouble.'

'Who was it who sent you, Jago?' Henry asked, picking up his towel and book from the roadside.

Boss-missus sent me. She say, you watch out for Mister Henry.' Jago replied, and a moment later, he had disappeared.

Henry continued to the Conti, wondering if Kasiah Taylor had just saved his life.

*  *  *

That night, a severe tropical storm swept through Broome, causing considerable flooding and damage around the town. Fortunately, it was the lay-up season, and most of the luggers and schooners were safely moored along the shoreline and in the mangrove-lined creeks.

Henry lay in his bed unable to sleep, partly because of the storm thrashing at the hotel buildings and partly because of his fight with George Peterson and the sudden, unexpected appearance of Jago. And, of course, because he knew for certain now that Tessa was soon to marry a man not worthy of her. But he had made up his mind; he would work at the hotel until the *Minderoo* arrived, and then he would travel back to Fremantle. He lay back, closed his eyes, and listened to the rain crashing down on the iron roof. He felt lost, but he knew he had to get on with his life. As he lay there, he thought of Kasiah Taylor kissing him and the smell of her perfume.

Lightning suddenly flashed across the small louvre window, followed by the loud rumble of thunder. His bedroom walls seemed to shake in fear of the thunder and the crashing of the rain on the iron roof. When it finally subsided, Henry heard a soft tapping— probably a fallen tree branch brushing against a wall, he thought. Then he heard it again. This time it was louder!

Tap . . . Tap . . . Tap!

Henry got to his feet, wrapped a towel around his waist, and went to the door.

'Who is it?' he called out, wondering if George Peterson was standing outside the door with a knife in his hand. Lightning flashed across the louvres again, followed by more thunder and the sound of heavier rain crashing down on the iron roof. 'Who is it?' he called out again.

'Henry, it's me. It's Tessa . . . Can I come in?'

'Just a moment,' Henry called back. The electricity had been taken out by the storm. He lit a candle stub, put it on his bedside cupboard, and unlocked the door.

Tessa stood in the narrow doorway, staring at him. Rain was crashing down behind her, flashing white in the lightning. Her clothes were soaked. Her long, dark hair was pasted to her face and shoulders. She had a distraught expression on her face.

'Oh, Henry, are you alright—? Mother told me you've been in a terrible fight with George and his friends,' she cried, her voice raised above the sound of the rain and thunder.

'Come in out of this storm, Tessa . . . You're soaked through! How on earth did you find me?' Henry yelled back.

'Jago brought me. He knew where to come somehow,' Tessa said, stepping inside.

'Is he outside somewhere?'

'He's waiting for me in Mother's car at the back of the hotel.

Have you been harmed, Henry? Have they hurt you?'

'I'm alright, thanks in the end to Jago showing up.'

'I'm so sorry, Henry. It's all my fault,' Tessa replied, sobbing.

'You weren't to know, Tessa, and there was no need for you to come here.'

'Oh, Henry—! Mother told me to come. She asked me if I was still in love with you. I've never stopped loving you, Henry.'

'But, Tessa, you're soon to be married.'

'I'm finished with George. It's over now after what he did tonight. I'll tell him tomorrow. Will you ever forgive me?' Tessa asked, reaching for him.

'Of course, I forgive you, my love,' Henry replied, taking Tessa in his arms, and pulling her wet body against him. 'I've never stopped loving you, Tessa.'

'There's something you should know, Henry—something that I have to tell you,' Tessa whispered as Henry held her.

'What is it, my love?'

'I've been in George's bed. We have made love. I wanted to wait until we were married, but he wouldn't wait. Can you forgive me?'

'Of course, I can forgive you. You were to be married,' Henry replied, kissing Tessa for the very first time.

Lightning flashed across the louvre window, filling the bedroom with flickering blue light, followed by the distant rattle of thunder. The storm was beginning to move away.

'You're soaked through, Tessa, and you're shivering. I'll get you a towel.'

Henry went to a wardrobe and picked up a clean towel. When he turned, Tessa was undoing her blouse.

'Oh! . . . I didn't mean I wanted you to get undressed, though,' he said, holding the towel out, his mind spinning.

'Do you have something dry I could put on?' Tessa asked, slipping her arms from her wet blouse. She wore nothing underneath. Her breasts were slick with water, and her dark nipples were erect with pleasure.

'I'll get you a shirt and a pair of my shorts,' Henry whispered, watching breathlessly as Tessa struggled out of her remaining clothing.

'Now you can give me that towel,' Tessa said, standing naked before him, her copper skin glowing in the flickering light from the candle and the lightning flashes.

Henry's heart was racing. He passed Tessa the fresh towel. 'Oh, Tessa, you're so beautiful,' he murmured, turning away.

'No, Henry, not that one. I want the one you're wearing.'

Henry turned back. He tossed the towel he was holding onto the bed, undid the one at his waist, and passed it to her.

Tessa took it, dropped it to the floor, and reached for Henry. 'Make love to me, Henry,' she whispered, just as another rain squall crashed down on the roof.

'Oh, Tessa . . . There's never been anyone else for me. I have loved you since the first moment I saw you so very long ago. I'm so sorry that I never wrote when I was overseas.'

'Shh, my love,' Tessa whispered.

Henry kissed Tessa's lips and then each of her wet, glistening breasts. Then he carried her to his bed. 'My darling, Tessa, I have dreamed of this moment,' he murmured, holding her wet body against him.

'I love you, Henry . . . I've always loved you.' Tessa whispered, moving her hips to the edge of the bed.

'Oh, my sweet love,' Henry murmured, kissing her breasts again and then her naked belly.

Outside, the rain continued to crash down on the iron roof, and lightning flashed across the louvre window, filling the little room with flickering blue light.

*   *   *

A while later, they lay together on the narrow bed, exhausted from their lovemaking. The rain had finally stopped, and it was strangely still. A frog started croaking from somewhere just outside the door.

'Will Jago still be waiting for you, Tessa?' Henry asked to break the silence.

'He won't leave until I go out to him,' Tessa replied. 'But I suppose I should go.'

'When will I see you again, my love?'

'Will you come for lunch tomorrow? I think Mother wants to talk to you.'

'Of course I will. It's Sunday tomorrow, and I have the day off.'

'Good. I'll send Jago for you at midday,' Tessa said, getting up. 'Do you have anything I could wear? My clothes are still soaked,' she said, picking up her wet clothes from the floor and dropping them again.

'Would a pair of my shorts and a clean shirt do?'

'That will do,' Tessa replied, sitting back on the edge of the bed. She kissed Henry and ran her hands down his naked body.

'You want me again, don't you?' She whispered.

'Yes, I do, my love,' Henry replied, kissing her copper shoulder.

'In that case, Jago will just have to wait for a while longer,' Tessa whispered.

# Chapter 18

# White China Plates

The following morning, just before midday, Henry was sitting on the front veranda of the Continental Hotel, waiting for Jago to arrive, remembering his night with Tessa. How strange life can be, he thought. Just when he was certain it was all over between them, things changed. All, it seemed, was because of the fight he had with George Peterson and his friends. His last memory of Tessa was watching her in his candlelit room put on a clean pair of his shorts and his best white shirt before she left. When she was dressed, he went with her to the door and kissed her one last time. Then he watched her run out into the darkness and light rain, carrying her wet clothes in her hand.

Henry woke from his reverie just as Jago parked the big Pierce-Arrow close to where he was sitting. He hurried down the veranda steps.

'Good morning, Jago,' he said happily through the open driver's window.

'You get in back, please, Mister Henry,' Jago replied with a flicker of a smile.

Henry remembered that Jago had been waiting for Tessa for several hours the previous night. He would have seen the clothes she was wearing when she got back to the car. He would have known they'd been intimate.

'Thank you for coming to get me, Jago,' he replied with a smile, climbing in the back seat. Henry couldn't conceal his happiness.

Jago never replied. He put the Pierce-Arrow in gear and drove off through the puddles. Henry saw him glance in the rearview mirror and smile again as he changed into second gear.

A short while later, they turned into the long, winding driveway of Kasiah Taylor's home on Walcott Street. As they passed through the gardens and drew closer to the house, Henry noticed a small round dining table set in place and covered with a white tablecloth under the big flame tree where the Pierce-Arrow usually parked. White China plates and silver cutlery had been placed in neat order on the white linen tablecloth. A small antique desk piano stood in the shade, a short distance away.

Jago parked the car near the house just as Tarni came down the veranda steps carrying a silver container of food. She smiled at Henry as he climbed out of the car and then hurried over to the table.

Henry looked around and noticed Jago had already disappeared. He made his way up the veranda steps. Tarni joined him just as he was about to knock on the door.

'Wait here for a minute, Mister Henry. I'll tell Kasiah you're here,' she said, hurrying past him and leaving the door open.

A moment later, Kasiah came out carrying an ice bucket filled with bottles of wine. She put it down and took Henry in her arms.

'Good afternoon, dear Henry. Tessa is still dressing. She won't be long,' she said, kissing his cheek.

Kasiah Taylor looked stunning. She was dressed in the same deep red and gold kaftan he'd seen her wearing the first time he'd visited. She was wearing fuchsia-coloured makeup above her dark, smiling eyes and glistening wine-red lipstick that matched the kaftan she had on. Her long, dark hair was tied back and held in place with a pair of gold and pearl shell clasps. Her dark skin shone like coal oil in the morning light.

'You look very beautiful today, Kasiah.'

'Thank you, Henry. How kind of you to say so. Come with me, and I'll get you seated at our little table. We'll be having our lunch outside today. I hope you don't mind.

'Not at all. The table looks very nice,' Henry replied, following Kasiah down the steps.

Kasiah put the ice bucket in the centre of the table and pulled back a chair. 'You can sit here where my darling Duncan used to sit, Henry.'

'Thank you,' Henry replied.

Kasiah leaned forward. 'I'm very pleased everything has worked out for you and Tessa. I thought your shorts and nice white shirt looked quite lovely on her when she came home last night,' she whispered, kissing Henry's blushing cheek.

'Thank you for helping us, Kasiah. I can't tell you how happy it makes me feel,' Henry replied.

'You are a part of our family now, Henry.'

'Thank you, Kasiah.'

'I'll go and see what's holding her up,' Kasiah said and hurried away.

A few minutes later, Kasiah and Tessa came down the veranda steps together. Tessa was carrying a jug of iced water and glasses. Close behind them came Juliette, holding a booklet of sheet music and a small stool.

Tessa put the iced water on the table and went to Henry.

'Good afternoon, Henry, my love,' she said, kissing him on the mouth, much to Henry's embarrassment.

'Hello, Tessa,' Henry replied awkwardly. He noticed Kasiah was smiling at them.

Tessa looked stunning. Her copper skin seemed to glow with happiness. She was wearing a fashionable dress of pale green silk with a row of sequins stitched around the low-cut neckline and a band of dark green frills at the hemline. Her hair was tied back and held in place with a pretty, silver-sequinned clasp. She was wearing a white hibiscus flower in her hair.

'You look very beautiful today, Tessa,' Henry said, getting to his feet.

'Thank you, my love,' Tessa replied, kissing him again.

'Would you like a glass of champagne before we start our meal?' Kasiah asked from across the table, still smiling.

'I suppose so. I've never drunk champagne before,' Henry replied.

'It's refreshing on a hot day like this. I think you will enjoy it.' Tessa said, lifting a bottle from the ice bucket, just as Juliette started to play Beethoven's *'Fur Elise'* on the piano.

*   *   *

Their lunch under the old flame tree that day would remain in Henry's memory for as long as he lived as one of the most enjoyable days of his life.

Unfortunately, when it was almost dark, something happened that changed things forever and set a new direction for his life. They had just finished their meal and were enjoying their third bottle of champagne when they heard a motor car turning off Walcott Street into the long driveway. Kasiah had heard it first. She put down her glass, stood up, and waited.

A moment later, a black Ford motor car came to a stop at the foot of the veranda steps, and two men got out. One of them was George Peterson, and the other was his father.

Something caught Henry's eye near the side of the house. Jago had suddenly appeared. He was standing in the shadows near some hibiscus bushes, watching the two men.

George's father came over to the table. His ruddy face was red with anger. George was close behind him.

'Good afternoon, Sean,' Kasiah began politely. She was still standing.

'What is the meaning of your daughter calling off her engagement to my son? They were to be married, Kasiah.'

'It's an unfortunate outcome, Sean, but it's what Tessa has decided.

'Arrangements have been made . . . I have paid for the

caterers. I've had a marque sent up from Perth on the Minderoo. I demand a proper explanation.' Sean Peterson shouted, slamming his right fist on the table.

George was looking pale and nervous. He had seen Jago standing near the side of the house.

'I think you should calm down, Sean,' Kasiah replied quietly.

'I will not calm down. This is an insult to my family,' Sean Peterson snapped.

'The decision was Tessa's to make, and that is what she has decided.' Kasiah said, turning to Tessa.

Tessa was frightened. She never replied, just nodded.

'Invitations have already been sent out. George is very upset. It makes no damn sense at all. Apart from that, their new home is almost complete. It has cost me a pretty penny too, I might add.' Sean Peterson argued.

'You are aware that your son and three of his friends attacked Tessa's friend Henry. If it hadn't been for Jago, he might have been killed!' Kasiah replied.

'It was just a little scrap. There's no harm in that. George told me this friend of Tessa's was interfering in his affairs,' Sean snapped back, staring at Henry.

'Regardless of that, Sean, Tessa has made her decision. She spoke to George on the telephone this morning and broke off their engagement. As far as I'm concerned, that's an end to the matter.'

'It most certainly is not an end to the matter. I have my reputation to consider, you black bitch. How dare you treat my son so poorly!' Sean Peterson snapped back, slamming his fist down again.

Henry stood up. His chair flew back onto the grass behind him. 'You will apologise to Kasiah for that remark right now, sir,' he called across the table.

'I most certainly will not apologise, you interfering bastard,' Sean Peterson snapped back.

Henry started around the table. He was white with rage.

'Please sit down, Henry,' Kasiah called out. 'I will deal with this.'

Henry went back and stood next to where Tessa was sitting and put his hands on the back of her chair.

Sean Peterson continued. 'Let me tell you something else, you black bitch, any hopes you may have had regarding me buying you out are now gone forever. I was warned not to deal with you. You're not to be trusted, you voodoo-believing fucking black Mulatto bitch!'

Henry left where he was standing and started around the table again. He couldn't be stopped this time. He was livid with rage. Sean Peterson would apologise, or there was going to be hell to pay.

'Stand down, Henry! Let me deal with this,' Kassiah called out in an assertive voice. At the same time, she put her hand up to stop Jago.

'Sean, I could not understand what Tessa ever saw in your son. But I would never have said anything to upset my daughter. George is nothing but a spoiled, self-opinionated bore, and I'm so glad that she's finally come to realise it.'

Sean Peterson was angry. His voice had become filled with rage. 'You will not be popular in this town when people find out the way you have treated my family, you black bitch!' he hissed.

I think you are the one who should be concerned, Sean,' Kasiah replied calmly.

'Concerned—! Why on earth should I be concerned?'

'I'll tell you why, you disgusting little man. Perhaps your son would like to know what sort of man his father really is. I'm sure your wife would like to know as well. On your last visit to my office, when you offered to buy me out, you told me you had never had sex with a black woman and that you had always envied Duncan being married to me. You said you'd like me to be your first. I think you imagined that I should have been pleased with your admission, and if I remember correctly, your exact words were, *'If you'd let me, Kasiah, I'd like to fuck you right now on that desk of yours.'* That was the moment that I slapped your face. You are a pig of a man, Sean Peterson. You should also know that at no time did I ever seriously consider selling my fleet to you. I only put up with your nonsense because Tessa and your spoiled son were to be married. But now things have changed. I have decided to offer a partnership to someone to help me in the future. Someone whom I have great confidence in and whom I trust implicitly.' Kasiah said with a cold, restrained voice.

'And just who would this person be?' Sean Peterson asked, his voice losing some of its venom. 'I take it that you have had a better offer than mine then.'

'That is none of your damn business, Sean. Take your son and get off of my property before I have Jago teach you some manners. And when you get home, please tell your dear wife that I look forward to seeing her again. We will have much to talk about.'

Sean Peterson turned to speak to his son, but George was already waiting beside their car. He stormed off.

'Take no notice of what that black bitch just said, George. It's all a pack of fucking lies,' he snapped when he got to him. 'You can drive. Get in the fucking car. We're leaving right now.'

George climbed behind the wheel and waited for his father. His face was white with fear. He'd noticed that Jago had disappeared from the side of the house.

Sean Peterson went to the passenger side and opened the door. He was about to climb in when he suddenly realised someone was standing right behind him. He turned and looked into Jago's dark, remorseless eyes.

Those sitting at the table hadn't noticed Jago move from where he'd been standing, and now Sean Peterson's car was blocking their view.

Jago smiled and shot his shaven head forward in a brutal headbutt. Sean Peterson's nose split open and broke from the impact with a sickening crunch. He fell back into the car, unconscious, blood spraying from his broken nose all over his white shirt and jacket.

Jago crouched, quickly tossing Sean's legs into the car after him, and slammed the door shut. Then he disappeared back into the darkness.

George engaged the gear lever and let out the clutch far too quickly. The car lurched across the lawn, crushing a hibiscus bush in his panic. He wrenched the steering wheel back, bounced onto the driveway, and sped off.

After George and his father had left, Kasiah turned to Henry. 'Will you stay for dinner, Henry?' she asked.

'Thank you, Kasiah. Yes, I would love to,' Henry replied.

'I'm sorry about the disturbance. It has ruined what could have been a wonderful day for you two,' Kasiah commented and turned to Tessa. 'Are you alright, my darling?'

'I am now. I have never seen George's father so angry. It frightened me, Mother.' Tessa replied.

The candles on the table suddenly started to flicker from an unexpected breeze, and light rain began to fall. They quickly gathered up the dishes and glasses and carried them up to the protection of the veranda. Henry and Juliette carried the little desk piano to a lower storeroom, while Tarni covered the table with a striped tarpaulin.

'I'm so sorry about all that, Henry.' Kasiah commented, opening the front door.

'It wasn't your fault, Kasiah. You weren't to know they were going to arrive. I think you put them both in their places rather well, though.'

'I'm sorry about the bad language, but I needed to make a point,' Kasiah replied.

'Don't concern yourself, Kasiah. I've heard much worse,' Henry replied as they stood together in the hallway.

'Mother, Henry, and I will go to the sitting room and listen to the phonograph for a while,' Tessa said, taking Henry's hand.

'Before you do, my darling, I would like to talk to Henry privately in the library,' Kasiah replied.

'I'll wait for you in the sitting room, Henry.' Tessa said, as her mother led Henry along the hallway into her study.

'Sit down, Henry, Kasiah instructed, going behind her desk.

'Is there a problem, Kasiah?'

'Let me ask you a question, Henry.'

'Please, go ahead.'

'Do you love Tessa, Henry?'

'More than you could ever know,' Henry replied.

'Do you wish to marry her?'

'Yes, I do, but I haven't asked her yet. I was going to speak to you first,' Henry replied.

'She loves you very much, Henry. I'm sure she'll say yes when you ask,' Kasiah said, smiling.

'I hope you're right.'

'What do you intend to do with your life now? Will you be staying in Broome?'

'Yes, I suppose so . . . Yes, of course, I will be,' Henry replied, wondering where the conversation was heading.

'I would like to offer you a partnership with me at *Taylor House Pearls*.' Kasiah said, with a serious expression on her dark, beautiful face.

'A partnership? Do you mean it was me you were referring to when you were speaking to George's father?'

'When I first met you, Henry, I saw something in your eyes—something that I liked. Sometimes things happen that are just meant to be. I think you were meant to be with Tessa and me. We both love you, Henry. You do know that don't you?' Kasiah said, staring into his eyes.

'And I love the both of you,' Henry replied.

'Well then, will you come and work with me? Will you accept my offer?'

'Yes, of course I will. But I have very little money to

invest, Kasiah.'

'You will not need money, Henry.' Kasiah said, smiling. Will you come and work with me or not?' Kasiah asked again.

'Yes, I will, Kasiah,' Henry replied. 'Yes, of course I will, and thank you so much.'

Kasiah came around the desk and took Henry in her dark arms. 'You will not be sorry, Henry, I promise you,' she whispered as she held him.

'Thank you, Kasiah. I will do my best for you.' Henry whispered back, his mind spinning with gratitude.

'I know you will, Henry. Now let's go and tell Tessa the news.' Kasiah said, taking Henry's hand in hers.

# Chapter 19

# The Gods of Love

Three weeks later, Henry Dawson and Tessa Taylor were married in the gardens of Kasiah Taylor's home. It was short notice, but more than a hundred people attended. Most of the local pearling families were eager to meet the young man who had stolen Tessa Taylor away from the well-liked and well-to-do George Peterson.

The occasion was a great success and enjoyed by all who attended. The weather was mostly agreeable, although rain had been forecast, but it held off for most of the day. A local band was hired, and an area in front of the house was set up with a portable wooden dance floor. The catering and drinks were organised by Henry's friends, Paul and Cheryl, from the Continental Hotel.

While the planning for the day was underway, Kasiah realised that because Tessa's father had been killed by the snake, she had no one to give the bride away, and it caused her great concern. Finally, she went to Jago and asked if he would give Tessa away, and to her great surprise, Jago agreed.

Tessa wasn't sure it was such a good idea, nor was Henry. But Kasiah insisted that it was something they should consider. She explained that Jago had been deeply troubled that he had failed to protect Duncan from the taipan. She told Tessa about him killing and eating the raw flesh of the snake in his belief that it would turn evil away from the family. After hearing this and realising Jago's absolute dedication to their family and understanding that his sense of failure at protecting Duncan from the taipan was still bothering him, Tessa and Henry finally agreed.

For Ahmed Bin Jago, it was the proudest day of his life. His usual stern, unyielding disposition changed the day Kasiah asked him into a smile that lasted right up until the wedding was over. From that moment on, Kasiah, Tessa, and Henry Dawson took the place of Duncan Taylor in his devotion to their safety.

Many who attended that day were surprised when they saw the swarthy, pig-tailed brute of a man dressed in one of his master's altered white suits leading Tessa Taylor down the garden aisle. But of course, the things that Kasiah Taylor did always gave the people of Broome something to talk about.

However, for Henry, it created another real problem: what was he to wear? Kasiah suggested one of Duncan's suits. She told him it could be altered, like the one they gave Jago to wear. But Henry was taller and much leaner than Duncan had been. Finally, Kasiah took him to a Chinese tailor in the town that Duncan had some-times used. Zhang Liu insisted that a suit could not be made on such short notice. He told them he was already very busy with other work she had asked of him and that he was very sorry. But when he noticed Jago staring at him through his shop window, he changed his mind, helped, of course, by the roll of banknotes Kasiah threw onto his cutting table. Henry was measured, and a white linen suit complete with a waistcoat and two extra pairs of trousers, one white and one black, were made with days to spare for final adjustment. Henry was so happy with Liu that he invited the old man and his wife to the wedding and insisted that they sit at the bridal table.

For Henry and Tessa, it was the happiest day of their young lives. It was as if the gods of love had found them wandering aim-lessly apart and finally bound them together.

The day after the wedding, Henry and Tessa boarded the S.S. *Minderoo* for their honeymoon. They were to travel to Fremantle by ship and then to Perth by train. After a few days in Perth, they would travel back to Broome on the *Minderoo* again. The pearling season had already begun, and that was when Henry's work with Kasiah would begin.

*  *  *

Henry struggled up the gangway, carrying their two heavy suitcases. Captain Bradford was waiting for them at the head of the gangway.

'Good afternoon, Henry Dawson. I'm told we are to have you as a paying passenger for this trip,' the captain announced, smiling and putting out his hand.

'Yes, you are, sir, And good afternoon to you. Captain Bradford, I would like you to meet my wife, sir. This is Tessa.' Henry replied, helping his new wife from the rickety gangway onto the deck.

'I'm very pleased to meet you, Mrs. Dawson. Although, I believe I remember you travelling with me when you were a much younger young lady.

'Yes, sir. I do remember. I believe we dined at your table.' Tessa replied.

'I must offer you my deepest sympathy, my dear. Your father was a good friend. He and your mother travelled with me many times. He will be sorely missed,' Captain Bradford acknowledged sincerely.

'Thank you, Captain. My father always spoke very highly of you,' Tessa replied.

'Now then, I have reserved our finest saloon-class cabin for you both. I think you will find it quite satisfactory. Cabin 11 has its own small bathroom and a pleasant outlook over the starboard side of the ship.'

'It will be a nice change from the crew's quarters,' Henry replied with a wry smile.

'It most certainly will, Henry. I'll have a porter help you with your baggage and get you to your cabin. After you have taken some rest, I'd like to invite you both to my table for dinner this evening,' Captain Bradford said, summoning a porter.

'We will look forward to it, Captain,' Tessa replied.

'Dinner is served on board between six and seven o'clock. If it suits you, six-thirty would be a good time for me.

'Well then, in that case, we shall see you at six-thirty, Captain

Bradford,' Tessa added.

Henry and Tessa followed the porter to their cabin. They waited outside while he unlocked the door and carried their bags inside.

'There's a jug of iced water on the bedside cabinet and fresh towels in the bathroom,' he said, putting their cases on the floor.

'Thank you very much for helping us,' Tessa replied.

'If you need anything else, just use the buzzer next to the bed. I hope you enjoy your trip,' the porter added, smiling, and handing Henry the key.

Henry thanked him, closed, and locked the door.

'This is nice, Henry. It's even bigger than the family cabin we had on the *Gorgon*.'

'Yes, it is very nice, Henry replied.

'I think I'll take a shower,' Tessa remarked, as Henry put their bags on a luggage table.

'When you're finished, I think I'll do the same,' Henry added, watching Tessa undo her blouse.

'Just think, Henry, we're married now. Isn't it exciting?' Tessa declared when she was finally naked. Her smooth copper skin was moist with perspiration, and her long, dark hair spilled down her back as she removed the sequinned clasp that held it in place.

'You're so beautiful, my love,' Henry replied.

'You do realise, Henry, that we haven't made love since that rainy night in your room at the Conti?'

I'm painfully aware of that. But I was staying at your home, Tessa. I thought it was the right thing to do. Your mother would have known if I went to your room,' Henry replied and continued, 'I just wanted to wait until we were on board the ship and on our honeymoon.'

'Mother wouldn't have minded. I think she expected it.'

'When I look at you now, I wish that I had.'

'Take off your clothes, Henry. Let's make love, and when we're finished, we can shower together.'

'A very sensible idea, my love,' Henry mumbled, undressing as quickly as his urgent fingers could manage to undo his buttons.

* * *

At exactly six thirty, Henry and Tessa Dawson arrived in the saloon-class dining room of the S.S. *Minderoo*. It was quite busy. Stewards were rushing about with plates of food and trays of drinks. At first, they couldn't see the captain at all. Then they saw him. He was sitting at a table with a small group of passengers. They watched him stand and wave them over. They waved back and made their way through the tables of the already-seated diners.

Tessa looked sensational. She was wearing one of the dresses her mother had gifted her for her honeymoon. It was jade in colour and made of silk. The collar was high and slightly rounded in the fashionable Cantonese style, so loved by the English and Australians living in the Orient in places like Hong Kong and Peking. It clung to her like a second skin—to her breasts, her waist, and her hips—and flowed, shimmering down almost to her ankles. Her dark hair was tied back from her face and fastened with an elegant silver and polished jade clasp. The perfume she was wearing, *Maderas de Oriente*, was another gift from her mother. Henry was wearing his brand-new white linen suit, white shoes, and a black open-necked shirt that suited his handsome, easy manner.

Captain Bradford was still standing when they reached his table. He gave Tessa a polite bow. 'Mrs. Dawson, you do look rather sensational this evening,' he said, offering his hand.

'Thank you, Captain. How nice of you to say so,' Tessa replied, smiling, and taking his hand. Tessa was quite used to men passing compliments on her beauty.

'And you look very smart this evening as well, Henry,' the captain added, reaching then for Henry's hand.

'Thank you, Captain Bradford,' Henry replied proudly.

'Very sharp indeed, young man. Now, before I show you to

your seats, I would like to introduce you to the other guests at my table this evening.'

Captain Bradford turned and looked at the older couple seated near him. 'These are my good friends from Port Hedland, Darby and Lois Bennett, well-known graziers from that area. The couple on the other side of the table are Connor and Angela Burke from Darwin. Connor is an investment advisor and stockbroker from our northernmost city. Both couples are travelling with us on holiday. This handsome young man is Henry Dawson, a good friend of mine, and his very beautiful wife is Tessa Dawson. They are recently married and from Broome. Tessa's mother is a well-known pearling fleet owner from there.'

Both couples got to their feet and shook Tessa and Henry's hands. As they sat back down, Angela Burke suddenly insisted from her side of the table. 'Tessa, you must come and sit next to me.'

Angela Burke was a very attractive 24-year-old redhead. Her husband, Connor, was considerably older, closer to fifty. A handsome, distinguished man with a shock of white hair, a fashionable moustache, gold-rimmed glasses, and sharp, calculating eyes.

'Yes, Tessa, come around here and sit next to my angel. Henry, you can sit on my other side,' Connor Burke suggested.

Henry escorted Tessa around the table, and they sat in their appointed seats just as Captain Bradford proposed a toast.

'If you would like to charge your glasses from the champagne bottles and stand again, I would like us all to wish Henry and Tessa the very best for their future together.'

The captain's guests got to their feet and raised their glasses, as did several diners at nearby tables who had been admiring the beautiful Tessa Dawson and her handsome young husband.

*   *   *

Their dinner with Captain Bradford that evening was a great success. Tessa was a hit with everyone, in particular with Angela Burke, and as the night continued, they became the best of friends.

Angela was fascinated with Tessa's skin colour and the way she was dressed.

'Tessa, your dress is fabulous. It suits you so wonderfully well. Where on earth did you find it?' She asked her in a quiet moment.

'It's a gift from my mother,' Tessa replied. 'It was one of hers that I've always liked. I believe it's called a *cheongsam*. Fortunately, she and I are the same size. She bought it while on holiday with my father in Hong Kong a couple of years ago. She knows a wonderful seamstress there. She only ever wore it once.'

'Do you think I could wear something so beautiful?'

'Yes, of course you could. I'm sure that with your lovely red hair and your wonderful ivory skin colour, it would suit you just perfectly. You and I could meet in your cabin tomorrow, and you could try it on if you like.'

'What a wonderful idea, and when we're finished, we could have lunch together,' Angela replied. 'Our cabin is 23. Would nine o'clock in the morning be alright for you, Tessa?'

'That would be perfect,' Tessa affirmed.

'Henry and I could get together as well. I'd like to learn a bit more about this pearling industry you're involved in,' Connor added, looking at Henry.

'I'm afraid I will not be much help on that subject. I've only recently joined Tessa's mother in the business, and I've yet to start working with her,' Henry replied.

'I think we should get together anyway, now that Tessa and Angela have hit it off so well.'

'In that case, I'll come with Tessa in the morning. While they try on each other's clothing, we could take a walk around the ship,' Henry suggested.

'I will look forward to it, Henry,' Connor replied.

# Chapter 20

# Surprise News

For Henry and Tessa, the remainder of the trip down the coast and the days spent shopping in Perth were spent with Connor and Angela. The four of them became inseparable. They shopped together and dined together each evening while they were in Perth, and on their last day in the city, they took a boat trip across to Rottnest Island and spent the morning with a guide showing them the sights of that unique island and its wildlife.

Connor and Angela were to have spent another week in Perth before travelling back to Darwin on a different ship. But Angela insisted that they return on the *Minderoo* with Tessa and Henry. She wanted to spend more time with Tessa before they went their separate ways.

Even though Connor was much older than he was, Henry found he enjoyed the older man's company immensely. Connor had a wealth of knowledge in the world of finance and investment. It was something Henry was interested in learning more about. He wanted to prove to Tessa and Kasiah that he was worthy of their faith in him.

On their return trip on the *Minderoo* and over drinks one evening, Connor told Henry about a new venture he'd been considering in the remote town of Pine Creek, some distance south of Darwin. He told him he'd recently had a visit from an old prospector with gold samples taken from a remote area some distance from the town. The prospector needed finance to purchase mining equipment and set up a workable gold mine, as he had little money of his own. Connor explained that he had sent the ore samples to a Perth laboratory for analysis and had picked up the report while they were in Perth. They indicated positive results worthy of further investment and exploration. He told him the old prospector would be waiting for him to return to Darwin with his decision on whether he would finance the mine in a partnership. Because of their friendship and their wives getting along so well, Connor decided to offer Henry a financial partnership in the new mine. But he went to great lengths to explain the possibility of the mine not being profitable and the risks involved.

Henry explained to Connor that he was only a recent and very minor partner in *Taylor House Pearls* and that he was not in a position to make such decisions, and because he had no money of his own to invest, he would need to speak to Kasiah and ask if she would like to meet with them when they arrived back in Broome and discuss the possibility of investing in the mine. This was agreed upon, with Connor explaining that he did not want to ruin their friendship by forcing Henry into anything he wasn't comfortable with. He told him that if he couldn't raise the money needed, he intended to finance the entire operation himself anyway.

* * *

The trip back up the coast was enjoyable for both couples. They spent an afternoon walking the streets of Geraldton and a morning in Port Hedland. Most nights, they dined with Captain Bradford. It was during dinner on one of those nights that the captain mentioned Henry's war record and his episode with the German fighter plane off the coast of North Africa, explaining that Henry's bravery had saved the lives of many returning wounded and crippled Australian soldiers.

'The lad deserves a medal for what he did that day,' Captain Bradford told them with great sincerity as they dined together.

Henry tried his best to play it down and change the subject. But Connor Burke was mightily impressed, and it seemed to further consolidate his friendship and respect for the younger man.

Their final dinner together before they were to arrive in Broome was spent with the captain, and as usual, they were enjoying themselves, sipping wine, and listening to his stories. But as the evening wore on, Henry noticed Tessa looked uncomfortable. Even Angela had noticed it and asked if there was something she could help her with. Tessa told her there was nothing for her to worry about and that she was sorry, but she had a bad headache and suggested that Henry should take her back to their cabin for some rest. Henry apologised, bid them good night, and took Tessa back to their cabin.

'Are you unwell, my love? Have I done something to upset you? All this mining talk was probably getting a bit boring. We have been going on a bit,' he asked when they arrived at their cabin.

'No, Henry, it's nothing you have done. I *am* feeling a little unwell, though,' Tessa explained.

'Would you like me to get you something? A glass of water, perhaps?'

'Please sit down, Henry. I have to tell you something that I don't think you're going to like.'

'What is it, Tessa?'

'I think I'm pregnant.'

'But . . . how could that be?' Henry asked, his mind spinning with concern.

'I'm so sorry, Henry. I'm almost certain I'm carrying George Peterson's child. You must surely hate me now.' Tessa whispered.

'I could never hate you, Tessa. Not ever, my love. But are you sure that I am not the father from that night when you came to my room in the Conti after my fight with George and his friends?' Henry whispered back his question.

'I'm quite sure, Henry. I've been worried for the last few days. I'm well overdue. I'm quite certain it's George's. Are you sure you don't hate me knowing that George is the father?'

'Don't say such things, my love. You are my wife, Tessa, and that will never change. But what are we to do about it?' Henry asked, concern showing on his handsome face.

'I will speak to Mother when we get home. I suppose I will just have to get rid of it somehow. She will know what to do. I'm so sorry, Henry. What a terrible start to our married lives together!' Tessa whispered and started to cry.

'Tessa, I love you more than you can ever know. We could keep the baby. No one needs to know that it's George's.

'Oh, Henry, do you truly love me that much?' Tessa sobbed, tears pouring down her cheeks.

'Of course I do. I will never stop loving you, Tessa, no matter what happens,' Henry replied, taking Tessa in his arms. Tears were misting in his own eyes.

'Oh, Henry, what have I done? I'm so ashamed,' Tessa whispered as Henry held her.

'Shh now, my love,' Henry whispered back.

# Chapter 21

# Monkey's Faces and Long-Tailed Lizards

The following afternoon, they arrived in Broome with an already-turning tide. The Minderoo was to remain in Broome until early the following morning.

Tessa's mood had lifted with the knowledge that Henry still loved her after hearing her unpleasant news and would support her through this difficult time. She would speak to her mother as soon as she was able. She was determined to not let it ruin their friendship with Connor and Angela. Tessa had never had a close friend. Her father, whom she had loved dearly, had kept her protected in so many ways. She felt comfortable with Angela. They got along so well—almost like sisters—and she was saddened that they must soon part company. They stood together on the upper deck and watched the crew toss their heavy lines down onto the long Broome jetty.

'I wish you weren't leaving tomorrow, Angela. I could speak to Mother. You could stay with us for a while if you wanted to,' Tessa said, holding Angela's hand.

'Connor doesn't like to impose. He's funny like that. But I do love him so, Tessa.' Angela replied, kissing Tessa's cheek.

'I'm going to miss you,' Tessa admitted.

'You must come up to Darwin and stay with us soon. We have a lovely new home with plenty of room.'

'Yes, we certainly will. But tonight, you're coming to meet Mother and have dinner with us. I'm certain you'll love her.' Tessa replied, just as Henry and Connor joined them at the railing.

'Well, we'd better get down and see if we can catch a ride into town. There's usually a horse-drawn carriage waiting at the jetty entrance. We can ring Kasiah from the Continental Hotel,' Henry announced.

'A horse-drawn carriage! That will be fun,' Angela said excitedly.

*   *   *

Twenty minutes later, they were enjoying a drink in the cocktail lounge of the Continental Hotel. While Henry was introducing Connor and Angela to his good friend Paul, the hotel manager, Tessa excused herself and went to ring her mother. When she came back, she was excited.

'Mother is sending Jago to pick us up. She's speaking to Tarni now about having something nice prepared for our dinner,' she announced, going to Angela and taking her hand.

'These two women are becoming inseparable, Henry,' Connor admitted.

'It certainly seems that way,' Henry replied, smiling at the two women.

A few minutes later, Jago came into the hotel and stood near the door so they could see he'd arrived.

'We'd better get moving,' Henry said, swallowing the last of his beer. 'Be careful what you say to Jago. He's not too fond of conversation.'

'Point taken,' Connor replied, downing his drink as well. They said goodbye to Paul and followed Jago out to the Pierce-Arrow.

'Miss Tessa, you sit in front, please. Rest in the back,' Jago grunted, opening the door for Tessa.

They watched Tessa climb silently into the front seat. She had never sat in the front with Jago before.

Henry smiled to ease the tension and ushered his new friends into the back seat, and they sat squeezed together in silence while Jago went to the front and used the crank to start the car. When he climbed in, he said nothing and drove them to Tessa's home.

It was almost dark when he turned into the driveway. Ungainly fruit bats were gliding across an already-rising moon in the distance. A moment later, the long shadows of the palms that lined the driveway were flitting under the Pierce-Arrow's wheels as they drew closer to the magnificent home now visible through the trees. Kerosene lanterns lit up the front veranda. Two had been placed at the foot of the veranda steps.

Jago parked the Pierce-Arrow under the big flame tree and climbed out. He went around the car and opened the door for Tessa. Once she had climbed out, he hurried away.

Henry helped Angela and Connor from the cramped confines of the back seat, and they joined Tessa at the front of the car, just as a dark shape appeared on the veranda.

'Is that my darling daughter and her husband back from their honeymoon?' They heard Kasiah call down.

'Hello, Mother. Yes, we're home at last.' Tessa called back, leading them up the steps. When she reached the top, she rushed into her mother's arms.

Kasiah kissed her daughter's cheeks and then her forehead and turned to Henry. 'Come here, Henry, and let me hold you.'

Henry went to Kasiah's outstretched arms and felt her crush him against her warm body. 'It's so good to be back, Kasiah. We've both missed you terribly,' he whispered to her.

'I've missed your handsome face as well, Henry Dawson. It's so nice to have you home again,' she whispered back, kissing his cheeks. 'Now then, you'd better introduce me to your friends before we go inside,' she said in a slightly louder voice, releasing him.

'Yes, of course,' Henry replied, standing aside. 'Kasiah, I would like you to meet Connor and Angela Burke, our new friends.'

Up until that moment, Connor and Angela hadn't moved from the top of the steps. They were entranced by the stunningly beautiful black woman looking at them in the light of the kerosene lantern. They stepped forward together. Connor spoke first.

'Thank you for inviting us to your home with such short notice, Kasiah,' he said, taking her outstretched hand.

'You are very welcome, Connor. I hope my daughter wasn't too much trouble for you while you were on board the ship,' Kasiah asked as she studied the distinguished white-haired man.

'Tessa was delightful company,' Connor replied, looking into Kasiah's dark, fascinating eyes. 'She and Angela have become the best of friends.'

Angela moved up next to her husband and put out her hand. 'I'm so pleased to finally meet you, Kasiah. Tessa has told me so much about you.'

'I hope at least some of it was true,' Kasiah replied, smiling, and taking her hand. 'Now, I think we should go inside. Tarni will have our dinner ready quite soon.' Kasiah took her daughter's hand and led them into the dining room.

The first thing Connor noticed in the dining room was the varnished sawfish mounted on one of the walls. It was huge; its dangerous-looking saw was more than five feet long. He had never seen anything quite like it. He cast his eyes around the tastefully appointed room. The long mahogany dining table had been set with white linen. Comfortable rattan dining chairs, of an Oriental design he had never seen before, sat against the table. Tall candles burned in a silver candelabra, guttering slightly from the slowly spinning ceiling fan. A huge glass vase of flowers sat in the centre of the white tablecloth. An ornate silver censer of incense sticks burned next to it, filling the room with the pleasant smell of sandalwood and cinnamon. A mahogany sideboard matching the table sat against a side wall. A bowl of pale pink frangipani flowers sat on its top, flanked on either side by ebony figures of naked African women with dark, pointed breasts. On the wall opposite hung the painting of a pearling lugger with a helmeted diver standing ready on the deck.

'Your taste in decoration is wonderful, Kasiah. What a very comfortable room,' Connor commented.

'Thank you, Connor. My husband and I travelled to the Orient quite often. Most of the furniture and ornaments you see here come from there. I'll show you the rest of the home after dinner. I think you will like what you see,' Kasiah replied.

A door suddenly opened. Tarni and Juliette came in carrying plates of food. Steaks cooked over a charcoal brazier were placed in front of each of them, along with small bowls of salad.

'This is our wonderful housekeeper and cook, Tarni,' Kasiah announced. 'She is also my dear friend.'

The Aboriginal woman gave them a nervous smile and stood back against a side wall.

'With her is Juliette, another dear friend. Juliette was once Tessa's governess and music teacher. Tessa assures me she no longer needs a governess, although I do sometimes wonder. Juliette is from Paris. She has been with us now for so long that she has become part of our family, and we all love her. She has been teaching Tarni some of her wonderful French recipes for us to try. The salad you are having this evening is one of her creations. She uses vegetables from our garden: lettuce, cucumber, tomatoes, red onion, and capsicum, all finely chopped and drizzled with a mixture of French mustard, vinegar, and olive oil. The mustard and olive oil we have imported from her home country just for her to use. I hope you enjoy it. It has a very different taste, probably because of the seed mustard and the olive oil.' Kasiah explained.

Juliette smiled proudly. '*Merci, Madame. You are too kind.*' She gave a polite bow, stepped back, and the two women left the room.

The steaks and salads were a great success, as were the two bottles of imported French burgundy. The dessert was another surprise for the guests and was thoroughly enjoyed. Tarni had made ice cream and topped each bowl with chilled lychees, diced pawpaw, and a drizzle of passion fruit pulp.

* * *

When they finally finished their meal, Kasiah lifted her wine glass, took a sip, and looked across the table at Connor. 'Now, Connor, Tessa told me when she rang from the hotel that you men have been discussing a business venture. Perhaps you could let me know what you have in mind?' She began.

'I would be glad to, Kasiah,' Connor replied, only to be interrupted by Tessa.

Mother, Angela, and I will leave you for a while. I want to take her to my room. She wants to try on some of my things to see if they suit her.' Tessa said, getting up and taking Angela's hand.

'Of course, my dear. Off you go and enjoy yourselves,' Kasiah replied, smiling at the two women.

Henry and Connor got to their feet and politely waited for the two women to leave the room.

'Let us start again. You were about to explain this gold mining venture of yours, Connor,' Kasiah said.

'I shall do my best, Kasiah. A few weeks ago, I was approached by an old prospector from Pine Creek. He showed me some samples of gravel and gold. He explained that he needed to raise capital to set up a mine. I've had the samples sent off to a laboratory in Perth, and they have come back very promising. To be honest, I intended to finance the complete operation myself. But because Henry and I and our wives have become such good friends, I decided to offer Henry a partnership in the venture. Henry has since informed me that he is not able to make such decisions without speaking to you first.' Connor explained.

'Henry has only to ask. I will always help him in any way I can. Can you tell me how this partnership would be structured?' Kasiah asked.

'I had in mind a 33 per cent partnership for Henry and the same for myself. The prospector would retain a 34 per cent share as well, which is quite generous considering he has no money himself to speak of,' Connor explained.

'And how much would we need to put up for this 33 per cent partnership?' Kasiah asked.

'I have done some earlier costings on mining equipment, shoring timber, and the labour and accommodation required. I think £5,000 should be more than enough for a 30 per cent stake in the operation,' Connor replied.

'That sounds quite reasonable. And does this man have a mining claim already?' Kasiah asked.

'Yes, he does. The area has been mined before, but many years ago. The mining claims are quite cheap at this time.'

'What do you think, Henry?'

'I have just one thought. Do the people of Pine Creek know the old man has been fossicking around the area?' Henry asked.

'Not at the moment, or at least I don't think so. But that will change when we take in our equipment. Men will need to be billeted locally. Probably at a local hotel initially,' Connor explained, wondering the point of Henry's question.

Henry continued. 'Once the word gets around, it might set off the beginnings of a gold rush. Perhaps we should take out mining rights on a much larger area? Then, if we're successful, we can expand. If not, we could sell the mining claims to others who are encouraged by our activity in the area and recoup some of our costs.'

'A sound and sensible proposition, Henry. What do you think, Connor?' Kasiah asked.

'A good idea, and I don't think it should add too much to our initial costs,' Connor replied.

'When you get back to Darwin, Connor, could you send me your costings and the assayer's report? I have a man here in Broome I would like to show them to,' Kasiah asked.

'I have them on board the ship. I could give them to Henry when we go back to the ship later tonight.'

'Thank you. If you leave your contact details and address with Henry, there will be a telegram waiting for you when you get back to Darwin with my decision,' Kasiah replied.

'I will look forward to it. Thank you for entertaining us so well this evening, Kasiah, but I suppose Angela and I should be getting back to the ship before too long.'

'You are welcome to stay for the night. I have a bedroom already prepared for you,' Kasiah replied.

'Are you sure it wouldn't be an imposition?'

'Not at all, Connor. I'll show you to your room now if you like. I'm going to bed myself very soon. Kasiah said, getting to her feet.

'In that case, we will accept. Thank you again for a wonderful evening, Kasiah. The meal and the wine were just superb. Please thank Tarni and Juliette for us,' Connor replied, getting up as well.

'Thank you. I will have Jago take you back to your ship well before it sails.' Kasiah added.

'I'll go and find Tessa and Angela. Angela will need to know which bedroom you'll be using,' Henry said, getting to his feet as well.

A short while later, Kasiah was showing Connor and Angela to their room.

'We only ever use this room for visitors. There is a lovely view of the garden in the mornings. If you open the French doors, you should feel a nice breeze tonight,' Kasiah said as she opened the bedroom door and led them inside.

'It looks very comfortable and quite roomy,' Connor replied.

'I hope you like the four-poster bed. We had it made in Singapore by a wonderful craftsman my husband knew there.'

'Tessa told us of your loss, Kasiah. You have our deepest sympathy,' Angela said, placing her hand on the beautiful black woman's arm.

'Thank you, my dear. I still miss him terribly. I think I loved him too much. But that is the way I am with love.'

Connor was silently admiring the furnishings. A huge rattan mat covered the polished hardwood floorboards. A cedar-bladed ceiling fan was spinning slowly on the decorative plaster ceiling. The heady smell of incense filled the room, calming his thoughts.

He looked at the intricate carving on the mahogany bedposts. Carefully carved monkey faces peered out from clusters of leaves and twisted vines, and here and there, tiny lizards with frilled necks and staring eyes wrapped their long tails around the dark timber. A white mosquito net hung knotted at the ready from a heavy brass hook above the magnificent bed. Bath towels lay folded on the silk cover.

'Oh, Connor, this room is just so lovely.' Angela whispered, walking over to the French doors, opening them, and peering out into the now-dark gardens. 'Thank you so much, Kasiah.'

'I'll leave you to get some rest now,' Kasiah replied, smiling. 'I hope you both sleep well.'

'Goodnight and thank you, Kasiah.' Angela and Connor replied in unison.

Once they were in the hallway, Kasiah turned to Tessa and Henry. 'Goodnight, you two. It's wonderful to have you home again. Tarni and Juliette have made up a double bed in your old room, Tessa. Enjoy yourselves.' She whispered, kissing her daughter's cheek.

'Thank you, Mother.' Tessa replied. 'It's so nice to be home with you again.'

Kasiah left them and went to her bathroom to shower before bed. She took off her kaftan and stood naked in front of the mirror with the shower running behind her. She knew that Henry and Tessa, and their friends, Connor and Angela, would be sleeping in each other's arms. Perhaps even making love while she stood naked in her bathroom. It was the way things should be. That thought made her realise that she missed the comfort of a man's arms around her at night. She missed the urgency of lovemaking and the peaceful sleep that followed it.

Kasiah looked at her naked body in the mirror. Her belly was flat and sleek. Her breasts were full and well-shaped. She was still a beautiful woman. Men lusted over her. Even women were attracted to her. But she had always been faithful to her husband. She had loved Duncan so completely, but now he was gone from her life forever. For some strange reason, looking at her naked body in the mirror with the shower hissing impatiently in the background made her feel lonely and unloved.

# Chapter 22

# A Night to Remember

Early the following morning, Henry and Tessa were saying their goodbyes to Connor and Angela in their cabin on board the S.S. *Minderoo*. Jago was waiting for them at the entrance to the long Broome jetty. Connor had just given Henry the assayer's report to take back to Kasiah.

'I will look forward to Kasiah's telegram, Henry. I sincerely hope we can join forces on this gold mine,' Connor affirmed.

'I hope so as well, Connor. But do try and enjoy the rest of your trip,' Henry replied.

When your season ends, you two should come up to Darwin and stay with us. It will be so sad if we lose contact,' Angela added, holding tight to Tessa's hand.

'We certainly will, my friend. I will make certain of it. Mother has been talking about having a holiday home built down in Perth for some time. I wonder if she would consider Darwin instead,' Tessa replied.

'We live on East Point Road, right across from the bay. It's a wonderful place to live. We get nice breezes most nights. I'm sure you would both love it. Come to think of it, there's a very nice piece of vacant land for sale right next to us. I'll show it to you when you come up.' Connor said, taking Henry's hand.

'That sounds very interesting,' Henry replied.

'I hope everything we're hoping for comes to pass, Henry.'

'As do I, my friend,' Henry agreed.

'Send us a photograph of that piece of land when you get back; if you don't mind, Connor and I'll show it to Mother,' Tessa added, putting her arms around Angela. 'Goodbye, my dear friend.'

'Goodbye, Tessa. Goodbye, Henry. Please tell your mother we loved our room last night. It made us feel like we were on our honeymoon again, didn't it, Connor?' Angela said, smiling at her husband.

'It did, my angel. That is, of course, when you finally left Tessa and came to our room.'

'That was the ship's horn. We had better be off,' Henry said, kissing Angela's cheek and shaking Connor's hand one last time.

Tessa started to cry. Henry took her hand, smiled at Angela, and they hurried out of the cabin. Nothing was said between them as they strolled back along the jetty to the Pierce-Arrow, and they sat silently in the back seat as Jago started the car. Henry knew Tessa was going to miss her new friend. But he wanted to ask if she had spoken to her mother about her pregnancy, and if she had, what advice had her mother given her? But he supposed she would tell him when she was ready.

A moment later, Jago climbed behind the wheel, and they drove away.

*　*　*

The following morning, Henry and Tessa woke up late. Kasiah had already left for her office. Henry was to start work the following day. At breakfast, Tessa waited nervously for Tarni to leave the dining room before she spoke to Henry.

'Henry, my love, I'm going in to see Mother soon and tell her I'm carrying George's child. She will know what I should do. Will you come with me?' she asked in a quiet voice.

'I think it might be better if you spoke to her alone, Tessa. Don't forget to tell her that I don't mind if we keep the child. You can tell her I would love it as if it were my own.'

Henry replied.

'Are you sure you won't come?'

'I'll stay here for the day. I want to write a letter to Captain Callaghan. I want to tell him that we're married now. He's been like a father to me. I'm sure he'll be happy to know it has all worked out well. I wish he could have joined us for the wedding. He could have given you away instead of Jago,' Henry said.

'It was what Mother wanted, Henry. You mustn't forget that,' Tessa replied.

'It did cause quite a sensation with some of the guests, from the looks I saw on some of their faces,' Henry added, smiling.

'I didn't mind. Mother said it made Jago very happy after what happened to Father.'

*   *   *

An hour later, Tessa arrived at her mother's office and tapped on the door.

'Who is it?' She heard her mother call out.

'It's Tessa, Mother.'

'The doors open. Come in, my dear.'

'I came in to ask for your advice about something. Do you have the time?' Tessa asked from the doorway.

'Of course I do. You look concerned, Tessa. Sit down and tell me what's bothering you.'

'I think I'm pregnant, Mother!'

'You're pregnant—!' Kasiah replied with a startled expression. You mean you're carrying George Peterson's child, don't you?' She added, getting up and going to her daughter.

'Yes, and I don't know what to do about it,' Tessa sobbed.

'Have you told Henry?' Kasiah asked, embracing her daughter.

'Yes, he knows. He told me he didn't mind. He thinks we should keep it. He said no one needed to know that he wasn't the father.'

'Well then, perhaps that's what you should do, my darling,' Kasiah replied.

'I would rather have it aborted, Mother. There's that old Filipino woman in Chinatown. I've heard she can be trusted to keep things quiet,' Tessa said in a soft voice.

'Tessa, that's a very dangerous thing to do. I've been told that old woman uses crude instruments. You might die. You could bleed to death, and what would I do if I lost you? What would Henry do?' Kasiah whispered, hugging Tessa to her.

'I think it would still be worth the risk. If George were to find out I was pregnant, he would want to be a part of my life again. I couldn't bear that, Mother.'

'I'm sorry, Tessa, but I won't allow you to do it. If Henry wants you to keep the child, then that is what you should do. Why take such a terrible risk? It could kill you. I just can't allow it, Tessa.' Kasiah said firmly, still holding Tessa in her arms.

'I wish I hadn't told you now, Mother!'

'Please don't say things like that, my darling. You're my life, Tessa. Promise me you won't think of doing something so dangerous—something that could take your life. Promise me, Tessa!'

'I promise, Mother,' Tessa replied and burst out crying.

'Everything will be alright. We'll talk to Henry together tonight,' Kasiah whispered, rocking Tessa in her arms.

'Henry should hate me, but he still loves me. He deserves better than me.'

'Is he outside?' Kasiah asked.

'He's at home writing a letter to his old captain,' Tessa replied.

'How did you get here?'

'I drove Father's old car,' Tessa replied, sobbing.

'I'll go and get Jago to take you home. I don't want you driving while you're so upset. You need to calm down and get some rest. We will discuss this with Henry when I get home.'

'Alright then, Mother,' Tessa whispered.

* * *

Henry was sitting on the veranda. There was a cool breeze blowing through the gardens. He'd finally finished his letter to his good friend, Captain Callaghan. It had taken him quite a while, as there was so much to tell him. He was married now, and he was about to begin a new life in the pearling industry. He told him he missed the ship and his friends and wished he could have joined them for the wedding, but he understood it wasn't possible on such short notice. He asked if his ship was returning on the coastal run, and if so, he would look forward to seeing him again when he was next in Broome. After he finished, he folded the letter and put it in its envelope. He would post it in the morning. He sat back in the easy chair. Tessa would be home soon. He was missing her already. He closed his eyes. He hadn't realised how tired he was. In what felt like only a moment later, he felt Tarni shake his shoulder. He'd fallen asleep.

'Wake up, Mister Henry. Kasiah wants you on the telephone. She said, you better come quick,' Tarni stammered.

Henry jumped to his feet. He'd been sleeping for a couple of hours. It was already late afternoon. He followed Tarni inside and picked up the telephone.

'Is everything all right, Kasiah,' he asked.

'Tessa is in the hospital, Henry. I've sent Jago to get you. He should be there soon!'

'What's wrong . . . Has something happened?'

'She's in the hospital, Henry. She's lost a lot of blood. She could die!' Kasiah cried out.

'Has there been an accident?' Henry asked, his heart racing.

'She's had an abortion, Henry, and it went badly for her. I told her how dangerous it was to do such a thing. She promised me she wouldn't do it, Henry!' Kasiah sobbed.

'She never said anything to me! I didn't think she would do such a thing . . . Henry whispered into the mouthpiece.

'Jago was supposed to take her home hours ago, but Tessa made him take her to an old Filipino woman she had heard about. Jago had no idea what she was going to do. When the old woman came out and told him he must rush her to the hospital because she couldn't stop the bleeding, Jago went into a rage. He struck the old woman. He thinks he may have killed her.'

'What did he do with Tessa?' Henry asked, his heart pounding in his chest.

'He tried to stop the bleeding as best he could and carried her to the car. She was bleeding terribly, he said. He raced her to the hospital. I have never seen Jago so upset. I've spoken to the doctor. He told me we were lucky Jago got her there so quickly. He said he must have taken towels from the woman's house and wrapped her in them to staunch the bleeding. You must hurry, Henry. She might die—!'

'I hear the car now. I'm on my way, Kasiah,' Henry replied, hanging up the phone and racing outside.

Kasiah was waiting for him at the hospital entry when Henry got there. She took his hand, and they hurried down a long corridor, only to be met by a doctor coming towards them. There was blood on his gown and sleeves.

'Is she alright, Doctor Burke?' Kasiah asked. There was a terrible panic in her voice.

'She will be alright, Kasiah. She has lost quite a lot of blood, but she'll be fine,' the doctor replied.

'Can we see her?' Henry asked.

'I've sedated her. She's sleeping now. She was extremely upset when she came in. I'm very glad that man of yours got her here so quickly. You can come tomorrow morning. You'll be able to see her then, and don't worry, she's going to be alright.'

'Thank you, Doctor,' Kasiah replied.

'I've told my nurses it was an unexpected miscarriage at home that caused the bleeding.'

'Thank you for being discreet, Doctor. I had no idea she would do something so silly,' Kasiah replied.

'I'm fairly sure I know who did this. I've just stitched up her face. I'm not sure what happened to her, but she looked very frightened when she came in. I hope she's learned her lesson and stops her wicked business.'

'Thank you, Doctor. We'll come in the morning,' Kasiah replied, taking Henry's hand.

Jago was waiting for them when they got outside. Kasiah went to him and put her arms around him. Jago tried to back away, but she held him.

'She is going to be alright, Jago. Thank you for getting her here so quickly,' Kasiah said in a soft, caring voice.

Jago looked relieved. But when Kasiah released her embrace, he whispered to her. 'If Miss Tessa dies tonight, then that old woman dies too!'

Kasiah never replied, but she shivered with dread. She knew Jago meant what he said. 'You can take us home now, Jago,' she whispered, relieved now that she knew Tessa was going to be alright.

Jago went to the car, held open the back door and stood aside while Kasiah and Henry climbed in.

When they arrived home, Kasiah called the staff together and told them that Tessa had had a miscarriage. She told them she was still in the hospital but that she was going to be all right. If they would like to visit her, Jago will take them in tomorrow afternoon.

Juliette stepped forward and replied for them all.

'We are so relieved that she will be alright, madame. *Dieu merci,*' she whispered. She went to Kasiah, kissed each of her dark cheeks, and hugged her.

'Thank you, Juliette,' Kasiah replied.

* * *

That night, Henry decided he had no appetite for dinner. He apologised to Kasiah, showered, and went to his room. He was feeling terrible. He should have gone with Tessa, and then this wouldn't have happened. But he was greatly relieved that she was going to be alright. He took off his bathrobe, turned on his ceiling fan, and got into bed. A faint breeze was coming through the French doors. He undid the knot that held his mosquito net in place and watched it fall over him. He closed his eyes and hoped he would be able to sleep after all that had happened.

Well, after midnight he was still awake, staring up at the folds of the mosquito net shimmering in the moonlight. Fruit bats were calling to each other in the darkness outside as they fed on ripe fruit in the mango tree.

A moment later, he heard a soft tapping on his door.

'Who is it?' he called out.

'It's Kasiah, Henry. Can I come in?' He heard Kasiah whisper through the door.

'Yes, of course. Come in.'

Kasiah opened the door and stood looking at Henry from the doorway. 'Were you sleeping?' she asked in a soft, tremulous voice.

'No, I wasn't Kasiah. Not after what has happened today,' Henry replied.

'I wanted to see if you were all right.' Kasiah whispered, tightening the sash around her silk bathrobe. Her feet were bare. She closed the door, walked to the bed, and sat down close to Henry. 'Are you sure you're alright?' She asked him again through the fine mesh of the mosquito net.

'I'm fine now that I know Tessa is going to be all right,' Henry replied. 'How long do you think she will have to stay in the hospital, Kasiah?' Henry was suddenly aware that he was naked under his bedsheet . . . He pulled the sheet up to cover his bare chest.

'Just a few days, the doctor told me,' Kasiah whispered back.

'I'm just so relieved that she's going to be alright,' Henry replied.

'Oh, Henry, this has upset me so much,' Kasiah sobbed. 'We could easily have lost Tessa!'

Henry pulled back his mosquito net and took Kasiah in his arms. 'She's going to be alright, Kasiah. You don't need to worry so. We'll go together and see her in the morning.'

'I don't know if I could survive if something happened to my Tessa,' Kasiah murmured. 'You do love her, don't you, Henry?'

'Yes, of course I do. She's my wife now,' Henry replied.

'Do you love me, Henry—?'

'Yes, of course, I love you, Kasiah. Very much so. You have been the very reason Tessa and I found each other,' Henry whispered into Kasiah's dark, beautiful eyes.

'Would you think it wrong if we stayed together tonight, Henry? I feel so afraid and lonely!'

'Yes, of course you can. I think it's right that we should be together tonight,' Henry murmured, lifting Kasiah's face and kissing her cheek to comfort her.

Kasiah turned her face and kissed Henry full on the lips. 'You do love me, don't you, Henry?' she whispered as Henry held her in his arms.

'Oh, yes . . . I do, Kasiah. I hadn't realised just how much until now,' Henry replied, pulling Kasiah to him and kissing her open lips in return. He felt her breasts crush against him through the thin fabric of her bathrobe. His mind was spinning with sudden, overwhelming desire.

'Tessa must never know about this, Henry,' Kasiah whispered as he held her. 'You must promise me.'

'She will never know, Kasiah . . . I promise you.'

Kasiah stood up, took off her robe, and laid it over the chair next to the bed. Yellow moonlight from the French doors washed over her coal-black, naked body.

Henry sucked in a deep breath of anticipation. He hadn't expected this to happen. Kasiah was beautiful . . . so very beautiful. He noticed the thin gold chain and the strange golden pendant with the ruby eye that hung between her dark, perfect breasts glint in the moonlight as she turned toward him.

'Oh, Kasiah, you're so beautiful,' he whispered, pushing the mosquito net to the other side of the bed and getting to his feet. He took Kasiah in his arms and kissed her lips again, passionately, and then each of her dark, burnished breasts.

'Henry, I told you you wouldn't regret coming to work with me. I told you then that I loved you. I think I have loved you since the day that I first saw you. Something strange happened to me that day that I cannot begin to explain. You were so young. It was something that I saw in your eyes. It was like a forbidden door into my future opened just for a moment, and in that fleeting moment, I knew you were destined to become a part of my life. To be my lover.'

'I do remember, Kasiah. I remember how beautiful you were. I'm so glad we met that day.'

'Make love to me, Henry, and when you are finished, I will make love to you . . . You will never forget this night, my love,' Kasiah whispered. 'But, Henry, we must remember. Tessa must never know.

'She will never know,' Henry whispered back, burying his face between Kasiah's breasts and feeling the heat from her dark body.

'Oh, Henry—! I want you so much.' Kasiah moaned, holding him tight against her.

They fell back onto the bed.

Henry could no longer control himself. 'She will never know, Kasiah. I promise you.'

'Oh, Henry . . . Oh . . . Oh . . . Oh, my sweet, impatient young love!' Kasiah whispered, pulling him hard into her nakedness.

A sudden, violent breeze blew through the French doors. The curtains flew apart and hung in the air for just a moment and then fell against the polished floorboards. A fruit bat squealed from somewhere just outside the window. . . It was still for a moment, and then Henry heard Kasiah whisper to him.

'Oh—Henry, my love . . . Tell me again that you love me,' she moaned, holding him, slowing his impatience.

'I do love you, Kasiah. I think I have loved you from the very first time that you kissed me outside the Tropicana Guest House.' Henry whispered into the moonlight-filled room. 'And I will love you forever.'

'And I love you, my eager young stallion,' Kasiah murmured a short while later. 'And now you must lay back on your bed and let me make love to you.'

'Oh, Kasiah, my love,' Henry whispered.

# Part 3

190

# Chapter 23

# Jeremy Bolton

Dawson House, Darwin
1997

Charlotte Dawson put down Henry's old journal. Her face was flushed from what she had just read. She picked up her mobile phone to check the time. It was three in the morning. She'd been reading for hours. She had fallen in love with the old man's story. It had taken her back in time to a terrible war that had cost the lives of so many young Australian men and women, a war in which Henry Dawson, although badly wounded, had become a hero, saving the lives of so many on board his ship with his bravery. He had returned from the war as a reluctant hero on a mission to see the young woman who had captured his heart so long ago, only to find she was soon to be married. But life can be strange and unpredictable, and it was proving so for Henry Dawson. A fight in the streets of Broome had sent his first love back into his arms and his life once again. But while Tessa lay in the hospital recovering from a foolish and dangerous abortion, her mother, the bewitchingly beautiful Kasiah, had visited him in his bedroom in the dead of night to tell him that she too was in love with him. But how can Henry love them both—and is it not a terrible sin for him to do so?

Charlotte wanted to keep reading, but it was late, and she needed sleep. She was to have her final meeting with Paul Rosenberg in the morning. *Dawson House Holdings* had now been transferred into her name. She had met with Henry's bank managers, accountants, insurance representatives, and a very professional stockbroker by the name of Damian Kerslake. Her meeting in the morning was to be a brief one. A final check to show her that everything had been done correctly and for Paul Rosenberg to be assured that she was comfortable with it all. When it was over, she would have lunch at a café in the city that she liked and be back at the old home for her meeting with the carpenter, Jeremy Bolton, at two o'clock. She put Henry Dawson's journal, the box of old letters, and bits and pieces in her bedside cupboard and turned off the light. She must try to get some sleep. But Charlotte knew she was going to dream of sailing the high seas with a young Henry Dawson and of the terrible storms of an almost forgotten war. She pulled the sheet up to cover her nakedness. It had been hot and humid during the day, and she wasn't yet used to Darwin's weather. She looked across the room at her closed door and imagined a soft tapping . . . She was also almost certain she was also going to dream of forbidden love.

*   *   *

The following morning, Charlotte woke from a dream-filled sleep to find Alice sitting on her bed, shaking her shoulder.

'Good morning, sleepyhead. Would you like me to make you a nice cup of coffee?' She heard her ask her.

'Oh! . . . Good morning, Alice. I've slept in. What time is it?'

'It's almost eight o'clock, Miss. I hope you slept well.' Alice replied.

'A little too well, by the looks of it. I had better get moving. I have quite a lot to do today.'

'You get yourself organised, and when you're ready, I'll make you a nice cup of coffee and get you something for your breakfast,' Alice said, leaving the bed and heading for the door.

'Just a coffee would be great, Alice. I'll just have a quick shower first,' Charlotte replied, holding the sheet up to cover herself.

A short while later, Charlotte was sipping her coffee in the little nook and listening to David mowing the lawns outside. Colourful rainbow lorikeets were flitting past the leadlight windows, alarmed by the noise. She put her cup down and looked at the tired old kitchen. Her meeting with the carpenter, Jeremy Bolton, later in the day was going to be important.

Alice came in carrying a basket of cleaning gear. 'Are you sure you wouldn't like me to make you some nice, scrambled eggs or an omelette, Miss Charlotte?'

'I'm fine, thank you, Alice.'

'I've finally finished cleaning the flat downstairs, Miss. If your mother decides to move up here, you'll need to have an electrician take a look at the fans and that old refrigerator,' Alice reminded her, pouring herself a glass of water from the fridge.

'After I've spoken to the carpenter later today, and if I've got time, I'll go into town and order a new fridge and electric stove for the flat and enquire about air conditioning for the house and the flat as well,' Charlotte replied.

'That will be a big improvement, Miss. Are you still thinking of buying yourself a nice new car?'

'I'll start looking tomorrow. Which reminds me, I might ask David to push the old cars out of the garage down below later and give them a good clean as well. Then, I'd like to have a mechanic take a look at them. I was thinking of having them both restored. It would be nice to drive Tessa's little car once in a while. It's such a pretty little thing. Do you think it would be disrespectful of me, Alice?'

'Not at all, Miss. I think it's a wonderful idea. You would need to get a new canvas top for it, though. The old one is in the boot, and I'm sure it's beyond repair by now. David and I could get in the garage and clean it up as well. There's such a lot of old stuff lying about in there.'

'If we can get them going again, you could come for a spin with me along East Point Road. With the sea so close and the roof down, it'd be a lot of fun.

'I would love that, Miss. I'd feel like a proper lady getting about the town,' Alice replied with a laugh.

'In that case, Alice, it's a promise. As soon as I can have

Henry's old cars restored and running again, we shall do it.'

'Do you want to know something, Miss?

'What's that, Alice?'

'I can see now that you and the old man are kin. He was always nice to me, and you're just the same.'

'How nice of you,' Charlotte replied.

'That's all right, Miss.'

'Getting back to this lovely old home, I'll speak to Jeremy about having a painter look at it as well. It's certainly well overdue.'

'All this work is going to cost you a lot of money, Miss.'

'I can afford it now. But I'd like everything we get done to be respectful to the memory of Henry and Tessa so that when it's finished, it will be something we can all be proud of,' Charlotte said, sliding out of the nook.

'It sounds exciting, Miss.'

'I'd better get moving,' Charlotte replied, carrying her cup to the sink.

'Leave that, Miss. You go and get yourself ready and head off.'

'Thank you, Alice.'

*　*　*

It was just after ten when Charlotte parked her rental outside the offices of Rosenberg and Gately. She adjusted her blouse. It was already sticking to her. The air conditioning in her rental car wasn't working properly. She was glad the offices were air-conditioned. She hurried inside.

'Good morning, Penny,' she greeted the receptionist with a warm smile.

'Good morning, Charlotte. Go on through. Paul is waiting for you,' Penny replied.

Charlotte hurried along the passage. The door was open to Paul Rosenberg's office. He was at his desk.

'I'm sorry I'm a bit late, Paul.'

'Good morning, Charlotte. Don't concern yourself. I've only just finished with another client. Please sit down, and I'll go through this summary of the transfers of *Dawson House Holdings* and some other bits and pieces with you. This is going to be our final meeting for a while. I need to make sure you're comfortable with it all,' Paul replied.

'Certainly, Paul. But I think I understand most of it already.'

'It's very important that you do, Charlotte.

Charlotte spent the next few minutes studying the paperwork that had been waiting for her on the desk.

'You've been very thorough and patient with me, Paul. I'm quite confident that I understand it all by now,' she said, finally pushing the summary back across the desk.

'Take that copy with you. Thanks to Henry, you're now a very wealthy woman, Charlotte Dawson. I hope you find much happiness with your newfound good fortune.'

'Thank you for everything you've done for me, Paul. You've been very professional.'

'It has been a pleasure, my dear,' Paul replied.

'I should get moving. I have quite a busy day in front of me. I'm meeting with a carpenter to get his thoughts on some work I'd like to be done on Henry's old home later today.'

'You mean Charlotte's old home.'

'It doesn't really feel like mine just yet, Paul; perhaps after I make some changes,' Charlotte replied, getting to her feet, and reaching for the solicitor's hand.

'Before you go, Charlotte, I'd like to invite you to my home this Sunday evening for dinner. My wife is looking forward to meeting you. I've invited some others I think you would be comfortable with. Now that you've decided to live here in Darwin, you need to make some new friends.' He handed a card to Charlotte. 'My home address is on the back. Six o'clock if you can manage it.'

Thank you, Paul. Six o'clock is fine. I'll look forward to it.'

Charlotte replied, shaking the solicitor's hand.

* * *

Three hours later, Charlotte had bought herself a brand-new silver Honda Accord from a local car dealer. It was to be delivered to the old home after the registration plates had been fitted the following morning. When she finished at the car dealer's, she took her rental back to their depot and caught a taxi to the restaurant she liked for lunch before heading home for her meeting with the carpenter, Jeremy Bolton.

* * *

Just after two, Alice tapped on Charlotte's door. 'Miss Charlotte, Jeremy is here. He's out in the garden, talking to David.

'Thank you, Alice,' Charlotte called back. She had been looking through the old box of photos and letters she'd brought up from the secret room. She put them away quickly and went to her bathroom, picked up her hairbrush, and ran it through her long blonde hair. She was wearing a pair of faded Levi's and a white cotton T-shirt that clung to her full breasts. When she finished, she went into the kitchen.

'You look very nice, Miss,' Alice remarked.

'It's just my old jeans and a T-shirt, but thank you, Alice. I won't wait for him to come to the door. I'll go down and talk to him in the garden. There are things I'd like him to look at outside first.'

'You watch out now, Miss. Jeremy's a handsome devil,' Alice replied with a mischievous smile.

'Just as long as he is a good carpenter, Alice. That's the most important thing,' Charlotte said, smiling and adjusting her jeans.

'The old man was always very happy with his work, Miss,' Alice called out as Charlotte disappeared down the hallway.

When Charlotte walked out onto the veranda, Jeremy Bolton was already coming up the steps.

'Good morning, Mr. Bolton,' she called down to him.

Charlotte studied the man coming up the steps. He looked to be about 35 years old, perhaps a little more. He was tall, slim, and very fit-looking. He was wearing tan work trousers with green knee patches and a military-style shirt with epaulettes. There was a pencil in one of the pockets. His face was tanned from hard work, and his hair was dark brown with a few strands of grey at the temples. She drew in a breath. Alice had not exaggerated. Jeremy Bolton was certainly a handsome devil.

'G'day there, Charlotte. Just call me Jeremy. You'd like me to take a look at a few things, Alice tells me.'

Charlotte was caught short for a moment, but by the time Jeremy reached the veranda and put out his hand, she'd composed herself.

'I'm Charlotte, Charlotte Dawson. I'm the new owner of this lovely old home, Jeremy. I'm glad to finally meet you.'

*My God, Charlotte thought. The man has the palest blue eyes I've ever seen.*

'The pleasure is all mine, Charlotte,' Jeremy replied, admiring the stunningly beautiful woman reaching for his hand. *Alice's description of her being very pretty was well short of the mark.*

'I think it is best if we go back down the steps. There are a few things I would like to show you before we go inside,' Charlotte said, brushing back strands of her blonde hair that had caught in the breeze coming across from the bay.

'David has the gardens looking great, as usual,' Jeremy remarked when they reached the bottom of the stairs.

'He certainly does a very good job,' Charlotte agreed.

'I envy you inheriting this wonderful old home, Charlotte. I've admired it ever since I was a boy. I used to ride my bike past here quite often on my way to go fishing on weekends out this way.'

'I'm glad you like it, Jeremy. That could be quite important,' Charlotte replied.

'Alice told me about Henry passing away. He was a hell of a nice old man. Just so you know, I've done quite a bit of work here before.'

'So, I've been told, and that's one of the reasons I had Alice call you. You've replaced some of the veranda floorboards, she told me.'

'That, and some of the roof sheets, and a couple of the gutters,' Jeremy replied. 'Just what are you thinking of doing this time, Charlotte?'

Charlotte liked the way Jeremy said her name. It sounded friendly—like they'd known each other for ages.

'I want to bring the old home back to its former glory. I have in mind a complete renovation. But of course, I'd like your professional opinion first.'

'What exactly did you have in mind?'

'For a start, I think the roofing iron and all the gutters should be replaced. There are still quite a few rusty sheets up there. Some of the fascia boards look like they may need replacing as well. The storm shutters and quite a lot of the windows are in very poor condition too. Some of them won't open anymore. In fact, any of the timberwork that needs replacing, I think, should be replaced. The old place could then do with a complete clean-up and paint job from top to bottom in the very same colours it is at the moment,' Charlotte began.

'That would certainly amount to quite a lot of work. But I do agree that it needs to be done. As you know, the windows are all made from timber. I would have to have them copied and made in a joiner's shop,' Jeremy replied, stunned by the sheer amount of work Charlotte was asking him to do.

'If you feel they should be replaced, please include that as well. The garage doors certainly need attention as well. They are very difficult to open. Perhaps suitably designed electric doors made from wood, of course, would be an improvement and a good idea.

'I'm guessing you've seen Henry's old cars then?' Jeremy said.

'Yes, I have. I'm thinking of having them restored and running again as well,' Charlotte replied.

'That's a great idea. They could be worth a lot of money these days. Especially the old Porsche. I could give you the name of a good car man, I know. He's a friend of mine.'

'Thank you, Jeremy. I'll get the number from you when we go back upstairs,' Charlotte replied.

'He knows his stuff, but he's not cheap.'

'Would he come to the house and take a look at them?'

'I'm sure he would. I could bring him around and introduce him sometime if you like,' Jeremy replied.

'Thank you. I look forward to meeting him. Now, let's get back to the work that needs to be done on this old house. There's quite a lot of work that needs to be done inside as well. Apart from a paint job, I'd like the kitchen replaced, but it must look exactly as it does now and in the very same colour. The bathrooms need to be renovated as well, but I'd like the tiles to be as close as possible to the existing ones. I'd like new toilets as well, but they would have to be of the old style with chains if they are still available.'

'I may need to import them from England. That's where the existing ones would have come from, I imagine,' Jeremy replied.

'Would all this be too much work for you, Jeremy—?' Charlotte asked.

'No, it wouldn't. But I should tell you right now that it will probably take a while to get done. I'd have to bring in other trades: plumbers, electricians, cabinetmakers, and painters. Also, I should tell you, it's going to cost you a heck of a lot of money. I hope you are aware of that.'

'I'm aware that it will cost a considerable amount, certainly, but I want it to be done properly. You need not concern yourself with the costs. Would a monthly progress payment take care of things?'

'That would suit me just fine. Would you like me to work out some costings for you?'

'That won't be necessary, Jeremy. You have come recommended, and knowing you've done work for Henry before is important and good enough for me. Would I have to wait very long for you to start?' Charlotte asked.

'Things have been a bit quiet just lately. I have a small job I'm finishing in the city at the moment. I could start next Monday if you like. How does that sound?'

'That would suit me just perfectly. We should go inside now,' Charlotte said, turning for the steps.

'I'm right behind you,' Jeremy replied, smiling, and following Charlotte up the steps.

'I'll show you the kitchen first and then the bathrooms. When we are finished upstairs, I want to get your thoughts on what should be done in the flat downstairs before you go. I'm hoping my mother will come up from Adelaide to live in it,' Charlotte said, leading Jeremy to the kitchen.

'It's starting to sound like you will have to get used to my ugly face being around the place for quite a while. This is all going to take some time to get done,' Jeremy replied.

'Alice thinks you're a handsome devil. Jeremy. They were her exact words. I suppose I'd have to agree with her on that. I think we could put up with having you around the place for a while yet.'

'Thank you, Charlotte. I'll take that as a compliment.'

'You may, Jeremy,' Charlotte replied with a mischievous smile.

*   *   *

That night, after she had eaten the meal Alice left for her, Charlotte showered and put on her silk bathrobe. She poured herself a glass of chardonnay and dropped in some ice cubes. She was very pleased with the outcome of her meeting with Jeremy Bolton. Work would begin on the old home next week. He seemed competent, and she liked a lot of his ideas. And importantly, she felt comfortable with him. His casual manner made her feel as if they had known each other for ages. She wondered if she should have taken him into her confidence and shown him the secret room. She may have to if he discovered anything odd beneath the house while he was working. She would give it some more thought.

Charlotte decided she would ring her mother first thing in the morning and tell her about the renovations. She hoped she had decided to sell her house in Adelaide and come up to live in the flat. She loved her mother dearly, and she was looking forward to seeing her again.

She went to her bedroom, opened her bedside cupboard, and picked up Henry's old journal. She wanted to read more of his fascinating story. She carried it back to the kitchen, switched on the light in the little nook, and slid into the seat. She took a sip of her chilled wine, smiled, and opened the journal where she had left off...

# Part 4

204

# Chapter 24

# A Bad Dream

Henry was dreaming. In his dream, a German fighter aircraft was strafing Kasiah's home. The lawn was being torn apart. The Pierce-Arrow was on fire; broken trees and bushes lay everywhere. A trail of bullet holes tore across the gravel drive toward the house. He could feel a terrible pain in his left thigh. He'd been hit. He struggled up the steps, concerned for those inside. The veranda was covered with the bodies of dead and wounded soldiers. Men were screaming and shaking their fists at the German pilot. He stumbled through the house, opening doors and searching for survivors, but the rooms were empty. Then he heard the deafening scream of the aircraft's engine as it turned back and raced down toward the house again. He must find Tessa and Kasiah! He must warn them of the danger! Finally, he reached his bedroom. It was the last room to check . . . He kicked open the burning door.

Even though the room was filled with smoke, Henry was certain he could see three people lying on the bed. They seemed oblivious to the sound of the approaching aircraft . . . He must warn them of the danger!

He started across the room. Through the smoke and dust, he could now see they were naked, but he couldn't see their faces. The mosquito net was torn to pieces and lay on the floor next to the bed. Sunlight streamed through a line of bullet holes in one of the walls. The room suddenly started to shake and vibrate from the approaching aircraft, and then he heard the chatter of its machine gun. Bits of broken plaster began dropping onto the naked bodies on the bed . . . He called to them, but they seemed to be taking no notice!

He stumbled across the room. He must warn them of the danger of staying in the bedroom. When he got to the bed, he stopped and recoiled in horror! He was one of those on the bed! He was locked in a writhing, carnal embrace with both Tessa and Kasiah!

*   *   *

Henry woke with a sudden start, the cold realisation of what he had done the night before flooded his mind. He'd betrayed Tessa. He had betrayed his new wife! He was wet with perspiration. He wiped his face with a bed sheet. Cockatoos were screeching from somewhere outside. It was almost dawn. He looked around the room . . . Kasiah and her jade green bathrobe were gone!

He lay there, remembering their lovemaking. He could still smell her perfume and her nakedness on his bedsheets and in his hands. She had done things to him that he would never forget. There was nothing he could have done to stop himself, not even if he had wanted to. He drew the mosquito net aside and sat on the edge of the bed. He couldn't remember sleeping, but he must have. He'd just woken from a dream that he wished he could forget. Guilt racked his thoughts. He felt as if he'd been under some strange erotic spell.

Suddenly, he remembered a conversation he'd had with Paul at the Continental Hotel one night when the two of them were having a few drinks in the beer garden after work. He'd just finished telling him that he had to give his notice at the hotel and that he was going to work for Kasiah Taylor.

'You've done very well for yourself, Henry. I'm glad things have finally worked out with you and young Tessa. She's a beauty all right,' Paul had replied.

'Thank you, Paul. It's a pity it had to be a fight to bring us together in the end, though.'

'She was far too good for that, George Peterson anyway. I'm

glad you sorted him and his mates out.'

'It was Jago who sorted them out in the end. George pulled a knife on me, and Jago just appeared out of nowhere. They took off like scared rabbits as soon as he showed up,' Henry added.

'Is there any wonder, Henry, that Jago is a dangerous man? I've heard stories about him that would make your hair stand on end.'

'I'm certainly glad he showed up that night, let me tell you. I asked him who told him to watch out for me. I thought it might have been Tessa. All he said was that Kasiah had sent him, and then he disappeared,' Henry explained.

'I like you, Henry, and I'm not sure I should be saying this, but be careful how you go with Kasiah Taylor.'

'What's that supposed to mean? She's been good to me, Paul. She's even offered me a partnership in her business now that I'm marrying Tessa.'

All I'm saying is to be careful with her. They say she uses her beauty to get her way with people. But then, I suppose there's no harm in that. Most of the men in Broome would like to spend a night in her bed anyway. Some have tried, but they've all failed.'

'If that's the case, then why are you warning me?' Henry asked.

'I've heard she knows the black arts, Henry. They say her father taught her things when she was a young girl.'

'What sorts of things?' Henry asked, smiling in disbelief at what Paul was suggesting.

'They say she knows how to speak to the dead. How to understand dreams. How to cast spells—all sorts of strange things. Her father was Toledo the diver. He was well known in Broome as a hoodoo man when he was alive. I'm told he taught her how to make charms from pieces of someone's clothing, from strands of hair, even nail clippings,' Paul replied.

'That's just silly gossip, Paul. It can't possibly be true. I met Duncan when I first got to know Tessa. He was a respectable businessman. He would have known if any of this had been true,' Henry insisted.

'Duncan knew what she was like, Henry. He'd heard the stories about Toledo and his hoodoo. He always knew what she was capable of, but he loved her anyway.'

'I know her, Paul. She's not like that. She's a wonderful, caring mother to Tessa, and in the short time I have known her, I've grown to admire her,' Henry replied. He was starting to get annoyed.

'You're not the only one, Henry. People admire her because of her beauty, and yet at the same time, they fear her.'

'Fear her—! Why would anyone fear Kasiah? It makes no sense, Paul,' Henry replied.

'When Duncan was killed by that snake, it got the town talking for weeks. They say the taipan is rare in Broome. And then there's Jago. He follows her everywhere now. They say he is having his way with her. Some say he was having his way with her, even when Duncan was alive. The man is an evil heathen, Henry.'

'I don't believe a word of any of this, Paul. They're just stories from people who have nothing better to do but gossip,' Henry said sharply.

'Just the same, I'd be careful if I were you.' Paul replied, and then he changed the subject back to the coming wedding.

*   *   *

Henry shook his head to clear his thoughts. He got up and removed his sheets and pillow covers. He would ask Tarni to wash them and remake his bed. He rolled them into a bundle and left them on the floor. He must find Kasiah and tell her how sorry he is for what happened last night. It must never happen again! She would understand. He put on his bathrobe and went down the hallway quietly, guilt filling his thoughts. He needed to shower away the guilt from his body. Just as he was about to reach for the bathroom door handle, it turned, and Kasiah came out wearing the same jade-green bathrobe she'd been wearing the night before. Her long hair was wrapped in a white bath towel.

'I'm sorry, Kasiah. I didn't realise you were in there,' Henry mumbled, taking a step back.

Good morning, Henry. Come in here for a minute. We need to talk. Kasiah said, holding the door open for him.

Henry followed her into the bathroom. He could smell the soap on her skin and sense her nakedness beneath the robe. He couldn't help it . . . He wanted her again.

Kasiah put her arms around him and hugged him for a few silent moments. When she spoke, her voice was full of emotion.

'What we did last night was very wrong, Henry. It was my fault. I was upset and feeling lonely. It must never happen again. We have to think of Tessa,' she whispered.

'I agree, Kasiah. It cannot go on,' Henry replied, his mind spinning with indecision.

'It was wonderful. But it must stop, Henry.'

'Yes, it must, Kasiah,' Henry whispered back.

 'Was it wonderful for you, Henry?' Kasiah asked, her voice a soft vibration in Henry's mind.

'I cannot begin to tell you how wonderful it was, Kasiah. I have never felt more like a man,' Henry replied.

'Last night, you were my tireless young stallion, but it cannot go on, Henry. It must stop now, my love.'

Henry reached for the sash that held Kasiah's bathrobe in place and pulled it . . . It fell open.

Kasiah didn't attempt to stop him or to cover herself.

Henry bent to her breasts and kissed her dark, erect nipples.

Kasiah tossed her head back and moaned at the sudden, un-expected pleasure it gave her. 'Oh, Henry, this is so very wrong,' she whispered.

Henry slowly slipped the bathrobe down over her dark shoul-ders. 'I want you now, Kasiah. I must have you again,' he mur-mured, laying it carefully over the bath edge.

Kasiah untied the towel from around her dark hair, knelt, and laid it on the hard floor next to the bath. Then she reached up and pulled Henry down with her.

'This must be the last time, Henry,' she whispered. 'You must promise me.'

'I promise you, Kasiah,' Henry replied. 'This will be the last time.'

# Chapter 25

# Visiting Time

Later that morning, Henry and Kasiah sat silently in the back seat of the Pierce-Arrow while Jago drove them to the hospital to visit Tessa. Henry had a grim expression on his face. He stole a look at Kasiah and noticed she was smiling at him. He looked at the car's rearview mirror. Jago was watching him. Did he know what happened last night?

'We must support Tessa now after what she has been through, Henry. She'll be feeling terrible this morning,' Kasiah said with a soft, caring voice.

'Yes, of course we must, Kasiah.' Henry replied.

A short while later, Jago parked the car. They climbed out and hurried through the hospital doors. Kasiah took Henry's hand and looked into his eyes as they walked. 'Are you alright, Henry?' She asked, concern showing in her dark eyes.

'Yes, I think I am now.' Henry lied.

When they reached the nurse's station, they were told Tessa's room number. A few moments later, Kasiah tapped on the door and pushed it open. Tessa was sitting up in her bed sipping a cup of tea.

'Hello, my darling,' Kasiah said, hurrying to the bed.

'I'm so sorry, Mother. What a terrible mess I've made of things,' Tessa replied, putting her teacup on her bedside cabinet and putting her arms out.

'Shh now, sweetheart,' Kasiah took Tessa in her arms. 'It's all over now, and you are still with us,' Kasiah whispered. 'Look who's with me. Poor Henry has been so worried about you.'

Kasiah got up, and Henry sat on the bed. He took Tessa into his arms. 'Oh, Tessa, I'm so glad you're alright. Will you ever forgive me, my love?'

'Forgive you for what, Henry?' Tessa asked.

'For not coming with you when you asked me to. If I had, none of this would have happened.'

'It's not your fault, Henry. It was all my doing, and I'm so sorry. Can *you* forgive me?'

'Of course I can forgive you,' Henry replied.

'There's something that I should tell you both, though. Please sit down, Mother,' Tessa said in a timid voice.

'Are there still some problems, Tessa?' Kasiah asked, sitting beside Henry.

'No, I'm alright now. But the doctor visited me just before you arrived and told me there is a chance I may never be able to bear a child. How silly I've been, Henry. I'm so terribly sorry,' Tessa said and started to cry.

'You're still with us, my love, and that's far more important to me,' Henry whispered, taking Tessa in his arms again.

'I'm sure there's still a chance of a child. Let's just see what the future holds. But for now, let's just concentrate on getting you back home with us first, Tessa,' Kasiah whispered. She was beginning to cry herself.

'Can you leave here today, Tessa?' Henry asked. 'We could wait and take you with us.'

'The doctor told me I have to stay here for another two or three days to be certain I'm fully recovered. He said I lost quite a lot of blood.'

'You were lucky Jago got you here so quickly,' Kasiah added, reaching for Tessa's hand.

'Thank him for me, Mother. I don't remember much of what happened now. I think I passed out just after he came in. But I do remember him being very angry. I was frightened that he might do something terrible to that old Filipino woman. He hit her in the face with such force that he knocked her through a wall. But he was so gentle with me. He wrapped me in towels and picked me up like I was a baby,' Tessa whispered, and then she started sobbing again.

'We had better let you get some rest, my darling. We'll come and see you again tonight. Today is Henry's first day working for us. There is much for me to show him and a lot for him to learn,' Kasiah said, kissing her daughter's cheek.

'Goodbye, for now, Tessa. You'll be back with us before you know it,' Henry whispered, kissing Tessa, getting to his feet, and taking Kasiah's hand.

*   *   *

Tessa stayed in the hospital for the next three days and nights, and just after midnight on each of those nights, Kasiah went to Henry's bed. Each night, they made love and lay in each other's arms until just before dawn. Time enough for Kasiah to return to her bedroom before the servants arose. On their final night together before Tessa was to come home, Kasiah almost didn't come at all, such was her concern that Tarni or Juliette should find out what had been happening. But finally, she pushed open Henry's door.

'Are you awake, my love?' she asked from the doorway.

'I was afraid you weren't coming,' Henry whispered. He lay naked on the bed. The French doors were open, and a cooling breeze was flicking at the sheer curtains.

Kasiah walked barefoot over and stood beside the bed. Moonlight fell over her dark body as she slipped off her robe.

'My sweet Lord, I will never tire of looking at you, Kasiah,' Henry whispered as he watched her.

'And I will never tire of looking at you, my urgent young stallion, and from what I see, you are already hungry for me again,' Kasiah murmured, running her dark hand over Henry's muscular body.

'After tonight, things must change, Kasiah. We cannot go on like this. I do love my wife.'

'It seems we have both lost our way, my love,' Kasiah whispered, kissing Henry's thighs.

'Oh, my Kasiah. I do love you.'

'You will not be the first man to have ever loved two women at the same time, my darling.' Kasiah murmured, kissing Henry's naked belly.

'But surely it will be far too dangerous for us to go on like this,' Henry insisted. 'We must try . . . We really must . . . Oh my Lord, Kasiah—!'

'We will find a way,' Kasiah whispered a while later.

'Tell me. Kasiah, does that strange golden pendant you wear have a meaning?' Henry asked. 'It's quite beautiful.'

'Yes, it does, Henry. It once belonged to my father. My mother gave it to me after the sea took him from us,' Kasiah replied.

'What is its purpose?' Henry asked.

'It's a talisman. It represents the evil eye. It is made from the purest gold, and the eye is a faultless Indian ruby. It is called the *Mata Jahat*. It protects the wearer from evil. My father was Juan Toledo, the diver. He was a shaman, a hoodoo man—a healer,' Kasiah replied, leaning forward, and letting Henry touch it.

'It looks very old and quite beautiful,' Henry whispered, running his fingers over the ruby and then over her dark, perfect breasts.

'It once belonged to a priest in my father's country. My mother told me it is quite ancient,' Kasiah explained.

'And have you used it to cast a spell over me, my love?' Henry asked in a soft voice, remembering Paul's warning to him.

'Perhaps I have, my virile young stallion, and if I have, are you angry with me for doing so?' Kasiah whispered back.

'I could never be angry with you, Kasiah. If it's a spell that you have cast over me, never lift it, and never stop loving me the way that you do,' Henry replied, lifting Kasiah to him and hungrily kissing her mouth and then each of her dark breasts.

'Make love to me, Henry. I want you to be rough with me tonight. I will show you how. Make us both remember this night, for it may be some time before we can be together again,' Kasiah whispered, pulling Henry from his bed onto the board floor.

216

# Chapter 26

# Tessa Comes Home

The following morning, Kasiah and Henry brought Tessa home. When Jago parked the Pierce-Arrow under the old flame tree and opened the back door, Tessa climbed out and put her hand on Jago's arm as he held the door handle.

'I'm sorry that I caused you so much trouble, Jago.' She told him sincerely, looking into his dark eyes.

'You no trouble for me, Miss Tessa. You Mister Duncan's little girl.' Jago replied, and then he hurried away.

'Let's get you inside now, Tessa. I think Tarni and Juliette have baked some cakes and made lemonade for you.' Kasiah said, taking her daughter's hand.

Henry led them up the steps and into the kitchen, where they were greeted by Tarni and Juliette with welcoming smiles on their faces.

Tarni went to Tessa and took her hand. 'You come and sit down, Miss Tessa. I've made you some of those nice jelly cakes you like,' she said, leading her to a chair. The Aboriginal woman loved Tessa as if she were her own child, such was the affection she felt for her and her mother.

'Don't fuss so much, Tarni. I'm quite alright now,' Tessa said, taking a jelly cake from the plate Juliette offered her.

'I've got your bedroom all ready for you and Mister Henry. I put some nice fresh sheets on the bed before you got here, just like Mister Henry asked,' Tarni said, smiling and filling a glass with lemonade.

Henry glanced at Kasiah and noticed she was smiling at her beloved daughter.

'Now, Tessa, if you think you will be alright, Henry and I have work to do at the warehouse. Jago has already left. There's a freighter due in later today, and we have a few tons of shell to get down to the jetty,' Kasiah said, helping herself to a glass of lemonade.

'I'll be fine, Mother,' Tessa replied, nibbling at her jelly cake.

'Before we go, Tessa, I have some important news. I haven't even told Henry about it just yet,' Kasiah said, glancing at Henry and smiling. 'I've decided to go ahead with the partnership in the gold mine up there in Pine Creek with your friends from Darwin. I posted the cheque to Connor a couple of days ago,' Kasiah announced.

'That's wonderful news, Mother. Conner and Angela will be so pleased,' Tessa replied, turning to Henry. 'So will you, won't you, Henry?'

'Yes, I am. I just hope it turns out to be profitable, that's all,' Henry replied, looking at Kasiah. 'Thank you for doing that, Kasiah.'

'I've also decided that it would be a very sensible idea for you and Henry to go up to Darwin and visit Connor and Angela for a week or two. Henry can then find out what the next steps will be with the mine. And, Tessa, you have just been through a terrible time. It will make sense for you to have a nice rest up there with your friends.' Kasiah added, turning to Henry.

'What do you think, Henry?' she asked.

'Are you sure you won't need me here to help you, Kasiah? After all, I've only just started working for you,' Henry replied. He was surprised that Kasiah hadn't told him about her decision before this.

'I'll be fine. The luggers will be at sea for some weeks yet. Captain Nolan, my fleet skipper, will be taking supplies out to them on the *Mina* in a couple of weeks. When he returns, there will be shell to crate up and store. We'll be busy then, but that won't be for a while yet. Besides, I have Jago and Paddy to help me in the warehouse while you're away.'

'Oh, Mother, what a wonderful idea. I'll write to Angela this afternoon. We could have a look at that piece of land that Connor spoke about while we're there,' Tessa replied excitedly.

'You could, my dear. I've been thinking about that as well. It would be nice to have a holiday home up there. Your father and I were always talking about doing something like that. We were thinking of Perth, but Darwin is very nice as well,' Kasiah said, enjoying the delight in her daughter's eyes.

'Can you afford to do something like that, Kasiah? It may well cost you a lot of money, and so soon after the mining investment,' Henry replied.

'Money will not be a problem, Henry. Just make sure that the land is suitable and that you both like it. You could send me a telegram if you decide to buy it, and I will transfer the money.'

'And when will we be going?' Henry asked as he tried to hide the disappointment he was feeling.

'The *Minderoo* is due here in a few days. You could go then. In the meantime, we had better get moving; we have a lot of shell to get to the freighter by this afternoon,' Kasiah replied.

Henry went to Tessa and kissed her cheek. 'I'll see you when we get back, my love.'

* * *

Kasiah was at the wheel as they drove to the warehouse. Nothing was said between them until they left the driveway and turned onto Walcott Street.

'Are you sending me away because of what we have done, Kasiah?' Henry asked.

'Perhaps I am, Henry. But it has been as much my fault as yours. I have been foolish, thinking it could continue. We both agreed that it must stop,' Kasiah replied.

'But I love you, Kasiah.'

'I am too old for you, Henry. I have felt a terrible loneliness in my heart ever since Duncan died. I should never have gone to your room that first night,' Kasiah admitted, looking briefly into Henry's distraught eyes.

'Do you mean that you no longer love me, Kasiah?'

'No, Henry. That is not what I meant at all. I do love you, and I will never stop loving you. It was meant to be this way. But for how long, I do not know. Perhaps it is only for the gods to know that.' Kasiah confessed.

Henry saw the tears forming in Kasiah's eyes.

'My love for you will never change, Kasiah. Your age has nothing to do with it. You must believe me.'

'Thank you, Henry.' Kasiah replied.

Henry reached across the seat and kissed Kasiah's cheek. 'I can never stop loving you, Kasiah,' he whispered to her.

'Henry, you must remember, you are married to my daughter—my darling daughter—my only child,' Kasiah said, turning into another street.

'And I love Tessa with all my heart as well,' Henry replied. 'I love you both, Kasiah.

'Let us see how you feel when you get back from Darwin. You are so young, Henry. Your love for me could change like the winds that change with the seasons.'

'It will never change, Kasiah, not as long as I breathe.'

'We shall see,' Kasiah said as she parked the Pierce-Arrow outside the warehouse. A horse and cart were already backed up to the open main doors. Jago was on the back, stacking crates of pearl shell.

* * *

Late that afternoon, after the shell had been carted to the freighter, Henry and Kasiah were back at the warehouse, enjoying a mug of tea before heading home. Jago and Paddy were busy cleaning out the warehouse and getting ready for the next load of pearl shell to be brought in by Captain Nolan and the *Mina*.

'I know you have explained a lot of what I need to know about this industry, Kasiah, but tell me, is the pearl shell still bringing good money overseas now that the war is over?' Henry asked.

'It has been quite stable for some time now, Henry. At the moment, we get £180 per ton for good-quality shell. What we just took to the freighter will return us almost £2,000,' Kasiah explained.

'That is a lot of money. Apart from buttons, what else is the pearl shell used for?' Henry asked.

'Because of its beautiful colours, it has many other uses. It is made into cigar and cigarette cases, hair combs, and clasps. Skilled jewellers can turn them into delicate brooches and beautifully shaped pendants. It is even used in expensive English and European furniture and as an inlay in musical instruments as well. All sorts of things.'

'I had no idea it was used so widely. But now that I come to think of it, Captain Bradford had a silver cigarette case that was lined with pearl shell on the inside. It was quite beautiful,' Henry added.

'The shell from the sea in this area is prized in Europe and America because of the brilliance of its colours. So exceptionally beautiful are some of the things I have seen made using it,' Kasiah explained.

'And what about the pearls?' Henry asked.

'The pearls are only found occasionally. Sometimes weeks will go by before one is found on any of our boats. Sometimes two or three in a single day. The pearl is a bonus—a very welcome bonus.'

'And where do the buyers for the pearls come from?' Henry asked.

'Buyers are operating in this town all the time. Most of them have contacts overseas.'

'Are they as valuable as I have heard?'

'Henry, let me explain things a little more clearly for you. Quite a lot of the pearls we find are baroque, smaller, irregular-shaped pieces suitable only for brooches, hat pins, and the like, still quite valuable though. Some are just hollow, mud-filled blisters caused by small marine boring insects drilling through the pearl shell from the outside and causing an irritation between the pearl muscle and the shell itself. When this happens, the pearl itself is usually full of mud and almost worthless. But not always. Sometimes a perfect pearl is found that way,' Kasiah explained. 'It takes the delicate skill of a surgeon to peel away any blemishes and marks, but sometimes it is worth it. There is a Cingalese man here in Broome that we use. He is fascinating to watch. Fortunes are made and lost in his little workshop.

'I certainly have much to learn,' Henry replied. 'What happens to the perfect pearls you *do* find?'

'I have quite a few in my safe at the moment. Usually, they are sold in Europe to buyers who supply bespoke jewellers and skilled artisans. They, in turn, sell their creations to the very wealthy, or to European royalty,' Kasiah explained. 'I'll open the safe and show you some of the ones we have at the moment. We have quite a good collection. Duncan would only ever sell what we needed to. He always considered our best pearls a sound investment to keep.'

Kasiah went to her safe and entered the combination. When she finished, she pulled open the heavy door, slid out a velvet-lined tray, and brought it back to her desk.

'They are quite beautiful, Kasiah. So many different colours.' Henry remarked.

'The pearl is judged by its weight, its shape, and the quality of its colour. Some are almost pure white; some have a rosy or silvery hue to them, as you can see by these,' Kasiah explained.

'They are simply beautiful,' Henry whispered, picking one of them up and admiring it.

'That particular pearl would weigh around 40 grains. There are some on that tray weighing 80 grains and more. Its value to us, when sold to a reputable buyer, would be somewhere in the vicinity of £100 per grain.'

'My goodness, Kasiah. I had no idea they were worth that much. That means this little pearl I'm holding is worth about £4,000.' Henry said, carefully putting the pearl back on the velvet tray. That's more than a tradesman could earn in years of hard work. Who on this earth can afford them, Kasiah?

'Only the very rich, Henry,' Kasiah replied.

'My God, Kasiah, you must be a very wealthy woman.'

'Yes, I suppose I am. And you are now my partner, Henry. Are you pleased?'

'I am stunned,' Henry replied.

'I have been very careful with you, Henry. I wasn't sure how you would react to the knowledge of my wealth. Most of it I must give credit to Duncan for. Does it change the way you think about me?' Kasiah asked.

'If you told me you were penniless, I would still love you, Kasiah,' Henry replied.

Kasiah got up and came around the desk to where Henry was sitting. 'Thank you for saying that, Henry,' she whispered, kissing him on the lips. 'And I promise that I will never stop loving you.'

Henry got up, went to the door, and locked it.

'Oh, Henry, this is so wrong. We will be going home soon. You must think of your wife,' Kasiah said, taking the pearls back to the safe and locking it.

When she turned, Henry was waiting for her. His braces hung at his sides. He had taken off his shirt. There were marks on his arms and muscular chest from handling the heavy crates of pearl shell.

Kasiah went to him and kissed him passionately on the mouth and then on each of the marks on his chest.

'We should be going home now, Henry,' she said, holding him in her arms.

'Soon, my love,' Henry replied.

'We've been working, Henry. I'm all wet with perspiration,' Kasiah whispered, undoing her dirty blouse.

Henry watched her take off her soiled clothing and lay them on the desk. He could see the perspiration between her dark breasts and on her naked belly.

'Look at me, Henry. I'm all scratched as well and wet all over with perspiration.'

'I don't care, Kasiah. Seeing you wet with sweat makes me want you even more,' Henry replied, kissing her mouth, her neck, and then each of her slick, perfect breasts.

Kasiah moaned softly with the pleasure it gave her. She reached over and turned off her desk light. The only light coming into the office then was from the small bar-covered window at the front of the building.

'I feel like a slut, Henry. This must stop. You promised me,' Kasiah whispered.

Henry went to her, took her hand, and turned her in a little circle in front of him. The slanting light from the window bars cast slowly moving stripes over her dark, naked body as she turned before him.

'You're no whore, Kasiah. You are the beautiful black goddess who has cast a spell over me. You're like a drug that I can't do without,' Henry whispered, kissing Kasiah's open mouth.

'And now, I feel a whore's fire beginning to burn inside me again. Do you see what you have done to me?' Kasiah moaned.

Henry lifted her onto the desk, his hands slipping on her slick waist.

'I want you just like this, Kasiah, all wet with sweat,' he whispered, pushing her legs apart. He left his dirt-covered trousers on and began undoing his fly buttons.

'Oh, yes, my love . . . Just like this. I want to feel that rough cloth against my thighs.

'I love you, Kasiah, more than you could ever know,' Henry whispered.

'Oh . . . Oh . . . Oh . . . Oh, Henry, my love. My wonderful, tireless love,' Kasiah moaned.

# Chapter 27

# Bitter Creek Gold

Three days later, Henry and Tessa were on board the S.S. *Minderoo* and heading north for Darwin.

For the four days it took them to travel from Broome to Darwin, they spent each night at Captain Bradford's table, listening to his stories and enjoying his company. On their final night together, the captain broached the subject of their trip to Australia's northernmost city.

'We have invested in a gold mine south of Darwin, Captain. We're meeting our partners in Darwin to discuss what progress has been made. You would remember them from our last trip—Conner and Angela Burke,' Henry explained.

'Yes, I do, Henry. Connor Burke is a very astute businessman. He is well known in Darwin. A very wealthy gentleman by all accounts. His wife is much younger, as I recall, but very charming indeed,' Captain Bradford replied.

'We have to thank you for introducing us, Captain. We have become very good friends, in particular Tessa and Angela,' Henry added.

'If Connor Burke is involved, your mine should be a worthwhile investment. Are you staying with them, Henry?'

'We are, Captain. For about two weeks. We hope to be able to catch a ship back down to Broome sometime after that,' Henry replied.

'It won't be the *Minderoo*, I'm afraid. We will be returning from Singapore in about nine days after arriving in Darwin. If you check with the shipping office, you'll be able to find out what ship is due around that time.'

'Thank you, Captain. This has been a pleasant trip with you. Very relaxing indeed. My wife is beginning to feel much better. Sea air is a wonderful cure-all,' Henry said.

'I wasn't aware that she had been unwell, Henry. In that case, I'm glad she is feeling much better. Was it something serious?' Captain Bradford asked.

'She had a miscarriage, unfortunately, and there was some bleeding,' Henry replied, turning to Tessa, and smiling.

'Thank you for your concern, Captain. But I'm fully recovered now.' Tessa said, looking up from her wine glass, her pleasant smile masking her thoughts.

'How very unfortunate for you, my dear,' Captain Bradford offered.

*   *   *

The following morning, they arrived at the port of Darwin. The day was fine and sunny, with a clear blue sky. The *Minderoo* was guided into a position near the busy port's main gantries for easy unloading of the cargo.

Henry and Tessa were at the starboard side railing, looking out for Connor and Angela among the milling crowd on the wharf.

'There they are,' Tessa called to Henry, pointing down to their waving friends.

As soon as the ship was safely moored and the gangway was in position, they hurried down the wooden ramp, Henry struggling with their heavy cases.

Connor and Angela rushed over to greet them.

Henry put down the cases when he reached the wharf.

'Let me help you, Henry,' Connor offered.

'Hello, Connor. It's nice to see you again, my friend,' Henry replied, reaching for Connor's hand.

Angela rushed into Tessa's outstretched arms. 'Oh, Tessa, how lovely to see you again,' she gushed.

'And you, my dear friend,' Tessa replied. 'I'm so glad you offered to put up with us on such short notice.'

'Oh, it's no bother at all. I'm just so pleased you decided to come so soon,' Angela replied, turning to Connor. 'Hurry up with those cases, you men. Let's get back to the car so we can go home and talk.'

Henry and Connor picked up the heavy cases and hurried after the two women. A short while after they had loaded their luggage into Connor's black Packard sedan, they were turning onto East Point Road, with the blue waters of Fanny Bay on their left.

'It's nice along here with the sea so close. Is this the road you live on?' Tessa asked Angela.

'Yes, it is,' Angela replied. 'It's lovely and quiet out here, and we're only ten minutes from the centre of town.

'And with the blue waters of the bay right across the road,' Henry added.

'That's the piece of land we spoke about,' Angela called out as Connor stopped the car on the side of the gravel road.

'It's quite large, around half an acre. Our place is right next door,' Connor explained, turning off the ignition.

'Oh, how perfect. We'd be neighbours if we decided to buy it, Angela,' Tessa said excitedly.

'There are already some nice, shady trees on it, and there's a level area toward the back where a good-sized home could be built.' Connor explained.

'It looks simply perfect. What do you think, Henry?' Tessa asked.

'Do you know the price, Connor?' Henry asked.

'It's quite expensive, and that's probably why it hasn't sold already. I rang the real estate people this morning, thinking you might ask. They told me the asking price is £200,' Connor said.

'Let's go over and have a walk over it for a bit,' Henry replied.

'I've brought my little box camera with me. I'd like to take some photos to show Mother when we get home,' Tessa added as they climbed out.

'Do you think you really might buy it then, Tessa?' Angela asked.

'Yes, we may do. Mother said it was up to us to see if we both liked it,' Tessa replied.

'How lovely that would be,' Angela said, putting her arm around Tessa as they crossed the road.

'We could give you a good builder's name if you decide to build. Our home is quite new, and we're very pleased with the builder we used.' Connor added while they stood in the shade of a young flame tree near the front of the land.

'What a wonderful spot. I can even feel the breeze coming from the bay right now,' Henry remarked.

'The builder we used has a draftsman working for him who comes from Queensland. His designs are just perfect for our climate,' Connor mentioned.

'Let's get home so we can get you unpacked and showered before dinner,' Angela said, reaching for Tessa's hand.

*   *   *

After dinner that night, the two couples took their wine glasses and went out onto the wide front veranda of Connor and Angela's new home.

'Your home is so beautiful, Angela. You must be very pleased,' Tessa said.

'Oh, yes, we are, Tessa,' Angela replied. 'And you will have the very same outlook if you buy the land next door.'

'You must give me your builder's name, Connor. I would like to contact him for some ideas before we leave,' Henry remarked.

'I'll ring him tomorrow morning and ask him to come out and meet you both if you like,' Connor added.

'That would be perfect. Kasiah has asked me while we are here to find out how the mine is progressing,' Henry asked Connor.

'You'll be able to take back very promising news, Henry. The old prospector has informed me that they are already bringing out gold in good quantities. He thinks the mine will be a great success.' Connor said.

'That's excellent news,' Henry replied.

'I've drawn up papers for you to sign while you're here. We've named the mine and the partnership 'Bitter Creek Gold.' Bitter Creek is the area where the mine is located,' Connor explained.

'A sensible choice,' Henry replied.

'My accountant would like to meet you both while you are here as well and take down a few more details. For taxation reasons, I've set up a limited private company with a total of 100 shares, with each share having a value of £150. I have divided it in the following way: 33 shares for *Taylor House Pearls*, 34 shares for *Burke Investments*, and 33 shares for Max Davies, the old prospector. That would enable me to manage all costs, including wages and accommodation for the miners. Those costs will be taken from the existing funds—and, as we continue, from the profits. At the end of each fiscal year, a dividend will be raised and distributed to each of the company's shareholders.'

'Very well done, Connor. My congratulations,' Henry replied.

'I am quite confident that we are on a winner with this mine. I think in a year or so it will make us very rich men,' Connor concluded.

'All this business talk is probably boring our wives. Perhaps Angela should take Tessa into the kitchen for coffee. While I get a decanter of port for us men.'

'That's an excellent idea, my love,' Angela agreed. 'Come with me, Tessa. I have some new clothes I'd like your opinion on.'

The two women got up and hurried from the veranda.

Connor and Henry got to their feet. After the women left, Connor turned to Henry.

'I'll go and get a couple of glasses and this very nice port I keep for special occasions. I have some excellent Cuban cigars you might enjoy as well.'

'I haven't smoked before, Connor. But I think with the news that the mine is progressing well, I should certainly like to try one,' Henry replied.

*   *   *

The following morning, Connor rang his builder and asked if he could call on him sometime in the afternoon. The builder agreed to be at Connor and Angela's home at three o'clock that afternoon. Connor then called the real estate company that was handling the sale of the land Henry and Tessa were interested in and handed the telephone to Henry.

'Hello there,' Henry began. 'I'm ringing to ask you the price of a block of land you have listed.'

'Good morning, sir. What particular property are you referring to?' the agent asked.

'You have a vacant piece of land listed out toward the end of East Point Road,' Henry replied.

'Oh, I see. That particular block of land is one of the best residential blocks we have on our books. The owner was going to build on it himself, but his current financial situation does not permit building at this time. The asking price is £200. I think it represents excellent value at that price,' the agent replied.

'I will make you a cash offer of £160 and no more. If you could get back to me before this day ends with an answer, it would be appreciated,' Henry said.

'That's quite a low offer, sir. However, I will take it to the owner and get back to you before the day ends. Could you give me your number?' the agent asked.

'I would prefer if we met in person. I could sign the offer this afternoon. I am staying with my good friend Conner Burke on

East Point Road. Do you know where he lives?'

'I do, sir. Mr. Burke is well known to us. And who will I ask for?'

'Mr. and Mrs. Henry Dawson. I look forward to meeting you later today. Five o'clock would suit us if you can manage.'

'David Brent is my name, sir. In that case, I will see you at five o'clock, Mr. Dawson. Thank you for the inquiry.'

'Goodbye, David,' Henry replied and hung up the phone.

At three o'clock, Connor's builder arrived and was shown to Connor's study.

'Mr. Thomson, I would like you to meet our good friends and business partners, Mr. Henry Dawson and his wife Tessa, pearlers from Broome.' Connor began.

'I'm pleased to meet you both,' Dale Thomson replied.

'My friends have been very impressed with the work you have done with our home, Dale. They would like to have a chat with you about the possibility of having you build a home for them. I will leave you with them so they can explain their plans in private with you,' Connor said, leaving them to talk.

'Where do you intend to build, Henry?' Dale Thomson asked after Conner had left the room.

'We hope to buy the piece of land right next door,' Henry replied.

'I know the block. A wonderful spot. And what sort of house did you have in mind?'

'We like the Queenslander-style home you have built for Connor and Angela. I'm hoping you could draw up plans for us for something similar. Initially, the house will be a holiday home. Perhaps later, we may decide to move here,' Henry began.

'I can certainly do that for you. Can you give some idea of the size?'

'It would need to be two stories, with at least four good-sized bedrooms upstairs, two bathrooms, a dining room, and a large sitting room. We would prefer the toilets to be inside, of course. Wide, shady verandas with French doors for the breezes would be nice. We would also need a separate flat downstairs with two bedrooms for our staff to use and garaging for at least two motor cars, and a storeroom if the plan allows. And if possible, a secure room below, accessible in some way known only to you the builder, and us,' Henry said. He was thinking of Kasiah's valuable pearls.

'I see,' Dale Thomson replied. 'A sizable job indeed. And do you own the piece of land yet?'

'I will, one way or another, by the end of this day,' Henry answered. 'I should also tell you that we will be returning to Broome in a couple of weeks. If possible, I would like to take back preliminary plans and sketches, if you can manage, to show my wife's mother, Kasiah Taylor.'

'I've heard of the Taylors from Broome,' Dale Thomson replied. 'Pearlers, I believe.'

'Do you think it would be possible to have this all done before we leave for Broome?' Henry asked.

'I will have them done and ready for you to take back. You have my word on that. I'll have some costings done as well,' Dale said, shaking Henry's hand.

'Thank you, Dale. I look forward to hearing from you.'

'It's been a pleasure to meet you, Henry, and you, Mrs. Dawson,' Dale Thomson said, shaking both their hands and leaving them.

'What do you think, Tessa? Did I cover everything we discussed on the ship? You do love the piece of land, don't you?' Henry asked Tessa.

Tessa was smiling at him. 'Oh, Henry, you were so masterful. Yes, I love the piece of land. I just hope we can get it at the price you have offered. It will be wonderful to be able to come here and live so close to Connor and Angela,' Tessa replied.

'We shall have it, Tessa, even if we have to pay the full £200, my love,' Henry replied.

At five o'clock, David Brent, the real estate agent, called at Connor and Angela Burke's home with the good news that Henry's offer for the block of land had been accepted.

'You have just bought yourselves a wonderful piece of land, Henry, and at an exceptionally good price. I must congratulate you,' David said, shaking his hand.

'Thank you, David. If you ring me here tomorrow morning with the settlement amount finalised, I will have the money wired to you before the end of the week.'

'I will see to it, Henry,' David replied.

'The land title and paperwork are to be in the name of Mrs. Kasiah Taylor, of Walcott Street, Broome, Western Australia. When you have it all finalised, please send the relevant paperwork to her at that address.'

'Thank you, Henry, and you, Mrs. Dawson. I will be in touch with you soon.'

*   *   *

Twelve days later, Henry and Tessa were preparing to board the M.V. *Kangaroo* for their voyage to Broome and home and were farewelling their friends on the long Darwin wharf.

Angela Burke was crying and hugging Tessa. 'Oh, Tessa, I wish you didn't have to leave so soon,' she sobbed. 'We've had such fun.'

'We will be back in a few short months, Angela. After we have spoken to Mother, I'll write and let you know our plans. I feel certain she will want to start construction on our Darwin home just as soon as possible,' Tessa replied with tears forming in her eyes.

'I do hope so, Tessa.' Angela said.

'Thank you for a wonderful time,' Tessa replied, kissing Angela's cheek.

Henry and Connor were standing a short distance away.

'Thank you for looking after us so well, Conner. We've had

a wonderful time,' Henry said, shaking Connor's outstretched hand vigorously.

'I'll keep you informed about the progress of the mine, Henry. I think it will make us both very rich men, with a bit of luck. Let me know if you would like me to do anything concerning your home construction here in Darwin,' Connor replied.

'I will, Connor. We will look forward to seeing you both soon. Goodbye for now,' Henry said, turning to Tessa.

'C'mon, Tessa, we had better get aboard.'

'I'm coming. Goodbye, Angela. Goodbye, Connor. Thank you for a wonderful time.' Tessa kissed Connor quickly and hurried after Henry.

# Chapter 28

# Captain John Nolan

Henry and Tessa's holiday in Darwin had been a wonderful experience for the both of them, but it had ended far too quickly. Connor and Angela had gone to great lengths to show them the sights of Australia's northernmost city. They dined out most nights, trying many of the different restaurants and hotels in town.

For Henry, holidaying in Darwin was a strange experience, with it being the town where he was born. Most of the places they visited he had neither heard of nor visited before. One day, on their way to somewhere for lunch, they drove past the old home in Parap where he grew up as a boy. The place where his drunken father had beaten him and his brother so many times that he couldn't count them.

When Henry looked out the window at the house, he remembered his beautiful mother. He remembered the night his drunken father smashed her face with his fists and broke her cheekbone. He remembered, as boys, he and his younger brother walking with her to the hospital. He remembered her sobbing in the darkness as he held her bloody hand.

He also remembered the morning he found his father hanging in the woodshed, a turned-up beer crate beneath his dirty work boots, his tobacco pouch on the wood chip floor nearby, and the smell of urine. His father must have wet himself as he hung there, struggling for breath in the darkness. He wondered if the wood-shed was still there at the back of the old house. He hoped in his heart it had been torn down.

Henry thought then of how much his life had changed and all that had happened to him since those long-ago days. He thought of how close he came to losing Tessa and the desperation he felt when he first learned she was to be married to George Peterson. And then he thought of Kasiah, her dark arms holding him against her naked body as they made love. He stole a look at Tessa. His breath caught in his throat. She was so beautiful. She was his wife, and he knew he could never stop loving her. Just for a fleeting moment, he felt confused and guilty. He was glad when Connor turned the corner, and the old house was gone again from his sight and his life forever . . . He said nothing of it to the others.

*   *   *

Four days later, they arrived back in Broome. Jago was waiting for them on the jetty to drive them home. Henry and Tessa hurried down the gangway to where he was waiting.

'Good morning, Jago,' Henry said, as Jago took their cases.

'Boss Missus is at the warehouse, Mister Henry. We take Miss Tessa home first, and then, if you want to see her, I take you there,' Jago said, turning to Tessa. 'We go home now, Miss Tessa.'

'Thank you, Jago,' Tessa replied. She thought for a moment that she should correct Jago. He should address her as Mrs. Tessa now. But she decided against it. She knew she would always be Miss Tessa to all of their employees.

They both fell in behind Jago and followed him to the jetty entrance and the Pierce-Arrow. Tessa climbed into the back seat while Henry and Jago loaded their luggage. A few short minutes later, they were driving down the long driveway to Kasiah's home on Walcott Street. The sound of the car approaching the house brought Tarni and Juliette onto the front veranda, and as soon as Jago parked the Pierce-Arrow beneath the old flame tree, they hurried down on their mission to see Tessa and find out if she had fully recovered from her recent ordeal.

'Hello, Miss Tessa. Are you well?' Tarni asked when she got to her.

'I am very well, Tarni. We had a wonderful holiday,' Tessa remarked, hugging the Aboriginal woman.

'Your mother has been so worried about you,' Tarni replied.

'Oh, Mother worries about me all the time, Tarni. Hello Juliette. It's so nice to see both of you again.'

'You look very fresh and very beautiful, Miss Tessa. It's wonderful to have you back home again. Tarni and I have made some jelly cakes for you,' Juliette said with a welcoming smile.

'You two spoil me,' Tessa said as Henry joined her with the cases.

'I'll take these to our room, Tessa, and then I'd better go and see if everything is alright at the warehouse. Jago's waiting for me.'

'I'll see you when you get back then,' Tessa said as they went up the steps.

'I'll probably have work to do. I'll get changed quickly before I go,' Henry replied as they continued to their bedroom.

'In that case, I shall see you at dinner, my darling,' Tessa said, reaching for Henry. 'We had a wonderful time, didn't we?'

'We did, my love. We had a wonderful time. Just wait till your mother sees the photographs of the block of land and the drawings the builder did for us,' Henry replied as he hurriedly changed his clothes.

'I'm sure she will love it. Goodbye then, Henry,' Tessa said, kissing Henry when he finished dressing.

*    *    *

Henry hurried down to the Pierce-Arrow and climbed into the back. He couldn't wait to see Kasiah again. He wanted to tell her how much he had missed her and how much he loved her. He was glad that Jago had suggested that he go to the warehouse when he got back from the ship. Kasiah must have instructed him.

A few minutes later, Jago parked on the street outside the warehouse.

'Kasiah in office, Mister Henry.' He said as he turned off the ignition.

'Thank you, Jago,' Henry replied, smiling, and climbing out of the back seat. He left Jago in the warehouse and tapped on the office door.

'Who is it?' he heard Kasiah call out.

'It's me, Kasiah. It's Henry.'

'Come in, Henry. It's unlocked.'

Henry had been thinking of Kasiah all day. He opened the door and stepped inside . . . There was another man in her office!

'Oh, Henry, how nice to have you back with us. Did Tessa come with you to see me?' Kasiah asked with a warm smile.

'Tessa's home with Tarni and Juliette.' Henry replied sheepishly.

'There was no need for you to come back to work so soon, Henry. You could have started back tomorrow morning.'

'It's just that Jago said . . .' Henry stammered.

'Did you enjoy your holiday up in Darwin?' Kasiah asked.

Something didn't seem right to Henry. Kasiah should have walked over and hugged him to welcome him back.

'We had a wonderful time, Kasiah. Tessa has some photographs to show you back at the house,' Henry replied, trying to gather his emotions.

'Henry, I would like you to meet our fleet captain. This is Captain John Nolan of our schooner, the *Mina*,' Kasiah said, noticing the sudden flush on Henry's face.

Henry studied the other man in the office. He was a handsome man and about the same age as Duncan would have been. He was taller than Henry and very well built. Henry had the distinct feeling that he had walked in on something.

Captain Nolan stepped forward and reached for Henry's hand. 'I'm pleased to meet you again, Henry. We met at your wedding, but by the look on your face, I think you may have forgotten me.'

Henry took the outstretched hand and shook it a little too vigorously. 'I can't say that I remember you, John. It was to be expected, I suppose. I met so many of Kasiah's friends that day. It was my wedding day, and I suppose I was a little nervous,' Henry replied, looking questioningly into Kasiah's dark, beautiful eyes.

'Henry, John has just delivered a sizable load of shell from a couple of the boats up near the eighty-mile. Jago and Paddy are sorting them at the moment. We've been talking about pearling for a while. John has suggested we send a couple of boats down to the Cossack area. He's heard that shell is quite plentiful there.'

'I see, and are you staying in Broome long, John? I expect you have plenty to keep you busy at the moment,' Henry replied.

'I certainly do, Henry. The *Mina* will be leaving Broome early tomorrow morning. I have supplies to take to some of the luggers up near the eighty-mile. Kasiah has just informed me that she will be sailing with me for the next week or so. She intends to take a break for a while. I suppose you would understand that having just come back from a break yourself,' Captain Nolan said with a pleasant smile.

'Oh, I see, John. Kasiah hadn't told me. A week or so, you say,' Henry replied, struggling to remain calm.

'You don't mind, do you, Henry?' Kasiah asked.

'Of course not. After all, you're the boss, Kasiah,' Henry replied with just a hint of sarcasm.

'Well, I suppose I'd better be off then. I look forward to seeing you early tomorrow morning, Kasiah. The tide will be full at around six a.m. If you could get down to the jetty no later than seven, it would be appreciated,' Captain Nolan said, kissing Kasiah's cheek and reaching for Henry's hand again.

'Nice to have met you again, John. Sorry that I forgot you, sir,' Henry said, shaking the tall man's hand.

'Goodbye, for now, Kasiah. It was wonderful chatting with you.' Captain John Nolan said and left.

Henry locked the door and went to Kasiah. 'Oh Kasiah, I have missed you so much,' he said, reaching for her.

'There was no need to lock the door, Henry. We have work to do out in the warehouse,' Kasiah said, kissing Henry gently on the lips.

'Was I interrupting something before, Kasiah?'

'No, you were not, Henry. John and I were discussing business.

'He seemed to be very familiar with you.'

'Perhaps he was. He was Duncan's best friend,' Kasiah replied.

'I have the feeling that he would like to be more than just your friend.'

'John has always been fond of me, Henry. But we are just friends and no more than that,' Kasiah replied.

'Did you miss me, Kasiah . . . Did you really miss me as much as I have missed you, my love?'

'Yes, of course, I missed you. It's a terrible thing to be jealous of your own daughter,' Kasiah replied, putting her arms around Henry's waist and pulling him against her.

'Do you still want me to unlock the door, my love?'

'Oh, Henry, we must talk about this. It must stop,' Kasiah said, as she watched Henry undo his shirt.

'I can't help it, Kasiah. I have missed you so.'

'This really must stop, Henry. We must try,' Kasiah said, undoing her blouse.

Henry bent forward, opened the blouse, and kissed her dark, perfect breasts.

'Please hurry, my love,' he whispered.

Kasiah removed her remaining clothing and looked into Henry's impatient eyes.

'I have missed you, Henry, and I do love you, my darling, but this must stop.'

Henry kicked off his shoes, took off his trousers and

underwear, and went to Kasiah. He put his hands around her waist and lifted her onto the desk.

'Oh, my love. I have been looking forward to this very moment,' he whispered.

'Henry,' Kasiah said softly. 'You are so young and so impatient.

'Must you leave on the *Mina* tomorrow?' Henry whispered.

'Oh, Henry . . . Yes, I must. But it won't be for long,' Kasiah whispered back.

'My dearest, Kasiah . . . Oh, my sweet lord, I've missed you so.' Henry groaned.

'Oh . . . Oh . . . Oh, Henry, my impatient young stallion. I've missed you as well,' Kasiah whispered, encircling Henry with her arms.

Out in the warehouse, they could both hear the crash of crates of pearl shell being stacked against the office wall.

'My love, I wish we could stay this way forever,' Henry moaned.

'Oh, Henry, my sweet young love, how wonderful you feel, Kasiah whispered, pulling Henry hard against her.

# Chapter 29

# The Mina

Early the following morning, Jago parked the Pierce-Arrow near the entrance to the Broome jetty and got out. He opened the back door for Kasiah, turned, and nodded to Paddy. Paddy slid behind the steering wheel.

Kasiah climbed out, straightened her clothes, and looked at Paddy. 'Take the car back to my home, Paddy. Give the keys to Tarni. She can take you to the warehouse. You have plenty of work to carry on with. There's shell to clean, sort, and crate. We should be back in about eight days or so. Goodbye for now,' she said to the Aboriginal man.

'Goodbye, Missus,' Paddy replied, driving off with a shudder and then a crunch as he changed into second gear.

Jago shook his head, picked up Kasiah's small case, and followed her along the jetty to where the *Mina* was moored. The tide was already beginning to fall. They had to climb down to the deck a short distance on a wooden ladder.

Captain Nolan was waiting for them on the rocking deck of the schooner.

'Good morning, Kasiah. It's nice to finally have you back aboard again.' He said as Jago lifted Kasiah from the worn old ladder.

'Good morning, John. Yes, it's been quite a while since I've been on board the *Mina*. She looks in great trim, though,' Kasiah said to the likable captain.

'She's certainly a very fine vessel, Kasiah,' Captain Nolan replied.

'Have the last of the supplies for the luggers been delivered to you, John?' Kasiah asked.

'They have, Kasiah. The last of them was loaded just a few minutes ago. We weren't able to get as much of the fresh fruit as we wanted, but I purchased some canned stuff from Kennedy's instead, as well as a couple of dozen watermelons and as many pineapples.'

'That should keep the crews happy,' Kasiah replied.

'This tide is running out fast. We'd better cast off and get cracking,' Captain Nolan said, turning and barking a command to his crew.

'I hope you don't mind, John, but Jago has come along for the trip. Now that Duncan is no longer with us, he likes to keep an eye on me,' Kasiah said, as the *Mina* already started to move away from the jetty.'

'It's a good thing for a woman to have someone to look out for her, Kasiah,' John replied, smiling at the swarthy, pig-tailed man standing behind Kasiah.

Jago looked away, rubbing the scar on his cheek.

'He'll have to bunk in with the crew, though,' the captain replied. 'I'll take your bag below now and get you settled.'

Kasiah said something to Jago in a soft voice that John couldn't understand. In Malay, he thought, but he wasn't sure.

Jago nodded to Kasiah and moved off toward the stern of the schooner.

'Thank you, John. Tell me, are most of the luggers still up near the eighty mile?' Kasiah asked when they got to the owner's cabin.

'They're all strung out up there somewhere—all 15 of them. We should meet up with the first of them tomorrow morning early,' the captain replied.

'They're bringing in quite a lot of shell if what you unloaded yesterday is any indication.'

'They seem to be. You know, Kasiah, there was no real need for you to come with us. I'm certain there is plenty for you to do back at the warehouse. I have everything under control with the boats.'

'I know you do, John. But as I explained, I just wanted to get away for a while and clear my head. You don't mind, do you?' Kasiah asked.

'Not at all. Duncan would often come along as well. He liked to keep an eye on the crews. He was a good man, your husband.'

'Yes, he was, John, and he's dearly missed.'

'As you know, he was my best friend. How are you managing without him, Kasiah?'

'Quite well, I think. I've just taken on a partner to help me,' Kasiah explained.

'Young Henry Dawson, I've been told. As you know, we spoke yesterday afternoon. He seems like a fine young man. I take it he and Tessa are getting along well?'

'They are, John. They've not long returned from a trip to Darwin, visiting friends. Tessa had been unwell. The trip did her the world of good.

'In that case, I'm glad she's on the mend.'

'Thank you, John,' Kasiah replied, lifting her bag onto one of the bunks.

'I'll leave you to unpack your gear. I'd better get back up top.'

'I'll see you in a while then,' Kasiah replied and began unpacking the few things she'd brought with her.

* * *

Kasiah had been struggling with guilt. She had fallen in love with her daughter's husband. Was it just loneliness that had made her go to Henry's bed that first night? Perhaps it was simply just that. She had loved her husband, Duncan, so completely, but now he was gone. It must have surely been loneliness in the beginning. But in her heart, Kasiah knew that wasn't the real reason. It was something else. It was something that happened to her the day that she invited Henry for tea at their home so long ago. She had seen into her future that day. Her destiny had come to visit her. Was it a wicked thing that she had done? Had she unknowingly cast a spell over Henry, as he had suggested? She knew she was capable of doing such a thing. Or was it possible a spell had been cast over them both by the fickle gods of love that taunt us all? Of that, she was no longer sure. But Henry had stirred deep emotions inside her. He had taken away her self-control. She needed time to think and to reason with herself. She also knew if Tessa ever found out what had been going on behind her back, it would break her daughter's heart.

Perhaps she should just tell Henry the truth: that she can no longer go on deceiving Tessa and end it completely. But a terrible loneliness gripped her heart at the thought of losing Henry's love and affection. The *Mina* was the opportunity she needed. Captain Nolan was a dear friend. He had delivered shell from the luggers two days earlier, and now he was to take much-needed fresh food and supplies to the men on the luggers stretched out along the eighty-mile beach. It would give her the time she needed.

She was going to miss Tessa, though. She seemed so happy when they talked last night. Her friendship with Angela Burke was a blessing for her daughter. A woman needs the company of other women. Duncan had never allowed her to have friends when she was young. He thought it would lead to trouble with boys. That was the reason he had for taking her out of school when she was just fourteen—the reason he had hired Juliette as her governess.

The talk of building the holiday home in Darwin and being able to stay in touch with their friends was all Tessa could talk about last night. However, having another home to go to on holidays was something that Duncan often spoke of as well. They could afford to do it, so why shouldn't they? Tessa had shown her the photographs of the land and the builder's drawings of the proposed new home. They were simply perfect. She agreed that it should go ahead, and just as soon as possible. She was remembering their conversation of last night . . .

'Do you really like it, Mother?'

'I do, Tessa, very much so. Is the flat on the bottom floor for me, my darling?' Kasiah had asked.

'No, Mother. Of course not. You will always be upstairs with us. Downstairs will be for Tarni and Juliette. They may need to come with us when we go on holiday,' Tessa replied.

'When I'm older, Tessa, you may not want me with you all the time.'

'Don't say such things, Mother. I will always want you near me. Anyway, where would Tarni and Juliette stay if we didn't build the flat?

'I love you, Tessa,' Kasiah whispered.

'And I love you, Mother. Why are you behaving so silly? Have you been feeling lonely now that Father is gone?' Tessa asked.

'Perhaps I have, my dear. But I'm so glad you're back from your trip, though.'

'And now you're going off with Captain Nolan. Do you have to, Mother? I want to tell you so much more about our trip to Darwin and all the places we went to.' Tessa said, kissing her mother's cheek and putting her arm around her shoulders.

'When I get back, we will have plenty of time to talk, my darling. It's only for a few days. Your father always spent time checking on the boats and the men. It is something I have to do, Tessa,' Kasiah replied.

'Oh, alright then. Is Jago going with you?'

'Yes, he is. Why do you ask, Tessa?'

'It's just that Henry's a terrible driver. He's still learning.'

'You'll get by alright. Goodnight, my darling.'

'Goodnight, Mother,' Tessa replied, picking up the photographs and drawings of the new home. 'I'll see you in the morning before you leave.'

'You will, Tessa,' Kasiah said, kissing her daughter.

Just remembering their conversation of last night made Kasiah feel terrible. Perhaps the only sensible thing was to end her affair with Henry altogether and do it just as soon as possible. She must accept that she is alone in life now. She finished unpacking her suitcase, took off her shoes, and hurried up on deck to watch the crew preparing to get underway.

# Chapter 30

# The Eighty Mile

Late the following afternoon, the *Mina* reached the start of the eighty-mile beach area. The sea was calm, and the sky was cloudless. Up ahead, they could see one of the luggers drifting along with a diver down on the sea floor, searching for shell. It was the '*Gerta.*' Two men were working the hand-operated air pump. They could hear the steady click-clack as they drew closer and began furling their remaining sail and preparing to drop anchor.

Kasiah watched the lugger turn slowly into the light breeze. She saw a man go forward and drop anchor. Another man was standing ready on the starboard side. He was holding a rope and an airline. Kasiah watched him signal the diver below with a haul-up on the rope. He was a Koepanger man, bare-chested, with powerful brown arms. She watched him haul on the rope and airline in a steady, practiced action and then stop to allow the diver to decompress. She saw him relax his muscular arms and light his pipe. She watched the smoke drift off on the breeze.

Kasiah knew this man. His name was Haziz. She had never liked him. In the few times she had been in contact with him, he made her feel unclean. He would undress her with his eyes. Duncan never noticed. He'd been below deck each time it had happened. Duncan liked the man. He thought him strong, reliable, and trustworthy. Kasiah remembered him smiling at her and licking his lips several times. If Duncan had seen him do it, he would have killed him in an instant. Such was her husband's temper. She had watched him beat a crewman, bloody and sense-less, once, just for looking at her for what he considered was far too long.

A short while later, Captain Nolan lowered a dinghy, loaded it with fresh supplies, and sent it over to the lugger. A few minutes later, it returned with a huge load of pearl shell.

Jago went forward to help unload the unopened shell onto the deck of the schooner. When they finished, Kasiah watched him crouch and study the pearl shell. When he stood up, he came back to where she was standing.

'Some fella bin lookin' for pearls in them shells, Missus,' he said with an angry expression.

'How can that be? The shell is all unopened, Jago? We are to open it ourselves.'

Captain Nolan came across to see if everything was all right. 'Can I help with something?' he asked.

'Jago thinks one of the crew on that lugger may be trying to steal pearls from us.'

'How could he know that? The shell is all unopened, Kasiah.'

Kasiah turned to Jago. 'How can you tell, Jago?'

'Salt, Missus. Bits of course salt on some of them big shells.'

Captain Nolan left them and went to study the pearl shell himself. A short while later, he returned.

'Jago has a keen eye. He's right; there are a few grains of coarse salt on some of the larger shell,' he said to Kasiah in a lowered voice.

'What does that mean, John—?' Kasiah asked.

'Let me tell you what Jago thinks may have happened. But we can't be certain, Kasiah. At night, when everything is quiet and very still, the pearl shell opens and gasps out its remaining life. But if there is the slightest movement, it quickly snaps shut. If a crewman who is aware of this approaches the pile of shell very quietly and flicks a few grains of salt into some of them, they will be unable to close because they will be trying to rid themselves of the salt. That crewman can then use a piece of stick to hold a shell open and his fingers or a piece of thin wire to probe the shell in the hope of finding himself a nice pearl. When he removes the stick, the shell will close after a short while to conceal his crime.' Captain Nolan explained.

'So, you think someone on that lugger is trying to steal pearls from us?' Kasiah asked with an annoyed expression.

'It seems that *may* be the case, Kasiah.'

'John, I want you to take Jago with you and go over to that lugger and see what you can find.'

Jago was already standing at the side of the boat where the dinghy was tied.

'It'd be that, Haziz. He's tried this before, but we've never caught him with anything on him. I'll go straight over now and see what I can find.'

'Take Jago with you, John,' Kasiah instructed.

'Is that necessary, Kasiah? The men fear him. He might kill someone,' the captain replied.

'Take him with you, John.'

Captain Nolan went to where Jago was waiting, and both men clambered down into the dinghy. Jago took the oars, and the captain cast off.

Kasiah looked across the 100 yards that separated the two boats. Haziz had begun hauling on his rope again. A moment later, the heavy copper and brass helmet of a diver broke the surface in an eruption of bubbles.

* * *

Kasiah knew only too well that the practice of allowing a diver time to decompress while diving at depth was an important one and had to be followed very carefully. In the early days of diving, many men had died from the bends, as it was known. Pearl divers sometimes worked at depths of 35 fathoms or more. If a diver was brought back to the surface too quickly, the nitrogen in his bloodstream would begin to fizz and boil, causing him terrible pain, paralysis, or, often, death. Time was needed at varying depths while ascending to allow the diver's blood to slowly release the nitrogen and return to normal.

There were many instances when a diver had been brought up too quickly, whether through impatience on the diver's part or from the inexperience of the man holding his air and lifelines on the boat. Nitrogen poisoning would soon become obvious from the diver's bloated appearance, bulging eyes, and sudden spasms of crippling pain. Because there is no way to decompress a diver once he's on the boat and suffering, what was usually done then was for the backup diver to quickly suit up and take him back down to the bottom, stay with him for several hours, sometimes even overnight, and then slowly bring him back to the surface in stages in an attempt to save him from a very painful death.

*   *   *

Kasiah continued watching as the dinghy drew alongside the lugger, and Jago lifted the oars and laid them to one side. Captain Nolan climbed aboard the *Gerta*, followed a moment later by the man everyone on the boats and in the town of Broome was afraid of—the powerfully built, fearsome Jago.

*   *   *

Santiago, the captain of the *Gerta*, greeted them both with a pleasant smile.

Jago walked off to one side of the lugger and stood there looking back at the schooner. A moment later, he picked something up from the deck, looked at it casually for a moment or two and then slipped it behind his back into his belt.

Santiago put down the watermelon he was holding. He was wondering why Captain Nolan had returned to his lugger.

'We got no more shell for you, Cappun Nolan. Thank you for the good tucker, though. We like them pineapples and these watermelons,' he said to the tall white man who was their pearling fleet captain.

'Get the crew together, Santiago; I want to have a talk with them,' Captain Nolan replied to the smiling Koepanger captain.

Santiago barked a command, and a few moments later, six men were lined up next to their captain.

They were all Koepangers, except for the cook and the diver. Katakana, the diver, was Japanese, and Jan Li, the cook, was Chinese. Holo, one of the Koepangers, was the backup diver. Every one of them was now watching the swarthy Jago standing at the side of the boat near where the dinghy was tied and wondering why he had come on board.

Captain Nolan stared at the crew and was silent for a few moments while Haziz finished helping the Japanese diver out of his suit, and then he spoke in a stern voice.

'One of you fellas has been trying to steal pearls.'

'No, sir, Cappun Nolan . . . Nobody steal em pearls. I watch 'em pretty good alla time,' Santiago jabbered as he suddenly realised why Jago had come aboard.

'Me no steal em nothing! Me alla time bin cook,' Yan Li, the cook, cried out from the line of men.

'Each man is to empty his pockets on the deck in front of him right now,' Captain Nolan commanded. 'And when we are finished here, I will be searching your bunks.'

Each of the men fumbled through their pockets and laid the contents on the deck in a pitiful little heap next to their bare feet. Pocket knives, pieces of rag, good luck charms, matches, and clay pipes lay in front of each man.

Jago suddenly left the side of the boat and walked along the line of men, staring into their frightened eyes. When he got to Haziz, he stopped. His dark eyes burned into the Koepanger's very soul. He had seen something in his eyes.

'You empty pockets all out,' he said with a menacing stare.

'Already pockets all empty out, Mister Jago,' Haziz replied.

Jago swung the marlin spike out from behind his back and hit the Koepanger in the side of the head with the blunt end. Blood trickled down his cheek from the long cut.

'Take it easy, Jago. We have no idea if the man is a thief yet,' Captain Nolan called out suddenly.

Jago never turned or bothered to reply.

'You, empty pockets all out, or you dead man,' he whispered into Haziz's frightened eyes.

Haziz started to weep uncontrollably. He put his hand into his trouser pocket, pulled out a small, perfect pearl, and handed it to Jago.

'Me first time ever steal em pearl! Me alla time sorry now, Mister Jago. Me alla time real sorry,' the big Koepanger blubbered.

In a blur of movement, Jago grabbed the man's right hand and pulled it toward him. Using the heavy blunt end of the marlin spike again, he smashed it onto his hand, breaking all four of his fingers.

Haziz fell to the deck, screaming in agony and staring at his mutilated right hand.

Jago turned the marlin spike in his hand, knelt, and pushed the point against the Koepanger's throat. 'You finished with the Boss Missus now . . . I see you near her; I kill you! You understand?

'Me no go near boss missus, Mister Jago! Me plenty sorry,' Haziz whispered back, staring into Jago's dark, terrible eyes. Tears were streaming down the Koepanger's face.

Captain Nolan was shocked by what he had just seen. It had happened so quickly that he hadn't had time to intervene. His face was pale when he spoke to Santiago.

'You will haul anchor right now and set sail for Broome, Santiago. When you get there, you are to take Haziz to the hospital. He is finished with *Taylor House Pearls*. He will get no wages. The man is a known thief now. He will never get work on the boats again.'

'Yes sir, Cappun Nolan. We haul em anchor right now,' the Koepanger captain replied.

'You are to wait in Broome until I return.'

'Yes sir, Cappun Nolan.'

Captain Nolan and Jago went to the side of the lugger and climbed down into the dinghy.

When they returned to the schooner, Captain Nolan went directly to Kasiah.

Jago went to the stern and sat silently, looking out to sea.

'Jago was right, Kasiah. That bastard, Haziz, had this pearl in his pocket,' he announced, handing the tiny pearl to her.

'Thank you, John. I couldn't quite see what was going on from here. Was there much trouble?' Kasiah asked.

'That man of yours is a terrible brute, Kasiah. He broke the fingers of Haziz's right hand for stealing. It happened so fast that I was unable to do anything about it. His face will need stitches as well. The poor devil wet himself in front of his shipmates,' Captain Nolan replied.

'Is that all that happened?' Kasiah asked.

'I've instructed the lugger captain to haul anchor and sail for Broome immediately. They are to take Haziz to the hospital when they arrive. They are then to wait there until we return.'

'Thank you, John,' Kasiah replied.

'I'm sorry if you witnessed any of it, Kasiah.'

'Don't concern yourself, John. I know what Jago is capable of. Haziz is lucky to be alive. Jago knew I was watching, and that is the only reason he didn't kill him.'

'My God, Kasiah, I suppose you are right,' John replied. 'Is there any wonder the men fear him so?'

'It's already quite late, John. Will we be remaining at anchor here until morning?' Kasiah asked.

'I think we should. Most of the other luggers are quite a way up the eighty-mile, probably a good three hours from here. We'll leave early in the morning.'

'Thank you, John. Would you join me for dinner this evening?' Kasiah asked.

'I'd enjoy that, Kasiah. The cook has a couple of nice crayfish in the ice box. I've put a couple of bottles of that white wine you like in there as well,' the captain replied.

'In that case, John, I'll go and shower now and see you at seven if that suits you.'

'I'll look forward to it,' the captain replied, turning to leave, and then stopping. 'Will Jago be joining us?'

'Jago will take his meals with the crew, John,' Kasiah said with a matter-of-fact expression on her face.

'As you say, Kasiah,' Captain Nolan replied.

# Chapter 31

# To Fair Winds

At exactly seven o'clock, Captain John Nolan tapped on the owner's cabin door.

Kasiah went to the door and opened it. 'Good evening, John. Come in,' she said to the likable captain of her fleet.

John stepped inside. He was carrying two bottles of wine. He was followed by the schooner's Chinese cook, Zhang Wei, carrying a tray of wonderful-smelling food.

'Old Zhang Wei has done something special for you this evening, Kasiah,' John announced, guiding the old cook to the narrow table near the settee and putting down the bottles of wine.

'And what have you done for us, Wei?' Kasiah asked, helping him place the bamboo bowls of food on the table.

'I make a special dish for you, Missus. Do you remember when you and Mister Duncan first got married? I do this for you then.' the old man said, laying out the two special plates he kept for the owner's use. Both were made from delicate white China and were decorated at the bottom and around their rims with Chinese good-luck dragons. From one of the bamboo bowls, he scooped out his famous fried rice with a wooden ladle; from another, he used chopsticks to heap his special crayfish dish, *Lobster Yee Mein,* onto the plates. And then from a tiny China bowl, he added thin slices of pickled ginger. Finally, on the small amount of room left on the plates, he added a mango, shredded green pawpaw, cucumber, and green chilli salad, onto which he drizzled a dressing made with sesame oil, soy, palm sugar, and Chinese rice vinegar.

'Thank you, Wei. I do remember this dish and that night. It was delicious. Duncan and I were on our honeymoon. It was our first night on board the *Mina* together. It was a long time ago. How wonderful that you remembered,' Kasiah said to the old cook.

'You were a pretty young girl then, Missus. Now boss man is gone. You need a man again. Captain Nolly is a velly good man. He likey you velly much,' Zhang Wei said, smiling and putting the empty bamboo bowls back on his tray.

'Get out of here, you old scamp,' Captain Nolan said, his face flushed with embarrassment.

Zhang Wei bowed several times, smiled, and left the cabin.

'Sit down, John, and I'll pour the wine,' Kasiah said, smiling.

'Please disregard what old Zhang Wei just said, Kasiah,' John replied.

'Now that I'm alone, I suppose he thinks I must have a man to guide me all the time. It's the Chinese way of thinking.'

'I sincerely hope that you haven't taken offence?' John replied.

'Not at all, John. But I think we should eat this wonderful food before it gets cold,' Kasiah said, raising her wine glass.

'I agree,' John replied, picking up his glass. 'In that case, here's to fair winds and following seas.'

'To fair winds and following seas,' Kasiah repeated the toast and then sipped her wine.

As the evening progressed, Kasiah found her good friend John Nolan's company very enjoyable. It brought back memories of her wonderful marriage to Duncan and much simpler times. They seemed to have so much in common, in particular the pearling industry. Duncan and John were about the same age, and they'd been best friends. Kasiah had almost forgotten how handsome the swashbuckling skipper of the *Mina*, as he was affectionately known in Broome, was until just now.

John had been married long ago to a pretty young English

woman who left him because she couldn't take to the Broome lifestyle with its humid wet seasons, rainfall, and remoteness. She was never comfortable with some of the Aboriginal people of the town. Their constant drinking, foul language, and fighting in the streets disgusted her.

'Tell me, John, are you happy with your lot these days?'

'Do you mean with my job, Kasiah?' John asked with a puzzled expression.

'I suppose I do. That, among other things,' Kasiah replied, sipping her wine, and studying the man sitting opposite her.

'I love my job with you, Kasiah. I always have in the eight years I have skippered the *Mina*. You pay me well, and the pearl bonus you pay us all is greatly appreciated. Which makes me wonder why someone like Haziz would ever attempt to steal from you.'

'I'm pleased to hear that, John.'

'Are *you* happy with your life, Kasiah?' John asked.

'At this very moment, I'm not so sure, John. My life seems far too complicated.'

'It sounds to me like you're missing Duncan.'

'I think you may be right. He was the love of my life. We had known each other since we were children.'

'Duncan was my best friend, Kasiah. But I always envied him being married to you.'

'Thank you, John. How nice of you.'

'Are you having trouble with Tessa? I feel that something is troubling you, Kasiah.'

'No, I'm not. Tessa is my life now, John.'

'Perhaps it's young Henry Dawson? I must admit, he seems like a fine young man, a handsome fellow at that. But he has very little experience in our industry, Kasiah.'

'I don't think it's Henry, John,' Kasiah lied. 'Perhaps I just need a break away from Broome. I'm enjoying this trip and *your* company, though.'

'Please don't take this the wrong way, Kasiah. But I must tell you that I have had strong feelings for you for many years. If your life continues to feel directionless and troubling, I would gladly offer you my hand in marriage,' John Nolan announced.

'Why, thank you, John . . . You were Duncan's best friend, and I've always liked you. Perhaps it would be wise for me to accept. Few people in Broome have more knowledge of our industry than you. But some unsettled things are troubling me at the moment. Could you ask me again in a month or so?' Kasiah replied.

'Yes, of course. Take as long as you like,' John said, relieved that Kasiah Taylor was even considering his offer of marriage.

'Thank you, John. You have lifted my spirits,' Kasiah replied. 'But I think it's time for me to climb into my bunk and get some sleep now.'

John stood up. 'Goodnight, Kasiah. I hope you sleep well. We'll be sailing just after dawn. I'll have Zhang Wei bring you breakfast when you're dressed and ready.

'Goodnight, John.' Kasiah went to John, put her arms around him, and kissed his cheek.

'Please be patient with me, John, and I will give you my answer very soon,' she whispered to him.

'Yes, of course, and thank you for a wonderful evening, Kasiah. I'll see you in the morning then.'

After John left, Kasiah took off her clothes and climbed into one of the two narrow bunks that lined the walls of the owner's cabin. She pulled away the single blanket and tossed it on the other bunk. It was quite hot, and there was no breeze coming from the aft porthole at all. The sea seemed mostly calm, with just a slight rolling swell rocking the schooner. She turned the knob back tight on the kerosene lantern, and the flame died out. She covered her naked body with the sheet and lay back on her pillows.

As she lay there, she thought of John's offer of marriage. It would make a lot of sense for her to accept. He was closer to her age. She knew he had just turned 40. She was two years younger. He was a skilled captain, and he knew their industry well. She knew he had desired her for a long time. He was discreet and careful, but she had seen it in his eyes when he looked at her. She had felt it on his lips when he kissed her cheek and, in his fingers, when he touched her hand. A woman knows when a man is attracted to her. She had feelings for him as well, but that's all they were—just feelings, just thoughts of what could be. After all, she was a woman, and John Nolan was a very handsome man.

Yes, it would be sensible for her to accept his offer of marriage. It would be accepted locally. He had been Duncan's best friend. Not that she had ever cared what the local people thought. She was a black woman, and she had grown up in a white man's town. But it would make a lot of sense. They could be seen together. They could dine together at the local hotels. All of the simple things that she couldn't do with Henry. She could even learn to love him. Surely, it was possible.

And then Kasiah thought of Henry and their lovemaking. It was always so wonderful. The way he kissed her; the way he touched her body with his hands and with his fingers. The way he kissed her mouth, her breasts, and her eyes. Sometimes, when they made love, it was as if they were one complete and wonderful being.

Henry loved her so completely, so absolutely, and now she had fallen in love with him in return. But it was always doomed to fail. After all, he was married to Tessa, her beloved daughter.

Kasiah knew then, at that very moment, that she must end it. Henry wasn't capable of doing it. He would be hurt terribly, but it must be done . . . It had to be done . . . He would eventually understand that it was for the best for both of them. Tessa must never find out what happened between them. It would break her heart. She would accept John Nolan's offer of marriage, and she would learn to love him. It was the sensible thing to do.

# Chapter 32

# A Cock-Eyed Bob

Just before dawn the following morning, Kasiah was woken from a deep, restful, wonderful sleep by an urgent tapping on her cabin door. She'd been dreaming of Duncan. She got up, wrapped a sheet around herself, hurried to the door, and opened it.

Captain John Nolan had a very worried look on his face.

'Good morning, Kasiah.'

'Good morning, John.'

'I have some rather unpleasant news. The bottom has fallen out of the glass. I think we are in for some rather rough weather. If you would like to dress, I'll have Zhang Wei bring you coffee up on deck.'

'Thank you, John. I'll get dressed and see you shortly then,' Kasiah replied.

The captain closed the cabin door and rushed away.

Kasiah hurried to her bed, dropped the sheet, and started to dress. It was still stiflingly hot in the cabin. There was no breeze coming through the cabin porthole at all. She slipped on a loose-fitting white cotton blouse, underwear, and a red sarong. Then she left the cabin and hurried barefoot up to the deck.

The sea seemed quiet and gentle in the pre-dawn light, as it had during the night. Their accompanying crested terns had all disappeared. It was strangely silent and unnerving. Kerosene lanterns

263

were burning in brackets along the deck and on the binnacle. Worried men were scrambling to unfurl sails and preparing to get underway. Kasiah could hear the rattle of the windlass lifting the forward anchor in the darkness. She went over to where Captain Nolan was in deep conversation with the bosun. They both turned to face her with concerned looks on their faces.

'Are we in for it, John?' She asked.

'I think we are, Kasiah. It's a cock-eyed-bob that's come out of nowhere. We're double-lashing everything down and setting sail for the rest of the luggers to see if we can get into a creek somewhere south of here and ride it out,' the captain replied.

Kasiah looked out over the port side. In the distance, she could just make out what was racing toward them through the dawn's early light. A terrible black thing covered the distant horizon, rolling and moving in on itself as it intensified and thundered toward them.

'Can we manage to get clear of it?' Kasiah asked, a worried expression flooding her face. The wind had suddenly picked up. The sails that had already been set luffed and filled, and the *Mina* swung about, and they headed briskly away.

'We should be fine if we can make a decent headway. This breeze may be just what we need. I have to go, Kasiah. I'll come back and see you just as soon as I can, Captain Nolan said with a hopeful smile. He turned, and he and the bosun hurried away to check the lashing down of loose items on the deck.

Kasiah went forward. She found a protected position near the dinghy and sat down on a coil of rope. In the distance, she could now clearly see the rolling black cyclone thundering relentlessly toward them through the grey dawn. A few minutes later, dark clouds began racing over them, and then it started to rain, lightly at first, and a few moments later, it began pouring down.

For the next hour, they sped toward the southwest and the rest of the fleet. Their hopes were high. Fifteen minutes after that, the cyclone caught them. It came at them as a strong wind and stinging spray at first, and then they felt its full fury as mountainous waves caught up to them and began crashing into the schooner. The sleek, well-built boat was thrown about like a child's toy.

Captain Nolan stayed with the bosun at the helm and ordered him to turn the *Mina* into the wind. At the same time, he called for the reefing of the mainsail and the foresail and the setting of a storm jib.

Men scrambled into the wildly rolling rigging. They were about two miles offshore, and already they could see the mountainous surf in the distance. They must drive into the wind and keep clear of the shore and the surf. It was their only hope.

Jago suddenly appeared next to Kasiah in the wind and lashing rain.

'Come with me, Missus,' he yelled at the top of his voice, grabbing her hand.

'I'm going back to my cabin, Jago,' Kasiah cried out in fearful reply.

'Cabin no good, Missus,' Jago yelled back, pulling Kasiah along behind him.

A huge wave suddenly crashed over the starboard side of the schooner and hit both of them. Kasiah lost her footing and slid across the deck toward the port side. She hit the railing at the same time as she felt Jago's powerful arm around her waist. She felt him lift her and carry her across the swaying deck to the mainmast.

'You hold on tight to the mast, Missus, storm soon gunna get worse,' he yelled to her.

Kasiah grabbed hold of a loop of rope connected to the base of the mainmast and held on. She was terrified. She watched Jago go to the railing and look back at the terrifying darkness that was almost upon them.

A short while later, Captain Nolan called for anchors to be dropped fore and aft. The cyclone was now driving them inexorably back toward the beach. The *Mina* would be smashed to pieces in the now-mountainous surf if they weren't able to stop her travelling astern. Now and then, when the wind allowed, Kasiah could hear the bosun bellowing commands to the crew and the faint rattle of the forward windlass.

For a while, the anchors held against the full force of the sea and wind. And then, with a terrible screech, the cables parted. One of them flew back across the deck and struck and instantly killed an unfortunate crewman in its path. He fell to the deck and was swept away into the boiling sea. A moment later, Kasiah saw another member of the crew struggle over to the railing to search for his shipmate in the waves. She watched him shake his head with grief and struggle away again.

The wind was screaming through the rigging now—a terrible, frightening sound. A huge wave suddenly lifted the schooner and turned her broadside into the full fury of the cyclone. Kasiah knew then that John must have lost all control. She clung desperately to her loop of rope and prayed. A moment later, the boat dropped into a great, cavernous valley of water, only to be lifted again and smashed by yet another monstrous wave. The sturdy, well-built *Mina* was starting to break up.

The yards broke first and fell into the sea, and then a terrible, rending sound filled Kasiah's ears as the foremast snapped and dropped into the sea as well. The sleek schooner was beginning to surrender to the might of the powerful cyclone.

Kasiah was still holding onto her rope, but she was crying now out of terrible fear as the deck rolled and lurched wildly beneath her. In one moment, she was sitting with her back braced against the mainmast and her feet against a deck block. In the next, she was hanging sideways across the deck but always clinging desperately to her loop of rope.

Suddenly, out of the gloom and driving rain, Kasiah saw the bosun. He was running to help her. John must have taken the helm and sent him to find her. A massive wave came crashing over the port side of the boat, and the bosun was gone, washed overboard. Kasiah screamed in desperation and huddled against the mast like a frightened child.

A moment later, Jago appeared. He was carrying rope to lash them both to the mainmast. As he struggled towards her, another great wave came up over the side of the boat. It came at him like a terrible, curling sea monster crashing down on him, smashing him to the deck and across the boards. Kasiah watched in horror as Jago too disappeared into the sea, leaving his rope slithering uselessly across the deck and dropping into the sea after him.

Kasiah screamed into the wind again. But no one could hear her!

The *Mina* suddenly fell sideways into another deep trough, and then another massive wave smashed against the starboard side. Just for a moment, she lifted with the wave, righted herself, turned downwind, and raced away like a hound fleeing its angry master.

Kasiah held onto the mainmast rope with every ounce of strength she had. Huge, terrible waves tore past her, lifting the schooner higher and higher. They were racing headlong, like some broken skeletal thing, for the distant shore and the now-mountainous surf . . . A moment later, another mighty wave came crashing up over the stern. Kasiah hadn't seen it coming. It smashed into her, tearing her away from the mainmast like a rag doll, lifting her across the deck and into the boiling sea. It drove her down below the surface, and then it lifted her again. When she came up, she gasped for breath and kicked away from the dying schooner with powerful strokes. Kasiah had spent her life by the sea. She was a powerful swimmer.

The *Mina* was now broadside into the storm again and breaking up quickly. Pieces of the sleek boat were flying through the air, driven by the insane wind: a broken spar, a piece of ripped sail, empty drums, empty crates, and pearl shell flying about like cannon balls.

Kasiah noticed the dinghy in the waves. It must have broken its lashings somehow. Another wave lifted her. She struck out for the dinghy, only to watch the mainmast smash it to pieces as the *Mina* rolled onto her side and began to sink.

Suddenly, Jago was with her. He was holding onto a broken part of a deck hatch cover. She was lifted again, and when the wave fell, he was beside her, forcing her to take the hatch cover. She looked into his eyes. It gave her hope. She grabbed the hatch cover and held on as they both swooped down into another great trough.

When she came up, she was still holding on to the hatch cover, but Jago had disappeared in the waves!

Kasiah had never been so frightened in all her life. The broken hatch cover Jago had given her was her only hope. She clung desperately to it as another great wave came at her.

*   *   *

Several hours later, the sea and the sky grew black, and a frightening darkness fell over the ocean. The waves were still smashing relentlessly into Kasiah's weary body, lifting her, and tossing her about, but she was still grimly holding onto her hatch cover. With the rise and fall of each terrible wave, she searched for Jago in the darkness, but he had disappeared. She was so grateful that he had given her something to hold on to. But in doing so he had nothing to hold onto himself. She hoped that his unerring devotion to her safety had not cost him his life.

The noise of the wind and the crashing of the waves were now like some terrible nightmare for Kasiah. Sometimes, as she was hurled down into another great valley of a wave, things bumped into her. Was it fish or pieces of the broken *Mina* . . . She dared not release her grip on her hatch cover to find out.

# Chapter 33

# A Song on the Beach

All through that dark, terrible night, Jago searched for Kasiah in the waves. Somehow, he was certain that he must be close to her, but try as he might, he could not find her. Once, in the darkness, something bumped against him.

'Is that you, Missus?' he screamed out, reaching about in the racing water with his hands and his feet, but it was just a piece of broken spar about three feet long. He grabbed for it and held on as he was lifted over the top of another great wave.

Jago felt no fear for himself, but he feared for Kasiah. He must find her. He must save her. He must not let her drown. He clung to his broken spar as he raced down into another great valley of churning seawater. In the darkness, he prayed to Allah that she still had her broken hatch cover. If she held onto it, it would save her.

* * *

Early the following morning, Jago was still clinging grimly to his piece of broken spar and searching for Kasiah in the waves when he noticed someone in a dinghy rowing towards him.

'Jago, is that you there?' He heard the rower bellow out to him above the screaming wind.

He knew that voice well. 'Yes, Boss, it's me, Jago,' he yelled back, clinging desperately to his broken spar.

It was Duncan Taylor!

'Where's my Kasiah, Jago?' Duncan yelled.

'She'll be all right, Boss. I gave her something to hold on to,' Jago called back.

'Find her, Jago. You must save her. Do not let her drown. Do you hear me? Do not let her drown,' Duncan screamed when he got to him.

'I hear you, Boss. I'm sorry about the snake,' Jago said to the man he loved more than he had loved his own father.

'Find her, Jago. You must not let her drown.' Duncan Taylor cried into the mad, insane wind.

Jago watched him row over the crest of the next wave and then disappear. He clung to his broken spar as the same wave lifted him high and then jettisoned him down the other side and into another great trough of racing water. He looked about for Duncan, but he had disappeared.

*   *   *

Several hours later, Jago noticed a long fold of sail and rope lift on a wave and roll by him. He looked about for Kasiah, hoping to see her clinging to her hatch cover, but she wasn't there. He mumbled another prayer to Allah and hoped that she was safe.

The waves no longer seemed so huge to him now, more like great rolling green hills against the dull grey metallic sky. He watched the fold of sail and rope race ahead of him toward the distant shore. Several small fish were following it, their tail fins breaking the surface.

A short while later, Jago thought he could hear the surf breaking onto a beach somewhere ahead of him. He let the next wave lift him. In the distance, he could just see the dull white of the sand hills. He let go of the spar and swam with all his might for the shore. Several minutes later, he felt sand beneath his feet. He tried to stand . . . The spar suddenly glided past him.

'You come back here,' he screamed at his broken spar.

A sudden rip started to drag him back into deeper water again. He waited for the next wave; when it came, he struck out and swam with the last of his remaining strength.

His father swam past him.

'Allah is with you, my son,' his father called to him.

'Allah be with you, father,' Jago called back to his father.

He kept swimming until, at last, he could feel the sand beneath his feet again. He looked along the surf for his father, but he had disappeared!

Another wave lifted him, driving him forward into the frothy shallows. He staggered through the foam onto the beach and collapsed on the wet sand. It was raining; he could feel it falling on his back and legs. He lifted his weary head. He could now see low, stunted bushes and white sandhills beyond the beach. He had made it. He was alive. He closed his eyes and thanked his god.

* * *

A while later, Jago woke. He wasn't sure if he'd been sleeping or if he'd been unconscious. The storm had subsided now. It was moving away toward the west. It was quieter. He rolled onto his side and looked around. The rain had completely stopped. Pieces of the *Mina* lay along the edge of the waterline. Some of it was rolling about in the surf. Dead and dying fish were everywhere. A stingray was flapping feebly next to a short length of frayed rope near where he lay.

He struggled to his feet and looked down at himself. His shirt had been torn from his body. The legs of his trousers were split and torn to his hips. His shoes and socks were gone. His thick leather belt was still around his waist, but his knife was gone.

He started to stagger along the beach.

A body lay near some broken bits of the dinghy. It was the old Chinese cook, Zhang Wei. He was with his maker now. He dragged the old man's body up onto the beach so the crabs couldn't get to him so easily and continued along the beach.

A huge piece of torn sail was rolling about against the water's edge a little further along. A small reef shark was caught in the canvas, its tail thrashing this way and that as it tried to escape the confines of the canvas and get back into deeper water. Further up, an oar from the dinghy lay on the beach, covered in long strands of dark seaweed. The rowlock was still connected to it. He remembered using it to row across from the *Mina* to the lugger just yesterday.

He staggered on. Another body was lying covered in broken weed near the shoreline, but much further up. He felt weak, but he kept going, and then he stopped. Tears poured down his dark cheeks as he dropped to his knees and screamed at his merciless god . . . It was Kasiah!

The storm had ripped away the clothing from her coal-black body. Seaweed torn from the depths of the ocean covered her face and shoulders . . . She was dead.

Jago went to her. He pulled the strands of weed away from her and lifted her gently into his arms. Her beautiful face fell against his chest. He carried her into the sea and washed the sand and remaining strands of weed away from her body. Then he washed her dark, staring eyes free of the sand and grit that had filled them. As he washed her, he sang an old, gentle song to her in Arabic that his mother had taught him when he was a boy and faced with the loss of a loved one. As he sang, he kissed Kasiah's forehead and closed her eyes with his fingers. Then, he lifted her into his arms again and carried her from the sea and off the beach into a little gully he had seen in the sandhills surrounded by low, windswept bushes. He laid her down gently and removed the strange pendant from her neck and put it in his pocket. He would rest now, and then he would bury her deep in the ground so that no animal could ever reach her.

Just as he had failed to save Duncan from the snake, he had failed to save Kasiah from death as well. He wished now that the sea had taken him. He had loved them both, and now they were gone from his worthless life forever.

He lay back and wept.

*   *   *

Later that afternoon, Jago tore low bushes from the banks of the little gully and placed them over Kasiah's naked body to keep away the birds, then he left her and went down to the beach again.

A light rain was falling, and the sea was almost calm. He found the oar he'd seen before and dragged it up onto the beach. Then he waded in and untied a piece of sail from a broken piece of the yard. Sea birds were screeching and feeding on the dead fish in the surf and along the beach. He looked back to where he had left Kasiah's body. There were no birds near her. He continued along the beach. More of the broken *Mina* lay along the shoreline: empty drums, broken pieces of the dinghy, a weed-covered cork lifebuoy, all manner of things.

Zhang Wei's body still lay where he had left it. He found another smaller piece of canvas and covered his face to stop the birds from taking his eyes. He would bury him later. He walked along the beach for a while longer, looking for more bodies, but there were none. He found a good length of rope lying in some weed. He picked it up and cleared away the weed. As he worked, he looked out to sea and thought of the *Mina* and her crew.

Only he had survived. Apart from the old cook and Kasiah, the rest must have gone down with her. He whispered a prayer to Allah for thanks that he had been spared. But he would gladly have given his life so that Kasiah could have lived.

A little further along, he found an old bailer shell on the beach. It was brimming with rainwater. He picked it up and drank the brackish-tasting water.

Jago carried his finds back to the little gully in the sandhills where he had left Kasiah's body. He carefully laid out the canvas sheet and lifted her naked body onto it. He arranged her legs together and her arms against her sides and tidied her long, dark hair as best he could. Then he pulled away the few twigs that had fallen onto her from the bushes. To Jago, she looked as if she were sleeping. He bent down and kissed her forehead one last time, and then he wrapped her in the canvas sheet and bound her with the rope. When he finished, he got up, picked up the oar, and began to dig.

It was almost dark when he finished the grave. He threw the

oar to the ground, climbed out, and lifted Kasiah's canvas-bound body gently in his arms. Then he carried her down to her final resting place.

For a while, he sat next to her, a terrible loneliness now gripping his mind and his soul. A while later, he stood up. Tears filled his eyes. He climbed from the grave and set about tearing more bushes from the edge of the little gully and covering Kasiah's body with them. He knew he couldn't bear to throw sand directly onto her. When he was finished, he stood silently, looking down at the pathetic, eternal resting place of the woman he had loved just as much as he had loved her husband. Tears poured down his dark cheeks as he fell to his knees and began scooping sand onto the bushes that now covered her.

When Jago had finally finished, it was dark, and his fingers were bleeding from the sand and the oar. He went to the head of the grave and stood there silently for a while, and then he sang a gentle Arabic prayer song to the woman now buried deep in the earth. When he finished his song, he laid the oar on top of her grave. He was weary now. He had done all that he could. He lay down to sleep alongside the grave.

The following morning, Jago woke from a troubled night. Duncan Taylor had visited him in his dreams, cursing him again and again for not saving his wife. The snake that had killed him was with him. In his dream, he killed the snake again by tearing its ugly head from its evil, sinuous body and then eating its flesh. But the head soon grew back, and the snake laughed at him. Then it slithered down the beach and disappeared into a black, terrible sea.

It was just before dawn when Kasiah visited him. She was dressed in a pretty white blouse and a bright red sarong. She was beautiful. The sea beyond her was still and quiet. She went to him and put her arms around him, just as she had done when she thanked him for taking Tessa to the hospital. She smiled and kissed his bleeding hands from digging her grave.

'Jago, you must take the *Mata Jahat* and give it to my Tessa now,' she whispered as she held him. 'It carries my everlasting love within it.'

Jago watched her take the strange pendant from around her neck and hand it to him. She was smiling when she spoke again, but her eyes were filled with sand.

'I know you tried to find me in the storm, Jago. I heard you calling to me, but it was already too late. I have always loved you, Jago,' she whispered, kissing his cheeks again.

When Jago woke, he got to his feet. His back and arms were aching from digging. He looked down at the grave. The sand above the grave was a different colour than the ground around it now, but there was nothing he could do to change that. A terrible sadness was threatening to overwhelm his sanity. He reached down, picked up the oar, and went down to the beach again. More of the *Mina* had been washed up during the night. A section of the forward mast and a part of a sail lay along the water's edge. Broken pieces of the hull were rolling about in the low waves, but there were no more bodies . . . Now he would bury the old cook.

As he stood next to the old man's body, he noticed something green sticking up out of the water, just beyond the broken mast and canvas. To Jago, it looked like plants growing in the surf. He went down to the waterline and waded out to see what it was. He smiled when he got there. It was pineapples—two of them bobbing about near the canvas. He carried them back to the shore.

*   *   *

Three hours later, Jago had buried the old cook, Zhang Wei, in a shallow grave in the sandhills. He could manage no better than what he'd done. His hands were bleeding much worse now, and his body was aching from the work. When he finished, he went further up into the low sandhills and found a shady spot. He was thirsty and hungry. He would rest for a while.

When he woke, some of his strength had returned. He went down to the beach to wash his bleeding hands in the seawater and try to find something to cut open one of the pineapples. He found a piece of steel strap fastened to the broken forward mast. He bent it back and tried to snap it off, but it wouldn't break. He left it. He would try again when his hands felt stronger. He waded out of the water and walked along the shoreline, searching through the flotsam. He found a dead flathead that the birds hadn't torn completely apart near a section of the dinghy and picked it up. A little further along, he picked up an old seashell. It had a broken edge that was quite sharp. He carried the fish and the shell back to his shade. Using the sharp edge of the shell, he cut open one of the pineapples and ate a part of it. Then he used it to cut open the flathead, slicing off pieces and wolfing them down. When he was finished, he ate the rest of the pineapple, its sweet juice quenching his thirst.

Then Jago lay back, rested, and tried to work out what he should do. Should he stay where he was and wait for someone to find him, or should he head off along the beach toward Broome?

Jago knew that Broome was at least a hundred miles away, but when the news of the loss of the *Mina* spread, search parties would be sent out to look for survivors. Some would leave from Broome and some from the remote sheep stations inland from the eighty-mile beach. At least he hoped that would be the case. He decided he would spend the rest of that day searching through the flotsam along the beach for anything useful, and in the morning, he would head off in the general direction of Broome.

After he had rested for a while, he went down to the water-line again and worked on the steel strap he had seen before until it broke away. Using the piece of strap, he cut away a section of the canvas sail, about six feet square, and then a much smaller piece. He would use the larger piece as a shelter and as a cloak to keep the fierce sun off of him as he walked. In among the floating debris, he found two more pineapples, but there was little else of any use to him. Later that afternoon, he found a small, half-alive stingray trapped beneath another shroud of canvas. He bashed it to death with a broken piece of the dinghy and carried it back to his shade for his dinner.

The following morning, Jago ate what remained of his sting-ray and then half of a pineapple. He made a carry bag from the smaller piece of sail and attached a makeshift strap. He filled it with his few belongings—his piece of steel, several sharp seashells, his bailer shell, and his remaining pineapples—and hung it over his shoulder. The larger piece of canvas he draped over his head and shoulders to shade himself from the sun. He was ready to leave.

He looked back toward the little gully where he had buried Kasiah two days before and whispered a loving prayer to her in Arabic. Jago knew that when the winds blew along this desolate, uninhabited part of the coastline and the tides rose and fell, they would spread the debris from the *Mina* for miles along the remote beach. He would never be able to find this place again or guide anyone to it. Strangely, that thought comforted him. He turned and set off along the beach toward Broome, more than a hundred miles distant.

*   *   *

The following day, just as he was about to set off again, a light rain started to fall. Jago dropped to his knees on the beach and scooped out a shallow hole in the sand. He laid his canvas cape on the ground and pushed it into the depression. Then he scooped up wet sand to put on each of the corners and waited. He hadn't tasted water for two days. His pineapples were gone now, and he was suffering.

A short while later, his canvas hollow started to fill. He reached into his carry bag and took out his bailer shell, scooped up the precious water, and drank it down until it was all gone, and then he waited for more to fill his little hollow. After he had drunk the last of the water, he stood up, shook the sand from his cape, and pulled it over his head and shoulders, enjoying the wet canvas where it touched him.

He looked along the beach into the shimmering distance into which he must travel. He was alone, and his world was a barren, lonely place. He set off again, thankful for the rain that had just quenched his thirst and kept him alive for a while longer.

As he walked, the only food he could find along the barren coastline was hermit crabs. Now and then, he would stop when he found one of their little round holes above the waterline. He would dig them out, crush them with his fingers, and eat them, legs, and all.

Later, in the heat of that day, Jago was visited again by Duncan Taylor.

'You must keep going, Jago. You have a long way to go. You must take care of my Tessa now. Do you hear me, Jago?' Duncan instructed him as he walked beside him.

'I hear you alright, Boss. I bin lookin after her for a long time now. I stopped her bleedin and took her to the hospital real quick, Boss,' Jago mumbled back.

'You couldn't stop that snake from killing me, though, Jago. And now, you have let my Kasiah drown. You have let me down badly, Jago,' he heard Duncan say.

'I can't talk no more, Boss. I gotta keep goin. I've got something in my pocket for Miss Tessa,' Jago whispered through cracked lips and stumbled on.

'You have let me down, Jago . . . You have let my beautiful Kasiah drown in the waves . . .

# Part 5

280

# Chapter 34

# An Old Photograph

Dawson House, Darwin.
1997

Charlotte Dawson put aside the old journal. How sad Henry's story had become. Kasiah was dead, drowned in a terrible storm, and buried in a nameless grave on a desolate coast. A grave no one would ever be able to find; no place for those who loved her to visit, no place to say a prayer or to leave flowers—only the lonely waves of the 80-mile beach and the ghost of old Zhang Wei to keep her company.

She slid out of the nook and went to her bedroom. There were tears in her eyes. She opened her bedside cupboard and took out the old box of letters and bits and pieces that Henry had left in his safe with his journal. She had read some of the letters that Henry had written to Tessa and others that Tessa had written back. Some had been in bundles and held together with ancient rubber bands that broke easily when she undid them.

Charlotte knew she would never be able to sell the old house now. It was so full of her family's secrets and memories. She lifted out the letters and paperwork she had already looked at and put them aside. There were only a few other things left in the old shoebox. One was a large, yellowed business envelope, which she opened. Inside were several sheets of a draftsman's plans and perspective drawings of the house she now owned. Included was a sheet of costs, suggestions, and details. The attached letter was headed by *Dale Thompson, General Builder, Darwin, and dated May 20, 1920.* Charlotte studied the plans. She wondered if the secret room beneath the home was drawn in, and it was. A separate page showed in careful detail how the narrow passage was to be concealed behind the bookshelves in the room noted as the sitting room. She put the plans and costs aside.

There was only one more item remaining at the bottom of the shoe box. It was another old, badly yellowed envelope. She picked it up carefully and opened it. Inside was a single, very old photograph. She slid it out slowly. Before she turned it, she read the faded words on the back.

*This is the last photograph I have of my beloved mother. I took it with the new camera I bought for our very first trip to Darwin. It was taken on the morning she left to go on our schooner, the Mina, to sail to the eighty-mile with Captain Nolan and deliver supplies to the luggers. The Mina was caught in a terrible cyclone not long after, and Mother never returned to us. It broke my heart. Tessa Dawson.*

Charlotte turned it over and stared at the somewhat yellowed old photograph. Kasiah Taylor was standing in front of a very beautiful motorcar. She was smiling at her daughter while she took the photograph. It was a frozen moment in time from more than seventy years ago. A dark, heavily built man was sitting behind the steering wheel of the motor car. He was bald-headed and stern-faced. This would have been Jago, the man who buried her in the sandhills all those long years ago. The magnificent old motorcar was parked in the shade of a huge flame tree. A thin Aboriginal man wearing baggy trousers and braces was standing in the distant background holding a rake—more than likely one of the gardeners.

Charlotte wished dearly that the photograph could have been in colour. But Kasiah Taylor was certainly very beautiful, even in black and white. She was a tall, proud, and perfectly proportioned woman. Her skin was as black as coal. Her dark hair was tied back from her beautiful face with a glittering clasp of some sort, possibly made from pearl shell and gold. She was dressed in a long, flowing silk kaftan that shone in the early morning light. Her dark arms were bare, and she wore simple leather sandals on her feet. Her eyes were dark and mysterious. They seemed to be smiling and yet sad at the same time. A handsome young man was standing by her side. From the expression on his face, it was obvious that he was not happily farewelling her. That man would be Henry Dawson, Charlotte's grandfather's brother. The old photograph perfectly portrayed the confusion Henry was feeling at that very moment. There was something in his eyes that told Charlotte everything that she already knew. So clearly, it was there—wonderful love, guilt, sadness, and confusion. But Kasiah's face was very different. Only love could be seen in her beautiful smile. A mother's love for the woman taking the photograph.

Charlotte wondered if Tessa ever knew of the love affair between her beloved mother and her husband. She hoped in her heart that she hadn't. She slid the photo back into its yellowed envelope and put it aside. She would have it restored and put into a nice silver frame. When it was done, she would place it on one of the shelves in the sitting room. She was certain that it shouldn't remain hidden away at the bottom of an old shoebox. She put the letters and paperwork back in the old shoebox and slipped it into her bedside cupboard. She got up, undressed, and climbed into bed. She needed to get some sleep. Tomorrow morning, Jeremy Bolton was to start the renovation work on the house. She was to meet with him to select bathroom and kitchen tiles from the samples he was bringing that he had promised were very close to the original ones.

Charlotte closed her eyes. She knew she was going to dream of a terrible storm at sea and a beach lined with wreckage. And a man digging a lonely grave in the sandhills.

284

# Chapter 35

# A Little Velvet Box

## Dawson House

It was a little over six months later that the renovations on Henry Dawson's old home were finally complete.

For Charlotte, the time went by very quickly. She had opened her little office on the ground floor of Paul Rosenberg's building in the city some months ago now. Each morning, she drove into the city in her new car, opened her office, and spent the morning reading the financial pages of the newspapers and trying to understand the complicated wonders of the financial world. Often, she would have paperwork to be updated and checked with Dawson House Holdings, dividends to be transferred into her various bank accounts, and taxation obligations to be taken care of. On occasion, she would need to see Paul Rosenberg briefly for legal opinions and help. Sometimes she would have lunch with him at a nearby restaurant that they both liked. She and Paul had become close friends. Often on weekends, she would spend time with him and his wife at their home. Paul often invited friends that he thought she might be romantically interested in, but no one that she met seemed her type. They were mostly successful businessmen or bank people. Charlotte preferred men with an outdoor persuasion. At two o'clock each afternoon, she would lock her office and drive home. On this particular day, when she arrived home, she was excited. All the work on the old home was going to be finally completed.

She went inside, made herself a cup of coffee, sat down in the little nook, and chatted with Alice. Outside, David was cutting back some of the red bougainvillea from the freshly painted arbour near the cane palms.

*   *   *

A short while later, Jeremy Bolton parked his Land Cruiser utility in the driveway of the old home. He had something to show Charlotte. He grabbed his satchel from the passenger seat and climbed out.

'The gardens are looking just great, David,' he said to the gardener as he hurried past and started up the steps.

'Thank you, Jeremy.' David called back, bending to pick up some of the thorny cuttings.

A painter was putting the finishing touches on the new white veranda railings as Jeremy went past. 'Good morning, Jeremy,' the painter said, smiling.

'It's looking great, Syd. Are you still going to be all finished today?' Jeremy asked.

'We'll be gone within an hour. I have two men finishing the woodwork in the flat downstairs at the moment,' the painter replied.

'Glad to hear it, Syd. It's been quite a job.'

'It certainly has,' Syd replied.

Jeremy knocked on the door. A moment later, Alice opened it and ushered him inside.

'Come in, Jeremy. Charlotte is waiting for you in the kitchen. I'll get you a cup of coffee.'

'Good morning, Alice, and thank you. That's just what I need.' Jeremy replied, following Alice to the kitchen.

Charlotte was sipping her second cup of coffee in the little nook. She slid out and stood up.

'Good afternoon, beautiful,' Jeremy said, kissing her on the cheek.

'Good afternoon, Jeremy. You'll have Alice thinking something is going on between us with talk like that,' Charlotte replied, smiling and sitting down again.

'Well, it's not from a lack of trying on my part,' Jeremy said, taking the mug of coffee from a smiling Alice.

'You just keep trying, Jeremy. You're starting to wear her down. She never looks happy unless you're around the place somewhere,' Alice declared.

'Only when the house is finished, Alice. I told Jeremy last week that we could go to dinner somewhere nice as a celebration when his work is all done,' Charlotte replied.

'Well, it's finally finished, or at least it will be in an hour or so. So how about tomorrow night I pick you up and we go somewhere nice and enjoy ourselves?' Jeremy asked.

I'd love to, Jeremy. And to be honest with you, I've been looking forward to this very moment. Now, what have you got there?'

Jeremy opened his satchel and slid out a cardboard carton.

'The knobs for the kitchen cupboards have finally arrived from Singapore.'

'Are they the same as the old ones?'

'Exactly the same. What do you think of them?' Jeremy asked, passing one to Charlotte.

'Oh, I love them. Thank you for going to all the trouble, Jeremy. Will you be putting them on today?'

'I certainly will be. I've just spoken to Syd outside, and he tells me he'll be all finished in an hour or so. Once I have these knobs on, I'll be all done as well. It's a big day, Charlotte. Are you pleased with it all?' Jeremy asked.

'I'm very happy with it. You have done a remarkable job. Alice and I finished putting up the curtains in the flat last night. It looks lovely down there as well,' Charlotte replied.

'Has your mother sold her home down in Adelaide yet?' Jeremy asked.

'Not yet. But she told me last night that there's someone interested in it at the moment. If it all goes through, she should be up here quite soon.'

'She'll be very comfortable down there now that it is all done. The new kitchen and bathroom look just great,' Jeremy added.

'I'm sure she will love it, Jeremy. Now, do you have your final account in that bag of tricks of yours?'

'I do, Charlotte, and thank you for trusting me with this job. It's by far the biggest renovation I have ever done. Six and a half long months of hard work,' Jeremy said, passing his final account across the table.

'I'll get my chequebook just as soon as I've finished my coffee. Thank you so much for what you have done with the old place. It has turned out even better than I ever imagined it would. I'm sure Henry would have liked it just as much as I do.

'I'm certain he would have, Charlotte,' Jeremy replied with a proud smile.

What do you think, Alice?' Charlotte asked the Aboriginal woman, who had become her close friend.

'He would have loved it, Miss Charlotte, and so would have his dear wife, Tessa,' Alice called back from the brand-new kitchen sink.

'Come and sit down, Alice. I have something to show you both.'

Alice wiped her hands, came over, and sat in the little nook. Jeremy did the same.

'What is it, Miss Charlotte?' Alice asked.'

'Last night I was going through the odds and ends in the bedside cupboards in Tessa's old bedroom, and I found this,' Charlotte said, pushing a small jeweller's box across the table.

'What have you found—? In all the time I have been here, Henry has never allowed me to go into that room. He always did the cleaning and dusting in there himself,' Alice remarked, picking up the tiny box. 'I vacuumed in there this morning, but I never touched anything.'

'Would you mind opening it, please, Alice?' Charlotte instructed.

'Oh, Miss Charlotte . . . Do you think I should?'

'Of course, I think you should,' Charlotte replied, smiling. 'I'm sure it won't bite you.'

Alice clicked open the little velvet-lined box. Inside was a beautiful golden pendant on a thin gold chain. The pendant was round and about the size of a gold sovereign. It was made of solid yellow gold, and in its centre, was a ruby set in a design that represented the human eye. Delicately engraved into its border was a ring of ancient Cyrillic letters.

Oh, my Lord, it's the amulet that Tessa had on when I first came here. I often wondered what became of it. She told me long ago that it protected the wearer from evil. It is called the *Mata Jahat*. It once belonged to her mother, she told me.' Alice crossed herself and whispered a prayer. Then she lifted it from its case and passed it to Charlotte.

Charlotte took the amulet and rubbed her fingers over the ruby. She had an odd expression on her face.

'There is something quite peculiar about it, though. I noticed last night that the ruby feels warm to the touch. How on earth could that possibly be explained?' she asked, handing the pendant to Jeremy.

'It does feel a little warm. Very strange indeed. It certainly appears to be very old as well—ancient in fact. I wonder what the symbols around the edge mean,' Jeremy whispered.

'I think you should wear it, Miss Charlotte. You are a part of the old man's family now,' Alice whispered, with a strange look in her eyes. 'It will protect you from evil.'

'I'm not sure about that, Alice. It didn't save Tessa's mother from drowning at sea in that cyclone all those years ago,' Charlotte replied.

'What cyclone, Miss Charlotte?' Alice asked. The old man

never spoke about Tessa's mother to me.'

'Oh, it's something I read about only recently.'

'Anyway, the sea is not evil, Miss Charlotte. That would be like believing that trees are evil if a branch falls on you or that the rain that falls and nurtures the earth is evil. There is no evil in nature. Only man can be evil. The amulet was made to protect the wearer from the evils of man,' Alice said, staring at the pendant in Jeremy's fingers.

'You two are beginning to frighten me with talk like that,' Jeremy replied, putting the pendant back in its box but not closing it.

The three of them were silent and in deep thought for the next few seconds while they stared at the golden amulet lying in its little velvet box . . . And then Charlotte spoke.

'It seems that you are a very wise and knowledgeable woman, Alice. But do you really believe that it could protect me from evil?' Charlotte asked Alice.

'Yes, I do, Miss Charlotte. I believe that there are many things in this world that we cannot begin to truly understand,' Alice replied. 'It would be wrong to fear it. Surely.'

'And you think I should wear it?'

'Yes, I do, Miss. It is a part of your family, and it belongs to you now. I have a feeling that Henry would have wanted you to wear it. I think it would be wrong to leave it in its little box forever,' Alice replied.

'That made me shiver, Alice. You'll have me believing in ghosts shortly,' Jeremy remarked with a peculiar expression on his tanned face.

'I'm sorry about that, Jeremy,' Alice replied.

'Would you pass the pendant to me, please, Jeremy? Charlotte asked.

Jeremy took the pendant from its velvet box and handed it to her.

'Would you put it around my neck and do up the clasp,

please, Alice?'

'Certainly, Miss Charlotte,' Alice replied, smiling with satisfaction, and taking the pendant from her. I'm sure it will protect you now, Miss Charlotte.

A few moments later, Charlotte stood up and tucked the amulet beneath her blouse. 'Thank you, Alice. I will wear it with pride and respect for Henry and Tessa and for her dear mother, Kasiah,' she said, embracing Alice.

'I'm sure Henry would be proud of you, Miss Charlotte,' Alice whispered, kissing Charlotte's cheek. There were tears in her eyes.

Charlotte turned to Jeremy. 'Now then, I'd better go and get my chequebook and give you your final payment, Jeremy, for a job very well done.'

'Thank you, Charlotte. I'll load up my tools and gear shortly. I must say, it's been handy having that old storeroom down below to use. I figured when I first started using it that it would probably have been used as a firewood store once.'

'I'm glad you found good use for it then,' Charlotte replied.

'There's something quite odd down there among all the stumps and bearers, though.'

'Something odd—? What do you mean? Is there something that needs doing with the foundations?' Charlotte asked.

'No, not the foundations. But directly below the main bathroom, there is a concrete structure that I initially thought might have been built to carry the weight of the concrete floor in the main bathroom. I suppose it still could be, but it's a strange way to have done it. As you know, the rest of the floors are hardwood.

'And they look so nice now that they have been sanded and polished,' Charlotte interrupted.

'And then I thought it may have been another storeroom with supporting columns inside, but there is no door, and part of it is beneath the ground, so I can't fathom what it is at all,' Jeremy explained.

Charlotte knew what it was, and she knew she would have to show someone sooner or later.

'I thought you would have eventually asked me about that. Perhaps you both should come with me,' she said, looking at Jeremy and then at Alice. 'Would you mind getting the keys from the pantry for me, Alice?'

'Do we have to go outside and clamber around down there between the stumps and the walls of the flat?' Jeremy asked. 'I've worn my best shirt and jeans for today.'

'No, we do not, Jeremy. Come on, Alice, you too,' Charlotte instructed, taking the keys from her a moment later and leading the way to the sitting room.

'What have you found, Miss Charlotte? I've worked in this house for over 30 years. I'm sure there is no place that I don't already know about, Alice remarked.

'I think you will be surprised by what I am about to show you, Alice,' Charlotte replied when they went into the sitting room.

'I love a good mystery. Just what have you discovered in here?' Jeremy asked as they watched Charlotte go to a section of the bookshelves at the farthest end of the room.

'Just stand back for a moment,' she said as she opened a cupboard and pulled a hidden lever sideways. A section of the bookshelves where she was kneeling moved apart.

'Well, I'll be darned. A narrow little passageway,' Jeremy remarked as Charlotte pulled open that section of the bookshelves.

'Follow me,' she said, leading them into the narrow passageway and then down six concrete steps, along another little passage, and down six more concrete steps. When they reached the door that led into the safe room, Charlotte inserted the key, opened the door, and flicked on the light switch.

Oh, my Lord,' Alice whispered.

'Wow . . . This must be what I was talking about. I think the main bathroom would be directly above us.' Jeremy remarked with an astonished look on his face.

'Henry told me about this little room in a sealed letter he left for me. I have only been in here once before. What I am about to show you, you must keep to yourselves,' Charlotte said as she went over to the safe and opened it.

'You have my word,' Jeremy whispered.

'I won't ever say a thing, Miss Charlotte,' Alice whispered as well.

Charlotte reached in, took out the contents of the safe, and carried them to the little table. She laid out the gold sovereigns, the bundles of banknotes, and then the trays of glittering pearls.

'Oh, my goodness, Miss Charlotte. And this has been here all these years.'

'Yes, it has, Alice.'

'You have a king's ransom here, Charlotte. I couldn't even begin to guess the value of all this—certainly several million dollars. What do you intend to do with it? Jeremy asked.

'I've been thinking about that. I'm going to ask my solicitor, Paul Rosenberg, for some advice on what I should do in the next day or so. For the moment, I intend to leave it all locked away in here.'

'The hairs are standing up on the back of my neck. I've been working here for the last six months, and I had no idea this room even existed,' Jeremy announced.

'It has been cleverly designed and built by a very capable builder,' Charlotte replied.

'It certainly has been, Charlotte. Very clever indeed,' Jeremy agreed.

'How wonderful for you, Miss Charlotte,' Alice said, sitting at the table and admiring the pearls. 'I had no idea it was here either. How clever the old man was thinking of doing it,' Alice remarked.

'There was something else in the safe. I've taken it to my room. It's a box of old letters and photos and an old handwritten journal. The journal was written by Henry many years ago. It tells the story of his and Tessa's wonderful life together, including when they first met. I've spent many hours reading it. It's like taking a giant step back in time. It's how I knew about the cyclone and Tessa's mother's death. It's so well written. I'll show it to you when we go back upstairs.'

'Oh, Miss Charlotte. How wonderful. I loved the old man. He was always so kind to me. Would you read some of it to me sometime? I'm not very good at reading and writing,' Alice explained.

'If you would like me to, I'd be honoured, Alice. It's a truly wonderful story, but very sad in places.' Charlotte added, turning to Jeremy. 'When we're finished, I could give it to you to take home and read if you wanted to, Jeremy?'

'I would rather sit and listen to you read it to the both of us, Charlotte,' Jeremy said in a soft but serious voice. He was still coming to grips with what he'd just seen in the little room beneath the house. 'Anyway, I'm sure you would do a much better job than me struggling with it. After all, you're the schoolteacher. I'm just a humble carpenter.'

'Let me lock all this up, and we can go back upstairs, and I'll show it to you,' Charlotte said, carrying everything back to the safe.

*   *   *

An hour later, after Jeremy had finished installing the new knobs on the kitchen cupboards, they were sitting around the little nook, drinking coffee, and looking at the contents of the old shoebox and Henry's handwritten journal.

One of the last things Charlotte showed them was the old photograph of Tessa's mother standing by the motorcar in the gardens of her home in Broome.

'Oh, my dear Lord, what a beautiful woman!' Alice remarked This is the only photograph I have ever seen of Kasiah. The old man only kept photos of Tessa in the house.'

'Read what's on the back, Alice,' Charlotte whispered.

Alice turned the photograph and read the faded lines.

'Oh, Miss Charlotte, how sad it must have been for dear Tessa to lose her mother like that all those years ago. I often wondered what happened to her. I think the flat downstairs was originally built for her to live in, you know.'

'And so sad for poor Henry. He loved her so much as well,' Charlotte whispered back.

'She was certainly a very beautiful woman,' Jeremy agreed, taking the photograph from Alice. 'I'm guessing that would be Henry standing next to Kasiah.'

'And that is the *Mata Jahat* she is wearing. You can see it quite clearly. You should have the photograph restored, Miss,' Alice said in a soft voice.

'I intend to,' Charlotte replied. 'Now then, this is Henry's old journal that I told you about,' she said, putting the photo back in its envelope and sliding the thick, leather-bound journal across to have it in front of her.

'Would you read some of it for us now, Miss Charlotte?' Alice asked.

'I shall have to start at the very beginning, and it will take a few readings to get it all done,' Charlotte replied, opening the journal.

'We don't mind at all, do we, Alice? It will be a good excuse for me to come and visit,' Jeremy said.

'You don't need an excuse to visit, Jeremy. I think we would soon miss you if you weren't wandering around the place,' Charlotte remarked.

'Thank you, Charlotte,' Jeremy replied, kissing Charlotte's cheek. 'Does that mean you're rather fond of me?'

'Let's not get too carried away,' Charlotte added.

'Would you two like me to leave the room for a while?' Alice asked, smiling.

'Not at the moment, Alice,' Charlotte replied, smiling back, and opening the first page of Henry's old journal.

*　*　*

Two long nights later, Charlotte reached the page she had arrived at during her last reading.

'All right, you two, that's enough for today. Go home and get some sleep,' she said to Jeremy and Alice.

'Oh, Miss Charlotte, what a wonderful story so far. I had no idea the old man led such an adventurous life,' Alice said, getting to her feet.

'Thanks for reading it for us, Charlotte. I'm thoroughly enjoying it.' Jeremy added, getting up as well.

'How about we continue on Sunday? Jeremy could cook us up a barbecue, and we could have a few drinks before we start,' Charlotte suggested.

'It's a date. How does six o'clock sound?' Jeremy replied.

'Six o'clock it is,' Charlotte repeated. 'Does that suit you, Alice?

'It certainly does, Miss Charlotte.'

'Alice, it's getting late. Jeremy will put your bike in the back of his ute and drop you off at home. You don't mind, do you, Jeremy?'

'No worries at all. Come on, Alice, it's time to go. Goodbye, Charlotte.'

'Goodbye, you two.'

* * *

The following Sunday, after the barbecue, Jeremy and Alice slid into the little nook with their drinks in their hands and waited for Charlotte to bring out Henry's old journal from her bedroom.

A moment later, Charlotte sat down, took a sip of her Chardonnay, and looked at the other two.

'Are we ready?' she asked them.

'We are, Charlotte. Please continue,' Jeremy replied, lifting his glass of red in a salute.

Charlotte opened the old journal to where she had left off in her last reading and began . . .

# Part 6

# Chapter 36

# The Gerta

Three days after the cyclone had destroyed the *Mina*, the lugger *Gerta* sailed into Broome. The cyclone had completely missed the town, although there had been considerable flooding damage from the heavy rain it brought with it. Everyone in the little coastal town was concerned for the safety of those on board the sleek and beautiful *Mina*. It seemed to have completely disappeared.

Santiago Batista, the captain of the *Gerta*, had been fortunate. In the afternoon, after he'd been instructed to set sail for Broome by Captain Nolan, he was in a state of panic. He had watched Jago smash Haziz's right hand with the marlin spike and then threaten to kill him if he went anywhere near their boss, Kasiah Taylor. He wanted to put as much distance as he could between himself and the fearsome brute Jago. That night, the sea was relatively calm, and the winds were slight and from the southwest. The moon was full and clear, so he sailed on until nine o'clock before dropping anchor. At dawn, he instructed his men to haul anchor, and they set sail again for Broome. The wind had picked up considerably by then, and they were soon making good speed. Astern and to the southwest, he noticed heavy clouds on the distant horizon. A late-season willy-willy was building up and moving toward the coast. It was heading directly for where they had left the *Mina*. Old Santiago hoped that Captain Nolan had moved away from there before dropping anchor last night. They would stand a chance if they had. If not, the storm was heading directly for them.

As the day progressed, the winds picked up and then came the rain. But the willy-willy caused the *Gerta* little trouble, as it was many miles off their stern by that time. It was still raining heavily as night came when he instructed his men to drop anchor again for the night.

Haziz had been in his bunk all this time, his face wrapped in a rag bandage and his broken fingers wrapped with a dirty handkerchief. He had been moaning constantly about the pain in his hand. After they had eaten their evening meal of curried pearl oyster meat, pineapple, and sliced watermelon, Santiago went to Haziz to look at his hand.

'Let me see hand,' he said to his crewman, abruptly, pushing his plate aside.

'Hand no good, Captain. All broke bad and swollen; alla time worse now,' Haziz moaned.

'You real lucky the boss Missus was on the *Mina* watching. You lucky Jago no kill you and throw you to the fish,' Santiago replied with a sneer.

'I alla time sorry bout steal em little pearl. I meet 'em pretty young white girl. She new in Broome. She loves me very much, Captain. I steal em pearl for her like she wanted.'

'White girl would leave you after you give her pearl. White girl no stay em with you. You coloured fella, Haziz. She leave you real quick after you give her pearl. You let me look at hand now,' Santiago insisted, taking Haziz's hand and unwrapping it.

'Hand no good. Hurt real bad,' Haziz moaned.

A moment later, Santiago left his crewman still moaning with pain. He went forward to a locker and pulled out a small bag of his personal items. From it, he took out a clay pipe and packed it with a mixture of dark tobacco and a wad of tarry opium. He lit the pipe, took a long, satisfying draw himself, and took it back to Haziz.

'You smoke this alla way till gone and pain go away, you silly fella,' Santiago instructed, smiling, and leaving Haziz to get some sleep himself.

* * *

Late the following morning, they sailed into Broome. An hour later, Santiago Batista and another crewman delivered Haziz to the hospital to have his hand and face seen to. They were greeted in the hospital foyer by Dr. Burke and a nurse.

'Where have you men just come from?' the doctor asked.

'We bin up near the eighty-mile,' Santiago replied.

'Have you seen the *Mina?*'

'We seen em *Mina*, three days ago up near the eighty-mile. They bring us some nice fresh tucker.'

'There's been a bad cyclone up in that area. A couple of stations in from the coast have recorded considerable damage. Some lives have been lost. Everyone is concerned for those on board the *Mina*. It hasn't been seen for some days now. It seems to have disappeared completely.'

'We see em big willy-willy coming. We sail em pretty quick and miss him. What about alla them other luggers up further?' Santiago asked.

'Fourteen luggers at the bottom end of the eighty-mile found safety in a creek and rode it out with only some minor damage, but nothing serious. They have not seen the *Mina*, though.' Doctor Burke replied, turning to the nurse. 'Bring this man into the theatre, nurse. You men, stay here. I'll come back and see you shortly. By the way, can you tell me what caused the damage to his face and hand?'

'He silly fella and steal em little pearl. Jago, he comes on board and hit him in face and broke his fingers pretty quick.' Santiago stammered.

'You wait here,' Doctor Burke instructed, hurrying over to the reception desk.

'Nurse, please ring the Taylors' home and ask Henry Dawson to get here as soon as possible.'

* * *

Fifteen minutes later, Henry arrived at the hospital.

'Do you have news of the *Mina?*' He asked the receptionist with an urgent tone.

'I'm afraid I don't, Mr. Dawson. If you could just wait here for a moment. Doctor Burke has asked two men to wait until you arrive. We have them in the staff room. I'll go and get them and let Doctor Burke know you're here as well.'

Two minutes later, the two men from the *Gerta* came out of the staff room. Henry had no idea who they were when they approached him.

'Are you men off one of the Taylor luggers?' he asked.

'Yes, Boss. Me, Santiago Batista, captain of the *Gerta*, one of Missus Kasiah Taylor's luggers. This other fella is Katakana, our number one diver,' Santiago replied proudly.

'Have you seen the *Mina?*' Henry asked with an urgent expression on his young face.

'We see em Mina a few days ago when they bring tucker to the eighty-mile,' Santiago said nervously.

'Do you think they may have been caught in the path of the cyclone?' Henry asked, concern obvious on his face.

'I think maybe they get caught in that big willy-willy alright, Boss,' Santiago replied.

'Why are you here at the hospital?' Henry asked.

Before Santiago could reply, a door opened, and Doctor Burke joined them in the foyer.

'I suppose you already know by now, Henry. These men are from the *Gerta*. They brought a crewman in to have his face and hand looked at. They've told me that Jago attacked him for stealing a pearl.'

'Have they any news of the *Mina?*' Henry asked, looking back quickly at the two men.

They say they were in contact with the *Mina* some days ago. But they have no knowledge of its whereabouts now, I'm afraid,' the doctor explained.

'Thank you, doctor,' Henry replied.

'Have you heard anything from the police, Henry?'

'The local police are still waiting for news from the stations before they do anything. The police from Port Hedland are speaking to the crews of the luggers at the southern end of the eighty-mile at the moment.'

'I suppose we will just have to be patient and wait then,' Doctor Burke suggested.

'I'm going to take someone with me and drive out to the La Grange Mission and head south along the beach on foot and see what I can find,' Henry replied.

'It might be wise to wait for more news from the stations to get through before you do that. Some of them are sending out search parties as we speak.'

'I'm done waiting, Doctor.'

'It's a long way out there, and over quite a bad road, I'm told,' Doctor Burke added.

'Thank you for all your help, doctor, but I'd better be off,' Henry replied impatiently.

'Good luck to you then,' the doctor called after Henry, watching him hurry out through the main doors. He turned and went back into the operating theatre.

304

# Chapter 37

# La Grange Mission

Henry hurried home to see Tessa. When he got there, the gardeners were sitting on the ground under the old flame tree waiting for his return to find out if he had any news of the *Mina* or Kasiah.

'There is nothing I can tell you men at the moment. As soon as we have any news, I'll let you know.' He called to the two Aboriginal men as he climbed out of the Pierce-Arrow and hurried over to the veranda steps.

Inside, the house was in a terrible state. Tarni and Juliette were sitting with Tessa in the kitchen. All three of them were crying when Henry walked in.

'Does the hospital have any news about Mother, Henry?' Tessa asked, her beautiful face wet with tears.

'Nothing really. The lugger, *Gerta*, has just arrived in town. I spoke to the captain, and he told me they took on supplies from the *Mina* a few days ago. Doctor Burke told me Jago attacked a man on board for trying to steal a pearl. The man had his fingers smashed and broken. Captain Nolan sent them back to Broome to get his hand attended to. The captain of the *Gerta* thinks the *Mina* may have been caught in the cyclone, but he's not sure, and that's all he could tell me,' Henry said, sitting at the table and taking Tessa's hand in his.

'What can we do, Henry? There must be something. We must find out if Mother is all right,' Tessa replied, sobbing.

'I'm heading into the warehouse to pick up Paddy. I'm going to drive out to La Grange and set out along the beach. The Port Hedland police are at Pardoo Station at the southern end, but I'm told they have no news at the moment.'

'Should I come with you, Henry?' Tessa asked.

'You stay here, Tessa. If you have any news after I leave, notify La Grange Mission on the telephone,' Henry replied, getting to his feet.

'Just a minute, Mister Henry. I'll get some food and water canteens for you to take,' Tarni said, getting up as well.

* * *

It was already dark when Henry and Paddy arrived at the La Grange Mission in La Grange Bay. The mission had been set up many years earlier as a government food distribution centre for the local Aboriginal people of the area. A police constable, his wife, and an Aboriginal tracker were stationed there.

Henry went to the main door and knocked. A young, fresh-faced constable answered the door. 'Can I help you?' he asked, with a thick German accent.

'Do you have any news of the *Mina?*' Henry asked.

'I'm sorry, but we haf no news at all. My tracker searched along the beach earlier today, but he has found nothing. I haf informed the Broome police of this an hour ago,' the constable replied.

'Would you mind if my friend and I stayed here for the night? We'll be heading off along the beach toward the south first thing in the morning,' Henry told the constable.

'You vil have to sleep on the veranda. We haf no room in the cottage, and I haf no spare beds. I haf spare mattresses, though.'

'That will suit us fine, and thank you,' Henry replied.

'If you come with me, I'll get you some food, and then you can help with the mattresses and blankets. My name is Herman Bauer.'

I'm Henry Dawson. Just give me a moment, Herman, and I'll go and get my friend,' Henry replied.

* * *

The following morning, at dawn, Henry and Paddy set out from the mission. Both men were carrying two large canteens of water strapped over their shoulders. Henry had a small canvas pack on his back. Inside were another two canteens of water, four cans of bully beef, two cans of sliced peaches, and a large packet of bush biscuits. Paddy was carrying a Winchester rifle for their protection. There had been a spearing recently of a Koepanger crewman from a lugger who'd been caught by tribespeople having intercourse with an Aboriginal woman not far from the mission station.

They set off along the beach with the sea on their right all that day, and all they found were several small pieces of torn sail and rope floating on the shoreline.

Paddy picked one of them up and studied it.

'Is it from the *Mina*, Paddy? Can you tell?' Henry asked, wiping sweat from his face.

'Hard to tell, Boss. Could be. Not too sure, though,' Paddy replied.

'It's getting dark. I think we should go over near those sandhills, have something to eat, and set up camp. We'll head off early in the morning and see what we can find further up,' Henry instructed.

'Righto, Boss,' Paddy replied, following Henry into the sandhills.

At dawn the following morning, the two men ate a bush biscuit each, drank some water, and headed off again. By midday, it was becoming unbearably hot, but they continued along the seemingly endless beach.

Henry imagined they must have walked at least thirty miles by that time. They couldn't afford to go too much further. At the end of the day, it would take them two full days to get back to the mission from where they were, and that was the limit of the water they carried.

A little further along, they noticed a short piece of spar, some canvas, and a length of connected rope lying on the beach at the high-water mark. A large male dingo was standing near it, sniffing the canvas. When they got closer, the dingo ran off into the sand hills. When it reached the crest of a stony ridge, it stopped and turned to watch them.

When they finally got to the canvas, Paddy picked it up.

'Is it from the *Mina*, Paddy?' Henry asked the Aboriginal man.

'If them other luggers are all right like they was tellin' you before, Boss, I reckon it must be,' Paddy replied, dropping it to the sand.

'We better keep moving then,' Henry said, looking out over the vast, shimmering Indian Ocean on his right and fearing the worst.

*   *   *

Three hours later, Paddy hit Henry on the shoulder.

Henry had been thinking of Kasiah. He looked at his companion. 'What's wrong, Paddy?' he asked.

'Someone's comin' along the beach, Boss,' Paddy replied.

Henry looked off into the distance and noticed a lone figure walking slowly towards them. Now and then the figure would stumble and fall to its knees, then get up again and continue toward them.

'That's Jago, Boss,' Paddy yelled excitedly, running ahead toward the stumbling figure.

'My God, I think it is,' Henry yelled back, following the Aboriginal man along the beach.

Jago was dragging a piece of ripped sail along behind him. He had a makeshift bag over his shoulder made from the same material.

'Jago . . . Jago . . . It's me, Paddy,' Paddy yelled to his friend long before they got to him.

Jago stopped and sat down on the wet sand. He looked at the two men approaching him. He was tired of being visited by ghosts.

'Is that you again, Boss?' he said, through weary, half-blind eyes when they got to him. 'You leave me alone now. I gotta get up and keep on goin.'

'It's me, Jago . . . It's Paddy . . . We have water,' Paddy said, sitting next to his friend and holding a canteen in front of him.

'You trickin me again, Boss,' Jago whispered, staring at the canteen.

'Have a drink, Jago . . . It's me, it's Mister Henry,' Henry said, taking one of his canteens from his shoulder as well.

'Mister Henry, is that you?' Jago whispered back through cracked lips.

'Yes, it is, Jago . . . Where is Kasiah? Is she safe?' Henry asked. He could wait no longer. He must know.

'Kasiah dead, Mister Henry. She drowned in the big waves. Everybody all dead, Mister Henry. Captain Nolan, old Zhang Wei. All gone now.' Jago replied, taking the canteen from Paddy, and lifting it to his lips.

'Are you sure, Jago—? We could go on for a while after you've rested,' Henry whispered, trying to hold back tears. The shock of what Jago had just told him was almost too much for him to bear.

'Kasiah dead now, Mister Henry . . . I bury her deep. No animal ever dig her up. Storm very bad only Jago alive now.'

Jago gave the canteen back to Paddy and showed Henry his hands. His palms were cracked and broken, and in places, they were still bleeding from digging Kasiah's and old Zhang Wei's graves more than a week before.

'Did you see her in the storm, Jago?' Henry whispered back. His heart was broken. 'Did you try and save her?'

'I saw her in big waves, Mister Henry. I give her a broken hatch cover, and then nother big wave comes, and I lose her. I searched, but I did not find her. So sorry, Mister Henry.'

'You be quiet now, Jago. You have another drink, but not too much,' Paddy said to his friend, and then he looked at Henry.

'No more talk, please, Mister Henry. You help me take Jago over near them sandhills. He proper buggered now,' Paddy said, picking up Jago's canvas sheet. 'We'll make a shelter with this and let him rest a bit.'

'Alright then, Paddy,' Henry whispered back. He had a terrible, lost expression on his face. Kasiah was gone from his life forever now, drowned in a terrible cyclone and buried somewhere in the sandhills further along the remote beach. His heart was broken.

*   *   *

Henry and Paddy spent the rest of that day resting with Jago in the lee of a high sandhill in the shade they made with sticks and Jago's piece of sailcloth. When it was dark, they ate a meal of bully beef and sliced peaches. Jago ate very little of the beef and only a few mouthfuls of the peaches. He needed rest and sleep badly. He had hardly slept at all for the last few days, such was his determination to return to Broome and his perceived obligation to look after Kasiah's daughter for the rest of his days. In his pocket, he still carried the strange pendant he had removed from Kasiah's dead body.

*   *   *

The following morning, Jago seemed much better. Henry and Paddy helped him down to the sea, and the three of them bathed themselves in the ocean. After they finished, they went back to their shelter and ate a little more of the beef, a bush biscuit each, and washed them down with water. They rested in their shelter until the middle of the morning, and then they headed back in the direction of the La Grange mission. Henry and Paddy were amazed at Jago's rapid recovery and his return to strength. He seemed anxious to get back to Broome as quickly as possible.

They spent the following night in the lee of the sandhills again, dozing, talking, and listening to the gentle sounds of the waves lapping against the nearby beach. The following morning, they ate a little more of the canned beef and biscuit and headed off again. By the middle of the afternoon, they had arrived back where the track that led to the mission station came down through the sandhills on their right.

Several Aboriginal men were walking up from the beach and saw them approaching. One of them was carrying a speared stingray. They ran back up the track to tell the constable they were approaching. A few minutes later, Herman Bauer came out of the track and onto the beach. He stood there, watching them approach for a while. Then he and the Aboriginal men ran down the beach to welcome them back.

'You haf found a survivor, Henry,' he said when he got to them.

'We have, Herman. This man is Jago. He is the only survivor of the *Mina*. The rest have perished in the cyclone,' Henry said sadly.

'*Mein Gott* . . . Such a terrible thing,' Herman replied.

The Aboriginal men had surrounded Jago. They were staring at him, marvelling that he had survived such an ordeal—an ordeal that began more than eight days before. One of them stepped up close and said something that Jago couldn't understand and touched him on one of his heavily muscled arms. Jago tensed at the unwelcome touch and hissed at the man in response. The Aboriginal man and his friends stepped back a comfortable distance, suddenly realising that this was a very dangerous man.

'Let us go back to the house and get you into the shade. You are all badly sunburned. I vil set out your mattresses and get some soft soap to soothe your burns. Then I vil have my wife cook you some food,' Herman said, and they set off along the beach for the mission.

'Thank you for your hospitality, Herman. Would you mind if I used your telephone to ring my wife when we get there?'

'Yes, of course. Just let me know when you are ready, and I will put a call through to the Broome exchange,' Herman replied.

'Just as soon as we get back, if you don't mind,' Henry said.

'Yes, of course, Henry.'

When they arrived back at the mission, Henry left Paddy and Jago resting on the veranda and followed Herman inside.

Five minutes later, Herman handed Henry the phone receiver.

'It is ringing now,' he announced.

Henry took the handpiece and waited. A moment later, he heard Tessa's voice.

'Hello, Henry, my love. Do you have any news about Mother?' Tessa asked.

'Yes, I do, Tessa. I'm so sorry, my darling. Kasiah has died. She drowned in the storm,' Henry whispered into the mouthpiece.

'Oh no—! Oh, Henry—! Are you sure?'

'I'm sure, Tessa. We found Jago quite a way down the beach. He was in a very bad way.'

'How does he know that Mother has drowned, Henry? He may have made a mistake . . . Perhaps if you went on, you might find her.' Henry heard Tessa's reply.

'Tessa, you must listen to me. Jago found Kasiah on the beach. She had drowned in the storm. He told me he tried to help her in the waves. He had given her a broken hatch cover to hold, and then he lost her,' Henry replied, crying now himself.

'Oh, Henry—! How can I go on without Mother?' Tessa sobbed. 'What has Jago done with her body? Oh, Henry, why has this happened?'

'Jago told me last night, after we had eaten, that he wrapped her in a piece of sailcloth from the *Mina* and buried her deep in the sandhills. He was very upset. He said before he buried her, he carried her into the sea and bathed her body to cleanse her of the storm, and then he sang a prayer for her,' Henry whispered.

'Oh, Henry, what will we ever do without Mother?'

'Jago was still suffering from his ordeal when he spoke to me later, Tessa. I think he may have been almost delirious. He told me Kasiah visited him while he dreamed. He says he has something for you, my love, but he won't tell me what it is. I asked him about it again this morning, but he would say no more.'

'Tarni and Juliette are crying now, Henry. They've been listening. I must go . . . When will you be home, my love?' Tessa asked.

'We will leave here in the morning. We should be back late

in the afternoon, provided we don't have trouble. The road is in a terrible state.'

'Goodbye then, Henry,' Tessa said in a soft, tragic voice.

'Goodbye, Tessa,' Henry replied.

*　*　*

Late the following afternoon, Henry, Jago, and Paddy arrived back in Broome. The news of Kasiah's fate and the fate of those on board the *Mina* had already spread through the remote pearling community. There was a gathering of locals outside the warehouse when Henry stopped to let Paddy out.

'I'll come and see you here in the morning, Paddy. Thank you for your help, my friend,' Henry said, reaching for Paddy's hand.

'You make sure Jago gets some rest, Mister Henry,' Paddy replied as he climbed out.

'Yes, I will, Paddy. Goodbye for now.' Henry drove away just as Sean Peterson approached the car. A few minutes later, he parked the Pierce-Arrow under the old flame tree.

'Here we are, Jago, you're home at last. How are you feeling?' Henry asked as they climbed out.

'I stay here, Mister Henry. You tell Miss Tessa I wait for her,' Jago said, dragging out his sailcloth bag. For some reason, he'd held on to it. All it contained was a piece of bent strap, a bailer shell, some smaller, sharp shells, and a couple of crushed hermit crabs.

'I'll go up and tell her, then,' Henry replied, just as Tessa, Tarni, and Juliette came out onto the veranda.

Henry hurried up the steps and reached for Tessa. 'I'm so sorry, Tessa. I wish I had better news, my love.'

'What are we to do, Henry? Mother was our guiding light. We will be so lost without her,' Tessa sobbed.

Tarni and Juliette came to Tessa's side, their concern showing on their tear-streaked faces.

'Tessa, Jago is waiting by the motor car. He wants to speak to you,' Henry continued.

'Do you know what he wants?' Tessa asked, looking into Henry's eyes, and searching for something to lift her spirits.

'I'm not sure, my love.'

'Alright then. You all go inside, and I'll go down and talk to him,' Tessa said, starting down the steps.

Jago was still standing near the front of the car when Tessa went to him.

'Oh, dear Jago, you have been through so much. I'm so glad you're back with us again,' Tessa said, embracing him.

Jago looked awkward with Tessa holding him so close.

'You wanted to speak to me,' Tessa said, stepping back and looking into Jago's weary eyes.

'I have something for you, Miss Tessa,' Jago said in a soft, caring voice.

'What is it? What can it be, Jago?' Tessa asked.

Jago put his hand in his pocket, pulled out the *Mata Jahat* pendant, and passed it to her.

'This is for you, Miss Tessa.' He said.

'Oh, Jago. It's Mother's wonderful charm with the ruby eye,' Tessa whispered.

'You must wear it now, Miss Tessa. Your mother visited me when I dreamed. She told me to say this to you. It will protect you.'

'Thank you, Jago . . . Oh, Jago . . . Did the storm hurt her body? Was she cut and marked badly?' Tessa asked, with tears in her eyes,

'No marks, Miss Tessa. She was beautiful, just like always. I sang a prayer for her when I washed her in the sea,' Jago said with kindness in his voice. 'She is at peace now.'

'Thank you. You are a good man, Jago.' Tessa said, wiping her tears away with her fingers.

'I tried to save her, Miss Tessa. I searched, but I couldn't find her in the waves. Very sorry.'

'I'm sure you did your best,' Tessa replied, noticing the tears welling in Jago's eyes. 'Tarni and Juliette are so glad you are still with us, Jago. They will visit you later. I will tell them to bring something for your burns. Thank you so much for bringing me this.' Tessa said, rubbing her finger over the ruby eye. 'I will wear it always.'

'It was your mother's wish, Miss Tessa,' Jago said, wearily picking up his sailcloth bag and hurrying away.

# Chapter 38

# Life Without Kasiah

For Tessa and Henry, life without Kasiah was proving to be very difficult. Tessa seemed lost without her mother. Kasiah's death was almost too difficult for her to come to terms with. There was no grave for her to visit, no headstone to read her mother's name from, and no place to kneel and pray or to leave flowers. Kasiah was simply gone from her life forever, and it was almost impossible for her to bear. Sometimes at night, in her bedroom, when a light breeze blew the curtains aside in the darkness or when the moon cast strange shadows against the walls, she would imagine it was Kasiah standing in her room looking at her. Her heart would race, and she would whisper into the darkness.

'Oh, dearest Mother, is that you?'

But there never came the reply she wished and hoped for— only heartbreaking silence. Afterwards, she would lie in bed, her mind in turmoil, hoping she hadn't woken Henry with her silly whispering.

Henry's grief was very different. He had to hold back the terrible feeling of loss that was threatening his sanity. He had to support his wife through her grief over losing her mother but carry his own heartbreak in silence.

It was when he was alone in Kasiah's office with the door locked that it was the most difficult time for him. He had loved Kasiah with every fibre of his being. Sometimes he would run his hands over the desk where they had made love, and he would sob in pitiful silence. Kasiah had been right when she told him that it *was* possible for a man to love two women at the same time. He loved Tessa, and that would never change. But sometimes, when they lay naked together and made love, he would stare at the pendant with the ruby eye between her copper breasts and think of Kasiah and wish that it was her he was making love to.

*   *   *

As time went by, Tessa's grief became easier for her to bear, helped in no small way by Tarni and Juliette. Juliette reminded her of her piano lessons one morning, and they began playing together again. And then Tarni began to take her for walks in the garden in the mornings after breakfast. Sometimes they would sit and talk by her mother's little pond and watch the rainbow fish swimming beneath the lily leaves. Slowly, she began to heal.

For Henry, there was always work that needed to be done. There was pearl shell to crate and stack in the warehouse, supplies to be purchased for the luggers, and sent out with their one remaining schooner, the *Minerva*. He still had so much to learn, and Kasiah was no longer there to teach him. But Paddy and Jago were always there for advice and help whenever he needed it. And so, Henry began to heal as well.

One night after they had eaten their evening meal, Henry and Tessa took their coffee mugs and sat out on the veranda. It was a beautiful Broome night. It was cool, and the stars were bright. There was no breeze, and fruit bats were flitting about in the moonlight.

'Are you happy, Henry?' Tessa asked.

'Yes, of course I am. Why do you ask, my love?'

'No real reason. Do you miss Mother?'

'Of course, I miss her.'

'I think you loved her just as much as I did, Henry.'

'Yes, I think you're right, Tessa,' Henry replied.

'I'm so glad that you did, my love,' Tessa whispered.

'Tessa, now that we own that property up in Darwin, I think

we should contact the builder and get started on building the new home,' Henry said, hoping to change the subject.

'Yes, I agree. When the season ends, we could go up and see Connor and Angela again. Angela was so supportive when I called her and told her what had happened to Mother. I wish we could just leave here and go and live in Darwin permanently. Life is just not the same here without Mother,' Tessa said, sipping her coffee.

'I agree with you. When the house is finished, perhaps we should just sell up and go. I've been approached already by people about selling the luggers,' Henry replied.

'What would we do about Tarni and Juliette, or even Jago?' Tessa asked.

'We could take them with us, Tessa.'

'I suppose we could ask them. But do *you* really want to leave here, Henry?'

'Yes, I do,' Henry replied. I think we both need a new start in our lives now that Kasiah is no longer with us.'

'What about this house? Should we sell it as well?' Tessa asked.

'It will ultimately be your decision, Tessa. Your mother has left everything to you. If and when you were to sell everything, you would be a very rich woman.'

'Yes, I suppose I would. In that case, I think we should sell it all and move up to Darwin just as soon as the new home is complete,' Tessa said with sudden determination.

'All right then. I agree. In the morning, I will ring the builder in Darwin, and you can ring Angela and tell her of our decision.'

'When should we speak to Tarni, Juliette, and Jago?'

'Let's do everything tomorrow. I'll contact a real estate agent as well about putting the business and the house on the market,' Henry replied.

'I love you, Henry,' Tessa said. Let's go to bed and make love to celebrate.' She got up and reached for Henry's hand.

'You are my only love, Tessa,' Henry said, taking her hand and kissing her cheek.

Chapter 39

# A Celebration of Sorts

It was the end of the lay-up season in Broome. That dangerous time of the year when cyclones could still come out of nowhere and destroy everything in their paths. The town's pearling boats were all safely moored along the creeks and shoreline, with their gear stowed away in readiness for the next season. It was a time for carrying out maintenance on the boats and for the white pearling families to socialize and engage in local and cultural activities while at the same time preparing themselves for the next season. But Boome was sweltering through a late-season heatwave that had lasted for many days, and to make it worse, there had been no rain for more than three weeks. The town's hotels were doing a roaring trade, with cashed-up pearling workers spending their days in their bars and their nights savouring the many delights of Sheba Lane.

It had been many months now since the *Mina* had been lost in the tropical cyclone, which the locals were now referring to as *Typhoon Mina*. Even though no bodies were ever returned to Broome for burial, it was now being talked about. Because it was the end of the season, it was decided among the local dignitaries of the town that a funeral celebration should be held in respect for those on board who had perished anyway.

*   *   *

When the day arrived, Koepangers wearing colourful paper masks and carrying streamers on long painted sticks marched through the streets of Broome as a mark of respect to their countrymen who had perished on the *Mina*. Chinese men wearing brightly co-loured smocks walked with them, beating little drums as a mark of honour for the old cook, Zhang Wei, a well-known and popular man in the Chinese community. The surly Japanese were there as well, carrying banners with the names of the many divers who had died from the bends over the years written on them in elegant pictograph characters. The town's mayor and local councillors marched in front of them all to show their respect for the crew of the schooner, her captain, John Nolan, and her owner, Kasiah Taylor, of *Taylor House Pearls*.

When the day finally drew to a close and the celebrations were over, most of the townspeople continued to the Continental Hotel for a buffet dinner and celebratory drinks. The well-dressed white women of the town, most of them the wives of local pearling masters and town merchants, sat together inside, sipping their gin and tonics and champagne cocktails. Their husbands sat with them, dressed in their immaculate tropical whites, drinking Scotch whisky and ice-cold draught beer.

Outside, the long hotel veranda was packed with well-dressed Malay men, Chinese, Koepanger, Japanese, and Filipino men sitting in their different groups drinking Chinese wine and bottled beer. The town's local Aboriginal people, while not permitted inside the hotel, were sitting in the dirt outside the veranda railing, chatting among themselves, drinking cheap flagon wine, but also enjoying the celebrations.

For the white pearling masters, the tales of previous cyclones and the damage that had been wrought by them over the years were among the main topics of conversation. But as the night wore on and more drinks were consumed, another subject was being discussed. It was the passing of the beautiful black woman, Kasiah Taylor, and her strange burial in the sandhills somewhere along the distant eighty-mile beach. Most of those present believed that every effort should have been made to have her body returned to Broome for a proper Christian burial in the local cemetery and not simply left in an unmarked grave in the sandhills. The news had spread that the heathen Jago had washed her naked body in the sea while chanting voodoo incantations to her dearly departed soul before burying her uncovered and naked in a shallow, unmarked grave where scavenging animals could easily dig her up.

Everyone in the town knew the man had an unhealthy obsession with Kasiah Taylor. It was whispered among many that he had been having his way with her for years. After her husband, Duncan, was killed by the snake, he was never far from her side. It was even being said among some that he had probably conjured up the strange snake with his heathen voodoo to carry out the terrible deed. When it was done, the brute had eaten the serpent like the uneducated savage that he was, thus enabling him to freely continue to have his wicked, ungodly ways with her.

To the God-fearing people of the tiny polyglot community of Broome, it was all just another reminder of the strange life and sad death of the beautiful Kasiah Taylor, the only child and daughter of Juan Toledo, the black hoodoo man.

* * *

Neither Henry nor Tessa attended the celebrations that night, nor did Jago. Only Paddy was there. He was sitting outside in the dirt with the Aboriginal people, listening to the strange tales that were spreading like wildfire, and shaking his head in disbelief.

Henry and Tessa were at home, looking at the photographs Connor and Angela had sent them of their recently completed home in Darwin.

'What do you think? Henry,' Tessa asked.

'It looks just perfect to me. It's taken a bit longer than we thought, but it's well worth it,' Henry replied.

'I just love it, Henry. It's a pity the photos are in black and white. I'd like to see how the green cupboards in the kitchen look,' Tessa said and then added. 'I'm so glad now that we went ahead with it.'

'So am I, Tessa. Connor asked me on the phone if we would like him to hire a landscape architect he knows to lay out the driveway and the gardens for us as a gift from him and Angela,' Henry said.

'And did you accept, my love?'

'I did. What a very fine gesture.'

'Have there been any more inquiries about the business or the house?' Tessa asked.

'There have been quite a lot of offers, more than we expected. But something quite odd happened yesterday.'

'Something odd, Henry?' Tessa remarked.

'Yes, quite odd, I thought. After all that has happened, Sean Peterson has made us an offer for the business and the house. The offer came to us through his solicitor and not personally.'

'And was the offer reasonable?' Tessa asked.

'It was more than reasonable. It was far above what we were asking. His solicitor's letter stated that the offer is for seven days only, and we must agree that the house is to be a part of the purchase,' Henry added.

'Oh, I see. I suppose it would take away the problem of selling Mother's house separately,' Tessa admitted.

'It certainly would. But what do *you* think of the idea, Tessa?'

'It seems a little odd to me. The boats I can understand, but the Petersons already have a beautiful home. I wonder why he would want to change, although our gardens are so much nicer,' Tessa replied.

'He is very determined about the whole thing. He wants the boats to increase his fleet's size, and he insists that the house is to be a part of the transaction.

'What do you think we should do?' Tessa asked.

'I think we should accept. I don't like the man or his son, but it's a more than reasonable offer.'

'What about our furniture, Henry?' Tessa asked.

'The furniture must go with the home. We are only to take only our personal things.'

'That could suit us, Henry. Moving everything all the way to Darwin on a state ship would have surely created a few problems anyway, Tessa said.

'In that case, do we agree?' Henry asked.

'Yes, I agree. I think we should sell to him and get things underway as soon as possible.'

'Have you spoken to Tarni and Juliette, Tessa?'

'I have. Juliette is happy to join us, but Tarni will not. She has a lot of family here in Broome. She wants to stay, but she would like to come and visit us after we have settled in. She is very sorry, but she says she could never leave Broome.'

'I suppose that's understandable,' Henry replied. 'You'll miss her though.'

'I told her I would send her a ticket on the *Minderoo* when we are settled,' Tessa said. 'Perhaps she may change her mind when she comes up.'

'If she doesn't, we'll have to employ someone locally,' Henry added.

'Do you think we should have gone to the dinner in the Continental, Henry? After all, it was for the crew of the *Mina* and Mother,' Tessa asked.

'I don't think so. Paddy has told me some of the things that are getting around the town about Jago and your mother and about him burying Kasiah out along that beach. Among other things, they're saying her body should have been brought back to the town for a proper burial,' Henry explained.

'I would have liked that as well, Henry. But, as you explained, Jago told you he would have never been able to find that place again. So, it would have been impossible.'

'I'm sure she is at peace up there, Tessa. However, I do believe that if I had asked Jago to try to find the place again, he would have refused.' Henry said.

'Do you think so?' Tessa asked.

'I'm quite certain of it!'

'Have you spoken to him about coming to Darwin with us, Henry?'

'I have, Tessa. He told me that wherever you go, he must go as well.'

'How strange. He could stay here in Broome if he wanted to. But then, I suppose, he has become a part of our family now. You don't mind, do you, Henry?'

'Of course not. I think I've grown quite attached to him. Anyway, I don't think Juliette would have come with us if Jago didn't agree to as well.' Henry added.

'She is very fond of him. They could live in the flat downstairs.'

'I was thinking the same thing,' Henry replied.

'Oh, Henry, I do miss Mother. She and I joked about her living in the flat. She thought it would be better for us when she got older to live downstairs on her own. I told her I wanted her upstairs to be with us always. You would have wanted that, wouldn't you, Henry?'

'Yes, of course, Tessa. I wanted her to be close. I miss her, you know,' Henry replied.

'I know you do. I've seen the tears in your eyes when you speak of her. You did love her, didn't you, Henry?'

'Yes, Tessa, I loved her very much, and I wish she was still with us.'

'Me too, Henry,' Tessa replied.

'I'm sure she would have loved this house,' Henry said, lifting one of the photographs in the hope of changing the subject away from Kasiah.

'I'm certain she would have, my love,' Tessa replied, reaching for Henry's hand.

'I will contact our solicitor in the morning and tell him we will accept Sean Peterson's offer,' Henry said, gathering the photographs together.

'I suppose I had better start packing then,' Tessa replied excitedly.

# Chapter 40

# Leaving Broome

Six short weeks later, Henry and Tessa were standing on the deck of the S.S. *Minderoo*, watching Broome disappear into the brilliant blue of Roebuck Bay and the Indian Ocean.

'How are you feeling, Tessa?' Henry asked.

'A little sad, I suppose. Broome was Mother's home. I do hope we have made the right decision.'

'It was your home too, Tessa. Will you miss it?'

'Yes, I probably will—at least for a while,' Tessa replied.

'Let's just look toward our future and try our best to make it work.'

'I'm sure we will do our very best, Henry. I just wish Mother was with us.'

'So do I, Tessa,' Henry replied. 'And so do I.'

'Where's Jago?' Tessa asked.

'He's still down in his cabin. I think it was a sensible idea to have separate cabins for him and Juliette,' Henry said.

'Juliette looked surprised when I suggested they could share a cabin if they wanted to,' Tessa replied. 'I'm sure she thinks we aren't aware of what's been going on for ages.'

'Good luck to them, I say, Henry said, smiling.

'We'll be in Darwin in four days, Henry.' Tessa said, reaching for Henry's hand.

'Exciting, isn't it?'

'It certainly is,' Tessa replied.

'I spoke to Captain Bradford about looking after our briefcase with the contents of your mother's safe in it. He has a safe in his cabin, which he said we could use.' Henry added.

'Father showed me the pearls he was keeping some time ago. Was there much else in it, Henry?'

'Your mother's will, of course, and quite a large amount of cash. There is more than £5,000 in Australian currency and quite a lot of American dollars and English pounds as well. And then there were the 205 English gold sovereigns I counted. I'm not sure what they are worth, but quite a lot, I would imagine.'

'Oh, my goodness! That much—!' Tessa replied. 'And do you have any idea what the pearls could be worth?'

'Not really. But your mother told me what one of them was worth a while back. I haven't counted how many there are, but there must be many thousands of pounds worth in the captain's safe at this very moment,' Henry replied.

'Let's just keep it all, Henry. We have no need to sell any of it. We could lock it all away in the safe you had installed in that secret room in the new house. Mother has left me so much money, and with what we received for the warehouse, the boats, and the house, there will be enough for us to live on for a very long time.'

'Don't forget the earnings from the gold mine. Connor has a dividend cheque waiting for us when we arrive,' Henry added.

'I am so looking forward to seeing them both,' Tessa replied excitedly.

'And they've said they don't mind us staying with them until we buy some furniture,' Henry said.

'Let's just buy a nice brass bed and a few other things and move in as quickly as we can manage, Henry. When we have more time, we could travel to Singapore to choose some nice furniture. I have the address of the shop that Father and Mother used in my notebook.'

'Perhaps Connor and Angela would like to come with us,' Henry suggested. 'They loved that four-poster bed with the carvings on the bedposts in your mother's house.

'Oh, Henry! We will have so much to talk about when we get to Darwin,' Tessa said, kissing Henry's cheek.

Broome had disappeared behind a long peninsula of cliffs and mangroves, and a light breeze had picked up.

'Let's go inside to the saloon for a while, Henry.'

'Yes, I agree. Let's get out of this breeze,' Henry replied, taking Tessa's hand.

# Chapter 41

# Spawn Of the Devil

Back in Broome, Sean Peterson and his son George were standing on the veranda of their new home on Walcott Street. Two of their men were carrying the sawn pieces of a beautiful four-poster bed down onto the lawns and throwing them onto an already roaring bonfire. Expensive French polish was curling back in the heat from the faces of peering monkeys and the bodies of long-tailed lizards carved onto the now-sawn pieces of the bedposts.

Father Ryan came up the steps to see the two men. He'd spent the last hour walking through the servant's quarters at the rear of the beautiful colonial home, cleansing the rooms of perceived evil.

'Well, I'm all finished down there. I've instructed your men to throw all the servants' beds and mattresses onto the fire, along with the rest of the stuff from their rooms. We have no idea what has been going on in them. Would you like me to go back through the rooms up here just to be certain I haven't missed anything?' He asked Sean.

'A sound idea, Father . . . And are you quite sure you have cleansed them all down there of the evil that must surely have existed in them from that heathen Jago?' Sean replied, rubbing the thin scar on the side of his nose.

'I have, Sean. I found a small prayer book in one of them. It was written in French. I couldn't understand a word of it, but it was bound to have been sinful, so I tossed it on the fire along with a sheet of paper I found attached to a wall in Jago's bedroom. It was written in what I imagined was Arabic. Some sort of pagan prayer, I expect. I have no idea what it said, but the fact that it belonged to that spawn of the devil was enough for it to finish up in the flames as well.'

'Thank you, Father. I'll give you your £100 when you have finished the rooms up here then.'

'You're being more than generous, Sean. The church and the congregation thank you.' Father Ryan replied.

'I'm just thankful you could come on such short notice, Father.' Sean said, smiling at the priest.

Father Ryan had walked over to the veranda railing. He was looking down at the men at the fire when he spoke. 'I'm glad you have taken my advice with that disgraceful bed. That thing is something only fornicators would own.'

'I'm of the same opinion, Father,' Sean replied, nodding in agreement.

The old Catholic priest turned and hurried back inside the beautiful home again.

George turned and looked at his father. 'Are you burning that black witch Kasiah's bed as well, Father?'

'Certainly not, George. That will be the bed your mother and I will sleep in,' Sean Peterson replied, a perverse smile on his ruddy face.

'Is that wise, Father?'

'The bed I decide to sleep in is none of your damn business, George,' Sean snapped.

'Which room will I be using, Father?'

'None of them until we have sold that house we had built for you out near Cable Beach. You can stay out there and cook for yourself until then. You should have used a little more common sense in your choice of a wife. What a damnable waste of money that was.'

'I'm sorry about that, Father,' George replied.

A moment later, Father Ryan hurried out through the front door. He was carrying a huge, varnished sawfish in his hands.

'I'm certain this has some occult meaning, Sean. If I were you, I would burn it,' he said to Sean.

'Toss it down then, Father. My men will see to it, and thank you,' Sean replied.

Father Ryan hurried back inside, taking a bottle of holy water from one of his pockets and thinking of his £100.

# Chapter 42

# A New Beginning

### June 3rd, 1922

The sky was clear, blue, and cloudless, and the weather was warm and pleasant. It was late afternoon on a Wednesday when the S.S. *Minderoo* steamed into Darwin Harbour.

Henry and Tessa had spent every evening of their trip dining with Captain Bradford. The captain was most intrigued by the bold steps the young couple was taking with their move to Darwin. He found their courage refreshing and inspirational.

'Well, I certainly hope it all goes well for you. It's a big move uprooting and starting on a brand-new adventure with your young lives,' he said to them over a glass of wine on their last evening together.

'I suppose it is, Captain, and thank you so much for your encouragement and well wishes. We are fortunate that we have such good friends as Connor and Angela Burke waiting for us in Darwin. I'm sure they will make the transition much easier for us,' Tessa replied.

'You are a brave young woman, Tessa Dawson. To have lost both of your parents in recent years must have been a dreadful blow for you to bear. Duncan and your dear mother had sailed with me many times, and I had always enjoyed their company immensely. They travelled with me to Singapore on a couple of occasions, where they spent time holidaying and shopping. If I remember correctly, you were with them on one occasion. You were very young at the time and probably don't remember. They fussed over you so,' the captain said.

'I think I do remember some of it, but as you say, I was quite young. Mother bought a lot of her clothing from Singapore. She knew people in several fashion houses there,' Tessa replied.

'It was such a terrible thing, your mother perishing in that damn cyclone. Very tragic indeed. She was still so young and beautiful. You must miss her terribly.'

'I do, Captain. So does Henry. She was our guiding light in so many ways, wasn't she, Henry?' Tessa replied, turning to Henry for confirmation.

'She was, Tessa. She meant the world to both of us, Captain. It was so unexpected. Her death is probably the real reason we decided to leave Broome and start in a new direction with our lives,' Henry acknowledged.

'In that case, I sincerely hope the move proves to be a great success for both of you. From our recent discussions, your new home sounds rather wonderful. I'll wager you'll be looking forward to seeing it.' Captain Bradford remarked.

'We certainly are, Captain. If you can manage it sometime in the future, we would love to have you visit us for dinner one evening,' Tessa replied.

'Why, thank you, Tessa. I would enjoy that. Are you having the telephone connected to your home?' Captain Bradford asked.

'I've been informed that it has already been connected, Captain. I'll get you the number from our cabin when we have finished our meal this evening,' Tessa replied.

'Thank you, my dear. In that case, when I am next in Darwin and staying over for a night, I shall contact you.'

'We will look forward to your call, Captain Bradford,' Henry replied.

* * *

The following morning, as the *Minderoo* eased her hull against the long Darwin jetty, Henry and Tessa were on the upper deck, watching the men on the wharf drag her heavy hawsers along to the sturdy steel bollards concreted into the sea floor. Standing with them were Jago and Juliette, their cases in their hands.

Neatly uniformed port officials holding clipboards stood at the ready, waiting for the boom to be uncoupled and freight to start to be unloaded. Cartage contractors had their trucks lined up, their drivers chatting together in little groups. Dozens of well-dressed locals stood behind a white-painted barricade, waiting for friends and loved ones to begin disembarking.

Henry took Tessa to the lower-level railing, and they searched the waiting crowd for their friends. Jago and Juliette went with them.

'There they are over there,' Henry said, pointing to Connor and Angela walking along the wharf toward the ship and the waiting crowd.

'I see them,' Tessa yelled, waving her hand to attract their attention.

Connor and Angela stopped. They'd seen them waving from the ship. They waved back and hurried along to the arrivals area.

A short while later, the gangway was secured in place, and the *Minderoo's* passengers began to disembark. Henry and Tessa, Jago, and Juliette were among the first of them. Henry, carrying a heavy suitcase in one hand and a briefcase firmly strapped to his wrist in the other, led them over to the barricade, and they waited to be allowed through. A moment later, an official swung open a narrow gate, and they hurried through the crowd to their friends.

Tessa went to Angela and put her arms around her. 'It's so wonderful to see you again, dear friend,' she said excitedly.

'Oh, Tessa, how lovely you look. I've missed you so much,' Angela gushed.

Henry put his suitcase down but kept his briefcase in his left hand. He reached for Connor's hand. 'It's a real pleasure to see you again, my friend,' he said.

'Glad to have you both back with us again, Henry. Is that your only baggage?' Connor asked.

'It is, Connor. The rest of our belongings are to be unloaded with the Pierce-Arrow and taken to your home address, as we discussed on the telephone. There's quite a lot of it: our bedding, clothing, and bits and pieces. The captain has informed me it could be a day or two before it's delivered, though,' Henry replied.

'I'm sure they'll ring me and let me know when to expect it,' Connor added. 'We'll have it delivered to your new home then.'

'You remember Jago and Juliette from Broome?' Henry said, turning to the two people behind him.

'I certainly do,' Connor replied, smiling at the silent Jago, and putting out his hand.

'Jago took the outstretched hand and stared into Connor's eyes, but he said nothing as he shook it.

Juliette stepped forward and reached for Connor's hand. 'Hello, Mr. and Mrs. Burke. It's very nice to see you both again.'

'I hope you find Darwin to your liking, Juliette.' Connor said, smiling pleasantly as he took her hand.

'Thank you, *Monsieur*.'

Angela kissed the attractive French woman on both cheeks. 'Welcome to Darwin, Juliette,' she said affectionately.

'*Merci Madame*.'

Connor turned to Henry and Tessa. 'Let's get moving. I imagine you'll be eager to see your new home.'

'We loved the photographs you sent us,' Tessa replied excitedly.

They hurried out of the port gates to the car park and Connor Burke's brand-new Duesenberg four-door sedan.

'I like the car, Connor. It looks new, my friend,' Henry remarked as they loaded their suitcases into the boot.

'It is. I took delivery last month. I had it imported from America. Everyone here at the moment is driving a black T-model Ford. Very boring. I hope you like the dark blue colour,'

Connor announced.

'Very smart indeed, my friend,' Henry replied.

'Unfortunately, it was only available in left-hand drive. But I'm getting used to it. The good news for you, Henry, is that I paid for it with my first dividend from the Bitter Creek gold mine. I have your cheque at home in my office waiting for you,' Connor explained.

'That's very good news,' Henry replied, holding the rear door open for Jago and Juliette.

'I will have to squeeze in with you two,' he said to them. 'Tessa, you can get in the front with Angela and Connor.'

A short while later, they were speeding along East Point Road with the sea to their left. Very little was said. Henry was feeling awkward sitting so close to the always-silent Jago. A moment later, the car slowed, and they turned into a newly paved driveway.

'Welcome to your new home,' Connor announced, turning off the ignition.

'Oh, my goodness, how wonderful it looks,' Tessa remarked.

'It's just perfect. Thank you for contracting out the garden work for us, Connor. It's greatly appreciated,' Henry said as they climbed from the sleek new car.

Recently planted palms lined the driveway, and lush lawns covered most of the front garden. Here and there, frangipani trees and hibiscus bushes had been planted. A sprinkler on a long spike was beating water over a part of the new garden where a clump of golden cane palms had been planted. Further up the driveway, the recently completed new home waited for them.

Tessa suddenly started to cry, surprising them all.

'What's wrong, my love?' Henry asked.

Jago was staring at Tessa, concern showing on his dark face.

'I'm so sorry. It's just that dear Mother would have loved this home, Henry. It's so perfect. I wish she was here with us today,' Tessa sobbed.

Henry tried to reply, but he found he was unable to. Tears filled his eyes as he stared at his wife.

Angela put her arm around Tessa to comfort her, and they continued along the driveway toward the home. When they reached the steps, Connor turned to Henry.

'You two are now the proud owners of one of Dawin's finest homes. I should tell you that it has attracted quite a bit of attention from locals during its construction,' he said, handing Henry a ring of keys.

'Thank you so much for all your help along the way, Connor. We couldn't have done it without you. Do you know if the downstairs flat is complete as well?' Henry asked when they arrived at the steps.

'It certainly is, my friend.'

'In that case, I would like to show Jago and Juliette their new home first so they can, unpack. Would you all mind waiting upstairs for us?'

'Certainly, Henry.' Connor handed Henry another set of keys. 'The last time we spoke on the telephone, Tessa told us you were going to bring staff with you. Knowing that, Angela and I decided to have the flat furnished for you in readiness. Nothing too expensive, just good, functional furniture. I hope you don't mind.'

'You have thought of everything, you two. Just let me know what we owe you, Connor.' Henry insisted.

'We'll talk of it later, my friend. The important thing is that they are comfortable and able to take care of themselves from the outset. There's fresh food in the icebox. I've filled the wood box with firewood, and there's more in the wood store next to the garage. Angela has been to the shops and filled the pantry with foodstuffs for them as well.'

'You two have been such a big help,' Tessa said, reaching for Angela's hand.

'I'm sure you would do the same for us,' Angela replied.

Tessa let go of Angela's hand and turned to Henry. 'Henry,

you go up with Connor and Angela. I'll take Jago and Juliette into the flat if you don't mind. I'd like to speak to them both in private,' she said, taking the keys from Henry's hand.

'Are you sure you're not too upset? I don't mind showing them,' Henry replied.

'I'm quite sure, Henry. You go on up. I won't be too long.'

Henry turned and led Connor and Angela up to the veranda, where they waited for Tessa to join them.

Tessa took one of the keys, unlocked the freshly painted door to the flat, and led Jago and Juliette inside. She closed the door, turned to them, and spoke to Jago first.

'This is to be your new home, Jago, for as long as you want it to be. You have been with us for a very long time, and I consider you to be a part of our family now. I hope you feel comfortable here. If there is anything you would like to talk to me about, please come and see me.

'Thank you, Miss Tessa,' Jago replied awkwardly.

'Juliette, I would like you to consider this to be your home as well. There are two bedrooms, a bathroom, and everything you need. I hope you find it comfortable.'

'Thank you, Miss Tessa,' Juliette said, kissing Tessa's cheeks and embracing her fondly.

'Jago, because we no longer have a business to run, I would like you to continue as our driver. As you know, our motor car is still on the ship. It should be delivered sometime tomorrow. I would also like you to take charge of the garden work as your new occupation.'

'I will do as you ask,' Jago replied, nodding politely.

'Juliette, now that Tarni has decided to stay back in Broome, we will need a cook and housekeeper. I would like you to take on that important position. I will try to find someone locally to help you as soon as I can.' Tessa said to the smiling French woman.

'I will be honoured, Miss Tessa. I will do my best for you, Juliette replied in her wonderful French accent, turning, and smiling at Jago.

Jago nodded, and for the first time that day, he smiled. 'You are very kind, Miss Tessa. We will not let you down,' he said.

'Thank you, Jago. I hope you both like it here with us in Darwin,' Tessa said, glancing at Juliette. 'Here are the keys; please make yourselves comfortable.'

'You are always so kind, Miss Tessa. When you are ready, we will look after you and Mister Henry just like before,' Juliette replied, hugging Tessa fondly again.

'Thank you, Juliette. I should also tell you that the house upstairs has no furniture at the moment. Henry and I will take care of that as soon as we can. For the next few days, we will be living next door with our friends. Please enjoy yourselves until then,' Tessa said, turning to leave.

'Goodbye and thank you, Miss Tessa,' Juliette said, as Tessa opened the door.

# Chapter 43

# The Mata Jahat

Connor, Angela, and Henry were waiting by the front door when Tessa reached the head of the veranda steps.

'How lovely the verandas are,' she said, smiling when she got to them. 'We could dine out here on nice evenings, Henry.'

'We'll need a nice table and chairs. Perhaps a small round one.' Henry replied, turning, and unlocking the heavy front door and pushing it open. Then he swept Tessa into his arms and carried her through into the wide entrance hall.

'This will be a new beginning for us, my love,' he whispered as he carried her.

Connor and Angela followed them into the hallway and waited while they embraced and kissed.

'Oh, Henry, just look at these polished floorboards. How absolutely beautiful they look,' Tessa remarked when Henry finally put her down.

They followed Tessa into the sitting room. The room was empty apart from a brand-new cedar-bladed ceiling fan with a brass boss and a long row of varnished timber cupboards and bookshelves.

'You will need quite a few books to fill those shelves,' Angela remarked.

'We have quite a lot coming with our belongings from the ship,' Henry replied. 'Tessa's mother loved to read.

'So do I, Henry,' Tessa remarked.

'I came to the house one day a few weeks ago to see how things were progressing, and this room was closed off while the cabinet-makers were finishing their work,' Conner remarked. 'I'm not sure what was going on, but I wasn't allowed in here.'

'I'm sure they would have had some good reason. Perhaps safety or something like that,' Henry replied, glancing at Tessa.

'I suppose that could have been it,' Connor agreed.

'Well . . . What do you think, you two?' Angela asked. Do you like what you see?'

'I love it. I can't wait to see the kitchen,' Tessa replied.

They followed her out of the sitting room and down the hallway to the kitchen.

'Oh, my goodness. What a wonderful room. Just look at the stove. It's so big. I'm sure Juliette will love it. And the little nook is just as I hoped it would look. Look how lovely the leadlight windows are,' Tessa remarked excitedly when they got there.

'You're going to need quite a lot of furniture to fill up all these rooms,' Connor remarked.

'At least we can use the seating in the nook until we buy a dining table, I suppose. That should be a help,' Henry suggested.

'We have furniture you can use for as long as you like, Henry. We have an old house we're renovating to be a rental in town. It was furnished when we bought it.' Connor told them.

'There is a lovely brass bed you could have as a gift. It's in very fine order,' Angela suggested.

'That would be perfect. We were thinking of buying a new one. Are you sure you don't mind?' Tessa asked.

'We're just glad to be able to help. And as I said, I'm sure you would do the same for us.'

'What did Juliette and Jago think of the flat, Tessa?' Connor asked.

'Jago didn't say very much, but I think he's quite happy with it. Juliette loves it, though,' Tessa replied. 'I had a talk with them about the work they'll be doing for us. Jago is happy to continue as our driver, and I've asked him to look after the gardens as well. Juliette will be our housekeeper and do most of the cooking for us. She's a wonderfully talented cook. I'll try to hire someone locally to help her with the housework as soon as I can.'

'I was a little surprised when I saw Jago with you,' Connor remarked. 'I thought he may have preferred to stay in Broome.'

'He's looked after my family for so long now, it would be strange not to have him with us. Apart from that, when we asked him if he wanted to come with us, he told us it was his duty to look after me now that Mother is no longer with us,' Tessa explained.

'It was a terrible thing, your mother dying in that cyclone. You said in your letter that Jago was the only one to have survived,' Angela said in a soft, caring voice.

'Yes, Jago was the only one. He was terribly upset. He told me he gave Mother something to hold onto during the storm, but then he lost her and never saw her again. He searched for her all through the night and the next day, but he couldn't find her. When he finally reached the shore, he found her on the beach. She had drowned in the storm. He carried her into the water and washed her body. Then he took her into a little valley he found in the sandhills, wrapped in a piece of sailcloth from the *Mina*, and buried her. He told me he prayed for her.'

'How awful for you, Tessa. Your mother was such a remarkable woman. So very beautiful. What a terrible shame to have lost her!' Connor added.

'It must have been awful for Jago. He was so upset when he told me. I asked him if Mother was badly marked by the storm. He told me there were no marks on her at all and that she was beautiful, just like always. The poor man spent almost two days in the water and then another six days walking along the beach after he buried Mother. We were all amazed that he survived such an ordeal. He might have died on that lonely beach if Henry hadn't found him.'

'Aren't you afraid of him, Tessa? He frightens the both of us,'

Angela admitted.

'Perhaps I once was, but not anymore. I think I understand him a little better now. There's one more thing that I should tell you both, though. Before he buried Mother, he took something from her body. He told me while he slept alongside her grave, she came to him in a dream. In the dream, she asked him to give this to me and to wear it always,' Tessa said, unbuttoning her blouse and pulling out the golden amulet with the ruby eye.

'Oh, my gosh! Tessa. It's so beautiful,' Angela remarked. 'It looks very old. Does it mean something?'

'Yes, it does. Mother told me when I was a child that it represents the evil eye. It protects the wearer from evil. It once belonged to her father—my grandfather—Juan Toledo. Juan Toledo was a diver on one of my grandfather's boats long ago. He was a Negro-Macassan. He came from the Dutch East Indies up on the Savu Sea. I was told he was a hoodoo man, a shaman. Some say he had a gift and that he was a healer. He died long ago.'

Angela put her hand on Tessa's arm. 'You have endured so much tragedy in your young life, Tessa.'

'I don't think of it that way. But I suppose you're right,' Tessa replied.

The stone is quite large—is it a real ruby?' Angela asked.

'Yes, it is. It's an Indian ruby and set in the purest gold. The amulet is called the *Mata Jahat*. Mother told me that it once belonged to a holy man in my grandfather's homeland.

'Can I touch it?' Angela asked.

'Yes, of course you can.'

Angela took the golden amulet in her fingers and rubbed them over the ruby. 'It feels quite warm, Tessa. I suppose it's because it was against your skin,' she remarked.

'The ruby is never cold, dear friend. It holds Mother's love. I suppose that sounds silly and childish?' Tessa whispered in a soft, tremulous voice. There were tears in her eyes.

'No, my friend, it doesn't . . . I love you, Tessa,' Angela replied.

'We both love you, Tessa.' Connor added, taking Angela's hand in his.

Henry went to Tessa and kissed her forehead. He ran his fingers over the golden amulet himself. His mind swirled with memories of Kasiah's dark body as he touched the ruby eye.

'And I will never stop loving you, Tessa,' he whispered.

'Our conversation has become a little sad, I feel. Let's go next door, and I will get you your dividend check from the mine, Henry.'

'Thank you, my friend,' Henry replied, wiping tears from his cheeks with his fingers. 'And is it progressing well?'

'Very well indeed. I have had to order a bigger stamper battery for them.'

'A stamper battery—? Henry said, puzzling over the word.

'Yes, it's a type of crusher they use to break down the aggregate to a more manageable size so that it can be more easily worked in the sluices. The one they've been using is not quite big enough for the volume they are bringing out of the shaft at the moment. We are opening a couple more shafts over the next few months as well,' Connor explained as they strolled down the driveway and made their way to the home next door.

Once they were seated in Connor and Angela's sitting room, Connor left them, returning a few seconds later with an envelope in his hand. He passed it to Henry. 'Your first dividend cheque, my friend. More than enough for your new furniture and a year's living expenses, I'll wager.'

Henry opened the envelope and looked at the cheque. 'My goodness. It has certainly proved very worthwhile. We have more than our initial investment back already,' he said, smiling.

Angela went over, sat on the arm of Tessa's chair, and put her arm around her shoulders.

'Let's all shower and dress and head into town for a celebratory dinner and some fun. We have to wish these two all the very best for their new life here in Darwin,' she said, looking at her husband.

# Dawson House

Darwin.

## 1998

'And so, I hope, dear reader, that you have found my story of interest. I began writing this lengthy journal the day after my dear wife, Tessa, passed away and finished it many years later. I was beside myself with grief on that first day, and I needed to do something to hold back the sadness that was threatening to overwhelm me and take away my sanity. Looking back now that I have finished it, I think I was driven to complete it in the end because of the great joy and good fortune I have had in my life, but also because of the need to finally admit to the world the sin of loving Kasiah, my wife's mother. Many times, I came close to telling Tessa about the affair, but I chose not to. Perhaps it was cowardice; perhaps it was something else. There were times when I thought that she knew or at least suspected that something may have happened between the two of us, but she never asked me. If she had, I am not sure that I could have deceived her any longer. Perhaps that was the very reason that she never asked.

*I'm an old man now, and I have seen all the people that I have loved pass away. My good friend Connor Burke died long ago. His wife, Angela, spent her final days at a rest home here in Darwin. Jago had a heart attack and died in our garden in 1955. Not long after that, Juliette left us to return to her beloved Paris. We were informed she passed away in her sleep in 1961, the year before my beloved Tessa died in my arms.*

*My love for Tessa never dimmed or diminished through all the days of our married lives together. She was everything to me, and her death became a blow that I was never able to deal with. I have been a truly lucky man to have loved two women so completely and received their love in return. True love is like a perfect pearl, so beautiful and yet so rare and difficult to find. I am fortunate that I have held in my hands two of the most perfect pearls that God has ever created.*

*Henry Archibald Dawson.'*


Charlotte closed the old, leather-bound journal and sat back on her side of the little nook. She looked across the table at Jeremy and Alice. Alice was crying. But Jeremy was silent. She smiled; she liked Jeremy. Perhaps she was even beginning to fall in love with him. He had done such a wonderful job of renovating the old home. He had been so professional and helpful. Now that the old house was finished, he was just as proud of the work he had done as she was.

'Well . . . what did you both think of Henry's story?' Charlotte asked.

'It was wonderful, Miss Charlotte. Thank you for reading it to us.' Alice replied, wiping her nose with a tissue.

Jeremy was silent. He was staring at Charlotte.

'I'm sorry, Charlotte, I was miles away. I thoroughly enjoyed it as well, and I must thank you for reading it. As you said, it was like a giant step back in time. I was just thinking to myself. As I told you before, I did work for Henry some time ago. He just seemed like a nice old man to me. I never thought for a moment that he had lived and loved the way that he had. I shall never look at an old person the same again.'

'I'm glad you both enjoyed it, as did I. Henry had a wonderful life; there is no question of that,' Charlotte replied.

'Well, I suppose we had better get your bike in the back of my ute and get you home, Alice. Oh, by the way, Charlotte, Dave, my friend from the body shop, will be delivering both of Henry's old cars in the morning. Would you like me to be here when he arrives?' Jeremy asked.

'Would you mind, Jeremy?' Charlotte replied.

'No worries. They're being delivered at around eleven in the morning. I'll be here to help you get them back in the garage.'

'Thank you.'

I'll see you at eleven then.' Jeremy announced, getting up.

'I'll see you in the morning, Miss Charlotte,' Alice added, sliding out of the nook.

*   *   *

The following morning, at eleven o'clock, as promised, Dave Perkins from the body shop delivered the two old cars that once belonged to Henry and Tessa with great fanfare. Charlotte, Alice, and Jeremy were drinking coffee on the veranda when they were driven into the driveway and parked in front of the wonderfully restored home.

'Oh, my goodness, how nice they look,' Alice remarked.

'They look almost like new. He's done a remarkable job. Just look at Tessa's little Porsche; it looks so lovely,' Charlotte said, getting to her feet. 'Let's go down and have a closer look.'

An hour later, after thanking Dave for his work restoring the two old cars and giving him his final payment, the beautiful blue Mercedes was driven into the newly restored garage with its electric doors. The red Porsche was left outside.

'C'mon, Alice, hop in. You and I are going for a drive. Jeremy, would you mind helping me put the roof down?' Charlotte asked.

'Just as long as you and I can go for a ride as well,' Jeremy replied.

'I've got a better idea,' Charlotte suggested.

'And what's that, beautiful?' Jeremy asked as he went around the car to help Charlotte with the catch she was having difficulty with.

Charlotte took Jeremy's hand when he finished with the catch and turned him toward her. Then she reached up and kissed him on the lips. 'How about you and I take it out for dinner somewhere nice tonight?' she whispered.

'See, Jeremy, I told you she liked you,' Alice said, laughing as she climbed in the Porsche.

'Wow. That was nice. It's a date. I know a nice little Thai restaurant in the city. Do you like Thai, Charlotte?'

'I certainly do, Jeremy,' Charlotte replied, kissing his blushing cheek quickly and climbing in the car.

A moment later, Charlotte started the Porsche and put it in gear. She waved to Jeremy, drove down the driveway, and turned speedily onto East Point Road.

Jeremy walked down the driveway after them. He stood under the old flame tree and watched the little red sports car until it disappeared out of sight.


End